GREEK MYTHS

A NEW RETELLING

CHARLOTTE HIGGINS

with drawings by
CHRIS OFILI

VINTAGE

Vintage is part of the Penguin Random House group of
companies whose addresses can be found
at global.penguinrandomhouse.com

Penguin
Random House
UK

First published in Vintage in 2022
First published in hardback by Jonathan Cape in 2021

penguin.co.uk/vintage

A CIP catalogue record for this book is available from
the British Library

ISBN 9781529111118

Drawings by Chris Ofili, 2021 (pencil on paper, 21 x 29.7 cm):
The Weaver (p.vi); *Birth of Athena* (p.18); *Athena* (p.21); *The Riddle of the Sphinx* (p.52); *Alcithoë* (p.55); *Narcissus Falls* (p.84); *Philomela* (p.87); *The Lovers* (p.116); *Arachne* (p.119); *The West Wind* (p.146); *Andromache* (p.149); *The Judgement of Paris* (p.174); *Helen* (p.177); *The Golden Fleece* (p.208); *Circe* (p.211); *Odysseus's Return* (p.242); *Penelope* (p.245)

Printed and bound in Great Britain by Clays Ltd, Elcograph S.p.A.

The authorised representative in the EEA is Penguin Random House Ireland,
Morrison Chambers, 32 Nassau Street, Dublin D02 YH68

Penguin Random House is committed to a sustainable future for
our business, our readers and our planet. This book is made from Forest
Stewardship Council® certified paper.

For James and Emma Higgins,
Tilda and Eleanor Lawrence

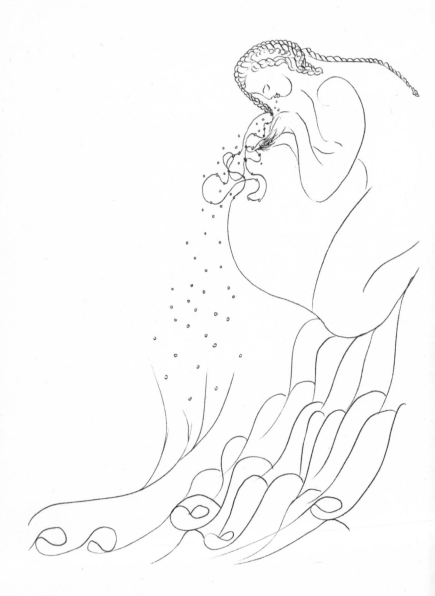

Yes! marvels are many, stories
starting from mortals somehow
    stretch truth to deception
woven cunningly on the loom of lies.

PINDAR,
Olympian Ode 1, 28–32,
translated by Frank J. Nisetich

A NOTE ON NAMES

Some characters from Greek myth are familiar to readers of English through Latinised or anglicised versions of their names; strict transliteration from the Greek can seem jarringly unfamiliar. I have chosen whatever form seemed most natural, which means I have sacrificed consistency. When the primary source for a story is Latin literature, I have given the relevant god their Greek name – Athena instead of Minerva, Zeus instead of Jupiter, etc.

CONTENTS

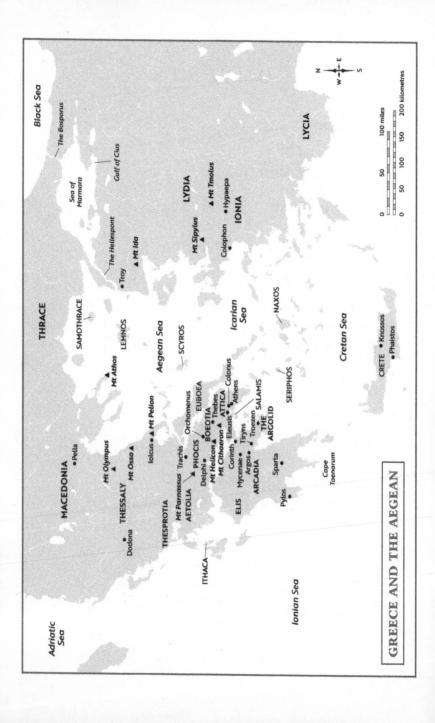

GREECE AND THE AEGEAN

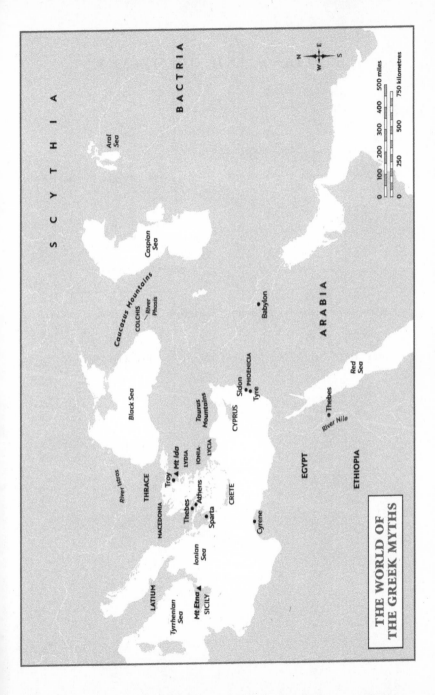

**THE WORLD OF
THE GREEK MYTHS**

TITANS AND OLYMPIANS

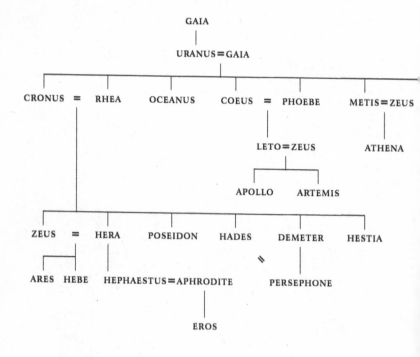

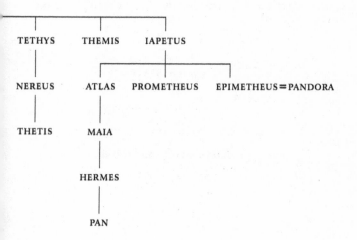

HOUSE OF CADMUS

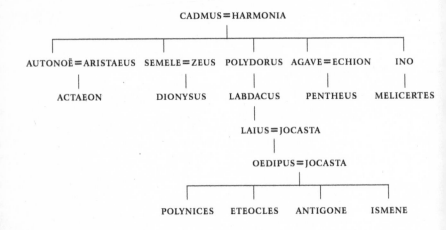

HOUSE OF TANTALUS

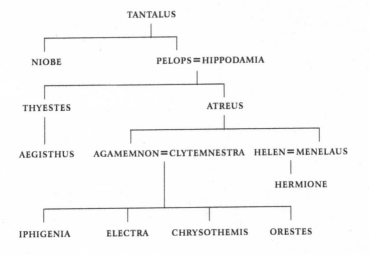

INTRODUCTION

Among my most treasured books as a child was a volume of Greek myths. My eldest brother, a sleep-deprived junior doctor at the time, bought it for me from a warren-like bookshop near his flat in London. The shop, sadly, is long gone, but I still have *Children of the Gods*, by Kenneth McLeish, illustrated by Elisabeth Frink. It infiltrated my childhood imagination – it was one of the things that set me on the path of studying classics, and becoming a writer.

Perhaps it was those pictures, those muscular pencil drawings, that made the greatest impression: Artemis, with her lean, athletic body; Hades, inscrutable king of the dead, magnificent and horrifying in his chariot, eyes shadowed by his dark helmet. Of course, the stories were marvellous too, strange and wild, full of powerful witches, unpredictable gods and sword-wielding slayers. They were also extreme: about families who turn murderously on each other; impossible tasks set by cruel kings; love that goes wrong; wars and journeys and terrible loss. There was magic, there was shape-shifting, there were monsters, there were descents to the land of the dead. Humans and immortals inhabited the same world, which was sometimes perilous, sometimes exciting.

The stories were obviously fantastical. All the same, brothers really do war with each other. People tell the truth but aren't believed. Wars destroy the innocent. Lovers are parted. Parents endure the grief of losing children. Women suffer violence at the hands of men. The cleverest of people can be blind to what is really going on. The law of the land can contradict what you know to be just. Mysterious diseases devastate cities. Floods and fire tear lives apart. For the Greeks, the word *muthos* simply meant a traditional tale. In the twenty-first century, we have long left behind the political and religious framework in which these stories first circulated – but their power endures. Greek myths remain true for us because they excavate the very extremes of human experience: sudden, inexplicable catastrophe; radical reversals of fortune; seemingly arbitrary events that transform lives. They deal, in short, in the hard basic facts of the human condition.

For the ancient Greeks and Romans, myths were everywhere. The stories were painted on the pottery that people ate and drank from; they were carved into the pediments of the temples outside which they sacrificed to the gods; they were the raw material of the songs they sang and the rituals they performed. Myths provided a shared cultural language, and a tentacular, ever-branching network of routes towards understanding the nature of the world, of human and divine life.

They explained the stars. They told of the creation of plants and animals, rocks and streams. They hovered around individual locales, explaining the origin of towns, regional cults and families. They reinforced customs and norms – sometimes offering a narrative justification for habits of oppression, not least of women and outsiders.

For a people scattered liberally across the Mediterranean and the Black Sea – Greek culture flowed out well beyond the boundaries of the modern Greek state – they also provided a shared sense of cultural identity. The tales in this book draw on sources by people writing not only in Greece, but in what we would now call Algeria, Libya, Egypt, Turkey and Italy. The world they filled with stories stretched from Greece to Georgia, from Spain to Syria, from Afghanistan to Sudan.

The Greeks often took a sceptical attitude to their own myths. The earliest philosophers questioned whether the events described in the old stories could really have happened. But even the staunchly rational Plato at times invented his own legendary stories to drive his philosophical points home. From him we have the idea of the lost city of Atlantis, and his *Republic* famously ends with the 'myth of Er', a haunting and strange story of the journey of human souls after death. No one could do without myths.

What we think of as 'the Greek myths' are the stories we find in the poetry, plays and prose of the ancient Greeks and Romans – a world also animated by an extraordinary surviving visual culture including ceramics, sculpture and frescoes. These myths deal with a long-lost past in which the worlds of immortals and humans overlap, and in which some exceptional humans can become almost divine. It is from this vast, contradictory, extraordinarily variegated body of literature that the tales in this book are taken.

Greek literature begins with the *Iliad* and the *Odyssey*, epic poems committed to writing somewhere between the late eighth and sixth centuries BCE, but drawing on a centuries-old oral tradition. These works, traditionally attributed to Homer, narrate stories from the Trojan War and its aftermath – versions, perhaps, of dimly remembered conflicts that took place in around the fourteenth to twelfth century BCE. At about the same time as the Homeric epics were written down, a Boeotian author called Hesiod produced his poem *Theogony*, which describes the origin of the gods and of human life.

Homer and Hesiod provided the Greeks with a bedrock of literary mythical stories. But they were just the beginning. Myths appear in a dizzying range of literature: the *Homeric Hymns*, for example; songs dedicated to different Greek gods, traditionally attributed to Homer, but almost certainly written at later dates. Then there are the *Odes* of Pindar, composed in the early fifth century BCE as victory poems for winners of Panhellenic religious sporting contests, and drawing on mythical stories for their poetic force. The great tragedians of fifth-century BCE Athens – Aeschylus, Sophocles and Euripides – almost invariably took stories from myth as their material. Later, in the great seat of culture and learning that was Alexandria, one of the cities established by Alexander the Great after his conquest of Egypt in 332 BCE, Apollonius of Rhodes wrote his epic poem *Argonautica* about Jason's quest to retrieve the Golden Fleece, and Callimachus wrote his myth-infused *Hymns*.

The Romans inherited the story-world of the Greeks' myths, absorbing and expanding it with their own distinctively flavoured narratives. Some of the stories I tell are, strictly speaking, Roman myths. Virgil's epic poem the *Aeneid*, which he was still working on when he died in 19 BCE, established a grand mythological origin for Rome; it was meant as both homage and rival to the poems of Homer. *Metamorphoses*, by Virgil's much younger contemporary Ovid, was finished around twenty years later. Mythical stories tumble out of that poem in almost bewildering profusion; it is the most brilliant ancient treasury of classical myths that survives to us.

From later on in the Graeco-Roman period, 'handbooks' of myths survive, prose volumes furnishing the reader with a guide to the most important stories. The best and most important of these, drawing on many early sources that are now lost, is the first- or second-century CE *Library*, by a writer known, somewhat confusingly, as Pseudo-Apollodorus. (The work was once attributed to a second-century BCE scholar called Apollodorus of Athens, but no longer, hence the prefix.) Also in Greek was the *Dionysiaca*, its subject the exploits and journeys of the god Dionysus. A vast, baroque and, I have to admit, sometimes exhausting work (the length of the *Iliad* and *Odyssey* combined), its author was Nonnus, who lived in the Greek city of Panopolis in Egypt in the fifth century CE.

It may sound paradoxical, but other important sources are those stories that no longer exist in their entirety. The works of Homer were once part of an 'epic cycle' that also contained long poems about the parts of the Trojan War not described in the *Iliad*, and about the deep past of Thebes, among other tales. These remain to us only as precis, mentions in other works, and brief fragments. In the case of tragedy, during the fifth and fourth centuries BCE Athens produced around a thousand plays by as many as eighty authors. Only thirty-two of them survive in full. Scholars, with patient, detective-like skill, have reconstructed what they can of lost works, drawing on fragments of ancient papyrus found in Egypt, assembling tantalising hints of a lost world of stories.

There was no canonical, fully authoritative account of 'the Greek myths' in antiquity. There were certainly versions of stories that dominated. Euripides' version of the Medea story, for example, became extremely popular, and you can see its famous final scene – the titular character magnificent in her dragon-drawn chariot – painted on Greek pots. But stories of the Greeks were endlessly variable, endlessly proliferating. It would be an impossible, Casaubon-esque task to gather all of their madly tendrilling versions into a single volume.

The dizzying variety of stories reflects the geography, politics and culture of the Greek world – scattered over a mountainous mainland, a jagged coastline, hundreds of islands, and the western seaboard of what is now Anatolia. From the eighth century BCE onwards, expanding trade networks also led Greeks to settle around the Black Sea, and on the coasts of North Africa, southern France and Spain. The same goddess might come with different associations, and differently weighted stories, in different city-states. (The city-state, *polis*, was the typical political unit of the Greek world. The thousand or so *poleis* were culturally distinctive in all kinds of ways and were often at each other's throats, both in myth and in lived reality.)

This bubbling, argumentative diversity is everywhere in classical literature. Disagreement on the details, I'd go so far as to say, is one of the most noticeable aspects of Greek storytelling about gods and mortals; ancient mythography is full of warnings along the lines of 'some people say this happened but other people, somewhere else, say that something different happened'.

For writers from antiquity onwards, this sense of branching choices has provided exhilarating freedom. A change of emphasis in a mythical tale could happen through compressing certain details in favour of expanding others. (A stratagem often used by the tragedians was to use an apparently minor episode in Homer as the seed from which to grow an entire plot.) It could happen through selecting a particular point of view for the telling, as Ovid does in his *Heroides*, a series of poems in the form of letters from female characters to mythical heroes. Stories could be radically altered: a playwright could perfectly well write a play in which Helen of Troy never actually goes to Troy. (I'm referring to Euripides' *Helen*, in which the Greeks and Trojans fight over a replica Helen made of clouds, while the real woman sits out the war in Egypt; the playwright was borrowing the idea from the sixth-century BCE poet Stesichorus.)

For the tragic playwrights of the fifth century BCE, myth also offered a means of confronting contemporary politics and society. Aeschylus's *Oresteia* trilogy is set in the distant aftermath of the Trojan War, but it also offers an origin myth – and thus a kind of legitimisation – for a new democratic order in Athens. Euripides' *Trojan Women* and *Hecuba* are also set at the time of Troy's defeat, but you can read them as reflections on the moral failures of the playwright's own day, as Athens poured resources and human lives into a grinding thirty-year conflict with Sparta. That's partly why the plays are still being staged now, their urgency and vitality undimmed. These stories of far away and long ago can be used by us as Euripides once used them – as lenses through which to see our own times more clearly.

For all these reasons, the modern reteller can never be some kind of faithful handmaiden of the stories. It is impossible. She is obliged to undertake the creative task of rejecting some tales in favour of others, of emphasising some aspects at the expense of others. She must choose where, and at whom, to point the camera.

In the compendia of mythical stories produced in the nineteenth and twentieth centuries, particularly those for children, the camera was usually pointed firmly at the figure of the hero. These characters – Heracles, Perseus, Jason, Theseus – were often subtly, or unsubtly, co-opted to offer models of male virtue for their young readers. Female characters were frequently relegated to the background as defenceless virgins, vicious monsters or grotesque old women. Homosexual desire was usually banished altogether. Nathaniel Hawthorne's volumes *A Wonder Book for Boys and Girls* and *Tanglewood Tales* provide excellent examples of this kind of tendency: his Theseus is a stout-hearted chap, unafraid of monsters; his Ariadne too virtuous a maid to abandon her family; his Medea reduced to a vindictive, jealous stepmother and ill-natured enchantress.

A complication for the reader (and reteller) is that the *'heros'* of ancient Greek literature was not at all the kind of person meant when the word 'hero' is used in modern English – the self-sacrificing military man whom Hawthorne might have had in mind, or the frontline healthcare worker we might think of today. The *heros* of Greek literature was an extreme and disturbing figure, closely connected to the gods. Achilles is by modern standards a war criminal who violates his enemy's corpse; Heracles murders his own wife and children; Theseus is a rapist. Some of the flattening-down of the strangeness and violence of the characters of classical literature has doubtless been an understandable consequence of retelling the tales with children in mind. But the Greek myths shouldn't be thought of as children's stories – or just as children's stories. In some ways, they are the most grown-up stories I know.

In recent years there has been a blossoming of novels – among them Pat Barker's *The Silence of the Girls*, Natalie Haynes's *A Thousand Ships* and Madeline Miller's *Circe* – that have placed female mythological characters at the centre of stories to which they have often been regarded as peripheral. And authors such as Kamila Shamsie (in her novel *Home Fire*) have used Greek myths as frameworks on which to hang modern stories. This book, however, is much more like an ancient mythological compendium than a novel. My work has not been to bring psychological insight to bear on a cast of characters as they develop through time, as a novelist might do, but to beckon the reader onwards through a many-storied landscape, finding a particular path through a forest of tales.

To emphasise the contrast between different approaches is not to devalue the old retellings, such as Roger Lancelyn Green's wonderful volume for children, *Tales of the Greek Heroes*, or Robert Graves's beautifully written *The Greek Myths*, which provides an intriguing monument to his own preoccupations, prejudices and theories. Rather, it is to underline the power of the Greek myths to produce resonance for every new reader and writer, and for every generation. Once activated by a fresh imagination, the stories burst into fresh life. The Greek myths are the opposite of timeless: they are timely.

My first concern when contemplating this book was to decide how to frame or organise my chosen stories. I considered the greatest of all compendia of myths: Ovid's *Metamorphoses*, an epic poem about legendary transformations. Its content is inseparable from its structure: the poem organically transforms as it progresses, seamlessly unfurling each new story from the last. The form itself is expressive. Nothing is stable, it says. Everything is contingent, matter is always on the move.

Clearly, I am not out to rival Ovid, but I realised that, like Ovid, I wanted the form of my chosen stories to be expressive in itself. I thought about other ancient authors who had framed mythological poems or compendia around various themes. One early text had used female characters as its organising principle: the fragmentary *Catalogue of Women*, once attributed to Hesiod. What remains is important and often beautiful; but it is a work that is largely concerned to establish genealogies of heroes, and the women's chief role is to give birth. There was also the lost *Ornithigonia* by Boios, about the mythical origins of birds; the little handbook of erotic stories, *Sufferings in Love* by Parthenius of Nicaea (said to have been Virgil's Greek teacher); and the fragmentary collection of star myths, *Catasterismi*, attributed to the Libya-born polymath, Eratosthenes.

I decided to frame my Greek myths as stories told by female characters. Or to be strictly accurate, my women are not *telling* the stories. They have, rather, woven their tales on to elaborate textiles. The book, in large part, consists of my descriptions of these imagined tapestries.

This idea is rooted in a recurring motif in classical literature: the idea of telling stories through descriptions of spectacular artworks, a literary convention known as ecphrasis. The first and most famous ecphrasis is the description of the scenes decorating the shield of Achilles, in the *Iliad*. Much later, in the first century BCE, the entire story of Theseus, Ariadne and the Minotaur was told by the Roman poet Catullus through a long description of the designs woven into a bedspread. A feature of ecphrasis was that the item under description could, at times, take on its own life as a narrative, escaping the status of an imagined object.

Specifically, though, the idea is inspired by the moments in classical literature when female characters take control of a story. On a number of striking occasions, this happens through the act of weaving.*

Take Helen of Troy. When we first encounter this most famous of literary characters, in book 3 of the *Iliad*, she is at her loom, weaving the stories of the struggles between the Greeks and the Trojans. She is the only person in the poem who has the insight to stand at a distance from the events unfolding in front of her, to interpret them, and to make art about them. Intriguingly, an early commentator on the poem, writing in antiquity, observed of this passage: 'The poet has formed a worthy model for his own poetic enterprise.' Both writer and character are, the early critic noticed, making art from the same material – the poet in verse, Helen in tapestry.

In the *Odyssey*, Penelope waits at home on the island of Ithaca for her husband, Odysseus. He has been away for twenty years, ten years besieging Troy, and another ten, who knows where. He's

---

* 'In the old myths, weaving was women's speech, women's language, women's story,' wrote the critic Carolyn Heilbrun in her influential essay 'What Was Penelope Unweaving?' (1985), collected in *Hamlet's Mother and Other Women: Feminist Essays on Literature* (The Women's Press, 1991).

probably dead. It is time for her to remarry. She tells the suitors who are harassing her that she will decide on a husband when she has finished making her father-in-law's winding sheet. Every day she weaves. Every night she unravels her work, delaying the decision. Describing this device, which is also a plot device, she uses the verb *tolupeuein*, which means to roll wool into rovings for spinning – or, metaphorically, to contrive a stratagem.

In Ovid's *Metamorphoses*, Philomela, an Athenian princess, has been imprisoned and raped. The perpetrator, her brother-in-law Tereus, has cut out her tongue to prevent her from telling anyone. But she weaves her story, and thus bears witness to the crime, moving the plot along to a gruesome conclusion.

In another part of *Metamorphoses*, a young woman called Arachne challenges the goddess Minerva (the Roman version of Athena) to a tapestry-making contest. Arachne weaves a design showing the terrible crimes committed by the gods; Minerva – who is, significantly, the goddess of winning – depicts the stories of the awful punishments that lie in wait for humans when they challenge the gods. Arachne will soon discover the consequences of her choice of design.

These are some of the characters who control the many narratives contained in this book. Athena herself begins; she invented the loom, after all, and possesses the cosmological insight to describe how the world began. Alcithoë, a weaver who appears in *Metamorphoses*, then tells us the tales of that most storied and ancient of Greek cities, Thebes. Philomela comes next – I have her weave love stories, as a kind of wish fulfilment, or charm against disaster. There's no strict chronology observed in the volume, although like many mythological compendia from Pseudo-Apollodorus onwards, I start with the creation of the universe and end with the aftermath of the Trojan War – at a point when it seems that the old world, where humans may consort with deathless gods, is gently slipping away.

Now that textile production has been mechanised into factory sheds, it takes a leap of imagination to consider that until the invention of the flying shuttle and the spinning jenny in the mid-1700s, the lives of most women, and many men, were dominated by the slow, laborious processes required to make cloth. Partly because few examples have survived from the classical world, and partly because they were long overlooked as mere 'women's work', textiles have only fairly recently taken off as the object of serious study. Now, though, they are being investigated in all of their aspects – sociological, economic, archaeological, literary, metaphorical, mathematical – and rightly seen as central to life in the ancient world.

It's sobering to think about the sheer time and work required to make cloth in the pre-industrial era. One scholar* has calculated that to make a single Roman toga, of about 4.2 by 4.8 metres, you would have needed some 42 kilometres of yarn, all handspun with a drop spindle. (The spinning wheel, invented in around 1000 CE in the Islamic world or China, later did this work faster.) Then there was the weaving. If one woman was labouring alone it could have taken her 120 days to produce the toga – if she was working ten-hour days, every day. (In practical terms, there was probably group work, not least by slaves, considerably speeding up the process.) And of course every single item of clothing in the ancient world – and every sail for every ship – would have required yarn to be handspun and handwoven.

The value attached to textiles is especially clear in the Homeric poems, where elaborate dresses are used as precious guest gifts, alongside golden cups and bronze tripods. Nearly all the female characters in the *Iliad* and *Odyssey* spin or weave – even the goddesses Calypso and Circe. Helen gives Telemachus a dress she herself has made, and tells him that his own bride should wear it on her wedding day (an intriguing gift given her own marital record). The powerful Queen Arete of the Phaeacians understands that something unusual is afoot in her palace when she recognises the clothing that Odysseus is wearing – as well she might, since she made it herself.

---

* Dr Mary Harlow, expert in Roman textiles, who kindly let me play on her warp-weighted loom and showed me how to use a drop spindle.

Despite the fact that textile survivals from the ancient world are so sparse, there are plenty of indications that real, non-mythical cloth could be woven with complex designs – most notably the textile annually offered in Athens to the sculpture of Athena Polias, which was said to have depicted the gods' battles with the Giants. In the Museo Civico at Chiusi, Tuscany, there is a beautiful skyphos (a kind of cup), dating from about 430 BCE. It is painted with a design of Penelope and her son Telemachus sitting either side of a great loom. On it, there is a half-finished cloth with a geometrical border along its length and, across its width, a band of winged horses and winged deities. Scholars long believed this kind of complicated pattern would have been impossible to create on so simple a device as a warp-weighted loom – but it is perfectly possible.*

Another vase, from about a century earlier, shows what looks like a contemporary, everyday scene of woolworking. On this lekythos (an oil flask), in the Metropolitan Museum in New York, two women work a loom, one packing in the weft threads with a weaving sword, the other using a shuttle that, owing to the width of the warp, she may need to pass along to her co-worker. Other figures weigh wool, spin, and fold finished cloth. One can easily imagine groups of women working together in such a manner, perhaps telling, or being told, stories. (In Euripides' play *Ion*, a work containing many references to pattern-woven textiles, the chorus of Athenian women recognise mythical scenes carved into the buildings at Delphi from the stories they have shared during their weaving sessions.)

Running through Greek and Roman thought is a persistent connection between the written word and the woven thread, between text and textile. The Latin verb *texere*, from which the English words text and textile derive, means to weave, or compose, or to fit a complex structure together. *Textum* means fabric, or framework, or even, in certain branches of materialist philosophy,

---

* Dr Ellen Harlizius-Klück, an expert on the algorithms, logic and mathematics of weaving, has demonstrated that it can be done, by simple dint of doing it herself on a reconstructed loom. At the time of writing, her impressive work was on display in the Museum for Plaster Casts, Munich.

atomic structure. The universe itself is sometimes described as a kind of fabric: Lucretius, in his first-century BCE scientific poem *On the Nature of the Universe*, describes the Earth, sea and sky as three dissimilar elements that are *texta*, woven together. *Texere* is related to the Greek verb *tikto*, which means to engender, to bring about, to produce, to give birth to. In turn the Latin and Greek words are related to the Sanskrit *takman*, child, and *taksh*, to make or to weave.

Greek and Roman literature is full of metaphors that compare its own creation to spinning and weaving. Ovid describes *Metamorphoses*, for example, as *'deductam carmen'*, a fine-spun song. When relating how he outwitted the Cyclops, Homer's Odysseus says: 'I wove all kinds of wiles and cunning schemes' – which you could read as a description of the shrewd design of the *Odyssey* itself. My book reasserts the connectedness of all this: text and textile, the universe, the production of ideas, the telling of stories, and the delicate filaments of human life. These are the lives that are so cunningly and ruthlessly manipulated by the Fates, the all-powerful ancient goddesses who spin, wind and finally cut the thread of each person's existence.

It is into their world, the Fates' world, that we step now. It is a thrilling and dangerous place, where the hooded stranger knocking on your door might turn out to be the king of the gods; where you might find yourself transformed into a swallow, or a kingfisher, or a stag; where a search for a lost husband might have you scaling the peak of Olympus to argue with the gods themselves. Are you ready? Then follow me.

INVOCATION

We mortals will never see you clearly. To us you are only ever vague shapes, never fully resolving into clarity, veiled in mist as you dance, barefoot, on the slopes of Helicon. Occasionally, we can hear you: you sing so sweetly that a fragment of your music, a heart-stopping phrase, sits trembling on the air for an instant, and then fades as quickly as it came, leaving us floundering to pull it to earth, to write it down, to make it our own. You are the poet's impetus, the astronomer's flash of certainty, the dancer when her body becomes the faithful servant of her mind. You are the moment a historian assembles the shards of the past and suddenly perceives a pattern. You come only to those who toil for you, painfully; and even then, your visits are erratic. Clio brings history, Euterpe lyric verse, Melpomene tragedy, Thalia comedy. Erato brings love songs, Polyhymnia sacred songs, Terpsichore dance, Urania knowledge of the stars. And Calliope, oldest and strongest of you all, brings epic verse.

Sing, Muses, of the Fates, the implacable ones, who measure out the thread of human life: Clotho spins it, Lachesis winds it and Atropos cuts it. They look frail, with their bent backs, their wrinkled faces. White, purple-hemmed robes cling to their ancient bodies; rose-red wreaths adorn their snowy hair. But they are stronger than, and almost as old as, anything living in the sky, on the Earth, or in the sea. Their work never ends: see how diligently Clotho coaxes out the soft wool from her distaff as she twirls her spindle, weighted by its whorl. These sisters are the authors of every existence. *They raise up the humble and dash down the mighty. They bring power and joy; they bring calamity, disease and terror. They know what has been, what is now, and what will be. They know when our world will end, when sea and land and sky will be consumed by sulphurous fire from pole to pole. Compared to these sisters even the gods, even Zeus himself, are as powerless as babies. Nothing happens that is not spun by them.*

Sing then, of the threads allotted by the Fates. Sing of gods and goddesses, sing of humans, sing of the spirits of trees and rivers. Sing stories that have the force of truth, stories embroidered and intricate. Sing the ancient web of tales – stories once told by goddesses, nymphs and women to the clattering music of the loom. Let thread be woven into new forms, fresh and bold and gleaming.

ATHENA

The world comes into being ✦ Gaia and Uranus ✦ the birth of the Titan gods ✦ Cronus, Rhea, the Cyclopes ✦ the birth and nature of the Olympian gods ✦ war between Olympians and Titans ✦ Typhon ✦ war between Olympians and Giants ✦ the creation of humans ✦ Prometheus, Epimetheus and Pandora ✦ Demeter and Persephone ✦ Phaethon ✦ Pyrrha and Deucalion

ATHENA

A thena had her workshop on Mount Olympus, near the mansions where the immortals feast on nectar and ambrosia and while away the unvarying bliss of their lives. In this great, high-ceilinged hall stood baskets of fleeces: some were unwashed, straight from the finest Arcadian flocks; some were clean and waiting to be combed, then roved into convenient lengths for spinning. On a chair lay her distaff, loaded up with wool; her muscular hand would send the patterned whorl whirling, drawing out even lengths of thread between finger and thumb and winding it up on her golden spindle. The room was dominated, though, by her magnificent, well-warped loom, which she herself had invented and built. It was taller than her and so wide that even she, a goddess, must walk up and down, up and down, as she passed the weft neatly through the warp threads, pressing them into place with her weaving sword, then adjusting the shaft before taking up the shuttle and sending the weft back again.

On her great web the goddess wove a border showing the origin of the world, casting back to an impossibly distant time before even she saw the light. All there was, back then, was Chaos: a chasm, a confused, formless morass. She picked it out in dark, swirling shapes, a wild abstraction. Back then, uncountable years ago, air and land and sea were intermingled. There was no Helios in his golden chariot, bringing light to the world in his daily journey through the sky. There was no Selene with her ivory horns, lightening the night with her milky glow. There was no Eos to draw night and day gently apart each morning with her rose-pink fingers. There was no fruitful, green-limbed Gaia. There were merely atoms, innumerable as leaves shivering in the wind on a thickly forested mountainside. And they were constantly obstructing each other, constantly at war. Cold fought with heat, wet with dry, weight with weightlessness. In strife the universe began, and in strife it would continue.

But nothing stays the same. There existed also a force, an agent of change. This force ceased the conflict of the elements, and separated them. Aether, the light upper air, sprang away from Gaia, the strong and ample Earth. She sculpted her body into mountain ranges and broad valleys; she smoothed her skirts into deserts and plains. Then the force unleashed the great salt seas; the waters flowed into their allotted places like a wave that floods a channel a child has dug on a sandy beach.

Gaia spontaneously gave birth to Uranus, the broad Heaven. Then together Gaia and Uranus had many sons and daughters, the generation of immortals called the Titans. Among them were Tethys, who presides over the sunless depths of the sea, the mother of a thousand nymphs; Oceanus, who belts the world with his fresh waters; the one-eyed Cyclopes; the giant Hundred-handers; and Iapetus, Metis, Rhea and Cronus. Oceanus filled the world with rivers: cataracts tumbled for the first time over new-made rocks; deltas separated into snaky channels; sluggish marshes spread. And since Gaia had been nourished by these waters, forests and grassy plains sprang up, plants rooting down and sprouting and spreading and flowering and offering their life-filled seeds back to the soil. In turn came living creatures in their bewildering variety: all those that inch their way across the Earth or soar or flutter above it, those that gallop across the steppes and those that burrow beneath the soil; those that scuttle across the sea floor or glide and flick their way through its waters.

But Uranus was jealous and frightened of his own offspring. And so he hurled them down into Tartarus – a prison far below the surface of the Earth. There the Titan gods languished, surrounded by adamantine walls that flamed with darkness.

Gaia was furious to see her children banished to this deathly place. She said to her son Cronus, 'Tonight I'll rescue you from that awful prison that's made from my own bones and entrails. I'll give you a sickle. Use it as a weapon against your father – and don't hesitate.'

When Uranus came to sleep with Gaia that night, Cronus was lying in wait. Just as his mother had instructed him, he swung the sickle, cutting off his father's genitals, flinging them into the sea. Later, out of the foam that gathered around the severed parts, a goddess was born: Aphrodite. Athena wove her as she stepped ashore on Cyprus, smiling and lifting her shining arms to the nymphs who came to attend on her. From Aphrodite's every step on the earth, violets and celandine sprang up; from her came delicious desire that unravels the wits of deities and mortals alike.

The Titan gods Cronus and Rhea reigned now, and the children they had together were the younger generation of immortals called the Olympians: Zeus and Hera, Poseidon and Hades, Demeter, goddess of the harvest, and Hestia, goddess of the hearth.

The next scene on Athena's border was the story of how Cronus in his turn came to be overthrown by his wife Rhea and son Zeus, establishing the Olympian generation of gods in power.

Cronus, like Uranus before him, became terrified by his young, strong children. And so, as each of them was born, he swallowed them. And out of fear he also imprisoned the Cyclopes and the Hundred-handers in the depths of Tartarus.

Rhea, like Gaia before her, was horrified. When her youngest, Zeus, was born, she tricked her husband by giving him a stone to swallow instead of a baby, and spirited the child away to Mount Dicte in Crete. There, in a glade in the impenetrable depths of the forest, the goat Amalthea secretly nurtured the young god. To distract the curious, she summoned the rowdy spirits called Curetes, who drowned Zeus's crying with their raucous cymbals.

When Zeus was fully grown he persuaded the shrewdest of the Titan immortals, Metis, to help him. She procured for him a certain drug. 'Feed this to Cronus,' she said. 'You'll soon see your brothers and sisters again.' He dropped Metis's herb into his father's nectar – which is what the gods drink in place of wine. Cronus first choked, then regurgitated all of Zeus's siblings, followed, last of all, by the stone.

Now that Zeus and his siblings stood together in freedom, war broke out between the generations, Olympians ranged against Titans, daughters and sons struggling against the father's flaming legions. Embattled squadrons of Titan gods filled the skies. Against them – storming, furious – ranged the ranks of the younger gods, and those of the older Titans whom they had enlisted as allies.

For ten years their battles blasted through the vaults of heaven – though a decade is like a heartbeat to these beings, who can never fight to the death. In the end, it was Gaia, exhausted by the conflict, who broke the deadlock. 'Zeus will win this war,' she prophesied, 'but only if he unleashes the forces of Tartarus.' So he descended to the bituminous depths of that prison, and negotiated with the Hundred-handers and the Cyclopes. In return for their freedom, the Cyclopes gave Zeus thunderbolts – and their loyalty.

Zeus now cast his new weapon, pale and blinding, through the fabric of the sky, ripping it end to end; then he hurled another, stronger, at his father: it fell like a white-hot sword thrust with inexorable force.

For the first time, Cronus felt pain rush through his body; in his agony he writhed and convulsed and bled – though immortals do not bleed as humans do, since it is not red blood but ichor, bright as gold, that flows in their veins.

Cronus sued for peace. Zeus imprisoned his Titan enemies, including his father, in the depths of Tartarus. The Hundred-handers became their prison guards.

When all of that business was done, Zeus turned to his most powerful brothers, Poseidon and Hades. 'There are three parts to the universe,' he said. 'The sky; the land and sea; and the Underworld. I propose we draw lots and divide these realms between us.' Poseidon and Hades agreed. Poseidon won the land

and the sea: when storms crash through the oceans, when the Earth trembles and cracks, tearing cities apart, it is his doing. Hades won the world below, where the faint ghostly traces of mortals crowd, insubstantial and insensate.

Zeus won the sky and became the king of gods, god of kings, storm-bringer, guarantor of justice, protector of a guest's right to hospitality. He reigned from his palace on Mount Olympus, where his sacred bird, the eagle, soared. His sister Hera, protector of marriage vows and families, became his wife. As a wedding gift, Gaia gave Hera trees bearing golden apples. She planted them in her garden in the land of the Hyperboreans, beyond the north wind. Athena's tapestry showed the goddess as she wandered through her beloved orchard, tended by the Hesperides, the daughters of evening. Nearby crouched Atlas, one of Zeus's Titan enemies. He was hunched in agony, limbs aching: he had been sentenced to carry the vault of the sky on his shoulders, keeping Gaia and Uranus apart, so they would never again become parents to powerful, unruly offspring.

Hera's children with Zeus were the ever-youthful Hebe, and Ares, the violent god of war, who delights in shattered corpses. But she had one child, Hephaestus, who was born without a father. The craftsman of the gods, wiry and strong, he worked day and night with his assistants, the Cyclopes, at a forge as hot and as powerful as a volcano. He walked with difficulty: one day, when Zeus and Hera were arguing, he had tried to intervene. Zeus hurled him down from Olympus; he fell for a whole day, and landed on the island of Lemnos, injuring his leg. He made marvellous and deadly things: a shield fit for the greatest warrior, engraved with scenes so detailed and vivid you could almost see and hear them; a net made from metal as silky and fine as a spider's web, but strong enough to imprison an immortal. He made a net like that to trap his wife, Aphrodite, and his half-brother Ares, when they slept together.

Athena wove a panel showing the story of her own birth. Zeus, in his lust for power, tried to rape the Titan goddess Metis. She used all her cunning to escape him, changing herself into myriad forms to try to wrest herself free from his terrible grasp, flicking desperately through shapes as you might through the pages of a book.

In the end, though, the threat of Zeus's thunderbolt defeated her. He had her caught in his iron grip; she became pregnant. Gaia prophesied again: 'If Metis has a baby fathered by Zeus, that child will be stronger than him.' Zeus's response was to swallow Metis whole. Later, he had Hephaestus extract the baby from his head with an axe. She came out fully armed, with a spear and a shield and a plume of feathers nodding from her helmet. Perhaps, if her father had not cheated Gaia's prophecy, Athena would have defeated her father, to rule on Olympus in her turn.

Athena is the goddess of winning wars, and she used to stride into battle alongside her favoured mortals, an owl accompanying her. She inherited all her mother's shrewdness: any mortal advised by her was strategic, meticulous and cunning. Inventive and practical, she was also the goddess of technology. She taught humans how to weave wood into the first ship; how to card wool and spin it; how to work the loom.

Beside the image of her own birth Athena made a panel of Apollo and Artemis, her luminous half-siblings, their deadly bows raised to kill mortals with unerring arrows. The twins' father was Zeus and their mother, the Titan goddess Leto, who gave birth to them on the island of Delos. Apollo, the sun god, was blinding, distant, vindictive. Fierce, virginal Artemis, both protector and hunter of wild animals, kept to the shadows and the woods.

When a human died suddenly in their prime, it was, likely as not, because Artemis or Apollo launched an arrow at them. Apollo used his arrows to send deadly plagues too, though he was also a healer. When the world was young, Apollo shot dead a tremendous creature called the Python, a child of Gaia. To commemorate his kill, Apollo founded the Pythian Games, where mortals competed in chariot races, running races and wrestling. And there, at Delphi, he also established his oracle: he used to whisper into the ear of his priestess, the Pythia, who gave prophecies to those who visited his sanctuary. But the oracle could trip the unwary. The Pythia's utterances were bundles of ambiguity from which questioners, as often as not, extracted only what they wanted to hear. In the forecourt of his temple were inscribed the words 'Know yourself', since it was only with self-knowledge that a human could unravel the confusing tangle of the priestess's words.

Athena wove her other half-brother, the shifty, untrustworthy Hermes – she showed him racing through the sky on winged boots, his snake-wreathed staff in hand. He was the son of Zeus and the nymph Maia, a protector of travellers, a messenger of Zeus, a prankster solemn only when accompanying the souls of the dead to Hades. For no reason other than to make trouble, he once stole cattle that Apollo was tending, herding them off into the mountains while his half-brother was distracted by a young man he was lusting after. Once he had them hidden, he sacrificed one of them. Then, idly playing around with the cow's entrails and the shell of a turtle, he constructed the first lyre. When Apollo finally caught up with him, he was so entranced by the sound made by the instrument that he forgot his fury, and traded the cattle for the lyre. Apollo brought the art of music to mortals, in all its mathematical precision and harmonious order.

The next scene on Athena's border showed two young Titan gods, Prometheus and Epimetheus, walking through the woods and glens of the Earth, far from the gaze of the Olympian deities. They were marvelling at the new creatures – men – whom Zeus had idly fashioned out of mud one day.

The gods, taken up with their own concerns, had mostly forgotten about these curious beings, who resembled them – or at any rate resembled them as much as a child's clay figure, wonkily moulded with clumsy fingers, can be said to be a likeness of a real person. But Prometheus was fascinated by the foolish, infantile creatures. They fed off wild berries and wandered through a world in which there were no houses, no cities, no governments; no ships, no trade; no war; no music, no literature, no philosophy, no knowledge of the stars.

'I feel sorry for them,' said Prometheus to his brother. 'All the animals around them are better suited to life than they are. Deer have speed, lions have strength, but these men have nothing special to recommend them. They are defenceless and stupid. They can't seem to find the pattern in anything. They look terrified every time the sun sets at night and rises in the morning. They must perceive the world as dreamlike fragments. And yet I have to admit, they intrigue me.'

'You're right,' said Epimetheus. 'It's as if Zeus left them half finished. The poor things can't even speak – have you heard how they grunt and howl at each other? They're not going to last long. Surely they'll die out and be forgotten – just another piece of Zeus's carelessness. What did he call them – "men"?'

'What I'm wondering,' said Prometheus, 'is whether I can teach them to be more resourceful. I think that, if they had some of the things that the gods are so jealously keeping for themselves, they might have a better chance. I think these mortals could be … magnificent, if only I could find a way to help them.'

Prometheus began to plot and plan.

He ascended to Zeus's halls on Olympus and, distracting the king of the gods with an arcane question of Titan-Olympian diplomacy, he pilfered a tiny finger of flame from a thunderbolt, hiding it in a fennel stalk. Then he went to the neighbouring palaces of Hephaestus and Athena where the two great gods toiled – Hephaestus at his forge, devising arms and armour for his fellow immortals, Athena in her workshop where she was experimenting with refinements to Apollo's skyborne chariot. As he talked to them, admiring their work, he waited till their backs were turned, then stole a handful each of their skill and intelligence, hiding them under his cloak. Then he went back down to Earth.

Prometheus now pitched a tent in a woodland glade where he knew the men sometimes gathered fruit, and settled down to wait. Sure enough, after several days, a few of them dared to approach him, though they'd soon enough skitter away like overbold lambs. Prometheus was patient, though, and very quiet and still, and as soon as the men came close enough to him – induced, perhaps, by the bowls of grapes and honey that he'd laid out on the grass – he took his handfuls of skill and intelligence and threw them at the humans. They drifted through the air and settled on the men's bodies.

At first, nothing much happened, and Prometheus began to worry, but, gradually, he saw something pass over the men's faces. First confusion, then fear, and then something else – something that seemed like curiosity. Prometheus could have laughed with delight. Instead very quietly, very slowly, he began to speak, hoping they would respond to his gentleness, if not to the meaning of his words. 'Please be calm, don't be frightened. I'm here as your friend, and I have wonderful things to show you – things that will make you almost as great as the gods that sit up there on Olympus. I'm risking a lot by being here, so don't let me down.' He held out his bowls of grapes and honey, and smiled.

And that was the beginning of it all. Over the following years, Prometheus lived among his beloved men. He taught them how to speak. He showed them how to build shelters to protect themselves from the worst of the winter weather. He taught them how to sharpen stakes into spears, how to plait nets to snare animals and fish. He guided their hands as they shaped flints into tools to skin their prey, and he gave them Zeus's fire so they could cook their food and warm themselves in the winter.

And all of this happened without Zeus noticing, because he had wars and lusts and amusements of his own to indulge, far away from the surface of the Earth. Until, one day, scanning the horizon from his palace, he noticed dozens of little trails of smoke curling up from the valleys below Olympus. And there – down among the trees – was Prometheus, demonstrating to a group of men how to shape an arrowhead. At once Zeus saw what had happened. Furious, he sent for Prometheus. 'What do you mean by this?' he asked the Titan, his thunderbolts crackling dangerously. 'You think you can steal from me? The god who defeated Cronus – are you mad?' Prometheus hung his head, but, quickly improvising, said, 'Great lord of clouds, storm bringer: forgive me. I only meant to show how brilliant your creation was. And those fires. I admit I borrowed a flicker of your divine thunderbolt. But see how I've taught them to burn offerings of meat to honour you and the other gods. I beg you to let them carry on. I think you might find them ... amusing.'

Zeus waved Prometheus impatiently away. He considered eradicating the men altogether. But then he thought again, and summoned Hephaestus and Athena. 'That cunning Prometheus has outwitted me, and you too. Look down there, deep in the valleys of the Earth – those foolish weak animals I made, those men, are now equipped with intelligence and skill and even fire. Nevertheless, there is room for improvement.'

Athena and Hephaestus went back to their studios and together worked on a new design. Hephaestus took soil and clay and moulded it into a form like that of a goddess. Athena warped her loom and made a marvellous robe in gleaming white – this she showed in her tapestry, a weaving within a weaving, lovely to behold. She designed a crown too, decorated with images of the remarkable creatures that inhabit the land and the sea. Hephaestus took her drawings and realised them in soft, lustrous gold, the detail so lifelike that you might have thought the dolphins on the crown were really leaping, the swallows really soaring. Then they dressed the figure in the robe and crown, and carried it down to Earth.

All the gods gathered, and a crowd of men too, with the brothers Prometheus and Epimetheus at their side. Hephaestus and Athena breathed on the figure. At first, nothing. Then, gradually, a change: you would have sworn that the clay arms were soft, and fleshlike, and veined. An eyelid seemed to twitch. Then the figure smiled, and the eyes opened, and there she was: a woman, strong and quick, a spark of shrewdness and humour in her eyes. 'Here you all are,' she said, looking around her, her steady glance taking in the forest glade with its dappled light, and the gods in their metallic splendour. Finally, her gaze lingered on the men, young and vigorous, their bodies muscled and hardened through the labour of their lives. 'What wonderful creatures,' she said. 'How beautiful men are. What a brave new world!' And she laughed.

The woman was named Pandora – meaning 'she who gives all'. She married Epimetheus, and together they had daughters, who became the companions, the sisters, the lovers of the men; and they became mothers themselves. Pandora did not unleash all the horror and grief into the world, as one poet – a man – has falsely claimed. With the arrival of women, the men ceased to be like children, innocent and ignorant. They began to know love, and joy, and the pain of loss, the ache of desire (often for each other): they became, in fact, fully human, with all the good and bad that that entails. Together, and guided by Prometheus, women and men learned new skills: they caught and domesticated the wild oxen, yoking them to ploughs; they learned to save seed and sow it every year, and harvest the crops, and store them safely against the lean times; they tamed and bridled horses, and Prometheus revelled in the joy humans found in a horse's strength and speed. Prometheus talked to them about the sun and the moon, about night and day, about the progress of the seasons, about rainbows and eclipses and the constellations. Hephaestus showed them how to forge metal into vessels, and knives, and horses' bits. Athena herself showed Pandora how to spin wool and flax, how to build a loom and weave. Prometheus demonstrated the art of blending herbs to make medicines; he showed them the patterns in birds' flight so they might catch a glimpse of the future; he guided them as they built temples to honour the immortals.

The humans began to observe the world around them, offering theories of their own about the nature of the Earth and the seas, of the wide, mysterious vault of the sky above and the broad circumference of the moon. They told stories round their fires; poets and philosophers arose among them.

But Zeus never dropped his grudge against Prometheus for stealing fire from him. He ordered his servant Cratos to take the Titan to the Caucasus mountains and shackle him with chains unwillingly forged by Hephaestus. Zeus sent his eagle to the exposed, desolate cliff where Prometheus was imprisoned. The bird clamped his great claws onto Prometheus's chest and tore relentlessly at his flesh until he had consumed his liver. Then the bird flapped lazily back to Olympus. The pain Prometheus suffered was incalculable – but his flesh was immortal, so overnight his wound healed completely. The eagle returned the next morning, and the next and the next, and the punishment was repeated for years that cannot be counted, until

Heracles eventually freed him. Prometheus's only solace, his only company, were the Oceanids, the daughters of Oceanus, who flew to him there and comforted him and told him stories of the world away from that harsh Scythian cliff.

In the centre of her tapestry Athena wove four great scenes, beginning with the story of the last great war in heaven – the Gigantomachy, the battle between the Olympians and the Giants. After Zeus's victory against the Titans, peace among the various generations of the immortals remained shaky and insecure. The Titans strained against their chains; Gaia herself was enraged at their humiliation. She gave birth to a new generation of immortals – enormous creatures who stood so high that their heads brushed gauzy Aether. Instead of having legs, the Giants' bodies were supported by twin snakes, each with scales as tough as armour. They began an assault on Olympus, flinging great boulders and burning oaks at the mountain citadel, hammering away with their missiles at the gods' palaces until fire took hold and charred the frescoed halls.

Finally an oracle told the Olympians that they would prevail in the war against the Giants only if they were helped by a mortal. So Athena set out to find Heracles. The son of Zeus himself and a human mother, Alcmena, Heracles was by far the most brutal and effective fighter among men.

Heracles now stood shoulder to shoulder with Athena, the mortal raining down arrows on the Giants while the Olympians used all their weapons. Hephaestus flung projectiles of red-hot metal; even the Fates, those ancient, powerful goddesses who spin, allot and cut the thread of human lives, fought with bronze cudgels. Athena took a boulder and hurled it; it landed in the sea, pinioning the Giant Enceladus beneath it, and it became the fertile and lovely island of Sicily. At last, the battle turned the Olympians' way. That was the scene that the goddess put right at the heart of her tapestry: herself fighting, with Heracles at her side.

Just when the gods felt they had the upper hand, though, Gaia sent one last creature to fight them – a child of hers, fathered by the echoing blackness of Tartarus. Typhon was larger even than the Giants. His body was like that of a vast man, but a hundred vipers of monstrous size took the place of his legs and he had multiple, snaky heads. From his mouths came a maddening hissing, and fire sprang from his eyes. Zeus, in his final desperation, took him on in single combat, pummelling him with his thunder, lashing and scorching him with endless electric bolts, like a boxer who, bloodied and recoiling, still manages to rain blows on his opponent though he's at the end of his resources, on the verge of collapse.

As the duel raged over the seas, Zeus hurled Mount Etna at him, which landed on Sicily, trapping Typhon beneath it. The creature's anger can still be felt today, as he groans and shifts, sending his sulphurous breath to the snowy peaks; even in our own times he has almost succeeded in escaping from his rocky prison to rage through the skies once more. That was the last great battle of the gods, when bounteous Gaia was defeated and despoiled by her own children and grandchildren.

Athena's second central panel depicted a group of goddesses wandering through a springtime meadow: Athena herself, the Oceanids, Artemis, Demeter's daughter Persephone, and Hecate, the great witch among immortals, who makes flocks fertile. The goddesses were gathering flowers: crocuses, violets and irises. Athena made the blooms gleam in shining, purple threads.

After a while they stopped to rest by the banks of a stream – all except Persephone, who kept on picking flowers, wandering further and further from her dozing companions. A pale narcissus nodded in the breeze, throwing up its delicate scent. Bending to pluck it, she felt a sudden chill, as if a thick cloud had passed in front of the sun, and with it, a pull of anxiety. It was like when you walk alone at night along a city street and sense the tap of footsteps behind you. You walk faster, you look straight ahead, and all the while you know it may be nothing, nothing at all.

As she stood up, she saw that a black chariot, drawn by black horses, had silently pulled up beside her. At the reins, towering over her, stood a god – a god who seemed to leach the joy from the spring air around him, and drain the light from the sky. 'Get in,' he said, smiling. 'No need for a goddess as lovely as yourself to walk. I'll take you wherever you want to go.'

'No,' she said, though she felt fear clutching at her gut. 'Thank you. But I prefer to walk.'

He laughed. She dropped the flowers. She turned and ran. He pulled viciously on his horses' reins, yanking them round, whipping them up in pursuit of the fleet-footed goddess. In a moment the only sign that anyone had been there was a scattering of crocuses, trampled. The other goddesses noticed not a thing – all except for one, who half saw, from the corner of her eye, a patch of darkness in the distance, and shook her head, and thought she must be dreaming.

Persephone was fast, but even so, she could not outrun the black horses: their driver was Hades, captain of the uncounted legions of the dead, a god stronger than all of the others except for his brothers Zeus and Poseidon. It was Zeus she called on now, her own father, praying for him to come and save her. But the protector of justice did not hear her. He was far away, in one of his temples, receiving offerings from humankind. And in any case: he had plotted all of this himself, with his brother.

Soon Hades caught up with her. His left arm held the reins, and with his right he reached down and scooped her up into the chariot, pinning her against his iron-cold body, his fingers digging mercilessly into her thigh, and all the while the horses galloped, taking her further and further from her friends. She struggled and screamed, now calling for her mother, Demeter.

As long as they galloped over the plains and hills, as long as she saw the sun and the sky, Persephone hoped that Demeter would hear her. But then, as they galloped near the foot of a range of bleak mountains, the earth cracked open and a chasm yawned. Hades drove his horses straight into it, urging them down, down, down. As the earth swallowed them, Persephone gave one final, desperate cry. Then the rocks above their heads groaned and shifted, narrowing the slice of bright warm sky until there was nothing left but the clammy, enveloping dark.

It was that very last scream that Demeter heard as it echoed from the mountains. Horrified by the sound of her darling's distress, she left the Olympian halls and flew through the skies as an eagle, scanning plains and mountains, searching for Persephone over land and sea. But she found no trace. No god or mortal could, or would, tell her anything; and no bird of omen dared to send her a sign. She dropped to Earth and roamed across the land for nine days, searching; she ate nothing, drank nothing, never paused to wash or sleep. Finally she found the goddess Hecate and questioned her. 'I don't know what I saw that day,' said Hecate, 'but it was *something* – a hole in the light, like a dark tornado. Helios must be able to tell you more.'

Without a word, Demeter turned and, with Hecate, flew straight as an arrow to shining Helios, the sun, as he travelled across the sky. They stood right in the path of his chariot, halting his blinding-bright horses. 'Respect me as an equal,' said Demeter, 'and speak the truth. Where is Persephone? Where is my daughter? I heard her voice crying out for me. You see everything and everyone, so tell me: has someone abducted her?'

'I do respect you and pity you, and yes, I will tell you the truth. It was Hades who took Persephone. He wants to marry her,' said Helios. 'She's safe – in the Underworld. I saw her running from him, screaming for her father, for you ... But listen, there's nothing you can do to change this. Hades arranged this with Zeus himself. And he won't make such a bad husband. Look at what power he has, how many souls he rules down there in his great kingdom of Erebus. She will be a great queen. It's all for the best.' With that he called out to his horses, and they sprang forward joyfully into the sky, soaring like birds towards the horizon.

Demeter didn't move at first. But then rage, terrible rage took her, and a grief yet more brutal than before. She plunged to Earth, fast as a kestrel that dives for its prey. Once there, she changed her appearance, wrinkling her clear bright skin, shrinking herself, bending her back, until she resembled a frail old woman. For months she wandered among humans, nursing her anguish, begging crusts from kings and swineherds, princesses and peasants; at times, she bartered for passage across the seas with merchants and fishermen.

She saw many cities, and learned the ways of many humans' minds. Some households greeted her kindly, giving her bread and olives and wine to stave off hunger, and asking no questions until she had eaten and drunk her fill; then, if she was lucky, the slaves would make up a bed for her in a corner of a house, piling up sheepskins and rugs to keep her warm. From other places she was shooed away with jeers and insults, or worse – perhaps a stool pitched at her head, or the farm dogs set loose.

One day, on the outskirts of a little town, she paused to rest by a well. As she sat there, in the shade of an olive tree, tired and hungry in her mortal's body, her heart aching for her lost child, four young women walked up the track, chattering to each other, laughing and joking; they had water jars with them, which they had been sent out to fill and bring back to their parents' house. As soon as she saw the homeless woman, Callidice, the eldest, said, 'I don't mean to intrude, but you seem all alone. Can't we help you in any way? I'm sure there are people in our town who would give you a bed.'

The goddess smiled, and told the sisters a tale. 'Thank you for your kindness, daughters. My name is Doso, and I've come here from Crete. Against my will, mind. I and some other women were rounded up and abducted by a crew of pirates. They took us across to the mainland. I was afraid they were going to sell us to slavers, so, while they were roasting meat and getting drunk, I managed to slip away and escape. Finally I found my way to this spring, but you're right, I'm in need of a roof over my head. So tell me, where am I, and whose house should I go to? I will gladly work. I can nurse children, or supervise younger women at the loom, whatever is needed.'

'I'm sorry to hear how you've suffered,' said Callidice. 'The deathless gods send us mortals so many bitter things to bear. But let me explain where you are: the nearest place is called Eleusis, and there are two or three families there that I'm sure would give you a place to sleep. But how would it be if we asked our own mother if she'd have you? If you wait here, we could go back and ask her now. We've a little brother who needs a nurse, and maybe, if our parents agree, you could live with us and help to look after him.'

The goddess nodded her head; the girls filled their water jars and ran back home. Demeter had no great expectation that they would return, but after a while, they did: the goddess could hear them before she could see them, laughing and chatting, and when they turned a corner in the ox-track and came into view, she could see their hair shining in the sunlight. The girls helped the goddess up and walked slowly with her back to the house of their parents, Celeus and Metanira, and when they reached its threshold, they ran towards their mother, who was sitting on a finely carved seat, smiling and hugging her little baby to her breast.

The old woman was behind the girls, and so they did not see her enter the room, as their mother did. As Demeter's sandal slapped against the doorstep, Metanira was sure she glimpsed, just for an instant, not a tiny, bent-backed old woman silhouetted against the morning light, but a goddess, tall and slender and strong. Quickly, though, the impression faded, and there was no one there but a ragged beggar. Nevertheless Metanira – fearful, full of awe – jumped up at once and offered the visitor her own seat. But Demeter kept her eyes modestly to the ground, and refused to sit until Iambe, the slave, thought to bring out a low stool, which she spread over with a sheepskin. And as the deathless goddess watched the mortal mother nursing her baby, surrounded by her chattering girls, she pulled her shawl tight round her face to hide her tears. She thought her heart would break with sorrow, as she remembered her own darling daughter.

For a long time Demeter sat there, shrouded in her own thoughts, saying nothing. Tactfully Metanira did not press her to speak, and when Iambe offered her a refreshing drink of barley, water and herbs, she refused it. At that, Iambe made a bawdy joke to make the visitor laugh – which the goddess did, despite herself. Her sombre mood was broken.

'Welcome, lady,' said Metanira. 'I can see that you are honourable; there is goodness and grace in your eyes. You've suffered a great deal. To lose your home, to be exiled, to be separated from your family – it's hard. But we would like you to make our house your own, if in return you'll help me take care of my little son, Demophon.'

'Here, let me hold him,' said the goddess, reaching for the child. 'I will indeed take care of him, and I promise you that while I'm watching him, he'll be safe from harm.' She jiggled him on her knee, and cuddled him, and smelled his delicious baby smell, and she whispered in his ear, 'Hades shan't have you – no he shan't.'

Demeter – or Doso as she was known to the mortal family – became Demophon's nurse. Each day had its rhythm: she played with him, soothed his tears, and, while he slept, she swept out the halls with Iambe and supervised the younger slave women as they worked on their spinning and at the looms. Meanwhile, everyone noticed how fast Demophon grew, outpacing the other children his age. His skin gleamed, his eyes shone, his hair grew thick and lustrous, he never suffered from the childish illnesses that afflicted his playmates.

Metanira had, more or less, shaken off the memory of the strange vision she had seen the day that Doso had arrived in her household. But after a time she became troubled by Demophon's incredible strength and vigour. Where on earth did it come from? As soon as Doso had started to care for him, he had weaned himself, quite suddenly. Then it occurred to Metanira: she never saw the nurse feeding him at all – no scraps of bread soaked in milk, no soft fragments of fruit, such as tiny children can eat. Perhaps that was all being discreetly managed out of her sight ... but still. Yet there was surely nothing to worry about – her child was happy and healthy. On the other hand, wasn't there something uncanny about his spurt of growth, his almost luminous bloom?

Metanira decided to keep a close watch on the nurse and her baby. All the next day she stayed near them, making little excuses to leave her loom to observe them as they played in the shady courtyard, or to check on him as he napped in his sheepskin-lined crib. And, though she could not have criticised Doso's patient, good-humoured care for her son, the mystery remained – when did the boy eat? Perhaps, she thought, the nurse was feeding him only at night, odd though that might seem. So she kept herself awake after the household had gone to bed and, when she judged everyone to be asleep, quietly padded out of her chamber to Doso's little room and softly pushed open the door.

For a second she froze. Then she screamed. She had seen a terrible, unthinkable thing: her child, her baby, in the fire – and Doso standing there, watching. She flung herself through the door, and, plunging her bare arms into the flames, pulled the child away. But Doso roared with fury and tried to snatch the baby back from Metanira's grasp; and as they fought, Demophon slipped right out of their hands and fell to the floor.

Doso turned to Metanira. 'You fool!' she said. 'You stupid, ignorant mortal. You have no idea what you've just done. Every night I've put Demophon into this fire, and every night I've been burning away a little more of his weak, pathetic humanity. I swear by the River Styx, the implacable water that circles the Underworld, that I would have made this child a god, to sit next to me in my halls on Olympus. Now, because of your blundering ineptitude, he'll die like the rest of you, even if he'll be remembered with honour because he once lay in my lap. Because I, Metanira, am not the feeble old woman you take me for. I am a goddess, the deathless Demeter, who brings blessings to immortals and humans.'

With that, her back straightened, her skin brightened. Old age fell away from her. She grew to a tremendous height. Her hair, no longer straggly and grey, fell thick and lustrous to her shoulders. A delicious perfume – like the breeze on a cool, harvest-tide morning – filled the room. A blinding radiance emanated from her. Metanira fell back in shock, and stumbled to the ground. 'Build me a great temple,' Demeter commanded, in a voice like summer thunder. 'I will dictate the rites you must offer to appease me.'

A white flash of light, and she was gone. Metanira's daughters, roused by the commotion, rushed in. Callidice picked the child up from the ground where he lay, trying to soothe and comfort him. But he wouldn't stop crying: he wanted his goddess of a nurse, not mere mortal sisters.

The very next morning work started on a new temple to the goddess. Still Demeter stayed on the Earth, avoiding the halls of her fellow immortals. Now that she had lost Demophon, her longing for her daughter redoubled. In her fury and sorrow, she withdrew her gifts of harvest and plenty from humans and gods alike. The whole Earth lay frozen in the goddess's grief. Nature was numbed.

No buds sprouted from bare branches; no shoots nosed their way through spring soil. All was grey and bleak. Day after day, week after week, month after month, there were only chill winds and squalling rains. Soon the sheep and goats had no hay left to eat; barns and storerooms lay bare. The people went hungry and grew thin. Even the gods became restless and discontented, since the mortals could make no smoking sacrifices of meat, send no rich perfumes wafting up to heaven for their pleasure.

Finally Zeus sent Iris – the gods' messenger, who rides on the rainbow's tail – to find Demeter. She found her sitting alone and furious in her own temple, the one that Celeus and Metanira had built in Eleusis, dressed in a robe of midnight black. 'Please, come back to Olympus, great goddess,' she said. 'It's Zeus's will – don't go against him. Your anger has gone on long enough. It's time to soften the soil, breathe life into the dormant seeds. There has been enough suffering now.'

Demeter turned to her and said, 'You can go back to Zeus and tell him that I will never return to Olympus, and no seed will germinate on Earth, until I have set eyes on my daughter.'

Nothing Iris said could move her, and so she darted back to the halls of Olympus. Zeus sent the other gods down to Eleusis, one by one, each with gifts and honours to offer to Demeter if only she would release the Earth from its wintry grip, if only she would let leaves unfurl and flowers bloom and seeds mature inside their husks. But she was implacable. She sent every god back to heaven with the same message. She wanted to see Persephone.

At last, the lord of the thunderbolt agreed that Persephone would be allowed to return to the upper air, but on one condition – she could stay permanently only if she had eaten nothing while dwelling in the halls of the dead. Demeter reluctantly agreed, and the king of the gods summoned Hermes and sent him down to Erebus, Hades' grim domain. There he found her, the beautiful Persephone, sitting apart from her captor in a chamber in his dank palace; she had become pale and thin, her divine bloom dimmed. Hermes bowed to them both, and said: 'Lord Hades, I come from Zeus. I know, sir, that you have no need of Demeter's gifts here, in your deathly kingdom, where nothing grows and nothing ever will. But she is angry and the Earth is dying. There will come a time when humans will cease to multiply – and then there will be no more souls left to populate your land. Demeter will not relent until she has seen her daughter. Please, let me take her with me.'

Persephone jumped up, her heart full of hope, hardly able to believe that she might see the lovely light again, the cloud-scudded sky. Hades, his face grim and set, considered for a moment. Then he came to a decision. 'I bow to the command of Zeus,' he said. 'Hermes, hitch the black horses to my chariot and you shall take Persephone to her mother.' As Hermes turned to obey, Hades addressed the goddess. 'Here, lady, let me help you with your cloak.' Suspecting nothing – feeling only shock at her sudden deliverance – she stepped towards him. As she came close, though, he clapped his hand – as cold and hard as marble – against her mouth. She felt something on her tongue. Involuntarily, she swallowed. Hades pulled his hand away. She staggered out of his grasp. 'Just a pomegranate seed,' he said. 'It's nothing. My little joke. Forget about it.' He smiled.

Persephone backed away from him, shaking, unsure of what had just happened – some game, she supposed, a cruel parting shot. Then she turned and ran out of the palace, where Hermes stood waiting in Hades' chariot. She climbed up beside him. 'Get me away from here, now,' she said. 'Just go.'

Hermes urged the horses on, and they galloped through the bleak, lifeless realms of the dead. And soon, the horses began to climb, ascending a track that led ever upwards, upwards. They leapt the River Styx, the fetid waters that circle Hades' domain, and came to the place where the rocks had closed over Persephone's head. The great stones creaked and shuddered apart, and there was a gust of pine-scented air, and the sight of the broad horizon, and they were out. Persephone laughed for joy.

They galloped on and on, the horses' hooves barely touching the ground, until they came to the great temple where Demeter waited. And as she sat there, she sensed her daughter coming to her, and she sprang up and ran down the temple steps, and Hermes pulled up the horses sharply, and Persephone jumped out of the chariot, and the two goddesses ran into each other's arms.

Deathless Demeter, who had thought she would live through the whole of eternity without seeing her dear daughter again, clung to Persephone as if she would never let her go, kissing her soft hair, her lips, her cheeks. And, as Persephone buried herself in that protective, strong embrace, she understood that Demeter's love was singular and inexhaustible; that she was loved by her mother as she could be by no other.

For a long time they stayed like that, their tears flowing.

After a time, though, Demeter felt an awareness of something – something not quite right. Gently freeing herself from Persephone's arms, she held her daughter's hands in hers, and said: 'Did he give you something to eat?'

'No,' said Persephone. 'All the time I was there I refused nectar and ambrosia. I couldn't bear to eat anything that came from him.'

'Are you certain?' said Demeter. 'You ate absolutely nothing, the whole time you were there?'

'Nothing at all,' her daughter replied. 'Except ... except after Hermes came for me, just before we left, he did something awful – he forced his hand over my mouth, and made me swallow something – but it was nothing, only a pomegranate seed.'

Demeter turned away briefly, and then looked again at her child, forcing a smile, stroking her long hair, and the two, mother and daughter, talked and comforted each other; and Hecate came too, to see her dear friend Persephone, and to promise her that she'd always be near her, whatever might happen. And after a time Rhea, Demeter's mother, the great Titan goddess, arrived, bringing with her a proposal from Zeus.

It was after Rhea and Demeter had negotiated together in private that Demeter drew her child to her again. 'Persephone, listen to me: Hades tricked you. There is a law: if you eat anything in Erebus, even a pomegranate seed, you must return there for ever. But Rhea and I have agreed this: you will go there for one-third of each year, and reign as queen of the dead. But you will also be able to come back to the upper air for two-thirds of the year, and be with me and the other deathless ones.'

She smiled through her tears, and as she did so, she loosed her grip on the living things of the Earth. Zephyr, the mild west wind, began to warm the soil. Not long after, the four goddesses – Rhea, Demeter, Persephone and Hecate – could hear the birds singing in the trees. Soon their song was drowned out by the screech of cicadas, waking up to the sun. Little by little, the Earth was reviving. Spring was returning. Meadows bloomed again with crocuses, and violets, and irises, and narcissi.

One of the Oceanids who had walked with Persephone, that day she was abducted by Hades, was Clymene; it was she that Athena wove next, in her third great central panel, showing the nymph as she wept all alone in the desolate north, shedding tears that hardened into amber. Clymene had brought up a son, Phaethon, on her small, rocky island. His father was Helios – but the god never paused his progress through the sky to visit the child. Phaethon pestered his mother daily for tales about his father, and screwed his eyes up against the searing brightness in the heavens, hoping against hope that he might pick out the outline of his chariot. As the boy grew older, he used to boast about Helios to his friends. But that only bored and irritated them. 'If he really is your father,' said one of them, 'why hasn't he ever been here? Maybe he actually isn't your father at all. Maybe that's just a story your mother told you.'

Back home, Phaethon raged against Clymene, blaming her for the loss that gnawed at him. 'Why did he leave us? What did you do to him? Are you sure he's my father?' he asked, over and over again. In the end, she said, 'If you really want to see him, go. You're old enough now. His palace isn't far from here – just travel east, you'll find it just below the horizon; it's where he spends every night. See how you like him when you meet him.'

Phaethon set off east and, after several days, arrived just below the horizon. His father's halls reared up splendidly in front of him, bright-pedimented; the boy felt very small. The remarkable doors, fashioned from pure silver by Hephaestus himself, were engraved with images of sea gods: shape-shifting Proteus tending Poseidon's seal flocks; and Triton, fish from the waist down and man from the waist up. Tentatively, Phaethon put his hands to the silver panels, and pushed.

He found himself in a vast hall. Everything around him gleamed: the porphyry and malachite floors, the golden, jewel-studded goblets standing on ivory-inlaid tables. The walls were frescoed with scenes of the Earth as Helios observed it from his daily passage through the skies: forests and rivers and plains and mountains and island-studded seas all set out in their order and harmony, just as Gaia had made them.

From the back of the hall came a heat and light so intense that Phaethon flinched. Through the blinding glare he was just able to make out a throne inset with hundreds of emeralds, and, lounging on it, a god with flaming hair and beard: Helios. Around him stood the Hours, the goddesses of the passage of time, and the Seasons – Spring wearing a coronet of narcissi, Summer garlanded with roses, Autumn with arms full of grapes, and frosty Winter, crowned with bare twigs.

'Phaethon, my boy,' said Helios. 'I watched you as you set out to find me here, and I'm glad to see you, truly I am. What can I offer you – food, drink? Or, a gift? How about those jewelled goblets I saw you admiring? I could give you a handful of emeralds from my throne; or a robe woven by the Hours themselves for your mother. Tell me, and I'll give it to you.'

Phaethon felt lonelier than ever, since he realised that he could never reach out and touch the fiery god, never feel his embrace. 'Father,' he said, 'I don't want a gift. I just want to know that you love me.'

'Ha! Of course I do,' said Helios. 'Every morning I see you from my chariot, check that you're still alive and whatnot. I'm very fond of you, and all of my children.' He gestured vaguely towards the rest of the world.

'Will you prove it? Will you truly give me anything that I want?' said Phaethon.

'What? Well, yes, that's what I said,' replied Helios, shifting in his chair. 'What will you have, then? I haven't much time, I'm afraid. Need to get on with bringing light to the world. The Hours won't like it if I'm late.'

'Do you swear?' said Phaethon. 'A solemn oath, sealed by the immortal Themis, protector of promises?'

'Yes, yes, anything you want,' answered Helios. 'I swear.' This time, there was a very definite edge of impatience in his voice.

'What I'd like, then, is to ride across the skies in your chariot. To do your work, just for a day. To prove myself your true son.'

An agonisingly bright shaft of light now shot out from Helios's glance, so that Phaethon staggered back and almost fell. The god seemed unable to speak, and turned his head away. Then he turned back to face the boy. 'I've been very rash, Phaethon,' he said. 'I should never have made that promise. I would do anything, anything to unsay it. But I'm afraid it's too late. Themis, the guarantor of oaths, is more powerful than me, and certainly more powerful than you. The only thing I can do is ask you to take back your request. Child, you're a mortal. Your years on this Earth are few. Don't cut your life even shorter. Listen: you'll never be able to control my horses. Only I can do that. Even I struggle – there are days when I've almost gone off course, when Tethys has been afraid I might plunge into her seas. And those constellations you mortals gaze at by night? They'll attack unless you manage a course through them. The Scorpion will try to lash you with its sting, the Crab's claw will swipe you out of the chariot if you're not careful. Look, my son, my child – anything else in the world I'll give you. But please, not this.'

Phaethon could hear the distress – perhaps, even, the love – in his father's voice, and he hesitated. But he was so blazing with desire to drive the chariot that he refused to change his mind. He was secretly determined to gallop low over his island, to show his friends and his mother what he was really made of.

Helios reluctantly gave in, bound as he was by his oath. 'Listen carefully,' he said. 'Don't use the whip on the horses. What you've got to do is hold them back, not urge them on. You'll see my sky-tracks, the furrows the chariot makes every day on its course through the heavens – follow them. You want to aim for a broad, smooth arc. Avoid the poles. Don't get too near the Earth, and don't fly too high, either.'

By this time, Selene, the Moon, was reining in her pale horses at her own palace on the western edge of the world, ready to join her mortal lover Endymion, who slumbers for all eternity in her chamber. Eos took her place at the doors of Helios's palace, her rosy flush beginning to wash the horizon with faint traces of dawn light. The golden-maned horses were brought out by Helios's grooms and, as they bucked and snorted, sweat foaming at their shoulders, their ears lying flat against their heads, they were hitched to the golden chariot by the grooms. Helios made one last appeal to his son. 'My boy, let me take the horses out today – you can watch from here, enjoy yourself in the palace – we can talk and feast together when I return tonight.'

But Phaethon ignored his father and leaped into the chariot, grabbing the reins. Clawing the air with their gold-flashing hooves, the horses careered forward, quickly outstripping Zephyr, the warm west wind. Helios became a mere blinding glint on the hillside, his cries of 'Hold them back!' lost in the rush of wind around Phaethon's ears, the beating of his own heart. The chariot, untethered from the ground, carrying a mere boy instead of its usual heavy load, tossed from side to side like a boat in a storm. The fiery-footed steeds panicked, the whites of their eyes flashing. They bolted away from the usual tracks.

It was all Phaethon could do to stay upright; the idea of holding the horses back, steering them on to their proper path, was a fantasy. He couldn't even remember their names. As they plunged and dipped and reeled, sky seemed like sea, sea like sky; then the clammy grey clouds enveloped them, cutting off every reference point, completely disorienting him.

All at once the clouds parted and the chariot emerged into the clear air. Phaethon looked down. He could see islands like pebbles in the blue; then the outline of continents; then the whole curving body of Gaia was revealed as a shining orb of blue and green. They climbed so high they were among the stars. Phaethon dropped the reins in fright, and the horses bolted even more wildly, plunging right towards the ferocious constellations. The Great Bear swung out a massive paw; Scorpio's vast curved sting was poised to strike.

By some miracle, they swooped clear of the heavenly predators. But there was trouble on Earth. Without the warmth brought by Helios's chariot, unseasonable snow fell. You might have thought it beautiful, this great muffling, dazzling white-out. But not for long. As the cold continued, children went hungry; old men and women began to freeze in their homes. Flocks died in the fields, crops were frosted and ruined, birds could no longer find food. Trees bent and fell, weighted down by the endless drift of flakes. Fish were trapped motionless in rivers of solid ice; the very oceans grew sluggish as they filled with floes. Cities were cut off, and fights broke out over the last of their stores. People began to starve.

It had never occurred to the mortal boy that his arrogance would result in such destruction, such misery, such damage to Gaia herself. But there was worse to come. The horses now swerved downwards, nosediving towards the Earth. Soon Phaethon could see mountains rushing up to meet them with terrifying speed. Now he could pick out cities clinging to hilltops, painted temple pediments, isolated cottages, ships at sea. At one point, he glimpsed his home island, the village, his mother's house – and how he regretted his childish desire to show himself to his friends in his father's chariot. Because now, they were far, far too close.

In the chariot's wake, fields dried up, grass yellowing, soil cracking. Wells ran dry and the gurgling springs became stale and dusty. The nymphs, the gentle nymphs of stream and brook, departed. In the mortals' fields, crops shrank and browned. Rivers narrowed to trickles, then dwindled to nothing, baring their dead and stony beds; the labyrinthine delta of the great Nile became parched and arid. River gods moaned and wept dry tears. The trees, once green-boughed havens for birds and beasts and insects, dropped their leaves, and forests became boneyards. In the mountains, glaciers retreated and shrank. In the cold lands of the Caucasus, where Prometheus lay pinioned to his rock, the ice that had once gripped the soil melted. Fertile plains turned to deserts. Animals and humans starved. Disease ran amok. At the extremities of the world, the poles that Helios had warned Phaethon against approaching, the sea ice thinned; water began to gush from ice caps. The oceans, swollen by the melting ice, began to devour the low-lying coasts, consuming towns and cities. The winds, roused to confusion and fury, swirled and raged.

At last Gaia herself could bear it no more, and lifted her head – her massy head, once green-meadowed, soft with moss, but now grey and ugly and pitted. She could hardly breathe, so polluted was the air. Her throat was parched, her lips were cracked, her eyes – once deep, mirrored lakes – were now empty craters. She cried out in her distress to the Olympian gods, feasting in their halls, oblivious. 'Zeus, king of gods, if you can call yourself that – wake up! Can't you see what's happening? You think you're safe on your mountaintop, but the fires will burn you too. Atlas can barely shoulder his load any more; he too will burn, and when he does Uranus will come crashing down upon us, and primal Chaos will reign once more. Is that what you want?'

Exhausted, she sank back down. Zeus leaped up from his couch, ran from his palace onto the dusty mountainside, and cast his glance over the world. At once he aimed a flaming thunderbolt. It travelled through the air like an arrow, and found its target: Phaethon. The boy, the foolish boy, hurtled through the heavens, ablaze, like a shooting star. He plunged, already dead, into the River Eridanus, far away in the western wilds of the world, near the garden of the Hesperides.

The horses, exhausted, eventually found their way back to Helios's palace. So riven with guilt and shame was the god that he almost refused to get back into his chariot. Selene had to help him; as she supported him through the skies she half blocked out his light, so that for a day his glow was dimmed. Clymene eventually found her son's body. And there, on the riverbank, she wept for him.

With Prometheus, Clymene had another son, called Deucalion, who married Pyrrha, the daughter of Epimetheus and Pandora. It was their story that Athena wove to complete her tapestry.

For all their ingeniousness and resourcefulness, the young race of mortals were also venal, violent and greedy. The shrewd and selfish among them snatched more grain than they needed, and hoarded it, and shored up their own power. They built palaces for themselves and called themselves kings. They made slaves of each other, the strong oppressing the weak. Wars were fought for land, and for riches, and for fame among themselves. They gouged great wounds out of the mountains in their search for iron and gold and silver and precious stones. They clogged the air with fumes as they smelted ore to forge their weapons. They felled entire forests to build their ships, sending the gentle dryads and hamadryads, the demi-gods of the woods, into exile.

And so Zeus – though perhaps it might be argued that the humans' vices were no worse than the Olympians' – decided to end it all. He summoned the Winds – Boreas, the north wind, Zephyr, the west, Eurus, the east, and Notus, the south – and commanded them to roam abroad, all at once, so that anarchy raged in the skies. It rained, endlessly. The rivers rose and swelled, becoming torrents. They burst their banks, engulfing towns and villages and farms, toppling palaces as easily as a child might kick over a sandcastle. Crops lay flattened and then disappeared, orchards and vineyards sank without trace, animals and people were carried away in the furious spate, birds stayed on the wing, exhausted, finding nowhere to land. Still the waters kept on rising, submerging even hilltop temples and the highest citadels. As Zeus had intended, the humans were dying – they were either overcome in their own homes or taken as the rising water outpaced their search for higher ground. Waves lapped at mountainsides; fish and seals swam through underwater forests; Nereids explored what had once been cities, marvelling at the submerged ruins of temples and palaces. The gods watched it all happen from the heights of Olympus, indifferent.

Prometheus, though, had long before foreseen what was to come, and had warned Deucalion and Pyrrha. In turn, they had tried to tell the other mortals about the impending flood, pleading with them time and again to change their ways – or if that was impossible, at least to make preparations to keep themselves safe. But no one listened to them at all. Following Prometheus's instructions, Deucalion and Pyrrha constructed a chest, and stacked it full of provisions. As the waters rose and tore apart their village, they got into their chest and launched it. Off it bobbed, whirling this way and that in the eddying waters, sometimes colliding dangerously with debris, sometimes borne off at terrifying speed. For nine days the chest floated like that, and Deucalion and Pyrrha lay inside, frightened and wet, but alive.

As Deucalion woke up one morning he realised that instead of rocking and juddering they were grounded and still. Gingerly he opened the lid of the chest and looked out. He did not know it, but they were on the very summit of the mountain called Parnassus, which resembled a rocky island in an immeasurable sea. 'I think we're safe now, for a while at least,' he said to his wife, as they clambered out onto solid land. 'But what about the world? What if it's just us – what if we're the only ones left?' In wonderment and fear they scanned the horizon. There was nothing but water and sky. Animals and birds had flocked to the mountaintop; but they were the only humans. They felt completely alone – as indeed they were.

Zeus took pity on the blameless Deucalion and Pyrrha, and commanded the rains and the winds to cease. The sun came out. The floods receded. Parnassus became, first, part of an archipelago, as other peaks emerged. Then hill ranges became visible, and finally the plains. Pyrrha and Deucalion explored their new domain, eventually stumbling on a little temple, half ruined, filled with silt and mud. Cautiously they approached it, and as they reached the steps, they bowed down and kissed them. Pyrrha said, 'Whatever god or goddess inhabits this temple, please tell us: are we the last mortals alive?' Nothing stirred. Then came a sudden breeze, a voice – a sound as if the wind itself were whispering. 'It is Themis who speaks: to replenish the race of humans, you must throw Mother's bones behind you.' Then nothing. The wind fell to stillness.

Pyrrha was in despair. 'Mother's bones? It doesn't make any sense at all,' she said. 'And even if we found our mothers' bones, which is impossible, since we have no idea where we are, I'm sure it would be a sacrilege to do as the voice said.' For hours they debated what the voice might have meant. As they walked and talked, Deucalion tripped and fell, stumbling over a rock. Righting himself, he put his hand on the bleached, pale stone. Pyrrha said, 'Rocks, Earth's bones ... Maybe that's the answer.'

'We can only try,' said Deucalion.

Each of them made a pouch of their cloaks and filled them with stones. As they walked, they tossed them over their shoulders. Pyrrha could not help turning to look, and what she saw was extraordinary: pebbles swelling and growing, turning into great chunks of matter. Each of these inchoate masses resembled a lump of marble as it is gradually, painstakingly chipped away at by a sculptor – a curve of an arm beginning to show here, the muscles of a leg there – until the entire figure is revealed. And as human forms emerged from the shapeless rocks, so their flesh softened, and they began to breathe, and move, and smile, and laugh – they were brand-new people ready to make their mark upon the Earth.

And so Athena completed her tapestry. As she cut the shining, elaborate work from the loom she pondered how little the flood had taught the mortals. They were still everything their predecessors had been: loving and violent; ingenious and shortsighted; generous and jealous; clever and destructive. Of all the things that walked upon the surface of the Earth, it seemed to her, there was nothing more wonderful, and more terrible, than humankind.

ALCITHOË

The daughters of Minyas *
Dionysus * Europa and the
bull * Cadmus and Typhon
* Io * Harmonia * Tiresias
* Oedipus and Jocasta *
Eteocles and Polynices
* Antigone and Creon *
Niobe * Actaeon * Semele
and the birth of Dionysus
* Ampelus * Dionysus and
the Tyrrhenian pirates
* Pentheus and Agave *
Alcithoë and Dionysus

ALCITHOE

It was the days when the young god Dionysus first came back to Greece – to his mother's city, Thebes, in the territory of Boeotia. The women there answered his call to worship him: they abandoned their looms and their distaffs, their husbands and children, and ran out into the countryside, right out to the wilds of Mount Cithaeron. There they joined the god's band of followers, the army of women he'd brought with him from the east.

They were wild, these maenads, these bacchantes, these followers of the god: they wrapped themselves in fawnskins, cut fennel stalks for staffs, wreathed their hair in ivy, and spent their nights in frenzies of dancing. In their ecstasy they tore wild animals apart, then sucked on the creatures' blood, tasting their savage, throbbing energy.

All this for Dionysus: the god who could make spasms of fear run through armies; who brought the solace of drunkenness to humans; who made it possible to be two people at once, both actor and character. He coaxed fruits to ripeness. He was the force that makes buds burst into flower. He was double-natured: ferocious and gentle; feminine and masculine. He was a dangerous god, a god whom it was best not to ignore.

Nevertheless Alcithoë, who lived in the Boeotian city of Orchomenus, not far from Thebes, did ignore him, so intent was she on her art. What did she want with wild nights on the mountains when there was work to be made? With her sisters to help her, she was weaving a great tapestry thickly designed with the many stories of Thebes, right from the time the city was founded by Cadmus.

She began, however, not with Cadmus, but with his sister, Europa.

Europa was a princess of Tyre, in Phoenicia – a land of bold, seafaring merchants, whose mountains were rich with cedar forests, their timber good to trade with Egyptian kings. One day, she was playing on the shore with her friends when a white bull shambled towards them. Where had he come from? No one knew: one minute he wasn't there, the next, he was. He was beautiful, shining-bright, gentle. He let the girls stroke his soft flanks, wreathe his horns in flowers. After a while, he bent his front knees and, with an ungainly lurch, lowered his bulk down to the sand. Europa sat next to him, fondling his ears and silky dewlap; bolder, now, she dared to clamber on his back. The bull didn't seem to mind. Indeed, after a moment he heaved himself back up and ambled along the water's edge. Europa was laughing with delight.

All of a sudden, though, the animal veered towards the sea and waded in. Deeper and deeper into the waves he strode and, then, with a jolt, he was swimming – swimming straight out towards the horizon at an impossible speed. Europa screamed, but it had all happened so quickly: her companions were dwindling figures on an already distant shore. Sea creatures – tritons and nymphs – surfaced from the depths, but they just laughed as she shrieked for help. Alcithoë wove the Tyrian woman as she clung on for dear life, the bull forging through the spume, the girl's pink shawl billowing behind her.

After a long time, they came to an island. Later, Europa learned it was called Crete. The bull clambered onto the beach. The girl, exhausted, slipped off the creature's back and lay there, bedraggled, semi-conscious, mouth full of sand. She knew what was coming next. She'd heard the old stories about the gods, their monstrous appetites. The bull mounted her. The bull raped her. The bull was Zeus.

Back in Tyre, Europa's family was sick with worry. Agenor, her father, sent out her brothers to look for her. Cadmus was one of them. For years he travelled from land to land in search of his lost sister.

It was the time of the war between the Olympians and the Giants, the great conflict that Athena had depicted at the centre of her tapestry. Gaia, the Earth, had recently sent her child Typhon – a vast snake-footed, snake-headed, human-bodied creature – to fight the Olympian gods. He had the upper hand: he had stolen Zeus's thunderbolts.

There was no way of retrieving them by force. That left trickery. Zeus commandeered the least likely being imaginable to help him: Cadmus, the young man whose sister he'd raped. 'Take these pan pipes,' he told Cadmus, omitting to mention Europa at all. 'Play them to Typhon outside his cave. I need him distracted. If you do well, I'll make you the guardian of cosmic harmony – and I'll let you marry the beautiful Harmonia.'

So saying, he disguised Cadmus as a shepherd and gave him his instructions. Once he reached Typhon's lair, deep in the Taurus mountains, the young man leaned faux-nonchalantly against a nearby tree, and began to play. Soon enough, the giant creature, bewitched by the music, slunk from the cave, one immense tentacle-like limb after another, followed by his many heads with their grinning faces and slithery tongues. That's how Alcithoë showed the scene, the mortal man entertaining the snake-footed giant.

'Hey, shepherd,' called Typhon after a while. 'Instead of annoying me with those pan pipes, why don't you give them to Zeus: he's probably at a loose end without his thunderbolts. Or here's a better idea, why don't you and I have a competition? Just for fun. You play your pipes, and I'll make some music with this thunder. And as a favour, when I'm king of heaven – which will be pretty soon now – I'll let you sleep with whichever of the goddesses you choose, even Athena if you like. Except Hera of course. That one's mine.'

Crafty Cadmus now pushed his luck. He knew that Typhon had taken not only Zeus's thunderbolts, but some of the sinews from the god's body; those sinews were also concealed in Typhon's cave. 'Sir,' he said, 'I could make an even better tune if I could play my lyre. But just now I can't – Zeus destroyed my strings in anger, just because I played better than his son Apollo.'

Eagerly Typhon slunk back into the cave and returned with Zeus's sinews, proffering them to Cadmus to use as lyre strings. 'Thank you,' said the human, handling the god's body parts with extreme care. 'Excuse me while I find my lyre.' He darted out of sight, pretended to string up his instrument, then started a new, sweeter tune on the pipes, imitating a lyre's gorgeous thrum. Typhon sighed with satisfaction and settled down to listen. He imagined Cadmus was playing a victory song for him, and his mind began to wander. He was so distracted, in fact, that he failed to notice Zeus creeping over to pick up his sinews where Cadmus had carefully placed them, then slipping into the cave to retrieve his thunderbolts.

Moving quickly now, Zeus veiled the fake shepherd in a cloud, making him invisible. Cadmus stopped playing. Typhon jolted awake from his pleasant reverie, then, alarmed, swished back into his cave. At once he saw what had happened, and was roused to a new fury. 'What are thunderbolts against me?' he cried. 'Mountains will be my shield, hills and oceans my swords, rivers my spears! I will unleash the Titans from their prisons! We will win a great victory! When I've defeated him, Zeus will take Atlas's job, lifting the world on his aching shoulders. Apollo will be my slave boy, playing his lyre to me while I feast at the side of Cronus! And on Hera I will father a new race of many-headed gods.'

Zeus laughed: with his thunderbolts back, he was unbeatable. Typhon was still dangerous, though: he grabbed entire forests and hurled them at the Olympians' stronghold. Zeus retaliated with thunder, hurricanes, slashing storms. But it was their last battle: Zeus prevailed, burying Typhon beneath Mount Etna, just as Athena had depicted on her tapestry.

Zeus did not forget the young human. 'You did well, Cadmus. You will be rewarded: you will found a great city and rule over a great people. It's time to stop tracking the white bull. Forget about your sister. She's on Crete, she's safe, mother to a child. You must go to Delphi, soon, to consult the oracle about the site of your new city. But first you must win Harmonia, the woman who'll become your wife.'

A lively breeze, fickle squalls. Dolphins leaping exuberantly through the spume, sails flapping, hawsers creaking. Cadmus and his companions set their course for the island of Samothrace, as Zeus had instructed them. It was officially ruled by a king called Emathion, but the real power in the land was the queen mother Electra, one of the bright-shining Pleiades. She was also the foster-mother of Harmonia, whom the goddess Aphrodite had conceived during her extramarital affair with Ares, god of war.

Once they'd anchored, Peitho, goddess of persuasion, disguised herself as a local woman and led Cadmus through the winding streets of the island's city, making him invisible from prying eyes. As soon as they were in sight of the royal palace she resumed her divine form, darting back up to the heavens. The young man gazed at the elaborate building – at the bronze steps leading up to pillared doors, at the gateway rich with carving, at the great dome at the centre, at the brightly coloured mosaics lining the walls – all the work of Hephaestus, picked out with equal skill by Alcithoë on her tapestry. Behind was an arboretum of pears, olives, cypresses, figs, pomegranates and laurels, with violets and hyacinths blooming underfoot. There were fountains, too: one for drinking water, another providing ingenious irrigation for the gardens. Before the palace stood rows of silver and gold dogs: automata who either wagged their tails in welcome or barked intimidatingly. For Cadmus, their metal tails thumped the ground.

Emathion and Electra welcomed the young traveller, and a great feast was served. At last, when everyone had eaten their fill, the hall fell silent. Electra beckoned Cadmus, and he drew his stool close to hers. 'Young man,' she said, 'now that you have rested and eaten, won't you tell us something about yourself, your family?'

The young man paused, drank deeply of his wine, then answered the royal lady. 'My name is Cadmus, son of Agenor of Phoenicia,' he said. 'For many years I have been travelling, looking for my sister, Europa, who was taken from us by a white bull.

'But if you would like to know about my family, let me tell you the story of my great-great-grandmother, Io, daughter of Inachus.'

'Io was, once upon a time, a priestess of Hera. But Zeus raped her. Hera was furious. Not with her husband, the perpetrator of the crime, but with Io, who had done nothing wrong. In her vengeful jealousy, the goddess transformed my ancestor into a cow, then tethered her to an olive tree, setting hundred-eyed Argos over her as a guard.

'Zeus, though, instructed Hermes to set Io free. The messenger god skimmed a stone at Argos and killed him, quenching those bright eyes – though Hera quickly transmuted them to a peacock's tail, from which they stare out, turquoise and unblinking, to this day.

'Io was no longer under guard – she was free. But how could she exist? She still had her human brain and heart, but she was locked into a strange body. None of her family or friends recognised her. She didn't recognise herself. She couldn't speak, couldn't make herself understood at all.

'At any rate, as soon as she was freed from Argos she was restless, always on the move, like a leaf blown on the wind. People said that Hera maddened her with gadfly bites, and she roamed the world to try to escape the stinging agony. But I think it was a different kind of pain she was running from.

'She went west, and gave her name to the Ionian Sea. She went east, to the borders of the Scythians, the nomad people of the steppes. In the Caucasus she found Prometheus, the Titan whose liver was ripped out each day by Zeus's eagle.

'At that point Io wanted only death. She intended to smash her life out on the Caucasian rocks. But Prometheus urged her to continue her journey, to find the Amazons in Cimmeria. Those fearless warrior women would guide her to a sea channel, he told her. She would swim across it, entering Asia. He told her too to travel then through the lands of the Graeae, the three swanlike sisters who share one eye between them; he told her to search out the land of the gold-hoarding griffins in Scythia, and their predators, the one-eyed Arimaspians. He told her to come, at last, to Africa. She would find rest at last there, by the Nile.

'It all happened as Prometheus said. The Amazons led her to a narrow ocean channel, which she swam: it has been called "cow-strait", or Bosporus, in her honour ever since. And when, after many years, she arrived in Egypt, she did indeed discover a certain peace. Her human form returned then, and she became the mother of many children. She was the first of our family to travel so far across the world. Few humans have explored as widely, few have seen the remarkable sights that she encountered. I have thought of her often while I've been searching for my sister.'

The story was told, the feast ended. Electra was about to retire for the night when a young man beckoned her to one side. It was the god Hermes in human disguise. He whispered in her ear: Harmonia, her foster-daughter, must be married to the visitor. Zeus decreed it.

Electra went at once to Harmonia's own room, and broke the news to her as she was preparing for bed. The younger woman was appalled, tearful. 'Please don't make me marry that awful, shabby, travel-worn man,' she said. 'I couldn't bear to leave you – and for a life on the road. This is my home. Surely there are plenty of men on the island I could marry? Please, Electra, don't make me.'

It was Harmonia's birth mother who persuaded her, in the end. Disguising herself as one of the girl's childhood friends, Aphrodite plumped herself down on her daughter's bed the next morning and started talking about how much she yearned for the handsome stranger: Alcithoë wove them like that, the two young women talking intimately together, but one of them really a goddess. 'I'd go anywhere with Cadmus,' said Aphrodite. 'I'd do anything to be in your shoes – I'd swap my mother and father, our palace, all the purple in Tyre for him. Imagine it, Harmonia. Sea voyages, freedom, adventure … Don't you long to see new places? Aren't you dying to get away from the island? And don't you think he's handsome? I keep thinking about what it would be like to touch his body, have him touch me … I honestly think I could die happy if I could spend a night with him.'

That night, Harmonia found her feelings about Cadmus shifting a little. And what of him? Well, she was the daughter of Aphrodite. She had inherited enough of her mother's allure to be irresistible to any human.

Soon Cadmus felt the call of the sea again. The marriage feast would wait; first he would take his new bride to Delphi, there to consult the oracle, as Zeus had instructed. He settled Harmonia snugly in the stern of his ship, then, well-travelled Phoenician that he was, expertly took the helm and set a course for Greece – Greece, to which he would introduce the technology of writing, a skill he'd learned long before from the Egyptians.

Over sea and land the band of Phoenicians travelled, and at last reached the sanctuary of Apollo at Delphi, tucked into the lap of Mount Parnassus. Once the appropriate sacrifices had been made, once the Pythia, the great priestess, had entered the innermost room of Apollo's temple and seated herself on the tripod, once she'd worked herself into the trancelike state in which she could hear the whispers of the god, she said: 'Stop looking for the bull that your sister rode away on. You'll never find it. That animal does not do the work of Demeter – he has never pulled a plough. He will never obey a cowherd's commands, or respond to a goad. The only master he knows is Eros. Let go of your homesickness, too. Instead follow the next cow you see. She'll lead you to your new home. Wherever she lies down and rests, that is where you must stop. There you will found a city, to be a home for you and your descendants.'

Just outside the sanctuary was, as it happens, a speckled cow. The Phoenicians regarded her expectantly. She looked up from her grass, gave them a blank stare, and chewed. Then she ambled off. Cadmus and his companions followed.

The cow stopped often to graze. She seemed to have no plan. She was an utterly frustrating guide, hesitant and meandering. But she never lay down. And for all her apparent dilatoriness, she kept making steady progress east – down the mountains, across fertile plains. Finally, on the third day, they came to a spring called Dirce, a lovely place overhung with verdant trees, the rocks making a kind of natural architecture around it. The cow, sighing, sank down to the earth at last.

Cadmus looked around him in satisfaction: she had chosen a fine place for a city, atop an imposing, broad plateau. Which was when he noticed the snake – a giant creature, green, with dark zigzags traced over his back, slinking out from behind a rock. Before Cadmus could even cry out, the animal reared up and lashed out, sinking its massive jaws into the thigh of one of his Phoenician crew, who dropped to the ground. It now flicked its body towards another of the companions, and its jaws snapped shut around his arm. Then another man went down, and another, the whole thing happening impossibly fast, and now it was Cadmus who felt his arms pinned to their sides by the ropelike coils, saw the flicker of the snake's tongue and the bright fury in his eyes.

For a second he was paralysed by fear – until Athena, goddess of winning, breathed confidence into his heart: what was one snake, she whispered, to a man who'd faced down Typhon? Straining every muscle in his body, now, he broke free of the creature's grip. Then, reaching for a boulder, he hurled it with all his might at the snake's head, pounding its brains into the dust. Finally, with a yell of triumph, he drew his sword and decapitated the animal, before holding the smashed, bloodied head up for all to see.

Away on Olympus, Ares, to whom both spring and serpent were sacred, let out a deafening cry of fury: for the crime of killing the holy animal, Cadmus and the god's own daughter, Harmonia, would now be destined to live as snakes in their old age.

But that was to come. Cadmus felt he knew what he had to do now – Athena filled his mind with inspiration. Carefully, he pulled the teeth out of the snake's mouth and filled his helmet with them. Then, he walked up and down, scattering them like seeds until none was left (although Athena skilfully took a handful when he wasn't looking – later she gave them to Aeëtes, king of Colchis).

Almost at once, the soil began to stir. First of all, sharp metal points began to nose up from the ground: ears of bronze corn? No: spear tips. Not far behind them were what proved to be helmets, and inside the helmets, grim-looking faces. Bronze-covered chests emerged next, then muscular legs in bronze greaves. The snake's teeth men clambered out of the soil, turned to each other, their faces contorted with hatred. They began to fight, slashing at each other until all of them were dead – or nearly all. Just five of the sown men survived. They joined the Phoenicians and became the first citizens of Cadmus's new city: Thebes.

One of the descendants of the warriors sown by Cadmus was Tiresias, a soothsayer who lived to a great age. Now, Tiresias had become a prophet in the following way. When he was young, he had come across two snakes, fighting each other. He struck them with his staff. As soon as he did so, he became female. Seven years later, when she saw the snakes again, she didn't hesitate: she struck them with her staff for a second time. The transformation was duly reversed, and Tiresias was once again able to enjoy the freedoms accorded to men.

Not long afterwards, Hera and Zeus summoned him. They wanted him to settle a dispute. 'Tell us, Tiresias,' said the king of the gods, 'do men or women get more pleasure out of sex? We cannot agree, and you are the only person qualified to judge.'

Tiresias hesitated. The god and goddess looked at him expectantly. 'Sex for me was more pleasurable when I was a woman,' he said, wondering which of the two he was going to offend more.

Tiresias, in a single sentence, had betrayed a great secret: that women's sexual appetites are at least as voracious as men's. That displeased Hera immensely, and to punish him, she struck him blind. Zeus, though, gave him a different kind of perception: the ability to see the future. He would often be consulted by the rulers of Thebes. Sometimes they would believe him, sometimes not. But he was always right. Tiresias had a daughter called Manto; her powers of prophecy, which she honed much later at Delphi, were even stronger than her father's, her utterances so beautiful that poets would write them down and pass them off as their own.

On the site of the future Thebes, Cadmus and Harmonia at last celebrated their marriage. Zeus consented to sit at the same table as Cadmus. Hephaestus gave the bride a finely wrought crown; Hera offered her a magnificent golden throne. Alcithoë wove the feast, immortals seated beside humans for almost the last time. The most marvellous wedding present, though, was a gift to Harmonia from her birth mother, Aphrodite: it was a golden necklace Hephaestus had made for her long before, after she'd given birth to her son, Eros. It was exquisite, complex: it took the form of a double-headed snake that coiled its way around the wearer's neck. Where the snaky heads met, in the centre, there was an eagle. Its wings were studded with jasper, moonstone, pearl and agate, its eyes picked out in rubies. From the sinuous snake-chain dangled likenesses of terns, dolphins, leaping fish – you could almost hear the crash of waves and hear the mew of seabirds.

But the necklace, like so many gifts from the gods, brought only sorrow to mortals. It passed down through the generations of the Theban royal house, until Harmonia's great-great-great-grandson, Polynices, used it to bribe a woman called Eriphyle. In return for the necklace, Eriphyle persuaded her husband Amphiaraus, the king of Argos, to fight on Polynices' side for the kingship of Thebes – against his own brother, Eteocles.

How did two brothers come to loathe each other so much that they raised armies against each other? To answer that, I must leave Cadmus and Harmonia behind for a while, and jump forward through the generations to tell you the story of the brothers' parents, Oedipus and Jocasta.

Oedipus grew up in Corinth, the son of the king and queen, Polybus and Merope. It was a happy and uneventful childhood, until, when he was on the verge of manhood, someone got drunk at a feast and started insisting that he, Oedipus, wasn't truly his father's son. The next day he questioned his parents, who brushed off the drunk's words, saying they were nonsense. But he wasn't satisfied: there was something jangling, something nagging at him about the whole strange episode. So he journeyed to Delphi to consult the oracle. There, he received a disturbing prophecy. He was doomed, the Pythia said, to kill his father and marry his mother.

In order to escape this awful fate he decided never to return home to Corinth as long as Polybus and Merope remained alive.

He took to the road, he hardly knew where. He was on foot and alone: all he had for company were his own unquiet thoughts and a good strong staff. He saw no one. Until, when he was approaching a three-way fork – one road to Delphi, one to Daulis, one to Thebes – a horse-drawn wagon came barrelling towards him, a cloud of dust in its wake. Riding ahead was a herald, who tried to push him off the road to keep the way clear. Oedipus, furious at the arrogance of it, held his ground, even when the man riding in the wagon, evidently the master, lashed out at Oedipus with his goad, shouting at him, striking him as if he were a recalcitrant ox or donkey. Oedipus, really angry now, hit back with his staff, feeling excitement surge through his body as the weapon smashed into the older man's skull. The man's guards tore Oedipus away from their master. Oedipus fought them all. Soon five bodies lay there, dead or as good as dead – and he was the only man standing.

It was not long afterwards that Oedipus's journey took him to Thebes, a city he'd always been curious to see. But the place was in chaos. Its ruler, Laius, had recently been murdered. And a powerful creature called the Sphinx, who had the head of a woman, the body of a lion and the wings of an eagle, was hunting and killing the citizens. She said that she would stop only when someone could correctly answer her riddle.

Her question was this: 'What walks on four legs, three legs and two legs?'* When he heard it, Oedipus just laughed – it was easy. He gave the answer and the Sphinx stopped troubling the Thebans. The people acclaimed him as their saviour and their king. In time he and Laius's widow, Jocasta, fell in love and married. They were perfectly suited to each other: like peas in a pod, everyone said.

---

* The answer is 'a human'. Crawls on all fours as a baby; uses a stick in old age.

Years passed in peace and prosperity. The couple had four children: the boys Polynices and Eteocles, who could never stop fighting with each other; and two girls – the passionate, principled Antigone, and measured Ismene, who was always trying to keep the peace between her siblings.

But gradually, the city slid into trouble again. The crops started to fail. The flocks stopped producing. Citizens started to get sick. Then they started dying, more and more of them. Thebes became a place of grief and loss, of confusion and pain. The citizens sent a delegation to the king, begging him to find some way of alleviating the crisis, of stopping the epidemic. Oedipus rushed into action, confident of his ability to set things right. First of all, he sent Jocasta's brother Creon to Delphi for answers. 'Find Laius's murderer, and send him into exile,' the oracle pronounced. 'Only then will the city's problems end.'

Now Oedipus set about investigating the crime vigorously, berating his counsellors for not having done so properly at the time of the old king's death. On Creon's advice, he also sent for the soothsayer, Tiresias. But that went badly: Oedipus and Tiresias argued after the seer, in his equivocal way, seemed to suggest that it was Oedipus himself who was the source of the city's malaise. The king sent him away in a paranoid fury, accusing Creon of having conspired with him: it was all a plot, he said, to overthrow him.

Jocasta now attempted to soothe her husband's fears. She told Oedipus about a prophecy she'd received, years earlier. 'Listen,' she said, 'there's something I've never told you before. I don't know why: it all happened a long time ago, and it was very sad. Laius and I had a child together, a boy. But a seer told us that Laius would be killed by his son. Because of this, he bound our baby's ankles together and had him left in the mountains to die. So, obviously, that son did not kill Laius. Laius was killed by bandits, at a crossroads. Don't you see? That shows you how much trust to put in seers like Tiresias – exactly none.'

Oedipus looked at her sharply. 'Where did you say Laius was killed?'

'At a crossroads. A place where three roads meet – one branch leading here, one to Delphi, the other to Daulis.'

'Why did no one ever tell me that? When was he murdered, Jocasta? Exactly when? It's important ...'

'Well, it was just a few days before you came to the city, I suppose. Things were so chaotic ... the Sphinx ... and then it was all such a relief ... and afterwards it seemed better to look to the future, not dwell on how Laius had died.'

'What did Laius look like? Was he an old man?'

'Yes, old enough – grey-haired. About as you are now, I suppose.'

'And was he on his own? Or did he have an escort?'

'There was a herald, some guards – five of them, I think. Does this matter?'

'Oh gods ... yes, it might matter. Were there any survivors?'

'Yes – just one.'

'What happened to him?'

'He came back to Thebes. It was just after you'd answered the Sphinx's riddle. But almost as soon as he got here he asked if he could be released from his duties, sent off to his farm in the hills, and of course I agreed ...'

'Do you know where he is now? Can you get him here?'

'Yes of course, but what's wrong?'

'I think it might have been me ... I think it might have been me who killed Laius.'

Jocasta and Oedipus took this awful possibility in: could Oedipus really have unknowingly killed Jocasta's first husband, his predecessor on the throne of Thebes? 'The truth must be faced,' said Oedipus, 'and the consequences taken.' He sent slaves to fetch the old shepherd back to the palace.

Just then, though, a messenger arrived from Oedipus's home city of Corinth, bringing unexpected news: Polybus, his father the king, was dead. Oedipus's shock and grief were tinged with relief: it proved, once and for all, that the prophecy about killing his father must have been false. He hadn't been near Corinth, hadn't seen Polybus for years. There was no way he could have killed him, even inadvertently. Jocasta was right, it seemed: prophecies were lies. 'Still, I must not go back to Corinth, even now,' he said. 'What if by some horrendous, strange turn of events I were to marry my mother?'

The Corinthian messenger cut in. 'Sir, there is no need to worry about that,' he said. 'Perhaps I shouldn't be telling you this, it's not really my place, but it seems it would set your mind at rest. Polybus and Merope weren't your real parents. They brought you up, of course – but Merope wasn't your birth mother, Polybus wasn't your birth father. They adopted you as a baby.

'I brought you to Corinth myself, sir, when you were a newborn. The royal couple, they hadn't been able to have children. They were delighted with you, thought of you as a gift from the gods, decided there and then to bring you up as their own. Really: you could return to Corinth whenever you want. You're safe.'

'I wasn't their child? What are you saying?' said Oedipus. 'If they weren't my parents, who were?'

The messenger replied: 'Sir, all I know is that you'd come from Mount Cithaeron, quite near here. Your ankles had been tied together – I undid the bonds myself. It was another man that gave you to me. A man from Thebes, in fact. I suspect you're actually from these parts. He'd know more.'

'Well, who was this man? What was his name?' asked Oedipus.

The messenger looked blank. Then one of the older citizens – one of those who'd been part of the delegation, begging Oedipus to find a cure for the plague – cut in, saying he thought it was the very same person who they'd already sent for, the survivor from the scene of Laius's death. But he should ask Jocasta about it, he said. Oedipus turned impatiently to his wife. 'What do you know about this, Jocasta?' he said. 'Do you know something about a baby left to die on Cithaeron – about me?'

'Oedipus,' said Jocasta, 'stop this. Stop asking questions. Trust me: you need to let this go.' She had become suddenly pale.

'Of course I'm not going to leave it,' he replied, incredulous. 'Don't you understand? I'm about to find out who I am. Who my real parents were. Surely you're not worried about me being the child of someone lowborn, or a slave? I'd expect better of you.'

Oedipus turned impatiently, and started chivvying the slaves about why the man who seemed to hold the clue to everything wasn't here yet – this shepherd who had been both witness to the murder of Laius, and the one who had given him, the infant

Oedipus, to the Corinthian all those years ago. Jocasta walked away without a word, towards her own room.

The shepherd arrived. An old man, nervous, evasive. Trembling with age and fear. Oedipus questioned him; interrogated him. In the end he admitted – yes, he had given a baby to the man from Corinth. The baby was from here, from Thebes. He was born ... in this house. The parents needed to get rid of the child because of a prophecy. A prophecy that the baby would kill his father. It was Jocasta that gave the baby to him. Yes, it was her own baby. Hers and Laius's.

'Why didn't you follow your orders? Why did you give the baby to this man from Corinth?' said Oedipus. 'I couldn't leave the little thing to die,' said the shepherd, who was in tears by now. 'I thought if the baby grew up far away from here it would be all right, the prophecy could never come true. But if you are who you say you are, I'm sorry ... I'm sorry.'

All the fragmented pieces of evidence in Oedipus's head now reassembled themselves, slotting together to reveal an appalling new image.

He, Oedipus, was the baby sent away by Jocasta and Laius. He was the baby who had been given to the Corinthians. Jocasta was his mother as well as his wife. He was the murderer of Laius, and Laius was his father. His children were his brothers and sisters. He himself was the answer to every riddle and every prophecy.

He went into the house. In his darling wife's room, he found Jocasta dangling from the ceiling, hanged by her own belt. Weeping, he lifted her down, kissed her, not knowing whether his caresses were for a mother or a lover. Then he took the brooches from her dress, one in each hand, and dashed the pins into his eyes, over and over again.

Creon and his own sons, Eteocles and Polynices, banished Oedipus from Thebes. The two young men planned to share the kingship of the city, ruling in alternate years. But after the first year Eteocles refused to stand down. Polynices – using Harmonia's necklace as a bribe – raised an army, appointing seven leaders to storm the seven gates of Thebes.

Oedipus, now blind, roamed Greece, his daughter-sisters Antigone and Ismene his companions and guides. At length he reached the sacred grove of Colonus, near Athens, where laurels grow and nightingales sing. Here he knew he must die – a prophecy had said so. He cursed his heartless son-brothers, calling on the gods to make them kill each other.

The civil war between Polynices and Eteocles ended as Oedipus had prayed: the brothers slaughtered each other. Creon, Jocasta's brother, took over the rule of Thebes. He forbade anyone to bury the body of Polynices, the brother who'd attacked the city. But Antigone refused to obey. It was wrong, she said. The gods demanded you offer funeral rites for family, no matter what they'd done. Every night she'd slip out of the city and sprinkle soil on Polynices' body, ignoring her uncle's unjust law. She did it alone. No one helped her, not even her sister Ismene.

When Creon found out, he punished her by walling her up in a tomb, leaving her there without food or drink. He was completely recalcitrant, utterly unbending. Even his own son, Haemon, who was betrothed to Antigone, could not persuade him to relent – 'slave to a woman', that's what Creon called him.

It was Tiresias who eventually convinced Creon to change his mind. He showed Creon the depths of his folly, foretold that his intransigence would lead to more death, to the death of Creon's own loved ones. But when Creon arrived at the tomb where Antigone had been imprisoned, intending to free her himself, he found a dreadful sight: the young woman had hanged herself, like her mother before her. His son Haemon had killed himself too, burying a sword in his own stomach.

That was the fate that Cadmus and Harmonia's descendants would suffer, many generations in the future.

For the time being, though, the young city of Thebes was a happy enough place, as it gradually grew up along the plain. Amphion and Zethus, the sons of Zeus and a mortal woman, Antiope, built its great seven-gated walls. Cadmus and Harmonia had a son, called Polydorus – whose son was Labdacus, whose son was Laius, whose son was Oedipus: the king who killed his father and married his mother.

They also had four daughters: Autonoë, Ino, Agave and Semele. Autonoë was the first to be married. The husband she chose was Aristaeus, the son of the god Apollo and Cyrene, a warrior among women, a wrestler of lions. Aristaeus was a beekeeper, skilled in the art of harvesting honey, that heavenly gift from the skies. Together they had a son, Actaeon, who was punished and suffered through no fault of his own.

It happened like this. One morning, the young man set off on a hunting expedition. It was that time of year when summer is about to slip into autumn. He had risen at sunrise and whistled up his beloved dogs: Blackfoot from Sparta. Tracker from Crete. Storm and Flight. Forest, still bleeding from an encounter with a boar. Fury, and Greedy, and Harpy with her pups. Blaze and Blackmane; Patch and Cyprian. Catcher and Racer and Barker and Chaser. They were alert, obedient, sniffing the air: a loyal entourage for the prince. Together they set off to Mount Cithaeron, and there they chased the boar, and the subtle hares with their black-tipped ears. He set nets for songbirds, and aimed his feathered arrows at soft-eyed hinds. And when he had spent the morning killing, when the sun was at its height, it was time to eat and take shelter.

Nearby there was a grove sacred to Artemis. It was a clearing overhung with pine and cypress, at whose very edge – secluded, hidden, overgrown with ferns – lay a cool and shadowed cave. Right at its entrance rose a spring, numbingly cold in the midday heat, that pulsed up through the grass to make a dancing, silvery pool. Here, the goddess liked to take her rest. She too had been hunting that morning. And now her nymph-companions were undressing her, taking her bow and arrows from her, pulling off her sweat-soaked tunic (if goddesses can be said to sweat) and her dusty sandals, brushing out her tangled hair and twisting it back into a neat knot. And some brought jugs of the cool, delicious water to pour over her muscular legs and strong arms – a thousand times stronger than any man's. In that cold pool she bathed, that goddess, that fierce and pitiless goddess who despised sex. That goddess who would shoot down mortals with her arrows as easily and joyfully as she would fell swift deer.

Our lives are full of choices. Some of them seem momentous. Most of them are mundane: whether to go out hunting, or whether to stay at home. Whether to stay on the plains, or clamber up the wooded mountainside. Whether to keep to the path, or to walk into the trackless forest. Sometimes the most ordinary of moments, the most banal of decisions, dictates our fate. So it was just then, when Actaeon, his mouth dry and his limbs aching, felt a desperate need for the touch of cold water on his body. As he skirted a wood, he sensed the sudden cooling of the air that means a spring is nearby.

He turned off the path. He walked into the woods. He fought his way through brambles and thorn bushes. He stumbled over hidden roots and lost his footing in ruts and cracks in the dry ground. The land itself was trying to warn him away: he took no notice; he was determined. At length he reached the edge of the glade. His dogs hesitated behind him, whining, sniffing the air. Actaeon strode on, took a sudden tumble down a steep bank, righted himself – and then was half paralysed with shock to find himself amid a group of women, their naked limbs gleaming in the wash of cool water.

For a second, nothing: mutual horror: that frozen moment was what Alcithoë chose to depict in her artwork. Then the women started shouting at him, and gathered round Artemis to protect her from the violation. The goddess turned instinctively for her bow and arrows. They were out of reach, lying on a mossy rock. The only thing close by was the spring water. She bent for a handful, then smashed it into Actaeon's face.

'Now go home and boast that you've spied on a naked goddess,' she said. 'If you can.' Immediately he felt something change. His head itched; he raised his hands to his forehead and felt antlers budding. At the same time those hands were hands no more: his fingers were closing in on themselves, hardening, and then they hit the ground as his back bent forward. He turned and fled, and was astounded at his new speed; he leapt away across the glade, the ground consumed between his – what? – hooves? As he passed a stream he saw his reflection, saw that he was made stag, and tried to call out, but no words came. As he hesitated, wondering whether to hide in the forest or to run to his grandfather's palace, he heard his dogs give voice. He longed to call to them, to tell them, 'I'm Actaeon, your friend, your master!'

Instead, he raced through the forest and over mountain crags; he fled across dried-up riverbeds and through ravines; hunted, he took the paths he had once taken as a hunter. At last the dogs gained on him and surrounded him in a gully. Blackmane was the first to savage him, leaping for his throat. Cyprian took his left flank, Patch took his right. They held their struggling master down while the rest of the pack – snarling, bloody-jawed – took their turn. Sometimes, as they feasted, they looked around for Actaeon: they could not understand why he was not here to enjoy the kill.

Autonoë searched for her son, tramping across Cithaeron's flanks, calling for him, calling. She saw the carcass of a young deer, flesh stripped from the bones; she even stopped and touched the still-warm pelt. She had no idea the creature was her own child.

One of Actaeon's cousins was the god Dionysus. Semele, daughter of Cadmus and Harmonia, was his mother – but she did not give birth to him, she was dead before he was born.

This is how it came about. One morning, when Eos was still staining the sky pink, Semele was driving her chariot, silver whip in hand, through the streets of Thebes. Hardly awake, she fell into a kind of waking trance. She half dreamed, half imagined that she was a kind of creeping, twining plant that she'd never seen before. It bore berries; they were unripe. A storm came, and lightning struck the plant, blackening and killing it. But the berries remained unharmed, and Zeus, king of the gods, picked them up.

Semele tried to shake off this curious vision, but it was deeply disturbing. Her father, Cadmus, advised her to sacrifice a bull; when she did so, blood from the animal spurted over her. She went to wash it off in the River Asopus, where, watching the gnats rise and dance over the water's surface as she swam, she felt free and alone. But she was neither of those things. Zeus was watching her from behind every rock and tree. His lustful gaze was in the very shafts of light that fell onto the water's surface. A god can spy on a woman as much as he likes, it seems, though a man may not, even by mistake, glimpse a naked goddess.

That night she woke to feel a presence, an invasion. Fear came for her first; then the merciless god Zeus himself. He attacked her as a bull, then as a panther, then as a lion, then as a snake that pinned her down and imprisoned her in his horrendous coils. When he was done, Zeus told her to ask him a favour. He promised he'd do anything she wanted, anything at all. Semele in her anger and defiance told him: 'Show me what you really are, not what you pretend to be. Show me your true form. Show me your thunderbolts.' Later, people said it was pride and stupidity that had made Semele demand to see the god's true form, or something that Hera had put into her head out of spite and jealousy. But no: it was fury, pure fury.

Zeus didn't want to keep his word. But he was compelled to, bound by his oath. Months later, he returned and made his shape his true one, savage and lethal. His thunderbolts, crackling with destruction, set her house ablaze; the fire consumed Semele herself. Zeus plunged his hand into the burning woman's belly and grabbed what was growing inside her. Then he gashed open his own thigh, stuffed the foetus into it, and sewed it up. That's how Dionysus was carried inside his father's body before his birth.

After he'd struggled out of Zeus's leg, the infant Dionysus was given by Hermes to his aunt, Ino, and her husband, Athamas; the plan was to shield the tiny god from Hera's anger by bringing him up as a girl. The plan didn't work. Hera sent the foster-parents mad. Ino threw herself from a cliff, with her son Melicertes. Instead of dying they were transformed into sea deities called Leucothea and Palaemon, who helped mariners when they were in trouble. Dionysus had to be spirited away to Nysa, a deeply forested mountain peak far away in the east, where he was raised in secret by the nymphs who lived there.

It didn't take him long to grow up – he was a god, after all. His first love was a young man called Ampelus. They were always together, whether hunting through the mountains, or competing in athletics. Dionysus couldn't be without his beloved; became anxious when he was out of his sight, worried in case some other god should come and snatch him away. He'd always fix it so Ampelus would win the competitions held among their friends – running races, swimming races. He loved to wrestle with his friend, straining against him until they hit the dust together, entwined, laughing. One day, though, Ampelus took it into his head to catch and ride a bull as if it was a horse. The animal, when he mounted, at first seemed gentle – but then took off at a gallop, as if some jealous god had stung him to madness. Ampelus was tossed to the ground and the bull rolled over him, breaking his back, killing him.

A satyr – a creature of the wilds, like a man but with goaty legs, and the ears and tail of a horse – found the body, and ran to fetch Dionysus. The god, weeping, strewed the still-lovely corpse with roses, with hyacinths, with anemones, and dripped nectar between his soft lips. So deep was his grief that the Fates unravelled Ampelus's destiny, and rewrote it. Which is why Dionysus, to his amazement, saw the young man's body change. His fingers became woody stalks, his curly hair thick bunches of fruit, his body a verdant mass of heart-shaped leaves: Alcithoë wove this miraculous metamorphosis of man to greenery. The new plant grew with incredible vigour, sending out shoots in all directions, twining itself around trees, producing more and more of the luscious purple fruit, which Dionysus now plucked and squeezed in the palm of his hand so that the delicious, sticky juice poured out between his fingers. Ampelus had become the ample vine, and Dionysus would teach humans how to turn it into wine – the intoxicating, glorious liquid that is the nearest thing we have to the gods' own nectar.

After the death of his lover, Dionysus travelled far and wide in Asia – to Arabia, to Bactria, to India, to Persia – gathering followers, his bacchantes and maenads, wherever he went. One day he was standing on the Ionian shore, looking west, out to sea. He was in the guise of a handsome young man, dark hair flowing round his shoulders. A band of pirates – Tyrrhenians from the western seas – were just then fitting out their ship, preparing to sail. The captain noticed him, his sumptuous clothes. Imagining he must be the wealthy son of a king, he barked out an order to his men. 'Get him! Bring him on board and tie him up. There'll be something in this for all of us, I reckon.'

The pirates approached the god in a snarling gang, swords drawn. The god only smiled – he didn't resist as the sailors bundled him on board their ship. The helmsman had the job of tying him up, knotting his hands and feet fast, while the others held him down. But the ropes refused to bind him and simply fell away uselessly.

The helmsman realised something was wrong. 'Hey, did you see that?' he said to his shipmates. 'This man – I don't think he's a man at all. He must be a god. We've got to let him go. If we don't, he could bring storms and get us all killed.'

The captain ignored him. 'Shut up and do your job,' he yelled. 'If you can't deal with him, we will. He'll tell us soon enough where all his rich friends live.'

The crew raised the mast and hoisted the sail. But all at once extraordinary things began to happen. The deck of the ship began to bubble with wine, its delicious mineral scent mingling with the tang of the sea. A vine snaked its way up the mast, growing at prodigious speed. It spread its foliage along the top of the sail and sprouted heavy bunches of fruit; intermingled with it was a clambering ivy, which put out its clustering, honey-scented flowers.

The men were terrified – 'Turn her round! Back to shore!' they cried. But Dionysus transformed himself into a lioness, and, with an almost casual grace, sprang for the captain. She felled him with a mere nudge of her great paw, then sank her jaws into his neck. The other seamen jumped overboard – though Dionysus changed them into dolphins before they'd even hit the water.

The helmsman, though, he spared. 'Don't be frightened,' said the deathless one, once he'd turned himself back into human form. 'I like you. I'm Dionysus, the god who roars like a lion. My mother was Semele, daughter of Cadmus; my father is Zeus. Take me to Greece, my friend. I want to visit Thebes.'

In amazement, the helmsman set a course. The great white sail stiffened to the breeze. The god lay in the stern contentedly, his cloak wrapped around his muscular limbs: that's how Alcithoë showed him, as the ship dashed through the water, accompanied by a school of leaping dolphins, its mast entwined in vines.

The king of Thebes at that time was Agave's son Pentheus: Cadmus, when he'd grown old and weary, had handed over power to his beloved grandson. Pentheus had heard rumours from the east of an effeminate young man who corrupted women, goading them to leave their homes and live in the mountains like animals. These women, he'd been told, spent their nights in drunken orgies, having sex out in the open, with whatever man came along, quite possibly, even, with each other … It was like a plague, he thought, this madness that had spread through Asia: horrible, disgusting, unnatural.

Now, it seemed, the disease was infecting his own people. The women had left, gone to the mountains to worship Dionysus. Houses were unswept, wool unspun, babies and children left to their fathers to manage as best they could. The young man who was orchestrating all this was saying he was the god Dionysus, that Semele was his mother and he'd been born from Zeus's thigh. Despite the obvious fraudulence of it all, Pentheus's own aunt, Autonoë, and even his mother, Agave, had joined in with the madness.

Pentheus managed to arrest some of the man's followers, women who'd come over from Asia, and had them locked up. But to his immense frustration, things were clearly out of his control. Even his grandfather Cadmus and that old fraud Tiresias had now got themselves up in ridiculous costumes of fawnskins and ivy crowns. They were making fools of themselves, hobbling around on their sticks, claiming they were going to go off to Mount Cithaeron to dance, to join in the rites of Dionysus. At their age!

Tiresias tried to convince Pentheus that he was wrong. 'Dionysus will be worshipped all over Greece soon; just because he's a new god, and a young god, you shouldn't discount him. He gave us wine, so humans can forget about their troubles. He helps us understand ourselves – to find the kind of truths you can't get at through rigid thinking, but only through intoxication.' Cadmus added: 'Even if he's not a real god, what have you got to lose? Play along with it. Look at how your cousin Actaeon died, all because he dishonoured a goddess. None of us wants that to happen again.'

All this just made Pentheus more furious, more determined to stamp the cult out. He sent his guards off to find and arrest the young man. He'd see all this end, and soon. The youth would die by stoning.

It wasn't long before the guards returned with the foreigner – he'd not struggled, but had come willingly, they told the king. Calm and unruffled, the disguised god refused to tell Pentheus very much about what the women were up to – these were religious rites, he said, not for the uninitiated to know about. He deftly sidestepped every taunt thrown at him: when Pentheus said how stupid foreigners were for getting involved in bizarre rituals, he just smiled, and said, 'Foreigners aren't stupid, just different.' Pentheus became more and more infuriated. 'Those women you brought with you from Asia – I'll make them slaves, put them to work at the looms,' he said. 'And as for you – I'll lock you up myself, in my stables.'

But Dionysus confused his senses. When the king thought he was marching the supposed young man off to prison, he was actually shackling a bull; the god simply watched, smiling, as the king struggled and sweated. After that, Dionysus put his head back and roared – a terrible roar like a bull's or a lion's but a hundred times louder, shaking the whole city like an earthquake. The sound destroyed the building where his maenads were imprisoned. The women stepped free from the ruins without a scratch on them. Finally, Dionysus set Semele's tomb alight: a reminder of the fire that had killed his mother.

Pentheus, in his confusion, assumed the young man had escaped – then was amazed to see him standing calmly in front of the palace. The king, seriously angry now, issued orders: the whole army was to march to Cithaeron and round up all the women there. Dionysus laughed. 'Try it – your army will be sent running by my women. Bronze, you'll find, is no match for fennel stalks. Why don't you let me summon the women here? They'll come willingly. There's no need for armies.'

'What, and become a slave to my own slave women? I don't think so.' Pentheus turned to his attendants. 'Bring weapons here! Quickly! We're leaving. Going to the mountain.'

But something shifted, now, in the atmosphere. It was hard to say what. Everything became uncannily still. No birds sang, no dogs barked. It was as if the air had thickened. The god said, quietly, 'So – you *do* want to see what the women are getting up to?'

'Oh yes,' said Pentheus. 'I'd give anything to see. I mean, it would be indecent. But if I could spy on them, maybe from behind a fir tree ...'

'They'd find you, though,' said the god. 'Men aren't allowed. They'll kill you if they saw you. But you could put on a dress.'

'I'd be ashamed ... but a dress you say? What kind? What else would I need? Accessories?'

'Yes – a long wig, a ribbon for your hair. A deerskin shawl, a fennel staff,' said Dionysus.

'I could never put on women's clothes. That would be disgusting ... I'll think about it,' said the king. 'Maybe I'll send my army out to the mountain. Maybe I won't.' He had a strange way with him, now, as if he wasn't seeing straight, as if he was drunk. He stumbled, rather than walked, back into the palace. 'If you do go there,' Dionysus called to his retreating back, 'you'll return in your darling mother's arms. A real treat for you. Richly deserved.'

On the peaks of Mount Cithaeron, far from the city, far from men, Pentheus's mother and aunt felt free for the first time in their lives. There were no drunken orgies here: just women of all kinds, rich and poor, living together, singing together, praising the god who'd given them their liberty. They didn't need lovely handwoven shawls and fine clothes – animal skins would do. And no need for domestic drudgery: the god showered them with miracles. When one woman struck her fennel staff on a rock, a bright fresh spring bubbled up. Another one did the same, and milk gushed forth. The animals around them were tame and gentle. Snakes licked their cheeks. Those women who'd recently given birth, whose breasts were full, suckled wolf cubs. They felt like young deer who'd outpaced the hunters' nets, who could run as swiftly as storms. They were full of the joy of the unpeopled wilds, of the shadowed woods. But they could be violent, too. When the villagers from the valley came to chase them off, they surged against them, this army of women, and sent them running back home. Then the bacchantes vented their fury on a herd of the villagers' cattle, tearing the animals apart with their bare hands, pulling out their entrails ...

As the shadows lengthened and dimmed into darkness, Autonoë, Agave, Ino and all the other maenads gathered together peacefully in a woodland clearing. Some were twining their fennel staffs with ivy, some singing songs in praise of Dionysus. All of a sudden they heard a voice, a deep, thunderous shout that they knew was the god's. 'Women, I've brought you the man who mocked me, who mocked you, who laughed at our holy rituals. Punish him!' A plume of fire rose up like a flare, sank down to nothing again. Then the women, quick as doves, were on their feet searching for the man who'd dishonoured the god – clambering up rocks, fanning out through the trees, rushing down into gullies ...

At last they found him. He was perched at the very top of a mighty pine, dressed in women's clothes. He had succumbed to the fascination, to the thrill of disguise and spying. The god himself had helped the king put on the headgear and the dress, laughing as he'd adjusted the get-up. Then the god and the man – the cousins – had walked together to the mountain. Dionysus had bent the tree down like a bow for Pentheus, saying that he'd get the best view of the rites from there.

First the women climbed a crag and from there threw stones and pine-bough javelins. To no avail: Pentheus's roost was too high. Then they used branches as crowbars, trying to uproot the tree. No good. At last Agave shouted to the others, 'Come on, make a circle, grab the trunk and let's get this wild animal.' They did as she said and, their strength inhuman, uprooted the pine – it came toppling down, the king of Thebes with it. Pentheus pulled off his wig and headdress, cried out, 'Mother, it's me, your son – Pentheus! Please, please, don't kill me, whatever mistakes I've made.'

It was too late. Agave was foaming at the mouth, her eyes rolling back in their sockets. She had been maddened by the god. She planted her foot on her son's ribs and seized his arm, then ripped it clean out of the shoulder socket. Autonoë and the other maenads flocked round, grabbed at him, screaming. One dismembered a foot, still in its shoe. Others stripped flesh from bone. The women played ball with his body parts.

Now Pentheus's body lay there in pieces, all over the forest floor – at one with nature in death if not in life. But Agave grabbed his head – that poor head – and fixed it to the top of her staff, as if it were a lion's head, a hunting trophy. She was so excited about her prize that she ran down the mountain, leaving her sisters and companions singing and dancing. She arrived back in Thebes, still out of her mind, still like a madwoman, covered in gore and blood, holding aloft the king's head – her boy's head. There Cadmus brought his poor daughter back to sanity, gently coaxing her until she understood the terrible thing the god had made her do. That's what Alcithoë wove: Agave, bloodstained, weeping, cradling the head of her own darling son, the unbending king of Thebes, whom she had unknowingly murdered.

Alcithoë was working away at the textile with her sisters when the priests ordered a feast day: Dionysus was to be honoured, officially. Work was to be set aside. But Alcithoë was determined to complete her masterpiece. 'I'm certain Dionysus will forgive us. After all, we are telling the story of his power, his greatness,' she said. 'Athena will protect us.'

The sisters kept on weaving. From outside, they could hear a clashing of cymbals, a beating of drums, cries of ecstasy. The sounds of worship mingled with the polyphony of their work songs, the thud of their weaving swords, the clink of their terracotta loom weights.

Into the open doorway, now, ran a woman, casting her shadow deep into the hall. It was a maenad, her dishevelled hair crowned by an ivy circlet. Her face was flushed, her clothes all over the place. She grabbed the door frame and caught her breath – she'd evidently just been dancing. 'Girls, what are you doing?' she asked the workers. 'Why aren't you outside with the rest of us?'

'We're busy,' said Alcithoë shortly. 'I'll worship the god when I'm good and ready. So if you could just leave us alone …' The young woman ignored her. In fact, she walked up to the loom and studied the work curiously. 'Why are you still weaving when even your own tapestry is telling you to stop? The god doesn't want you to work. The god wants you outside, in the woods, on the mountains, away from all this domesticity. You don't seem to understand Dionysus at all. You don't seem to understand your own art.'

'You should mind your own business,' said Alcithoë. 'I'll not take lessons in religion from you, whoever you are.' The woman smiled. 'Say what you like. But see all this knotting you're doing, all this tying together, all this neatness and tightness? It's the opposite of what the god wants. Dionysus wants things undone, unravelled, dissolved. He wants you wild, not civilised; in the country, not in the city. He wants you free, not shackled to the endless production of things. What you're doing here is for Athena, not for him. And today, Dionysus is telling you to stop.'

'For the last time,' said Alcithoë, 'will you get out of my house?'

It was then that the unwelcome visitor, the maenad, changed. A soft dark pelt grew from her shining skin. Horns sprouted from her forehead. She dropped to all fours, and instead of hands and feet, there were hard horn hooves. A huge black bull stood before them, raging and snorting. Alcithoë and the others screamed and dropped their shuttles and distaffs, scattering in all directions. Then, in the blink of an eye, there was no longer a bull, but a roaring lion, shoulders taut with muscle. Then, no longer a lion, but a sleek leopard, tail lashing in fury.

The girl, it seemed, was the god, the immortal protector of the clinging vine and the throttling ivy – who now turned Alcithoë and the other women into bats. They flapped, screeching, into the rafters.

But what of the great tapestry, almost finished as it was? All at once, the face of the cloth frothed with young ivy leaves, obscuring Alcithoë's designs, burying her tales of Thebes in green foliage. The dangling threads of warp and weft became vine fronds. The purple hues in the lovely textile gave their colour to bunches of plump, ripe grapes. The beams of the loom dripped with nectar and milk.

The god changed form again, turning himself – herself – back into a maenad. She paused at the loom to admire her handiwork, observing with pleasure how she had transformed tales of a grand and tragic city into a glorious, unruly thicket of living green. Then she left the house of Alcithoë and began, once more, to dance.

PHILOMELA

Philomela, Procne, Pandion, Tereus ✤ Iphis and Ianthe ✤ Narcissus, Echo ✤ Pygmalion ✤ Deianira and Heracles ✤ Atalanta, Meleager and the Calydonian boar hunt ✤ Melanion and the Golden Apples ✤ Pyramus and Thisbe ✤ Eros and Psyche ✤ Itys

PHILOMELA

I t is true that Philomela and Procne quarrelled and bickered just like any other sisters. But they worked easily together at the loom, intuiting each other's movements, passing the shuttles back and forth, back and forth, singing to remember the complex patterns they had devised. On summer evenings they'd set up their work outside, in the palace courtyard. They'd watch the swifts darting easily through the air, wishing that Zeus would turn them into birds, so they could find the secret places of the cliffs, so they could soar over the seawashed coasts and rivers.

Their father, King Pandion of Athens, was at war with King Labdacus of Thebes. From the earliest times, the two cities had viewed each other with suspicion. They lay close enough together – a long day's walk between them – for hostility to simmer endlessly at the interlocking borders of their territories. This current bout of violence had dragged on for years. A breakthrough came only when Pandion negotiated an alliance with King Tereus of Thrace – a wild, rugged country far away in the north, famous for its equally wild, rugged men. With the Thracians' help, Pandion soon defeated the Thebans. Tereus was, after all, a son of the war god Ares himself.

The Thracians – pale, tattooed, trouser-clad – rode into the city and were honoured as saviours of Athens. To seal the friendship between the people of Athens and those of Thrace, Pandion offered his daughter Procne in marriage to Tereus. The kind of sacrifices that had so recently been offered to placate the gods of war were now given to Hymen, god of the wedding feast, and Hera, protector of marriage. Philomela helped to dress her sister in a magnificent saffron robe; the wedding torches were lit; joyful songs were sung. Before long, Tereus and his bride set out for Thrace.

Without her sister, the days spread solitary and long before Philomela. To fill them, she turned to the loom. She devised a spectacular design for a tapestry, and told herself that when she had finished the work, the sharp stab of loss in her heart would have dulled.

To begin, she made an elaborate border, filled with stories of love and desire between humans.

She began with the tale of a pregnant woman called Telethusa, who lived in lovely Phaistos on the island of Crete. Her husband had told her that, if she were to have a girl, he would be reluctantly obliged to take that baby and expose her on the mountains. Despite her tears, he remained unmoved, absolutely determined that it must be done.

Not long before her time came, the Egyptian goddess Isis came to her in a dream. She was magnificent: her golden headdress of cow-horns sat on her forehead like a crescent moon, and between the horns lay a bright sun disc. 'Don't worry,' said the immortal. 'Whatever you have, bring the baby up as a boy. I will be at your side if you ever need my help.'

And so when Telethusa gave birth to a little girl, whom she called Iphis, she kept the sex of the child concealed from everyone – especially her husband.

Growing up, Iphis enjoyed playing with boys, fighting with boys, riding with boys, hunting with boys – and also adored and doted on a girl called Ianthe. As the two grew up together, they fell in love. Eventually the young people went to Iphis's father, and asked permission to be married, which was gladly granted.

As the wedding day approached, though, Iphis became increasingly agitated, and went to Telethusa to ask a mother's advice. 'What can I do? Ianthe thinks I'm a man. What will happen on my wedding night? Will she hate me? Will she humiliate me? I've deceived her for years – not about the depth of my love, but about my body.'

Telethusa was as anxious as her child. Over and over again she found excuses – bad omens, ill health, disconcerting dreams – to put off the wedding. Ianthe, meanwhile, was eager to be married, and prayed continually to the god of marriage, Hymen, to speed things up.

When the wedding could be delayed no longer – when it was fixed for the following day – Telethusa went to the temple of Isis, and prayed to the Egyptian goddess in desperation. 'Remember, great goddess, that I have worshipped you all my life,' she said. 'Make this wedding a day of happiness and not of grief. Please help us. Please find a way for my child to be married to Ianthe.' To her amazement, the altar seemed to tremble. The sculpture of the stern goddess, seated stiff and upright on her throne, appeared almost to smile, and the golden sun disc of her headdress glowed.

Telethusa thanked the goddess, weeping with relief, and went back to her child. 'Trust in Isis,' was her advice. The marriage was duly celebrated, and Ianthe gazed lovingly at her Iphis as the rites were performed – that's how Philomela showed them, delighting in each other, as Hymen, who makes wedding torches flare, smiled on them.

Afterwards, the couple walked hand in hand to their bedroom, and there they took pleasure in each other's bodies, and in their own. Whatever it was that the goddess had wrought, whatever form love's metamorphosis had taken – that was theirs to know. It is possible that Isis transformed Iphis into a man, as is often claimed. It is possible that they lived together, as two women who adored each other. All we know is that they were happy. And Iphis, whether you are imagining a woman or a man, was beautiful.

✤

Next Philomela wove the story of Narcissus, a beautiful young man who was consumed by self-love. He was the son of the nymph Liriope, who'd been raped by the lustful River Cephisus when she was wading through his waters. Liriope adored her little boy, and went to see Tiresias the prophet to consult him about his future. 'Will Narcissus live a long and happy life?' she asked. 'Only if he never knows himself,' came the opaque answer.

Narcissus grew up into a beautiful youth, desired by both girls and boys. But he was immune from all their charms. One admirer he cruelly rebuffed was the nymph Echo, who had been condemned by Hera never to speak her own words, but only to repeat those of others. She used to follow Narcissus around as he taunted her. If he said, 'Why ever would I want to kiss you?' she'd reply, wistfully, 'I want to kiss you.' If he said, 'I'll die before I'd dream of touching you,' she'd repeat, 'Dream of touching you.'

But Narcissus went too far: he turned down the advances of another boy so rudely and arrogantly that the youth prayed that Narcissus himself should be rejected just as harshly. And the gods nodded their consent.

There was a clear pool in the forest near where Narcissus lived. Its waters were glittering, silvery; it was fringed by soft grass and shaded by a ring of trees. No one and nothing went there – not shepherds with their flocks, not even wild birds. But nevertheless, led by a strange impulse, Narcissus one day stumbled into this secret place. Thirsty, he bent to the water, intending to drink. As he did so, he saw a beautiful youth seemingly trapped in that glassy surface – and another kind of thirst came.

Narcissus reached out to touch the boy, but as soon as his hand pierced the surface, the face in the water seemed to fragment and disappear. He tried talking, but though the figure seemed to be speaking, Narcissus couldn't hear him. For a long time he crouched there, never moving, and the silent boy just gazed back: Philomela wove Narcissus leaning over the pool, and she picked out his reflection in matching threads, too.

'Please, can't you come and talk to me? I mean you no harm,' Narcissus would say to the boy in the pool. Echo would try to warn him of his error, whispering to him urgently, 'Harm!'

A long time passed. Echo's body, in the end, faded away, so that all that remained of her was her voice: we sometimes hear it now, as she vainly tries to communicate with mortals, repeating our words. Narcissus stayed like that, transfixed as if he were a marble sculpture, until he died. A creamy-golden, delicately scented flower grew up on the same spot: a narcissus.

Philomela now wove of an artist's lust for his own work. Pygmalion was a sculptor who lived alone on the island of Cyprus. He felt that no woman was good enough for him. And so he decided to make an image of the perfect female.

He carved a life-size statue from white marble: a beautiful young woman reclining on a couch, just as she was waking from a deep sleep. One of her breasts was exposed, as if her dress had slipped while she slumbered. The rest of the body was covered by a robe's complex, undulating folds, carved by Pygmalion with surpassing mastery. The feet were shod in elegant stone sandals. A stone bracelet in the form of a snake wound its way around one of the arms.

As the work went on, Pygmalion became more and more attracted to his creation. He kissed the chilly lips. He fondled that cold, hard breast. He ran his hands up and down the strong calves.

At night he began to lie with the statue, on its marble couch. In the dark of the small hours he pleasured himself against the figure's cool, unyielding surfaces. Sometimes he would imagine that the sculpture was responding to his caresses. At these times, he'd feel the stone grow warm, as if it were living flesh. Then, all too quickly, he'd remember that the only heat came from his own body. He'd grow angry, sometimes. 'Why are you so stubborn, so unresponsive, so ... frigid?' he'd say. At those times he would strike the statue's face. But it was his own flesh that suffered after these one-sided encounters. Afterwards, he'd be contrite, fussing around her, bringing her gifts: pearl earrings, a pendant.

In due course, the great feast of Aphrodite came round – the most important day of the year on Cyprus, since the island is sacred to the goddess of love. Pygmalion made his offerings and prayed hard. 'Please, great goddess, bring me a wife who is *exactly* like my sculpture,' he said. Aphrodite understood, as she understands all of our most secret and shameful desires. The torches in the temple burst into a fiercer flame. Pygmalion was overjoyed by the sign and rushed home.

There, in the studio, he approached the sculpture. He was nervous but also terribly excited. He kissed the statue, gently, on the lips. Was it his imagination or did there really seem to be a suggestion of warmth, this time? There was! The white stone was changing, taking on the subtle hues of human skin. Where unyielding ridges of masonry had once been, now there was soft flesh and silken fabric. This was what Philomela decided to show in her tapestry: the instant when stone became human, when masonry moved.

And what about the woman? Into her newly wide-awake brain was rushing a host of confused images. At first came a sensation of violence and pain – pointed objects bursting her matter away under repeated, rhythmic blows; something relentlessly abrading the surface of her. A sense of herself trapped and locked within an impossibly heavy form – like that nightmare you sometimes have when you can't move your limbs at all, no matter how hard you strain.

She sat up. She blinked in the new bright light. Nothing made any sense. She was not sure what to do with her ability to move, but some instinct told her to reach for the floor with her feet. She tried to stand but she was like a newborn animal. And so she slid to the ground. And then tried to heave herself up again.

'Not like that!' cried Pygmalion, suddenly furious. 'Go back to the couch. Lie down. Please. I arranged you so beautifully.' She had no idea what he was saying, but every newly awakened instinct in her body was telling her to get away from him. He made to grab her, but in truth he was terrified. This is not what he thought he had made, this dishevelled woman with sweat glinting at her clavicle, this woman shrieking like something escaped from Hades, this woman now staggering towards the door and her liberty.

Looking down from Olympus, Aphrodite smiled to herself, then shrugged, and started to comb out her long, shining hair.

❧

Next to that scene Philomela wove the story of Deianira – an expert charioteer, skilled in the arts of war – who killed her husband Heracles, the most savage warrior who ever walked the Earth.

In truth, it was not the first time that he was overmastered by a woman. Once, as penance for a murder, he had been obliged to spend a year as a slave of Queen Omphale of Lydia. First he was ordered to rid her territory of robbers and raiders. Then she brought him back to the palace and made him dress in women's clothes. While he toiled away in the weaving sheds with the female slaves, she went about in his lionskin and carried his club.

Deianira, it should be said, did not kill Heracles by force. No mortal could have done that: he was a human above all other humans. Once he even fought Thanatos, the god of death, to bring a perished wife, Alcestis, back to her husband, Admetus. He battled alongside Athena to kill Giants; he even, once, used his bow, his deadly bow that was a gift from Apollo, to shoot the shape-shifting fighter Periclymenus, when he had turned himself into a bee.

No, Deianira did not mean to kill Heracles. It was a terrible mistake.

This is how it happened. Long after he had completed the twelve Labours for which he was so famous, Heracles made war on the people of Oechalia. When he won – as was inevitable – he took the king's daughter prisoner, and brought her to his house in Trachis. The truth was that he was infatuated with the beautiful young woman, whose name was Iole. Deianira had no idea what to do. She didn't want to harm or punish Iole – in fact, she felt sorry for this woman who had lost her family, who was now a slave. But she did want Heracles back.

And then she remembered the dying words of Nessus, the Centaur.

A long time before, just after Heracles and Deianira's wedding, Nessus had offered to ferry the couple across a deep river. First he carried Heracles on his back, then he swam back for Deianira. But in midstream, she felt his hands all over her ... Heracles, watching from the far bank, saw the assault from afar and shot the Centaur, who stumbled ashore only just alive. As he bled out, he muttered to Deianira: 'Gather the blood from my wound. It will bring Heracles back to you, if he ever strays.'

Just as Nessus had told her to, she had kept that blood all these years, hiding it away in a tightly stoppered pot. Now she poured it carefully – it still seemed fresh and liquid – over a tunic that she had woven for Heracles. Then she set off in search of him. She found him in his great hall, sitting on a bench, his immense club leaning beside him. She sat down next to him and offered him the tunic with words of love – that's how Philomela showed them, sitting side by side for the last time.

Heracles took the garment, and pulled it over his head, humouring her. But as soon as he had it on it seemed to cling to him, just as stone carved to resemble fabric seems to cling to a statue's surface. He broke into a sweat. He screamed in pain. The skin of his face and arms became mottled and discoloured. The strength of his body – that body that had killed thousands – failed him. He collapsed.

This was Nessus's revenge. His blood was infected with the poison Heracles had smeared on his arrows: the venom of Hydra, the many-headed serpent he had killed as one of his Labours. Maybe you could say that it was not Deianira who killed Heracles in the end, nor Nessus, but Hydra herself – she who had once inhabited the swamps of Lerna, terrifying all mortals who came near her.

Those Labours were the result of the fury of Hera, who loathed Heracles because he was the son of her errant husband Zeus and a mortal woman, Alcmena. To punish Heracles – though he had done no wrong – the goddess cursed him with a fit of madness, in the midst of which he murdered his first wife, the Theban princess Megara, and their children.

When the insanity passed, when he realised in grief and shame what he had done, he asked the oracle at Delphi how he might atone. The Pythia, Apollo's priestess, told him to offer to become a servant to his kinsman, King Eurystheus of Tiryns. It was Eurystheus who set him those seemingly impossible tasks, the famous Labours.

It was scenes of those Labours that decorated the chamber in which the helpless hero now writhed with pain. The frescoes showed how he had killed the Nemean lion, taking his skin as his prize. They showed how, with the help of his lover Iolaus, he had killed Hydra, swiping off her serpent-heads while the younger man seared the stumps to prevent two new ones from growing out of each wound.

They showed how he had captured the beautiful deer from Ceryneia and then the boar of Erymanthus – he did not kill these creatures, but brought them back to Eurystheus alive. They showed how he had used his bow to shoot down the birds who thronged around Lake Stymphalos. How he had cleaned out the filthy stables of King Augeas. How he had captured a wild bull at the behest of King Minos of Crete, and tamed the man-eating horses of Diomedes in Thrace. How he had snatched the belt of the Amazon Hippolyta – she had offered it to him freely, even though it was a precious gift from Ares, but he killed her anyway. How he had herded the cattle belonging to Geryon – he whose three bodies, and three pairs of legs, were joined at a single waist. How he had killed the dragon that guarded the apples in the garden of the Hesperides.

They showed how, last of all, he descended to the Underworld to capture Cerberus. Hades had said he could take the savage, three-headed dog on condition he used no weapons, so Heracles crushed the beast with the sheer force of his arms until the whimpering animal submitted to his will. It was those same arms that now hung slack and weak by the dying man's sides.

That is how Heracles' mortal life came to an end. But when he was lying on his funeral pyre a change came about. From this abject death the gods relieved him: they swept him up to Olympus and gave him immortality. Hera no longer loathes him; she loves him second only to her husband, Zeus. He lives in everlasting peace among the mansions of the gods, in a different reality and with a different wife, the ever-youthful goddess, Hebe.

Now, Philomela wove the story of Atalanta who, though she despised love for a long time, eventually found a worthy lover.

As soon as she was born, Atalanta's father Iasius, who had wanted a son, ordered her to be taken away to the Arcadian mountains and there left to die. As the squirming infant lay on a crag, scarlet-faced and bawling and utterly defenceless, a bear loped over to her, moving heavily but gracefully over the rocky terrain. She nudged Atalanta curiously with her long snout, gave her an exploratory lick, opened her terrifying mouth – and picked her up, quite gently. She took little Atalanta back to her den, where she was raising her two newborn cubs. She treated the baby exactly like one of her own, at first suckling her, then teaching her to eat berries and fish and nuts and roots.

When Atalanta was a toddler, and the cubs were preparing to leave their mother and fend for themselves, a group of mountain-dwelling hunters found the girl – a filthy little savage, but perfectly healthy – and took her away from her bear foster-mother to bring up themselves. From an early age she was skilled with the spear and the bow, as strong as any boy, and as fast as a hind on her feet. Her adoptive family were rough men but kind, and they taught her all their skills. She swore her allegiance to Artemis, the protector of the hunt, the guardian of celibacy; and the goddess admired and delighted in her.

Atalanta wanted adventure, she loved competition, and she was determined to prove herself. When Jason was assembling companions to join him to adventure across the seas in search of the Golden Fleece, she volunteered, but he turned her down, convinced that a woman would disrupt the discipline of the *Argo*'s crew. Later, though, after the Argonauts had returned to Greece, she challenged one of them, Peleus, to a wrestling match. Peleus thought this was something of a joke, and nearly refused, because what glory would there be in fighting a woman? He changed his mind when he saw her broad shoulders, her muscled arms. She was beautiful, too, with the kind of features that seem boyish in a girl and girlish in a boy.

Atalanta won the wrestling match, gripping Peleus in a headlock that had him choking for mercy.

Later, the Aetolian fighter Meleager assembled another team of companions to hunt and kill the Calydonian boar, a creature that was ravaging his father Oeneus's realm. Among them were ex-Argonauts and other famous champions: Castor and Pollux, Theseus and his Lapith friend Pirithous, young Nestor of Pylos, Peleus – and Atalanta. The expedition was chaotic. Before they set off, some of the men said they wouldn't hunt alongside a woman. Meleager, though, threatened to cancel it altogether unless they withdrew their complaints. Then, when the hunt was finally under way, two Centaurs, Hylaeus and Rhaecus, decided to try to attack Atalanta. Fools: she heard them blundering through the trees behind her, boasting about how they would take it in turns to rape her. She reached for her quiver, turned, and sent a pair of arrows flying in superb, accurate arcs – one for each gullet. She left them to bleed out on the mountainside.

At last the boar was trapped in a woody valley, beneath a rocky bluff she couldn't climb. She was a huge beast with tusks like scimitars; now, cornered, she was deadly. She charged at one of the youngest fighters, Enaesimus, and impaled him; she would have got Nestor, too, had he not scrambled up a tree. Peleus flung his spear at her, but in the confusion hit Eurytion, king of Phthia, and killed him. Atalanta let loose an arrow, and caught the boar behind the ear: blood poured out of the wound, staining her bristles. Ancaeus was so enraged that first blood had gone to a mere woman that he flung himself into the boar's path, wielding an axe, shouting, 'My weapon's better than any woman's – watch this!' He held his weapon high above his head ready to bring it crashing down on the animal's skull; but before he could, she thrust at him with her gleaming ivory tusks, leaving his guts spilled out on the forest floor.

In the end it was Meleager himself who finished her off with his sword, and she lay there, panting, huffing, her magnificent bristles smeared with blood, the light in her eyes dimming to darkness. Meleager presented her tusks to Atalanta, as a prize for first blood.

Atalanta's fame was now so great that her father Iasius made it known that he would welcome her back to his court. She didn't want to leave her old companions, the wily hunters of the Arcadian highlands, but they persuaded her to go, telling her she'd soon outgrow their harsh lives – she should go and enjoy the plenty and luxury of the court, they said.

Iasius made much of his long-lost daughter, joking that if he hadn't left her to die all those years ago, she wouldn't be the great athlete she was today. The truth was that he wanted Atalanta to marry. He was eager to arrange a wedding for his own political and diplomatic purposes.

Atalanta was furious. 'That's impossible! I've sworn allegiance to Artemis and taken vows of celibacy,' she said. 'The goddess punishes anyone who's disloyal to her.'

Iasius was unmoved. 'You know as well as I do that girls grow out of their vows to Artemis in the end,' he said. 'You've had more than enough chance to run wild in the mountains.'

This argument went on and on, until a solution occurred to Atalanta. 'I promise I'll marry the man who can beat me in a race,' she said. 'Let any man challenge me. These are the rules – if I win, he dies. If he wins, I marry him.'

Iasius agreed. Atalanta marked out a racetrack in a level green valley. Halfway along the course she thrust a stake into the ground. She would give all of the contestants, she announced, a generous start. She would start to run herself only when her opponent drew level with the stake.

A surprising number of young men took up the challenge. For every one of them, almost his last sensation was the pounding tread of Atalanta's feet at first crescendoing behind him, then fading as she shot ahead. Each was executed at the finish line.

At last a young man called Melanion appeared at Iasius's court. He found Atalanta thrilling, her speed glorious. He marvelled at her beauty – not when she was dressed as a princess, but when her limbs were shining with sweat and her face was flushed from exercise. He was an athlete, too, tough and strong. He loved life in the mountains – the buzzards soaring above and the scent of pine in his nostrils. The more Atalanta saw him, the more she was drawn to him. She found herself dreaming about him, desiring him. She ached to touch him.

Melanion knew he could never win Atalanta fairly, so he turned to that queen of cheating, the goddess of love. Always keen to get one over Artemis, Aphrodite was happy to help: she gave him three golden apples, plucked from the garden of the Hesperides. Melanion immediately saw how he might use them. So he challenged Atalanta to the footrace.

Just as the rules dictated, Atalanta gave him a long head start, setting off only when he had already run half the course. But as he ran, Melanion let fall one the golden apples, and there it now lay in the grass, glinting irresistibly in the sun. As she sped along the racetrack she saw it. She hesitated, stopped – and scooped up the shining treasure. Melanion was still ahead. She had lost time.

Using his advantage, he ran on, kicking up another spurt of speed, and dropped the second apple. Again she paused and dipped to grab the precious fruit. Even so, she was gaining on him – so he flung the third apple with all his might well wide of the track. She dashed towards it, snatched it up as quick as a Harpy, and sped back to rejoin the race.

That is how Melanion cheated in the footrace to beat Atalanta by the merest whisper, his body lunging forward as he crossed the line. But as soon as she passed it in her turn, she let drop the golden apples, indifferent to them, and stepped towards him with a smile.

Melanion and Atalanta indeed got married, and she never told him whether she had let him win. However – and at moments of human joy there is often a 'however' – Melanion forgot to thank Aphrodite for her help. The goddess resolved that they should be punished. When they were out hunting together one day, they decided to rest from the midday heat in a cave. What they did not realise, though, was that the place was sacred to Zeus. By making love there, they were defiling a shrine. As they lay there, bodies entwined, fierce and wild and greedy for each other, their fingers began to curl and sprout claws. Their necks grew tawny pelts, their mouths erupted with long sharp teeth. When they finally fell apart from each other, breathless and exhausted, they understood. They had changed form. They were lions.

If lions could be said to laugh, they laughed. Their transformation may have been intended as a punishment, but it felt like a reward. To hunt side by side, to live together freely and equally, to pad up the loneliest peaks and haunt the remotest glens – that was true happiness for Atalanta and Melanion. It was as lion and lioness that Philomela wove them.

In the final part of her border Philomela showed the Babylonians Pyramus and Thisbe who, despite the bitter enmity of their families, loved each other in secret. The only way to communicate was in snatched conversations through a tiny gap in the wall that divided their gardens. And so they made a risky plan: they'd each slip out of their homes during the night and meet outside the city. Their rendezvous was by the tomb of King Ninus – the mausoleum that Queen Semiramis, that most resourceful of monarchs, the conqueror of Ethiopia, had built for her husband.

Thisbe arrived earlier than Pyramus and waited under a mulberry tree, its branches heaving with juicy white fruit. But as she sat there, in the dead of the night, she saw a lioness approach, fresh from the kill, her jaws bloody. Thisbe ran into a nearby cave, dropping her shawl in her haste – which the lioness sniffed curiously, staining it with the blood from her jaws. When Pyramus eventually arrived, that's what he saw – his lover's bloodstained shawl, a lioness's footprints in the dust. His mind leaped to the worst conclusion. Grief swallowed him. He drew his sword and plunged it into his stomach.

At last Thisbe dared to imagine the lioness had gone, and came out from her hiding place. 'Pyramus? Pyramus, are you there?' she called softly. That's when she saw him. She rushed to him, held his bleeding body in her arms, calling him back to life – but he was already dead. She took the sword, cradled it as if it were her friend. She closed her eyes, and she stabbed herself.

The blood stained the white berries on the tree beneath which the lovers died. From that day, mulberries have been purple. Their juice dyes your hands sticky crimson, like blood.

✣

In the centre of the tapestry, Philomela wove scenes telling the story of Psyche and Eros – whose love endured many trials.

Psyche was the youngest of three daughters of the king and queen of a distant land. And she was beautiful. More beautiful than her sisters. More beautiful than any human. More beautiful, some said, than Aphrodite herself. Which is where her troubles began. People started neglecting their duties to the goddess. They started to worship Psyche instead. Aphrodite was angry, and summoned her son, Eros, god of desire.

'This girl must be punished for her presumption,' she said. 'I want you to make sure she falls in love and marries a creature that everyone despises and fears.'

But Psyche didn't want anyone to worship her. She hated her beauty – or, rather, the effect it had. People treated her not as if she was a flesh-and-blood person with real feelings, but as if she were some kind of perfect, stony sculpture.

She stayed at home, saw no one, became more and more unhappy. Her parents, too, were worried, fearing she would never find someone to love her properly. So her father consulted the Delphic oracle.

The answer, as so often, was unwelcome. The message came that the king must leave his daughter, dressed as if for her wedding, on a deserted mountaintop outside the city. There she would be married to a monstrous, winged husband armed with stinging arrows, a creature even Zeus found terrifying.

The king and queen reluctantly began preparations for the grim wedding. On the appointed day, when Psyche was ready to lead the procession up the mountain, her grief-stricken, guilt-racked parents tried to stop the whole thing: they couldn't leave their child to this awful fate. But Psyche told them to be calm, to let her go. 'There's no alternative: no one can get away with being compared to a god,' she said.

And so the sad group set off from the palace, climbed the mountain, and tearfully performed the marriage rituals though there was no bridegroom to be seen. Finally they left Psyche there. Alone, she wept and shivered and wished she were dead.

After a while, though, she felt a warm gust of air ruffling her dress, disturbing her hair. Then the breeze – Zephyr, the west wind – seemed to envelop her. She found herself lifted, and blown gently down to a hidden valley on the other side of the mountain, a place no human could ever have reached on foot.

Zephyr set her down on the grass and, lulled by the gentle motion of the flight, she fell asleep. When she opened her eyes at last, she saw above her the blue sky over-laced with blossom-covered boughs. She was in an orchard, and it was the most pleasant place imaginable.

She got up and began to explore, and found that behind the orchard was a substantial, well-built house. She knocked – then, hearing no answer, pushed open the door. As she wandered through the empty rooms, at last she heard a voice, which seemed to come from the building itself. 'Psyche, don't be afraid,' it said. 'All these rooms are yours. Rest, enjoy yourself.'

Amazed, Psyche took the advice of the disembodied voice and bathed and rested. When she felt hungry, a delicious meal arrived of its own accord, borne on golden plates by unseen hands. Invisible hands strummed harps, too, and invisible choirs sang to her. When night fell, though, she became afraid: what if this beautiful house and this army of unseen slaves were just a trick to calm her before the terrifying dragon, her new husband, arrived? She lay there, rigid on her bed, fearing the very shadows.

After some time, the door opened quietly and Psyche could hear the soft tread of *something* coming in. Her heart pounded, but the thing, whatever it was, possessed two feet and did not seem obviously dragonlike. Through the darkness she heard a voice – a soft, sexy voice. 'Don't be afraid,' it said. 'I am your husband and I love you. I can't let you see me, but here is my hand.' She felt a soft brush of fingers (not scales) on her wrist. She felt hands and lips caressing her. She felt herself returning the touch. The warm and delightful body she encountered, with its smooth cheeks and soft curly hair, seemed to her to be a young man's. But she couldn't see him at all. And in the morning, he was gone.

The next night, the unseen husband returned, and the next, and the next. Psyche's nights were full of pleasure, and the days passed easily enough. One night, though, when her husband returned, there was a new note of seriousness in his voice. 'Your sisters are going to come looking for you,' he said. 'I'm warning you: however upset they seem, don't listen to them.'

Psyche took the advice badly: how could she ignore her sisters, let them think her dead, leave them to endure grief for no reason? And she missed her family so, so much. She was lonely.

She was still upset when he returned the next night. 'Do what you like,' he said in the end. 'Zephyr can bring them down here in safety. But it won't end well. They'll want to know what I look like. And I promise you: bad things will happen if you try to find out.'

The next day, Psyche was walking in the grove when she heard from above the faint sounds of voices calling her name. Her sisters! At once she asked Zephyr to blow them down to her from the mountaintop. They seemed delighted to see her. But they grilled her: who was her husband? Where was he? What was he like? Flustered, Psyche invented a story that he was a young man who spent most of his days out hunting. And, in something of a hurry to get rid of them, she gave them each a gift of jewellery, and asked Zephyr to take them back up to the mountaintop.

The sisters set out towards the city. But they hadn't been walking long before envy started to nip and sting at them. 'She has all the luck – money, a young husband, numerous slaves,' said one. 'How come our parents married *me* off to an ugly old man who's terrible in bed?' said the other. The first sister said, 'From the day she was born, everything's been about her. I've had enough of it.' The second one said, 'I think it's time we cut her down to size, don't you? I tell you what, let's not mention to anyone that we've seen her.' They began to make a plan.

That night, when Psyche's husband returned, he said, 'Don't you realise you're in danger? Your sisters are not good people. They mean to hurt you. Listen: whatever you do, don't let them persuade you to find out what I look like. This is important, Psyche. You're going to have a baby, and if you do as I say, the child will be a god. If you don't, she will be a mere mortal.'

Pregnant! Psyche was overjoyed. 'But if I can't see you, then at least let me see my sisters.'

Reluctantly he agreed. The next day, the sisters returned, and Psyche delightedly told them about her pregnancy – which made them even more jealous. They started quizzing her again about her husband. Under their joint interrogation, she floundered. 'He's a much older man,' she said at last. 'He's a merchant, he's always travelling.'

After Zephyr had wafted them back up to the mountaintop, the first sister said, 'Which one really *is* her husband, do you think? The young Adonis out with his hunting hounds, or the rich old man?' 'Do you know,' said the other, 'I don't think she's ever actually seen him.' The pair started to refine their plan.

The next day, they came to the top of the mountain and flung themselves off it in the direction of the grove – and were given a somewhat bumpy landing by Zephyr, who was tired of carrying them about. 'We're so worried about you,' they told Psyche. 'We've discovered something awful about your husband. He *is* a dragon, exactly as the oracle said. People have seen him flying about, hunting for sheep and goats: the farmers round here are terrified of him. He's waiting for you to have the baby. After that, he's going to eat you. Probably, he'll eat the baby, too.

'But listen: we've found a way to get you out of this. Before you go to sleep, light a lamp in your room and hide it under a jar. Then, when the monster is asleep, take this dagger, uncover the lamp, and by its light, cut the creature's throat.'

It never crossed Psyche's mind that her sisters were tricking her. She took the dagger and that night followed their instructions: she lit and hid the lamp, she concealed the knife, and she went to bed with her husband as normal. Once he had gone to sleep, she uncovered the lamp and held it in one trembling hand. With the other, she picked up the dagger.

The lamplight showed her no monster, no diabolical, flesh-eating dragon, but a beautiful young man, his naked limbs draped over the bed as elegantly as if a sculptor had carved them – the god Eros. She gasped, and couldn't help reaching out to touch him, as she had so many times before, but this time touch was joined to sight, and her pleasure was all the greater. She ran her hands over his smooth skin, over his luxuriant hair, over the snow-white feathers of the wings that were folded behind him, and finally over the arrows that lay in a quiver beside him. And, perhaps because her hands were shaking so much, she pricked her finger on an arrow-point, so that a little globe of blood bloomed there. No one escapes the contagion brought by Eros's arrows, and her desire for him now became overwhelming: she began to kiss him greedily, and as she did so, a drop of hot oil from the lamp fell onto his skin. At that, he started up from his sleep. In a glance he saw what had happened. And just like that, he unfurled his wings and without a word flew out of the bedroom, up into the sky, and was gone.

But not without Psyche: she had grabbed hold of his ankle as he darted out of the window. As he flew, so she clung, until, when her strength was about to give out, he circled close to the ground so she could drop down safely – then flitted up to the top of a nearby cypress tree. 'I warned you about listening to your sisters,' he said. 'You shouldn't have tried to look at me. They'll get what's coming to them, you can be sure of that. But I'm afraid you'll suffer, too.' And with that he swooped away, tacking across the sky until he was a mere dot in the distance.

Psyche had never felt so alone. In her despair she tried to throw herself into a river, but the compassionate waters cast her back onto the bank. That's where the goat-legged god Pan found her, and tried to comfort her. 'Whatever's wrong?' he asked. 'Is this about a man? Well now. If I were you, I'd pray to the great god Eros.'

Psyche laughed through her tears, despite herself. She paid her respects to the deathless god, dried her eyes, got up, and started walking with a new sense of resolution, a plan forming in her mind. She journeyed all the way to the house of her eldest sister, and she rapped on the door. After they had embraced with feigned affection, Psyche said, 'I came here to tell you: I did everything you suggested. But you were wrong, what I saw wasn't a dragon, but the most beautiful man you've ever seen: Eros himself. He was so angry with me that he threw me out of the house, saying that because I had broken my promises, he was minded to marry you instead.'

She had barely finished speaking when her sister pulled on her cloak, pushed past Psyche, and dashed off to the mountain.

She flung herself off the crag, expecting to be floated gently down to the enchanted grove. But Zephyr was elsewhere, blowing gentle breezes in Thessaly. So the sister plunged down the mountain, was smashed against the rocks, and died. Psyche set out for the next sister's house, where she told the same story. She too rushed out towards the mountain, and died in the same way.

Psyche continued her search for her husband, roaming from town to town, asking for him everywhere. But Eros was on Olympus, languishing in bed in Aphrodite's house, bemoaning the injury he'd suffered from the hot oil Psyche had spilled. Aphrodite wasn't there: she was bathing and swimming in the sea, the element that she loved, and in which she'd been born. The result of this joint neglect of human affairs was serious, and at length, a seabird took it upon himself to find the goddess and warn her. 'You're needed, my lady,' he told her. 'The world is out of joint. No one has seen either you or Eros for a long while. Affection and friendship are leaking away. Everywhere is growing full of harshness and anger. No babies are being conceived, except in loveless, violent union.'

'Where is my son? Why is he not attending to his duties?' asked Aphrodite.

'I'm not sure. There is a rumour that he's otherwise occupied with a girl called Psyche –'

'What! That same Psyche who claims to be better than me? I can see precisely what's happened here. He must think I'm some kind of pimp, having her for himself after I've given him orders to punish her. Wait till I get my hands on him ...'

Magnificent, she shot up from the sea, sending seawater cascading from her body: droplets caught the light, and rainbows shimmered in the air. In an instant she had flown to Mount Olympus, where she found Eros groaning with pain on his sickbed. 'First, you disobeyed my instructions,' she said. 'Second, you actually had sex with the girl – the very person who set herself up as my rival. Third, I suppose you want me to treat her like some kind of daughter-in-law. You must be mad. I've a good mind to adopt one of my slaves and give him your wings and arrows. Any of that useless lot would make a better son that you.'

She stormed out of the house, where she immediately bumped into Hera and Demeter, her fellow Olympians, who sympathised with her – but urged her to be kind to Eros. Why? Because they, along with all the other gods, feared his arrows more than anything else in the world.

Meanwhile, Psyche scoured the desert and the wilderness. She searched the trackless depths of forests. She walked until her feet were cut and blistered, until her legs could carry her no further, and she slumped down where her strength gave out – on the steps of an old mountain shrine.

After she had rested a while, she began to look about her, and saw that there were offerings to Demeter laid out, but all in a jumble: there was a stack of dusty old sickles, scattered ears of wheat, a messy heap of barley. She tidied everything up, leaving a swept floor and neat piles of offerings, all the while praying to Demeter to help her. At last she heard a voice wafting through the temple like a warm autumn breeze. 'Poor girl,' said the goddess. 'Here you are tending to my temple, when Aphrodite has marked you out for punishment.'

'Dear, kind Demeter,' said Psyche, 'let me stay here for a while, at least until Aphrodite is less angry.' The goddess pitied her – but not enough to help her. 'The best I can do for you is to let you go unharmed,' she said. 'Aphrodite is my friend.'

Psyche, choking back sobs, left and walked on. Eventually, in a pleasant, tree-ringed grove, she saw another shrine, this time belonging to Hera. She stumbled inside, fell to her knees, grasped the altar and prayed. 'Great queen Hera, protector of families, I beg you to help me.' A blinding light came from the entrance of the shrine – so bright that Psyche dared not look round. She heard a voice like thunder. 'Even though my friend Aphrodite is eager to punish you, I will allow you to leave my temple in safety. But I can give you no more help than that. You must find your own way.'

The light faded. Psyche limped out of the temple, and she wept until she had no more tears left.

At last, as she lay on the stony ground, staring up at the stars, she made a decision. If there was no escaping Aphrodite, then so be it. She would go to the goddess herself. Take the battle to her pursuer. After all, Olympus was the one place she hadn't looked for Eros.

Psyche walked and walked until she found herself in the foothills of Mount Olympus, the heights of which no mortal had scaled before, whose crags are dusted with snow and blurred by mist. Furiously determined, the pregnant woman hauled herself up that mountain, slipping on scree, willing herself to cross precipitous ridges, straining her muscles as she felt for handholds and footholds and wrenched her body towards the gleaming palaces of the immortals.

At last she arrived at the imposing bronze doors of Aphrodite's palace, and all but collapsed on the steps. Two of the goddess's slaves found her there and, screaming in excitement, dragged her inside. Aphrodite greeted her with contempt. 'So you're finally making a visit to your mother-in-law, are you? You must be a fool if you think you're married to my son. That baby you're carrying – it's a bastard.'

She grabbed Psyche by the throat and slammed her against the wall. 'You're an ugly little thing, aren't you? I guess you get men to sleep with you by playing the attentive handmaiden. Well, let's see how good you actually are at slaving.' She flung an enormous heap of seeds – hemp, sunflower, millet, lentil and even tiny black poppy seeds – on the ground. 'Sort these into piles. I'll come and check on you at nightfall.' She turned on her heel and headed out to attend a wedding feast.

Psyche looked despairingly at the enormous pile of seeds. There was no way she could sort them by dusk. But the ants who lived in Aphrodite's palace felt sorry for her, and brought all their thousands of brothers and sisters and cousins, and set about the work on her behalf. Psyche watched in wonder and gratitude as the clever and organised creatures, moving with the coordination and skill of tiny soldiers, laboured until there were five neat piles.

As the sun sank, Aphrodite returned, and choked back her dismay when she saw that Psyche had completed the task. 'I don't believe for one minute you did this yourself,' she said. She hurled a crust of bread at Psyche and left. Meanwhile, she set a guard to watch discreetly over Eros, who was in another wing of the palace, and had no idea that Psyche was there.

The next morning, Aphrodite came to the young woman again. 'See that pasture?' said the deathless one, pointing out of the window. 'There are sheep grazing in it, sheep with fleeces of pure gold. I want you to bring me some of that golden wool. By nightfall.'

Psyche set off for the meadows, doubting she would be able to do as the goddess said. But the reeds growing by a river advised her, their thin, windblown voices full of pity. 'Don't attempt to go near the sheep now, in the heat of the day: they will be angry, and gore you with their horns, or bite you with their poisonous teeth. Wait until the late afternoon, when they grow gentle and sleepy, and search the bushes in the next field over: you'll find fragments of their wool caught on the thorns and twigs there, ready for you to collect and take back to the goddess.'

Psyche thanked the reeds, and did exactly as they said. But when she returned with the shining wool, Aphrodite merely scowled, flung her a crust and left the room. The next morning, the goddess returned, and said: 'I've got another job for you, human. You see way up there, that mountaintop in the distance? There's a spring there that feeds the Styx and Cocytus, the rivers that flow round Erebus. I'd like a drink of cool water from it. Take this crystal jug and have it for me by nightfall.'

Psyche set off, despondent. As she neared the spring, she saw how impossible the task really was: the waters tumbled down in a vertical recess of a sheer slope, surrounded by innumerable writhing snakes. The creatures taunted her, telling her how useless she was, how hopeless her task, how pointless her life.

But then, a golden eagle, his tawny wings like ragged sails, landed on a nearby crag. 'You'll never get to that water yourself,' he told Psyche. 'But I can do it for you.' He seized the jug in his claws and, evading the darting tongues of the snakes, flew to the spring and filled it with the deathly liquid. Psyche thanked him and returned with it to Aphrodite's house.

The goddess bit down her anger; she simply grabbed the jug from Psyche, flung her a crust and left. The next morning, she returned. 'I'm giving you one last task,' she said. 'Take this box to

Persephone, queen of the Underworld, and ask her to put some of her exquisite beauty in it, just enough for one day. Then bring the box back to me. Now go. Hurry.'

Psyche realised that it was all over. Even the most famous fighters had struggled to return alive from the Underworld. Heracles had done it. Theseus had done it, but only just – when he had gone there with his friend Pirithous, intending to rape Persephone, the two of them had been tricked by Hades into sitting on Chairs of Forgetfulness. Heracles, in the end, had rescued Theseus – but Pirithous was still there, gawping like a newborn in the grip of an endless present. How was she, Psyche, a pregnant woman, going to manage a journey to the Underworld and back? How was she even going to find it?

She set off, not really knowing where she was going. On the plains below Olympus, there was a high tower, standing quite alone in the landscape. She climbed it, intending to throw herself off – the only certain route to Hades, she reasoned, was death itself. But before she could step into oblivion, she heard a mysterious voice – the voice of the tower itself. 'Psyche, don't. This isn't the right way,' said the tower. 'With my help, you can complete the task. But you need to do exactly as I say.

'You must journey to Taenarum, the southernmost tip of this land, and there you will find a cave that leads to the Underworld: there the path, though dark and shadowed, is clear. But before you set out towards those gloomy depths, leaving the upper air behind, take a barley cake in each hand, and put two coins in your mouth.

'When you have travelled a long way down the path, and you're nearly at the gates of Hades, you'll pass a lame donkey driven by a lame man. The man will ask you to help him pick up some sticks that have dropped from his load, but you must pass him by, saying nothing. It's a trap set by Aphrodite to make you drop one of the barley cakes – don't fall for it.

'When you arrive at the River Styx the boatman, Charon, will demand a fare to ferry you across: let him take one of the coins directly from your mouth. When you are in midstream, the corpse of an old man will beg you to help him into the boat: harden your heart and ignore him. When you disembark, you will pass three women spinning and weaving wool, who will ask you to lend them a hand: walk on by. You will be confronted by Cerberus, a three-headed, ferocious dog – throw him a barley cake. That will distract him and you'll be able to get past. Finally, Persephone will welcome you to her house and offer you a delicious feast, but you must accept only a crust of bread. When she has given you what you've come for, leave at once. Use the remaining barley cake to distract Cerberus again, and the second coin for Charon as he ferries you back.

'But the most important thing is this: do not, under any circumstances, open the box and look inside.'

Everything went well at first: Psyche ignored the lame old man, the corpse and the weavers. She paid Charon, fed Cerberus, and, when Persephone welcomed her, she accepted only a crust of dry bread.

She told Persephone of her task. The immortal goddess nodded gravely, filled the box and silently handed it back. Psyche thanked her, put it safely in her pocket, and set off to the world above. She fed Cerberus, paid Charon, and just when she was nearly back to the light and the sky, she thought to herself, 'I don't see why I shouldn't, after all my efforts, check what's in the box.' So she opened it. But inside Persephone had put not beauty, but sleep – the deep, dreamless sleep of the Styx, of Hades. Right where she was, she slumped down and fell into a profound slumber.

But by this time Eros was better. And less angry. And wiser. And missing Psyche dreadfully. He flew down to her where she lay, gently wiped the sleep from her face, and woke her with a tiny prick from one of his arrows. He and Psyche kissed each other for a long time, made plans together, and, entwined in each other's arms, flew up to Olympus on his great beating wings. Just as they had decided, he set her down at Aphrodite's house, while he went off to plead his case with Zeus.

Zeus listened, and called a council of all the gods. Philomela wove the scene: the Olympians assembled together among the clouds to hear the word of their king. 'I decree,' he said, 'that the marriage of Eros and Psyche shall stand. And, Aphrodite, this young woman, who roamed the world to find her lover, who fulfilled each of the impossible tasks you set her, is worthy of your son – more than worthy, if truth be told. I shall make her immortal.' With that, Psyche was brought before him. He himself gave her ambrosia to eat and nectar to drink – and she became a deathless goddess.

Zeus commanded a second marriage feast: this time a feast of the gods, and a feast full of joy, not mourning. Philomela wove this too: the most splendid wedding ever seen. Dionysus and the gods' cupbearer, Ganymede, served wine; the Hours strewed roses; the Graces made sweet scents swell in the air; Apollo and the Muses, Pan and the satyrs, sang wedding songs. After the eating and drinking was done, Eros and Psyche went to bed and made love in the bright Olympian light, feasting their eyes upon each other. When, several months later, their daughter was born, they called her Pleasure.

And so Philomela finished her great tapestry, alone in her chamber in Athens. If she had hoped that the time and the work would soothe the ache she felt for her sister Procne – so abruptly married to King Tereus, sent so far away to Thrace – she was wrong.

Not long afterwards, though, Tereus himself arrived at the Athenian court, bringing a message: would Philomela come to Thrace? Would she visit Procne and Itys, her sister's little boy?

The Thracian king was explaining the request to old King Pandion when Philomela herself came into the hall. As soon as Tereus saw her, for reasons he couldn't have explained, he was overwhelmed by bitterness and jealousy, by a desire to overpower and to possess – though he kept his feelings hidden under his charming, swaggering exterior.

When Philomela understood what Tereus was suggesting, she rushed to her father, throwing her arms around him, begging him to let her go – an embrace that Tereus watched lasciviously, imagining himself in her father's place. Pandion agreed. A great banquet was laid out: a feast of farewell. Tereus hardly ate, but he drank a lot. He was excited, his mind full of scenarios, plans.

The next morning they set out, all Athens cheering them off from the harbour. Philomela was still watching the shoreline fade away into the horizon when the atmosphere abruptly changed. Tereus came up behind her, too close, and then he was on her, grabbing at her ... He dragged her below. She was so shocked she forgot how to struggle. He chained her up. Then he raped her, day after day. Soon she felt as if this was the only life she'd ever had, imprisoned, waiting for her sister's husband to sate his hateful appetite on her body.

At last they made landfall in Thrace. Tereus locked his sister-in-law in a house in the woods, not far from his palace. It was a pleasant place, well furnished. Philomela was to want for nothing except, of course, her freedom. And one other thing. The day they arrived, Tereus ordered his men to hold Philomela down. He took out his dagger. She swerved and bucked, at first; then she offered up her throat like a taunt. 'Go on, kill me,' she said, 'I'm as good as dead anyway. But by the gods, my ghost will haunt you every day of your life!' But he didn't want to kill her. Instead, he forced open her mouth, and hacked out her tongue. 'I'm sick of the sound of your voice,' he said, as she choked.

When Tereus returned home, he told his wife Procne that Philomela had fallen ill and died on the voyage. Procne was beside herself with grief. Tereus, shameless, visited the house in the woods at regular intervals.

For a time Philomela lived in complete despair. Of all the stories she had ever imagined for herself, this was beyond the worst. Her situation seemed hopeless: the place was remote, and well guarded, the garden walls high. She had no voice. She could not tell anyone the truth.

But then she realised two things: first, she could listen. She began to pick up all kinds of things from the slaves and the guards. She learned, for instance, that the palace wasn't far off. And that Procne was in it, alive and in mourning for a sister. And she realised that there was a fragile kind of sympathy between her and the slaves who ran the house under Tereus's orders. They felt for her – and she for them.

In the house there was an old, rather ill-made loom. One of the slaves happened to discover it in a storeroom, and set it up. Philomela ignored it for days. Then, quite suddenly, she understood. She walked over to it, appraising it with an expert eye. She found some skeins of white yarn and some of purple. She prepared the warp, wound wool onto shuttles. She began her work, her hands adjusting to the familiar routine. She planned a design. Scene one: two girls watch swifts from a palace window. Scene two: one of the girls marries a king. Scene three: the other girl on a ship, in chains. Scene four: a tongue is severed. Scene five: this house, here, now. She wove this part as accurately as possible, observing the landmarks she could see from the windows.

It took a long time to make. Tereus was completely incurious; he never looked at the textile. When she had finished, one of the slaves cut the fabric off the loom, understanding by Philomela's gestures what was to be done.

Procne the queen was sitting at her own work in the palace when a slave brought her a gift: a precious, finely wrought textile. As soon as she unfolded it she recognised the work, just as you'd recognise your own sister's handwriting. She set out alone on horseback from the palace, and, using the tapestry as her guide, found her sister's prison. Ordering the confused guards aside, she beat on the door until it was opened. The sisters held each other tight. 'He has destroyed the thing most precious to me,' said Procne. 'So I will destroy the thing that's most precious to him: his manhood, his power over the future.'

The two women mounted Procne's horse and galloped to the palace. Procne made straight for her son Itys's room. She took the baby into her arms and kissed him through her tears. Ever so tenderly, she laid him down in his crib, then held a blanket over his face until he died. They went to the palace kitchen. Procne dismissed all of the slaves, telling them she was going to cook for her husband herself tonight – a private feast, just the two of them.

Later, the king dined lavishly, eating and drinking his fill. 'Bring me my son,' he said to Procne at last. 'I'd dearly love to see him.'

Procne laughed. 'See him? You've eaten him,' she said.

She opened the door: there was Philomela, clutching the baby's severed head – all that was left of him now. Tereus, ashen, started to gag. Then he unsheathed his sword, and lunged for the women, grabbing his wife by the hair and cutting her throat, seizing and killing her sister. But something miraculous happened. Tereus began to diminish and shrink. His striped cloak sprouted feathers. He was transformed, but kept his proud, martial crest: he was a hoopoe.

And the women? They didn't fall. They flew. They darted on new, slender wings out of the hall, out of the palace, to freedom. Philomela became a nightingale, her mournful, throbbing song as artful as the tapestries she'd once designed. Procne became a swallow. When you next see one, look carefully – the gash of blood at her throat is still there.

ARACHNE

Arachne + Athena, Poseidon and Cecrops + Ixion + Tantalus + Niobe + Marsyas + Daphne + Orithyia + Creusa and Ion + Callisto + Leda + Ganymede + Danaë and Acrisius + Dictys, Perseus and Polydectes + the Graeae + the Gorgons + Andromeda and Cetos + the origin of the spider

Arachne wasn't descended from the gods; she wasn't even royal. Her father, Idmon of Colophon, was a dyer. His work was to harvest thousands upon thousands of sea-snails from the shores of Phocaea. He'd crush their spiny shells, steep them in salt water for days, then boil up the liquor. Then, he'd dip fleeces into the vats. It was like the work of an enchanter: what began as dull-white wool would emerge from those vessels shimmering with subtleties of purple and scarlet.

Despite Arachne's ordinariness in other ways, she was famous for her skill as a spinner and weaver. People would come from miles around to her workshop at Hypaepa, beneath Mount Tmolus. It was a pleasure to see how deftly she combed the wool into fluffy clouds; how she attached handfuls of it to her distaff, then drew out the even, strong thread between her thumb and index finger, setting the whorl whirling as she did so. But it was in the design and invention of her tapestries that she really excelled. So vivid and alive were her scenes that you'd think the characters in them were really moving; you could almost hear them speaking.

It was evident to everyone that Athena herself had trained Arachne. And not a day passed without Arachne hearing someone saying so. But she, secure in the brilliance of her artistry, denied it. And there came a day when she was so irritated by the remarks that she found herself saying, 'I've heard enough about Athena. She can challenge me to a competition if she must. If she wins, she can name her penalty.'

It was a throwaway remark. And so Arachne was not at all on her guard when a stooped, grey-haired woman said to her, 'Take care, Arachne. You can boast that your weaving is better than any other mortal's. But never, ever compare yourself to a goddess. If I were you, I'd apologise right away.'

Arachne was so angry she almost struck the older woman. 'This is outrageous! I'll not take advice from you. You're practically senile! As for Athena – if she is really so bothered about me, I'm sure she'll come herself.'

'She's already here,' said the old woman.

With trembling, blue-veined hands she cast aside her shawl. All at once, instead of the tiny figure hunched over a stick, there stood a young goddess, erect, refulgent, magnificent. On her head gleamed a bronze helmet, made by Hephaestus – its horsehair crest brushed the beams of Arachne's workshop. In her hand was a spear, and slung over her breast was the goatskin aegis, the sign of the power she shares with her father, Zeus. A thousand snakes writhed from it like living tassels.

Arachne's assistants and slaves, all the nymphs of Tmolus who were gathered in the workshop, all the visitors who had come to admire her work, fell back in terror and bowed their heads in reverence. Only Arachne herself, flushing slightly, stood her ground. 'You still think you can compete with me?' said Athena, her voice ringing out strong and clear. Arachne stared belligerently at the goddess, her arrogance intact. She gave a curt nod. The competition was on.

The goddess pulled off her helmet, laid down her spear and threw off her aegis. Both of them, immortal and mortal, hitched up their skirts. Standing side by side now, working with extraordinary speed and skill, they set up a pair of tall, sturdy looms. They measured out the warp threads, attached them evenly from the beam, then tied on the terracotta loom weights in neat bunches, fixing the threads to the heddle bar with knots of wool. The preliminaries over, the real labour began: the women began to send their shuttles flying through the shed, neatening the work as they did so with sharp taps of their weaving swords. They used precious purple yarn, and real gold thread too, but they also blended together many other tints – everything that madder and saffron, woad and oak bark could produce – to create marvellously subtle effects. It was like when the sun comes out just after a shower, and a rainbow arcs over the sky. You can see the colours, distinct and shimmering, and yet at the edges the hues seem to shade into each other and you can hardly tell where one ends and the next begins.

Both the weavers, goddess and human, told ancient tales on their webs. Athena began by setting her immortal hands to weave a border of olive branches – you could almost feel the narrow, papery leaves between your fingers. At the centre was a scene showing herself as the winner of a great competition. The contest she chose to depict was not one against a mere, puny mortal like Arachne, but against one of the greatest of the deathless Olympians.

It was the time of the first king of Athens, Cecrops: he was man from the waist up and snake from the waist down. Poseidon and Athena were vying against each other to become the city's patron, and they both offered gifts to the king. 'I will give you the most precious thing of all: water,' said the god of the oceans. He slammed his trident down on the rock of the Acropolis, and up burst a spring. But Athena turned to the king and said, 'That spring, Cecrops, is of salt water – it will bring no good to your people. This is what I'll give you instead.' She struck her spear on the thin, stony soil – and up sprouted a wizened, silvery-leafed olive tree. Poseidon mocked the goddess: 'What an absurd idea, a tree – and not even an impressive thing like an oak or a pine.' He plucked one of its small black fruits, tasted it, and quickly spat it out again. 'Disgusting,' he said, puckering his immortal lips.

'I advise you to think carefully, Cecrops,' said Athena. 'Appearances are deceptive: the olive tree will bring Attica great wealth. Its fruit can be pressed for oil, which has a thousand uses.

You will never starve with this tree. Though it looks feeble it is tough and long-lived.'

Cecrops chose Athena, and named the new city after her. To this day, her temple, the Parthenon, crowns the Acropolis.

In each corner of her tapestry Athena added tales of humans' arrogance and impiety. She told the tale of the Lapith, Ixion, who had once lived in friendship with the Olympians. But a violent madness took hold of him. He wanted to marry Dia, daughter of his relation, Eioneus, and promised him remarkable gifts: drinking cups of gold and silver. But he never made good on his pledge and, frustrated, Eioneus seized his horses as security. At which point Ixion invited Eioneus to his house, apologising and assuring him that he would soon hand over everything he'd promised.

He did quite the reverse, though: he threw Eioneus into a pit filled with burning coals, killing him. So serious was the offence that no mortal would agree to purify him. In the end it was Zeus who, in a rare moment of leniency, decided that he himself would cleanse Ixion of his crimes. But the king of the gods was rewarded by yet another act of violence: the mortal tried to rape the goddess Hera. Zeus discovered it, though, and put an image in Hera's place, a mere cloud, but one so accurate that Ixion imagined he was impregnating the goddess herself. The cloud gave birth to the first of the Centaurs, who ever afterwards warred with Dia's children, the Lapiths.

As a punishment for his violence, Zeus fixed Ixion to a wheel and set it to whirl, eternally – that is how Athena wove him, revolving in torture.

Athena showed Tantalus, another man who, when the world was young, was a frequent guest at Olympian feasts; gods and goddesses used to return his visits at his palace in the foothills of Mount Sipylus in Lydia. But Tantalus tried to steal nectar and ambrosia from the immortals for his friends, so that they too could become gods. He also attempted to test the Olympians' powers of perception. He killed his own son, Pelops, and served his flesh to them at a feast. All the guests understood what he'd done immediately, except for Demeter, who ate a little of the terrible meal before realising. The horrified immortals brought Pelops back to life. But he was lacking a shoulder – the part that Demeter had mistakenly eaten – and so she fashioned him an ivory prosthetic.

For his offences, Tantalus was punished in the Underworld. He was condemned to stand for ever in a pool of limpid water, overhung by a grove of beautiful fruit trees, all of them heavy with ripe fruit: figs, pomegranates, apples. But whenever he stooped to take a drink of the water it drained away. And whenever he reached for the fruit the trees shrugged their branches out of his reach. Athena showed him like that, tantalised for all eternity; such was her skill, you could almost taste the soft pink flesh of the figs, feel the scarlet pomegranate seeds burst against your tongue.

In the third corner of her tapestry Athena showed Tantalus's daughter Niobe, the wife of Amphion, one of the builders of the walls of Thebes. Together they had twelve children, six girls and six boys. Recklessly, she boasted that she'd had more babies than the goddess Leto, who was mother to only two, Apollo and Artemis. The immortal twins were outraged and descended to Earth. Athena wove Niobe's children as they ran for cover, tried to hide, as the deathless siblings picked them off with their arrows, just as if they were hunting deer. The grief-stricken Niobe returned to Mount Sipylus, where she prayed to Zeus to turn her into a rock. The god assented; stone spread over her body like clinging ivy. Ever after, water dripped from the boulder, like tears.

In the fourth corner of her work, the goddess wove the death of Marsyas. He was a satyr of Phrygia – one of those wild creatures who haunt the mountains, like a man except for his goaty legs, horse's tail and ears. One day he spotted a strange object – it seemed to be made from deer bones – lying on the forest floor. He didn't know it yet, but it was a set of double pipes, the musical instrument called the aulos. Athena herself had invented it, but when she saw her reflection in a pool, she hated how her cheeks bulged and her face flushed as she played. So she threw the pipes away.

Curious, Marsyas now picked them up and examined them. He gave them an exploratory blow – and made a hideous honking sound. But he persisted, and eventually he became a wonderful player of the aulos – so confident, in fact, that he challenged Apollo himself to a contest. The god of music accepted, and the nine Muses agreed to be judges. 'Let's say, shall we, that the winner can do absolutely whatever he wants to the loser,' said Apollo. Marsyas, the foolish creature, agreed.

The god was the first to play. The music rippled out from the lyre, the notes trembling delicately on the air. His music spoke of nature – the sun glancing off water, the wind as it rushed through the trees. It seemed to those listening that nothing could surpass it. But then Marsyas took up the pipes. His music, plangent and wistful, reminded the listeners of the endless mortal cycle of fury and wrongdoing, of loss and love.

The Muses were about to anoint Marsyas the winner. But Apollo cut in. 'How about another round?' he said. 'Since you have two pipes to play, it's only fair that I be allowed to use my other instrument – my voice.'

Without waiting for disagreement, the god began to sing, accompanying himself on the lyre. The immortal voice was so honeyed and rich, the harmonies so complex, that the Muses had little choice but to crown him the victor.

It was time for Marsyas to pay the price – to let the victor do anything he wanted to the loser. Apollo, with cold calculation, stripped the satyr naked, then bound his ankles and wrists. Now the cruel work began in earnest: the god used his bare hands to slice the satyr open, scooping away his skin, flaying him alive – soon it was as if Marsyas was one enormous wound. The creatures of the wood wept in pity and horror; the very sky glowered. That's how Athena showed Apollo and Marsyas: the god radiant and tranquil, his gleaming cloak woven in purple threads; the satyr's face contorted by terror and pain.

Arachne, for her part, designed a pattern showing the gods' crimes.

She began her border with the nymph Daphne, the daughter of the river god Peneus, whose dearest desire was freedom to roam the woods and mountains.

But a god's pitiless gaze can penetrate everywhere, and as soon as radiant Apollo caught sight of her, he burned with greed. Imagine a forest fire: animals and humans flee from it in panic, powerless against its onslaught. Smoke chokes the sky; no rain relieves the catastrophe. The horizon glows a sickly red. That's how fiercely his lust blazed.

It was spring. Daphne was walking in her beloved Thessalian hills. Beneath her feet the young grass was vivid green, the ground alive with iris, euphorbia, asphodel. On the mountaintops the snow lingered still, but Zephyr, the gentle west wind, was already coaxing the world into its freshest beauty.

But then she felt something change. The birds stopped singing. The bees fell silent. Some god, she sensed, must be nearby. She swung round, and there he was, smiling at her, blinding bright. 'Don't be afraid,' he said. 'I'm not a woodsman or a shepherd, I'm a god, I'm Apollo – lord of Delphi, protector of Lycian Patara, master of Ionian Claros, champion of the island of Tenedos. I'm Zeus's son, the seer, the archer, the healer, the musician.'

She understood. And every sinew, every fibre in her body screamed 'No'. She turned and ran.

Daphne was fast, fast as a hare. Soon she could feel her heart begin to pound, her breath begin to rasp – still she ran. Behind her she heard the rhythm of the god's relentless tread, louder now and louder; then she saw his shadow creep up beneath her feet. Was he actually reaching for her tunic? Grabbing at her, like a dog snapping at his prey? Terror gave her new impetus. She felt the pursuing feet recede. But a deathless god has strength to spare, and soon she sensed him gaining on her, felt him anticipating his victory like a hound who can almost taste his victim's flesh.

The nymph began to pray to Gaia, whose knuckles are hills and whose eyes are lakes. The goddess heard her. She found herself arrested mid-stride. She screamed, she tried to go on but she couldn't – it was as if she were lashed to Mother Earth. She felt legs fusing, feet rooting, fingers sprouting, voice failing, sensation fading. Apollo's hands were on her, but instead of belly and breast he was touching hard, nubbled branches; instead of hair and hands, leaves; her trunk had become ... a trunk. That's how Arachne showed Daphne, capturing her in shining green threads as she mutated between nymph and laurel tree, the god lunging in vain for her body as it receded into bark.

Daphne could no longer speak; all she could do was sigh when the wind passed through her leaves. A darker, slower consciousness took her. When Apollo tore off a frond of her leaves to make himself a laurel crown, she found herself ... indifferent.

Next Arachne wove the story of Orithyia, the princess of Athens who was stolen away from her family by Boreas, the north wind. She was taken when she should have been safe, when she was walking in procession to the temple of Athena, carrying a basket of barley for the goddess.

What she felt was an iron-cold lash of air, the kind that steals your breath from your lungs and knocks you off your feet. Her basket was ripped from her hands; she was lifted roughly into the air, cold arms circling her waist like a vice. She glimpsed her friends, her father Erechtheus, her mother Praxithea, diminishing – she tried to cry out to them but her words were stolen by the gale. Soon they were flying higher, higher, Boreas's wings lashing the seas and whipping the waves to fury so they battered the coastlines: that's how Arachne showed the girl, abducted by a storm.

Boreas took her to his stronghold in Thrace, let her drop on the bank of the river Erigonus, and, wrapping himself in a black cloud, raped her where she lay.

Arachne wove Orithyia's sister, young Creusa, as she roamed about the slopes of the Acropolis – she was on the north side of the hill, where the crag is at its steepest. There Pan has his sanctuary: a simple cave nestling among the rocks, niches for offerings carved into its damp walls.

She was picking yellow crocuses, gathering them up in a fold of her dress; the delicate flowers radiated their own golden light. All of a sudden Apollo was upon her, blond hair full of blinding sunshine. He dragged her, as she screamed for her mother, into Pan's sanctuary. There he raped her – telling her it was a holy act in honour of Aphrodite, telling her to keep quiet about it. She endured it, all the while staring at crocus blooms, tumbled and trampled on the ground. Afterwards he left her to stumble back to her parents' house.

In her shame, she hid her pregnancy. But in the months that followed, her girlish, inept fingers made the baby a blanket, weaving into its centre the traditional design that her family used: the image of a Gorgon, bordered with snakes. When she gave birth to a boy in secret, alone and afraid, she hadn't finished the work, but she cut it off the loom nevertheless, and wrapped the tiny baby in it. She put a little necklace on him, too: a chain of intertwining snakes that all the royal Athenians are given at birth. Finally, she crowned his head with a small chaplet of young olive leaves, picked from the sacred tree that the goddess had brought forth from the soil of the Acropolis. Then she crept out into the night, back to the steep northern slope of the crag, and, weeping, laid the baby down in Pan's cave, on the very spot where she'd been raped. Surely the god's conscience would be pricked, he'd find a way to look after his own child? But when she came back later, she was distraught to find the baby gone – taken by wild dogs, she feared, or the lurking, hungry wolves that haunted the mountain slopes.

Later, Creusa was married, to a nobleman called Xuthus – not an Athenian, but a man who had been an ally in her father's war against the Euboeans. No babies came, and Creusa's secret rage against Apollo grew. Eventually Xuthus decided they should travel to Delphi: there he would ask the oracle how they could have a child. There, at the god's shrine, the Pythia told him: 'The very first person you see when you leave this temple – he shall be your son.'

Dazed, he left the building. Right outside was a young man – an attendant, it seemed, who was sweeping the steps. Xuthus bounded up to him and embraced him. 'My son!' he cried.

The boy thought the older man must be mad, and listened in wonderment as the richly dressed stranger told him that he should prepare to come to Athens, to be made a king's heir. Ion – for that was his name – knew nothing about his real parents. All he had known, all of his life, was this temple, this steep mountainside: he'd been brought up as the child of the sanctuary, and the Pythia was the nearest he had to a parent. Now he'd found a father – but the boy desperately wanted to know who his real mother was, and Xuthus couldn't tell him. 'It must have been before I got married,' he said. 'Perhaps she was some woman I met worshipping Dionysus, out on the hills one night. But I'm sorry: I can't remember.'

Creusa had come here to Apollo's temple – to the sanctuary of the god whom she hated, who had raped her – and now her husband had been given a child, but a child that emphatically wasn't hers. The injustice of it ripped through her. For the first time she bore witness to what had happened to her when she was a girl – she poured it all out to a loyal slave who'd known her all her life. In her rage against the god, she decided the boy, this interloper, must die: the very idea of a stranger becoming king of Athens was unthinkable. Her slave agreed to poison the boy's wine, and they would have succeeded in murdering him had it not been for Ion himself: just as he was about to drink he heard one of the servers speak an ill-omened word, and he ordered the wine to be taken away. Then a dove came and sipped from the discarded cup, and, with a shiver of pain, died. The server was questioned and admitted what he'd done. Ion hurried to find Creusa, now, determined to punish her for attempting to kill him.

As Creusa and Ion confronted each other, the Pythia intervened. She had certain things belonging to Ion, she said, which she'd kept hidden all of his life – the things that he'd arrived with when Hermes had put him, as a tiny baby, into her arms. The things were an ineptly woven blanket decorated with a Gorgon's head, a necklace in the shape of intertwined snakes, and a tiny crown of olive leaves. And so, by these tokens, son and mother were reunited. Athena came to them in person to explain how Apollo had ordered Hermes to take his newborn son from Pan's cave to Delphi. But Apollo himself? He stayed away.

Next Arachne wove Callisto, daughter of Lycaon, king of the Arcadians. She was an ardent follower of Artemis, and, like the goddess herself and all her disciples, had sworn to stay celibate. A hunter she was, and the goddess's favourite.

One day, after a solitary morning, when the sun was high and hot, she found a shaded grove to rest in. She unstrung her bow, took off her quiver, and pillowed her head on her arms, making the springy turf her bed. She soon fell asleep.

She woke to a dark shadow falling over her face. It was Artemis, smiling. 'Where have you been?' said the goddess. 'Did you find good hunting grounds? I've missed you.' Callisto raised herself up on one elbow and smiled. 'Lady Artemis, you're greater to me than Zeus himself, if he'd forgive me for saying so ...' She was about to go on, about to describe her morning spent on the mountains, when, to her amazement, Artemis dropped to the ground beside her, close to her. Now a shining hand reached for her thigh, a goddess's perfect mouth dipped for her lips. Callisto was frozen in shock: what was happening, what was the goddess *doing*?

Then the disguise slipped. Instead of a goddess, there was a massive, bearded god looming over her: it was Zeus who was holding her down now, pawing her breasts. Callisto fought and kicked, trying to roll away, free herself from the terrible grip.

She could have overcome any woman or man, but with the king of the gods, it was a one-sided contest. As soon as he'd finished he was gone, a flash of light ascending to Olympus. She was left there alone. After a while, she saw Artemis coming towards her. Callisto struggled to her feet, about to run, thinking it was Zeus back for more. Then she saw the goddess's companions behind her, jogging to keep up with her wide stride: it really was Artemis. Automatically, she turned and joined them, but nothing was the way it had been before. She shrank into herself, hardly spoke, kept to the back.

If Artemis noticed any change in her former favourite, she seemed indifferent. Months passed. Callisto refused to recognise the signs of her own swelling body. The companions were ranging through the hills together one hot day when Artemis called a halt. The sun was just past the zenith, it was time to rest and bathe in the clear-cold river. 'We're alone here, no prying eyes,' said the goddess. 'Let's swim.'

The others stripped, plunged in, wincing at the cool, laughing. Only Callisto hesitated, standing back on the water's edge. 'Come on, the water's lovely,' the others cried. She had no choice. She pulled off her tunic, exposing her body. Her companions saw her pregnant belly – there was a second of silence, then they were surrounding her, screaming, holding her down, calling to the goddess to look at her. Who said, without emotion, without mercy: 'Don't pollute these pure waters with your shame. You need to leave, now. Don't ever come back.' That's what Arachne wove: the implacable goddess sending innocent Callisto away.

Callisto couldn't bring herself to return to her father's house. She stayed in the woods and the mountains. She avoided humans. Quickly, she became ... feral. She found that it was easier to move on all fours. Her hands hardened into pads, her nails lengthened into claws, her shoulders became mountains of muscle. Hair sprouted from her arms, her chest, her back. There were no words for her to speak, no human voice left to her. She became a bear – perhaps it was Artemis who had made the change, perhaps Zeus, perhaps Hera.

Soon she gave birth to her baby, Zeus's son, and suckled him in her leaf-lined den in the woods. But one spring day, some goatherds who tended their flocks on the mountains saw the child and snatched him away from his mother.

Callisto's bearish grief, her animal fury, was all in vain. Her child was lost to her. The goatherds gave him to King Lycaon. Arcas, as he was named, grew up in his grandfather's house quite ignorant of his parentage, his ursine origins.

Meanwhile Callisto gave herself up to her new wild existence. Sometimes she'd make for the river, her lethal jaws clamping down on the squirming fish; sometimes she'd strip the bushes of berries, or withstand the furious bees to steal their honey.

Many years passed. One day Arcas, now a young man, was out hunting. He happened to come across a rugged old she-bear. She stood up on her hind legs, roared, and showed her teeth. Arcas, terrified, gripped his spear.

But then something changed. She dropped down to all fours, sniffing the air, and moved tentatively towards the boy. A memory was stirring. She was trying – though her face remained bearlike and inscrutable – to show the young man that she meant no harm.

But Arcas didn't recognise his mother. How could he? He was afraid of her ravening jaws, her destroying claws. She couldn't make him understand. Her voice could only growl, she couldn't utter the words she wanted to. Her son raised the spear, took aim ...

But Zeus stayed the boy's hand, his son's hand, and turned them both, mother and son, into constellations. She is the Great Bear, he is the Little Bear. They shine above us still.

Beside Callisto, Arachne wove Leda, wife of King Tyndareus of Sparta. Zeus raped her too, this time disguised as a swan. All Leda knew was a white-out, a suffocating snowstorm, webbed claws tearing at her thighs, the engorged, jabbing beak, the thrashing, snakelike neck. There was no escape from the prison of those heavy, sail-like wings – that's how Arachne showed her, fighting for breath, trapped by a vicious faux-bird. Later, Leda would have not babies, but eggs: from one hatched the Dioscuri, the future Argonauts Castor and Pollux; from the other hatched Helen and Clytemnestra.

The final scene on Arachne's border showed the beautiful Ganymede. It was the middle of the day, and the Trojan shepherd was resting on a mountain plateau. His head cupped in his hands, he was half dreaming, half watching an eagle's distant shadow as it poured itself easily over rock and river and gully.

The bird soared closer. The boy could hear its lazy mew, now, but he had no idea what was happening – not even when he saw the dark shadow rushing towards him, not even when he could see quite clearly the bird's indifferent eyes, its yellow-lipped beak, its dangling talons like bundles of knives. Then a ragged sweep of tawny wings darkened the sun, and Ganymede cried out in pain and shock as claws gouged his flesh. He was caught aloft like a fish on a hook.

Zeus – he had disguised himself as his own sacred bird – carried Ganymede all the way to Olympus's peak. The boy became the immortals' cupbearer, serving them at their feasts. His father, Tros, was heartbroken. The king of gods gave him a pair of swift horses, supposed compensation for a lost child.

In the centre of her tapestry Arachne showed yet another mortal woman raped by the king of the gods: Danaë. She was the daughter of Acrisius, king of Argos. But Acrisius desperately wanted a male heir, and consulted the oracle. The answer came: 'Your daughter will give birth to a son who will kill you.'

Acrisius's response to this prophecy was to construct a prison for his daughter beneath his palace. It was bronze-walled, impregnable. No man, except for him, was allowed to go anywhere near it. He made sure Danaë was fed, had the company of a slave, her old nurse. But this life of dark confinement was a life of torture.

Zeus can see everything – even the underground strongholds constructed by mad kings. In his endless greed he decided he must have the mortal girl. He dreamed up his strangest shape-shift yet: he turned himself into a mist of gold, like dust motes when they are lit by a streak of sunlight. In this form the father of the gods nudged himself through a tiny crack in the walls of Danaë's prison, and impregnated her as she slept. So Arachne wove the scene, her heart full of black fury.

As time went on, Danaë read the signs of her body: she was pregnant. But how? She was at a complete loss. A hundred dreadful scenarios ran through her head. Her slave was as bewildered as she. Then, hesitantly, the old nurse told her about the strange phenomenon she'd seen, weeks ago – a shaft, seemingly, of sunlight, a golden glow that had moved around the room then hovered over Danaë's body, pausing at her ... lap. That was the word she used. She had thought her eyes had been deceiving her. But maybe not.

In the end Danaë could find no other plausible explanation. The gold that the slave had seen must have been a god in disguise. She'd been raped.

It was a disaster, of course. How could she keep a baby secret? She couldn't. Soon after her little boy was born, Acrisius heard him bawling. He rushed down through the house to the bronze cell, beside himself with rage and fear. 'How did you do it? Did you sell your body to one of my soldiers? Or did a slave bring someone in from outside?'

'Father, please, no one has been here, I promise,' she said. 'I haven't laid eyes on a single man except for you. But listen, my nurse said she saw something that must have come from a god, when I was asleep. A sort of apparition of gold.' Acrisius cut her off. 'Of course you did it for gold! I should have known. You're all the same, you women. You all have your price.'

Danaë pleaded with her father. 'Send me away, Father, and I promise I will never come back, nor will the baby,' she said.

Even Acrisius couldn't bring himself to murder a daughter and a grandson. But he planned to do the next best thing, a kind of indirect murder. He ordered his slaves to build a large wooden chest. His workmen set about the task, not knowing its purpose, constructing a fine piece of joinery: its feet were in the shape of lion's paws, and its fittings were bronze. When it was ready, he returned to Danaë's prison. 'I have been considering the situation,' he said. 'Since that's what you want, I will send you away. Come with me.'

He led Danaë and her baby out of the bronze prison, into the world: she was dazzled by the brightness of the day, overwhelmed by the endless-seeming space. When at last they reached the sea, she expected to see a ship being readied for a voyage. But no: there was nothing but a large wooden chest with feet like lion's paws. 'Where's the ship, Father?' she said.

'The chest *is* your ship,' said Acrisius, and at his signal the guards rushed forward, seizing the young woman and forcing her inside it. The child was more or less thrown in after her, then the oak lid crashed down. Now came blow after blow as nails sealed it closed, and a series of awkward lurches as the men heaved it into the sea. Danaë sensed they were being towed out, into the open water; she screamed for help, but none came. Eventually the men's voices receded. They had been cast adrift. Danaë understood that her father meant them both to die. Which they clearly would, quite soon. She had neither water nor food. The chest was not so much their ship as their coffin. Danaë, half submerged, brine slapping round her thighs, tried to keep the weeping, squirming baby above the waterline. She managed to get him to feed for a while and then, just as if nothing terrible were happening, he fell asleep. She cried, now, remembering that once upon a time she'd been happy and loved; that once there had been no reason to weep at all. 'I'm so afraid,' she crooned to the child, 'but you don't mind, little Perseus, you're sleeping, all full of milk, in this terrible wooden prison. You don't care about the waves crashing over your head, you don't care about the howling wind, snug in your purple blanket. Thank the gods you don't understand what I'm saying, how desperate all this is. Go to sleep, little baby. Go to sleep, terrible ocean. Go to sleep, endless suffering. Father Zeus, please help us, please change your mind about us.' At last, exhausted and frozen, she felt her consciousness begin to ebb. Still she held the child tightly to her, giving him all the warmth she could.

The following morning, some time before sun-up, a fisherman from the island of Seriphos was setting his course for home when he realised he'd caught more than fish. A large object was bobbing around, tangled in his nets. It was draped in seaweed; it wasn't at all clear what it was. As the sun rose, as he rowed towards the shore, he caught sight of a friend taking a morning walk along the beach. 'Hey, Dictys,' the fisherman cried, 'can you help me with this?' He jabbed his finger in the direction of his strange catch.

'What is it?' shouted Dictys. 'A shark? Some kind of sea monster?'

'No idea,' said the fisherman. 'But it might be valuable. A gift sent by Poseidon, maybe.'

The fisherman jumped down from the boat, Dictys waded in, and between them they managed to haul the mysterious object onto the beach. It revealed itself to be a beautifully made chest. 'It's a dead weight, whatever's inside,' said the fisherman. 'What do you think? Some king's treasure, lost overboard?' Men and women from the village sauntered down to see what was going on. Someone ran back and brought a crowbar. At last the lid was off.

No treasure. No golden drinking cups, no precious swords or armour. Just a dead girl, pale and sodden. Some of the villagers silently took in the fact of her fine gold earrings, the pretty beads around her neck, the fine – though waterlogged – fabrics in which she was dressed. Then Dictys said: 'Dear gods, I think there's a baby in there.' He reached right down into the chest and pulled something out from a fold in the girl's shawl. Deep within the shimmering purple fabric was tucked a tiny, fragile human.

'For the love of the gods, give me something dry,' said Dictys. 'It might be alive.' Someone handed over his rough woollen cloak. Dictys tried to warm the little creature. 'Come on, come on, come on,' he muttered, willing life into the child. And then, there it was – a weak squirm, a faint bleat, a miniature hand forming a tiny fist. 'Shame the mother's a goner,' muttered the fisherman. 'Are you sure?' said Dictys. 'Come on, let's get her out.' A dozen hands reached into the chest and lifted the woman, none too gently, onto the beach. Where she promptly opened her eyes, groaned, and threw up.

The kind and gentle Dictys took the young mother and her child into his own house. She was afraid and silent at first. But, gradually, Danaë and Perseus slotted into life on the island, and people almost forgot the strange way they'd washed up on their shore. Perseus played with the village boys, learned to swim in the sea. He was strong – Dictys used to joke that his early adventure in the chest had toughened him up. But of course he was strong. He was a son of Zeus.

Danaë never stopped worrying that her father would somehow hear about the fisherman who'd caught a woman and her baby. But many years turned without disaster. All there was to worry about, increasingly, was Perseus – and, though it took her some time to realise it, Dictys's brother, Polydectes, the king of Seriphos.

Perseus's problem was that he was getting too big for the island. He was taller, tougher, faster than the other boys. Polydectes had brought him to his own house to train and exercise with the pick of the island's young men. But as the years turned, the king became more and more jealous of the boy. Perseus was becoming a threat.

For all her attempts to fade into the background, Danaë had drawn Polydectes' attention too. He wanted her in his bed. But not as a wife. No – he had much grander plans for his marriage.

Away on the mainland, in the town of Pisa in Elis, there lived a princess called Hippodamia. Her father Oenomaus had become obsessed by her, wanted to have sex with her. And so he'd told her suitors that they must beat him in a chariot race to win her, and if they failed, he'd kill them. Many men had taken up the challenge, but Oenomaus's horses were a gift from the god Ares, and always won. Consequently, there was an increasing number of young men's heads displayed on spikes outside the palace.

Polydectes was determined, nevertheless, to compete for her hand, and so he gathered all his young warriors together, demanding that each contribute his best horse. He also knew Perseus hadn't a horse to his name. When it came to his turn, the boy said: 'I might as well fetch you a Gorgon's head, sir, as bring you a horse. As well you know.'

This was an even better answer than Polydectes had expected. Without missing a beat, he said, 'Go on then, boy – bring me a Gorgon's head. That would be a fair substitute.' Perseus looked at him and laughed. Polydectes did not join in. 'That's an order,' he said. 'Go on, get out of here.'

Perseus, dumbfounded, stood up and left. Polydectes inwardly rejoiced. There was a young man he was never going to see again. With him out of the way, it was only a matter of time before he'd have his hands on the mother.

Perseus walked back to Dictys's house completely despondent. How was he going to kill a Gorgon and bring back her head? All he knew about Gorgons was that there were three of them, sisters, who lived a very long way away, but nobody knew quite where, and they could turn you to stone with a glance.

His mother and Dictys tried to calm him. Did it really matter? Couldn't he just go on as he was before? It was, surely, a far better life to tend your garden, to harvest your olives and prune your vines, than to tread the perilous path of a warrior.

That night, as Perseus lay awake, the god who takes particular care of boys on the verge of manhood came to him. 'Listen to me,' he said. 'I'm Hermes. Your father is the king of the gods, Zeus. That makes you my half-brother. We will make sure you manage to complete the task that Polydectes has set you – Athena and I. Before you find the Gorgons, you must find their sisters, the Graeae. And after you've found the Graeae, you must find the nymphs.'

Perseus looked bewildered. 'Thank you, Lord Hermes,' he said. 'But who are the Graeae? Why do I need to find the nymphs? What nymphs do you mean?'

'Don't worry,' said Hermes, 'I'll help you. First, the Graeae. Come with me.'

Hermes took Perseus by the hand, and suddenly they were aloft: the god's winged boots had strength enough for two. Like a pair of migrating birds they coursed east through the sky, until they reached the borders of Scythia, where, as dawn broke, they landed on a rocky mountainside.

'The Graeae live inside this mountain,' said Hermes. 'Only they can tell you how to find the nymphs – and you need the nymphs, because they will give you what you need to kill a Gorgon. But the Graeae won't want to help you, so listen carefully.

'They have only one eye between them. Each uses it in turn. When they are passing it between them – when none of them can see – that's when they are vulnerable. That's when you need to grab their eye. Then you'll be able to force them to do as you want. Oh, and by the way, when you get to the Gorgons, you'll probably want this.' He put a short, curved sword into Perseus's hand.

'There's the cave entrance,' said Hermes, pointing to a narrow gap in the rock.

'Won't you be coming with me?' asked Perseus. But the god's boots had already lifted him high into the air, and soon he was no more than a speck on the horizon. Perseus was alone.

There was nothing for it. He ducked into the crevice. As his eyes adjusted, he realised he was in a narrow tunnel, which soon opened out into a broad cave, dimly lit by a glance of sunlight from the outside. There, three women sat, facing each other in a circle. Their cheeks were bright and unlined, but their hair was grey. Perseus had the feeling he was in the presence of almost fathomless age. One of them was wearing, he noticed, a dress the colour of saffron. But the most striking thing about them was that they had no eyes – just empty sockets.

They were murmuring to each other in low voices, and at first didn't notice Perseus at all. Then they froze. 'Didn't you hear something, Pemphredo?' said the woman in the saffron dress, in a bright, clear voice. 'I think I did, Enyo,' said the other. 'Would you look for us, Deino?'

The third woman, who had her back to Perseus, now turned. A single gleaming eye shone from her face. Perseus felt it boring deep into him. 'I see a boy,' said Deino, 'a boy who is the son of Zeus. A boy who would like to be a man, and a warrior, and a killer of monsters.'

'Is that what he thinks of creatures like us? That we're monsters?' said Pemphredo.

'Let me see,' said Enyo. She held out her hand. To Perseus's horror, Deino reached into her face, plucked out the eye, and dropped it into the outstretched palm of her sister, who pushed it into one of her own sockets.

'Yes, I see. Strong, ambitious,' said Enyo. 'He wants to kill one of our sisters. A Gorgon.'

She took the eye from her socket and held it out towards Pemphredo. Which was when Perseus darted forward and grabbed the eye before Pemphredo could reach for it. He tried not to think about the feel of it, delicate and damp, in his hand.

'Where's our eye, Enyo?' said Pemphredo.

'I've just handed it to you, sister,' said Enyo. 'Don't you have it? Or did that greedy god's son steal it?'

'Careless,' said Deino. 'Now he'll be wanting to ask us a question.'

'I want to know where the nymphs are,' said Perseus, in a voice that sounded much higher and shakier than he would have liked. 'Tell me how to find the nymphs, or I'll throw your eye off the mountain.'

Deino sighed. 'Just go north, boy,' she said. 'And if you've finished with our eye, we'll have it back, thank you.'

She held out her hand, but Perseus dropped the eye on the ground so that the women had to feel around for it on the cave floor. As they cursed him, he ran – down the tunnel, out of the cave, into the open.

And now what? He was on his own, no sign of human life on this barren spot. There was nothing for it but to turn north as the Graeae had said. He began to walk. He walked all day. Evening came: still no nymphs. He was starting to despair. Had the Graeae been deceiving him? What did 'north' mean – how long was this journey going to take? Days? Months? At last, as the sun set, Perseus felt he could go no further. Tired and hungry, he lay down in a forest clearing and fell asleep.

It was still dark when he woke – to the sound of laughter. A dream? No. He opened his eyes to see three beautiful young women standing over him. 'We're the nymphs, Perseus,' said one of them. 'Don't look so scared – didn't you want to find us?'

Trying to shake off his confusion, Perseus sat up. 'Please, I need your help to kill a Gorgon,' he said.

'Oh yes, we know,' said the second nymph dismissively.

'We've got your stuff,' said the third. He saw that her arms were full. 'A pair of winged boots, so you can fly about like Hermes. A cap of invisibility: put it on, and no one will be able to see you. A bag to put poor Medusa's head in.' She dumped it all on the forest floor.

'Who's Medusa?' said Perseus.

'Don't you know?' said the second nymph. 'One of the Gorgons. There are three of them. Only one is mortal – that's Medusa. Obviously, it's her you'll have to kill. If you decide you're really going to do it, of course.' The women turned away, arm in arm. 'Goodbye, Perseus,' they chorused.

'Wait,' he called to their retreating backs. 'How will I find them, the Gorgons?'

'Just ask the boots,' called one of them over her shoulder. 'They'll take you.'

They melted into the trees. Perseus jumped up and ran after them, but there was no trace of them at all.

He walked back and surveyed the items the nymphs had left. Tentatively, he put on the cap, and saw his own body fade to transparency – disconcerted, he took it off again and stuffed it inside the bag, which he slung over his shoulders. Then he took off his own worn sandals and tried on the winged boots. As soon as he'd laced them up he felt them tugging at him, the way a skittish horse might pull at the mouth. 'Take me to the Gorgons!' he said, trying to sound more commanding than he felt. At once he was climbing through the chill night sky, then coursing high above the forest, always westwards, towards the land of the Hesperides.

It was morning when Perseus sensed he was losing height. Lower and lower he flew, until his toes skimmed the grass and he was walking normally again, in a lush green meadow.

At once he was aware of someone, or something, beside him. He turned and to his astonishment there was the immense figure of – surely – a goddess beside him, her bronze helmet glinting in the sun, a spear in her hand, a bronze shield strapped to her back. 'Perseus,' she said, smiling, 'I'm going to help you kill a Gorgon. Come with me.'

'Lady Athena,' he said, and bowed. 'Thank you. But how will I kill a Gorgon if she can turn anything she sees into stone?'

'Trust me, Perseus,' she said. 'I will show you how. You must not look at her directly: you'll watch her reflection in my shield.'

They walked on, Perseus almost trotting to keep up with the goddess's huge stride. Soon he began to notice something remarkable – the landscape was dotted with incredibly lifelike sculptures. There was a stone fox, skulking beside a hedge; a stone hare, caught mid-dash; a stone man, too, standing in the middle of a field. The goddess laughed. 'They aren't statues, Perseus. Not exactly. They all used to be living creatures, before the Gorgons saw them.'

At last, Athena put her finger to her lips and pointed. In the shade of a tree lay three figures, asleep, breathing evenly. Two of them were remarkable-looking, formidable: they had enormous golden wings, arms of bronze, tusks like a boar's, and snakes for hair. The third was like an ordinary human woman – except that she too had splendid golden wings. 'That one,' said Athena, pointing to the third. 'That's Medusa. She's mortal. She's the one to kill. Take my shield. Have ready the cap of invisibility. The Gorgons' wings are faster than your boots.'

Perseus took a deep breath and unsheathed his sword. Then, as silently as he could, as if he were stalking a hind, he edged closer and closer. That's what Arachne showed in her tapestry: Medusa sleeping, her wings folded, her face peaceful, just before Athena and Perseus killed her.

Medusa sighed and stirred. Quickly, Perseus turned his face away, using the shield's mirror-like surface to look at her. He gripped the sword harder, edged closer. The girl's eyes flicked open. 'Please don't,' she said quietly, without moving. 'It wasn't my fault. She hates me, but it wasn't my fault.'

'What do you mean?' said Perseus. 'What are you talking about?'

'I was raped. Poseidon raped me in Athena's sanctuary. She said I had defiled her temple, but it wasn't my fault. He took me when I was walking in a meadow. There was nothing I could do ...'

At that moment, a number of things happened at once. Perseus heard snuffling, groaning: the other sisters starting to wake. At the same time something came at him like a whirlwind. It was Athena, shrieking in anger, her voice a war cry. She was grabbing his sword-arm now, and he felt it smashing down, propelled by the inhuman force of a goddess. Through the mirror of his shield he saw the sword slice easily through Medusa's neck. Her head rolled away into the grass.

'Grab it,' cried Athena. 'Put on the cap. Fly!' Dumbly, Perseus bundled the head into the bag around his shoulders, shoved the cap on, then urged his winged boots into the air, as the other Gorgons – their names were Euryale and Stheno – wept in grief and fury. They rocked the headless body of their sister in their arms, looking about them in vain for her killer.

Athena was nowhere to be seen. Perseus urged the boots on. He didn't care where. What he didn't see, as he flew south, was what happened next. As Euryale and Stheno looked on in wonderment, a splendid winged horse appeared, miraculously, from their sister's blood: Pegasus, the child of Medusa and Poseidon.

The magical boots swept Perseus onwards to the coast of Ethiopia. There, as he soared above the shore, he spotted a statue of a woman on the end of a rocky promontory. Further back stood a small group of people, who appeared to be in mourning. Curious, he flew back, swooping lower, and realised that the statue was not a statue at all, but a young woman, chained to the rock. Perseus dropped down beside her.

'Who are you? Why are you chained up like this?' he asked, half mesmerised by her beauty. 'My name's Andromeda,' she said. 'My mother boasted that she was more beautiful than the Nereids.

So Poseidon sent Cetos to us as a punishment. Now a priest has told my parents the only way to get rid of him is by letting him take me.'

'Who's Cetos?' said Perseus. Andromeda flinched. 'He's coming,' she said. The young man followed Andromeda's gaze. A great dark shape was gliding just beneath the surface of the sea – bigger than a ship, the largest living thing he'd ever seen. The creature's body broke the surface, glistening in the sun, then dived, coiling over himself until the giant banner of his tail rose into the air, water pouring off it in runnels. Then he sank into the depths like a disappearing tower, leaving a foamy wake behind him.

When he rose up again to the surface, that was when Perseus struck. He charged headlong through the air, Hermes' blade in his hand, and slashed at Cetos's shining black flanks over and over again until the sea ran purple with his blood. At last the sea creature was dead, his body adrift like a giant wreck. From the shore, Perseus heard the people cheering.

He married the princess. Andromeda's parents, Cepheus and Cassiopeia, blessed the union. At the wedding feast, bards sang of Perseus's exploits: how he'd outwitted the Graeae, found the nymphs, defeated the savage Gorgons, and killed the murderous monster, Cetos.

It was some time before he and Andromeda journeyed back to Seriphos. They found the old house by the shore empty, furniture overturned, stores ransacked, slaves gone. The villagers were silent and jumpy. In the end it was the old fisherman who told Perseus what had happened. His mother and Dictys had fled, disappeared. No one knew whether they were dead or alive. Polydectes had come looking for them – the rumour was he wanted to kill his own brother and take Danaë to be his slave.

Perseus set out at once for Polydectes' house. In the great hall, the king was surrounded by his men, feasting and drinking. As Perseus strode in, his sword drawn, silence fell. He walked straight up to the king. 'I've brought you the Gorgon's head,' he said, 'just like you asked.' He reached into the bag that was slung round his shoulders. He grabbed Medusa's head by her hair. He pulled it out and held it up, triumphant, and her sightless eyes turned them all into stone.

Dictys and Danaë were found: they'd been hiding in a distant sanctuary, trusting to the gods to protect them. They married at last, and Dictys became the ruler of Seriphos. Perseus returned the magical items – the cap of invisibility, the winged boots – to the gods, and Athena afterwards wore Medusa's head on her aegis. Perseus did end up killing Acrisius, just as the oracle had foretold – an accident, striking the old man with his discus in an athletics competition. Neither had realised who the other was beforehand. He couldn't bear to become the ruler of Argos, his grandfather's city, and so he swapped with his cousin, Megapenthes, and became instead the king of Tiryns.

Arachne had finished her tapestry. The two artists stood back and surveyed each other's work. Athena took in her rival's pattern, examined the border that showed the gods' violent acts, the central scenes of Danaë raped and Medusa about to be killed, by her. She understood the woman's accusations: they were eloquent, though woven in wool. 'How can the gods call themselves gods when they behave like this?' Arachne asked, gesturing towards the figures on her textile. 'Explain it to me: the gods make laws for humans, and then refuse to follow those same laws themselves. And we're supposed to call that justice? Look at your tapestry – yes, you've shown the sins of humans. But when humans are cruel or violent, they're only following the gods' example. Admit it – you can't find fault with my tapestry. There's nothing untruthful in it. You know I deserve to win.'

'You stupid girl,' said Athena, 'can't you see what's in front of your eyes? My tapestry isn't about human wickedness. It's about how no one, not even Poseidon himself, can beat me in any contest. It's telling you that you can't win. Ever.'

She grabbed Arachne's tapestry, tore it off the loom and ripped it to shreds. Then she battered the girl's head with her shuttle of boxwood, three times, four times, knocking her to the floor. Arachne shrank – diminished almost to nothing. Her father and her friends thought she had vanished. But no: Athena had turned her into a spider, an arachnid. A punishment, you might think, but you could also consider it her prize. To this day she draws out her shimmering threads not from a distaff, but from her own body. And still she weaves her strong and skilful web.

ANDROMACHE

Andromache at Troy ✦ Alcyone
and Ceyx ✦ Baucis and Philemon
✦ Icarus ✦ Apollo and
Hyacinthus ✦ Aphrodite and
Adonis ✦ Aphrodite, Anchises
and Aeneas ✦ Orpheus ✦
Cyparissus ✦ the origin of the
frog ✦ Picus and Circe ✦ the
origin of the magpie ✦ Eurydice
in the Underworld ✦ the Golden
Bough, Hydra, Chimaera,
Bellerophon, Pegasus, Harpies ✦
Charon and Cerberus ✦ Caenis,
the Furies, Sisyphus ✦ Orpheus
in the Underworld ✦ the death
of Hector

ANDROMACHE

The palace was at the topmost point of the city of Troy, shaded by a stand of pines. The king and queen, Priam and Hecuba, had their quarters at the centre of the house; on each flank were those for their eldest sons, Hector and Paris. It was here, in Hector's part of the house, that his wife Andromache spent her days, in a north-facing room cooled by the endless winds that blew through the city.

Below her spread away the plain, the sea, and the life-giving river, Scamander. But for years she had been confined – to this room, this house, this courtyard, these temples, these streets, all bounded in by those city walls, whose great blocks had been heaved into place by the gods Apollo and Poseidon themselves in the time of King Laomedon. Within these mighty defences she felt imprisoned but also protected: Troy was under siege by the Greeks, the same Greeks who had slaughtered her parents and brothers when they'd sacked her home town, Cilician Thebes.

The invaders had come to take back Helen, the arrogant, beautiful daughter of Zeus who had left her husband, Menelaus of Sparta, because she preferred to be here in Troy with her lover, Paris. When the Trojans refused to hand her over, the Greeks had remained, building their camp on the beach, and the war had dragged on, deadly and exhausting, for nine years. Helen, meanwhile, wafted through the city unconcerned, in a shimmer of veils and perfume, worshipped by Paris, loved like a daughter by Priam, and even respected by Hector.

Andromache often begged Hector not to go out to the battlefield, to stay and defend the city from within its walls. But he never listened to her. The call of glory and honour was too powerful. In her heart Andromache knew what would happen. Hector would die. The Greek warrior Achilles would kill him: he was the better fighter, the son of a goddess. Troy would fall. Their baby, Astyanax, would not be spared: the enemy would never let Hector's heir grow to manhood. After the killing and the burning and the looting, she would be taken away, to toil as a slave in some Greek woman's household.

The love Andromache had once felt for her parents and brothers, she now poured into Hector – whom she'd come here to marry in that other time, the time before the war, in a ship loaded down with cups of silver and ivory, with bracelets and necklaces and purple textiles. That day all the people of Troy had thronged at the Scaean Gate to greet her, choking the streets with their chariots and carts. The air had been heavy with myrrh and cassia and frankincense, and singers had poured out their prayers.

All of that might as well have happened in another world. Now, only the loom soothed her unquiet mind, made the days pass. She wandered the earth in her work as she could not in life, weaving woodland groves and mountainsides and wild creatures; and she edged the work with an elaborate border of twining flowers.

She wove the origin of the lovely halcyon, its plumage a flash of turquoise – which later generations call a kingfisher, though the birds are quite different in their habits. The halcyon got its name from Alcyone. She was married to Ceyx, the son of Phosphorus, the morning star. They were sublimely happy together – as happy as Baucis and Philemon, who, old and frail and poor as they were, once offered Zeus hospitality, when he walked the Earth in human form.

Baucis and Philemon spread their humble table with all they had for the stranger: cheese and olives, wild plums and apples. And when Zeus left, he turned their cottage into a temple, which the old couple tended as priestess and priest for their remaining years. When the end of their long lives came, each sprouted leaves, their wrinkled skin hardened to bark, and they became two trees growing from a single trunk. But whereas Baucis and Philemon were unassuming and humble, Ceyx and Alcyone dared to compare themselves to the gods. One night, Alcyone whispered to her husband, 'Do you think any lovers in the world are as lucky as we are? I can't believe even Zeus and Hera are as much in love.'

As punishment for their presumption, Zeus stored up trouble for them, afflicting Ceyx with an intolerable restlessness. In the end, he decided that the only thing that would alleviate his sense of disquiet would be to visit the oracle at Delphi, across the sea. Alcyone begged him not to go. 'Ceyx, please: listen to me. People were wrong to let Athena teach them how to build boats and weave sails ... The sea is dangerous. There are monsters out there, deadly cliffs and rocks. Every day ships go off course, run aground, are hit by storms – the seabed must be covered with wrecks. I'm sure the gods didn't intend mortals to construct these unreliable wooden vessels, to set out on these dangerous journeys. Don't you know what happened to Icarus, when his father tried to master the skies? Daedalus made wings for them both from feathers and wax, so they could escape from Crete and the court of King Minos, but Icarus, even though his father warned him not to, flew too close to the sun and the wax melted. He plunged into the sea and was drowned. Please, Ceyx, stay at home. Or if you must go, take me with you.'

But Ceyx had his way in the end. To soothe Alcyone's misgivings, he promised to return to her within two months.

When his ship was provisioned and ready to leave, Alcyone came to the harbour to see them away, though the sight of the sailors busying themselves on deck was almost too much to bear. Just then Ceyx too felt he would have found any pretext to delay the voyage. But the captain was impatient to be off, and issued the command: the ropes were loosened, and the crew bent to the oars. For a long time Alcyone stood there at the harbour, waving her husband goodbye; when his figure receded, too small to be seen, she followed the billowing white sails until they too faded out of sight. Only then did she return to her chamber, flinging herself on her bed; but the echoing room and the empty space beside her only reminded her more deeply of the part of her that was gone.

All day a stiff breeze sent the ship smartly on its way; the sun shone in a clear sky. But as evening came, the air suddenly felt much cooler. Tall, dark clouds banked up in the sky. A stronger, more aggressive wind began to threaten. At an order from the captain, the crew hurried to take in the sail, to batten down the hatches, to make fast what could be made fast. But soon his commands were swallowed by the howling wind, the drumming rain. War seemed to break out between the sea and the sky; the wild waters roared. Andromache wove the scene.

The ship rolled dangerously, now pitching, now plunging. Chaos reigned: men were shouting, securing oars, bailing out; waves were dashing themselves against the deck, pounding it as a battering ram pounds the gates of a besieged city. All at once a wave burst through one of the hatches, infiltrating it like a soldier who, scaling the walls of a city, finally gains the battlements, though most of his comrades have been pushed back, repelled by arrows shot by the citadel's defenders. He hesitates, triumphant, before pushing on inside the stronghold to open the way for hundreds of his comrades to swarm inside – they will kill the men and boys and take the women and girls. That's what it was like as the waves inundated the ship.

Like the terrified citizens of a defeated city, the sailors prayed to the gods to take pity on them. But when they saw that no help was coming, that the gods had abandoned them, they thought of their wives, and their children, and what rushed into each man's mind as they hovered between life and death, was the memory of simple, ordinary things – the feel of a child's soft hair against his calloused hands; a wife's quick smile as she turned from the loom to greet him.

The same was true of Ceyx. As the mainsail splintered, as the ship was torn apart, his thoughts were only for Alcyone, and much as he longed to see her face one more time, he thanked the gods that she was safe on land, that it was he, not she, who was about to die. Soon enough the last great wave crashed over the deck of the ship, sucking her down, grabbing her as if she were some spoil of war. Every man aboard was dashed all to pieces; poor souls, they perished. As the night ended, as the seas gradually calmed, Phosphorus rose, cloaking himself in clouds of grief when he saw that his son was dead.

At home, Alcyone, who had no idea what had happened to her husband, busied herself with her work, counting the days, imagining how they would walk around their gardens together when he returned, how they would sit together on the bench outside their house, watching the light change as it struck the distant mountainside, sharing a cup of wine together. Every day she went to Hera's shrine to pray to the goddess to keep her husband safe. At first Hera looked away, simply ignoring her. Eventually, in irritation, the goddess summoned the immortals' messenger, Iris. 'I want you to send a dream to Alcyone,' she said. 'Every day she is defiling my altar by offering prayers for a man who has received no funeral rites.'

Iris shot down to Earth on her opalescent rainbow's tail, to the far-distant land where the Cimmerians live, on the edge of Ocean at the very borders of the world. It is a land that Helios never brightens, a land where the mortal inhabitants must ever grope about in the dusk. Near there, in a remote and silent grove, lies a cave. Silent, that is, but for the moan of doves, the murmuring of bees and the immemorial glide of the River Lethe, whose waters lull all to sleep. Andromache wove the poppies and wild valerian and springy chamomile that grow there in profusion; in the dewy air of constant evening, their scent rises like an enchantment. There, in that cave, was Hypnos, nodding and dozing on his couch; but as Iris entered, her gown shimmering with radiant water droplets, he jerked abruptly awake, disturbed by the light.

'Lord Hypnos – you who bring peace and ease to mortals – I greet you and honour you. Hera asks you to send a dream to Alcyone, telling her that her husband is dead.' Iris could say no more; she was overcome with exhaustion and could not stop yawning, and so she fled outside and mounted her rainbow, soaring far above the narcotic fumes of Hypnos's grove, and gulping mouthfuls of the fresh upper air.

Hypnos now issued orders to his son Morpheus, who can disguise himself as any man or woman in a dream. He flew on silent, dark wings until he reached Alcyone's house. He found her peacefully asleep, one arm outstretched as if to her husband – the husband whose corpse was now being pushed this way and that by the never-ending rhythm of Tethys's currents.

Morpheus blurred his features and made himself look just like Ceyx. Not Ceyx as his wife had known him, handsome and laughing and strong, but Ceyx in the throes of death, dripping, his tunic ripped, his flesh bruised and bleeding. 'Dearest,' said the dream image, 'you were right: I should never have gone to sea. A storm came. Our ship was broken up. Everyone died. I died. I love you still – more than ever. But now you must stop praying to Hera, and instead offer prayers for the dead.' In her dream Alcyone cried out in despair. Three times she tried to put her arms around Ceyx's neck; three times her arms found not the warm skin of her beloved, but empty air.

Waking, she felt dread overwhelm her. She rushed out of her room, out of the house, to the shore. She was weeping, beside herself. She waded out into the waters, becalmed as they were, now. Overhead Phosphorus shone palely; day was about to break. Deeper and deeper she waded, praying for the sea to take her too, wanting nothing but to be subsumed into the element in which her lover lay.

She slipped beneath the water, and would have drowned – but the gods raised her up from the water. She shrank; and as she did so her skin sprouted feathers of iridescent turquoise and dazzling orange, with flashes of white at the neck. Her face sprouted a long, sharp beak; her shoulder blades grew wings. At the same time, two Nereids found Ceyx's corpse. Whisking the water with their fishtails, they dragged him to the surface. Zeus breathed life back into his cold body; the Fates allowed it. In another instant he too had shrunk, grown feathers and taken wing in a rush of aquamarine. He flew, straight as an arrow, to Alcyone. As halcyon birds they were reunited: that's how Andromache wove them. Every winter they made their nests on the waters of the sea. Every winter, the seas became calm for a week of halcyon days, while they tended their eggs.

Nearby, Andromache wove a clump of scented hyacinth flowers, which had sprouted miraculously from the blood of a mortal, Hyacinthus. He was a young man from Amyclae, near Sparta, whom Apollo loved; and he loved the god, too. Apollo took him to all his favourite lands, driving him in his swan-drawn chariot. One day they decided to rest in a secluded meadow. There they stripped to exercise, and Apollo feasted his eyes on the beautiful youth who, though a mortal, was strong and swift, with a head of thick-curled locks: the god longed to make him immortal so that they could be together for all eternity.

That day, they ran races together, and threw the javelin, and wrestled, laughing as they sparred; Apollo let Hyacinthus win, making his deathless limbs weak, dampening his outrageous Olympian strength. Next they decided to compete at throwing. Apollo began. The bronze discus almost floated under his hand. His body was like a whorl, as a spinner's deft fingers sent it twirling. The discus flew away from him.

Hyacinthus ran eagerly towards the point where he judged its flight would end, ready to pick it up and have his turn. But the jealous Zephyr had been spying on them for some time. He wanted the mortal for himself – and since Hyacinthus had eyes only for Apollo, he decided to punish them both. He blew a sudden gust of his westerly breeze, sending the discus off course.

Propelled by immortal force, the discus struck Hyacinthus in the head. He cried out and collapsed. Apollo covered the ground between them in a divine blur of speed – no pretence at human sluggishness, now. Summoning all his medical arts, he tried every way he knew to heal the mortal, washing him in nectar, trying to give him ambrosia to swallow. But the man's life was ebbing away. Apollo wept, calling his name over and over again, pleading with him, commanding him to stay alive. In the god's arms Hyacinthus faded like a violet crushed underfoot, like a plucked poppy that drops its scarlet petals. From his blood sprouted the hyacinth, each petal inscribed with 'AI', a memory of Apollo's wail of grief as his lover died. The close-packed fragrant blooms are an eternal reminder of his beautiful curls.

✣

In another part of the tapestry, Andromache wove a different tale about a deathless deity and a mortal: Aphrodite and Adonis. He was a beautiful young man whom Persephone loved too. In the end the goddesses settled it between them that Adonis should spend a third of the year with Persephone, company for her in the cold loneliness of Erebus, and two-thirds of the year with Aphrodite, whom he, like all men, found irresistible.

Surely Aphrodite would have eventually become bored with Adonis – as she grew bored with Anchises, another of her mortal lovers. Anchises was a young Dardanian, as beautiful as a god, whom she noticed once as he tended cattle on Mount Ida, not far from Troy, with his comrades. Day after day she watched him as he strode out with his herds into the hills, then settled himself under a tree to doze the afternoon away, or play enchantingly on his lyre.

When it was his turn to stay away from the pastures and guard the byres, Aphrodite seized her chance. She transformed herself into the likeness of a beautiful young woman, dressed in a robe as bright as fire and shimmering with elaborate embroidery. Shyly she approached him. Anchises abruptly stopped playing, the music dying mid-phrase.

'Lady,' he said, 'tell me, please, which of the immortals you are – Artemis? Or Leto? Or Aphrodite, or Themis, or grey-eyed Athena? I'll build an altar to you and make sacrifices to you all my days, and I pray that you'll give me strong sons and let me live out my old age a happy man.'

Aphrodite laughed, and answered, 'Why do you think I'm a goddess? I'm only a mortal – the daughter of the king of the Phrygians. I come from a long way from here, but I can speak your language – I was nursed by a Trojan slave. I was in the meadows with my friends when Hermes snatched me up into the sky. I was terrified, but he gripped me hard, and we soared through the heavens for days, over cities and plains and fields and mountains and regions that seemed entirely untouched by humans – we flew so far I thought I would never set my foot on land again. In the end, he came down just near here –' she waved vaguely behind her – 'and he told me that it was the gods' plan that I should find a certain Anchises, and marry him. I was just about to despair of seeing any human life at all when I heard your beautiful music. I don't suppose you have heard of someone called Anchises, have you?'

Anchises swallowed. 'Lady: I am Anchises, prince of the Dardanians,' he managed to say. She smiled. 'Well, Anchises, if you're willing, I think we should straight away go and find your parents and prepare for our marriage, since that is the will of the gods. And if you send a messenger across the mountains to Phrygia, I am sure that my father will send you a magnificent dowry of gold and beautiful woven things.'

She gazed at him, and her glance sent a dart of sweet desire into his body. 'Come here,' said Aphrodite, holding out her hand. He took it, then lightly she touched his strong back, his neck, his hair, breathed in the exciting, ephemeral scent of humanity. They kissed. 'I swear to you,' she whispered, 'that no human or god will stop me until I've slept with you. I don't care if Apollo himself comes after me with his arrows – I'll die happy if only you take me to your bed, right now.' Wordlessly he led her to his cottage, and to his bed, and gently, carefully, he took off her lovely jewels and her precious dress, and she, laughing, took off his rough tunic, less gently and carefully, and together they made delicious love, and afterwards Anchises fell into a deep sleep.

Aphrodite slumbered for a time, too. Then she lay awake, pondering how to let the human down gently.

At length, Anchises stirred; he had the feeling that the sun was shining directly onto his eyes – which seemed wrong, in his dark little cottage. Then he realised that the entire room was bathed in radiance not from the sun, but from the immense figure that stood at the end of the bed, her head brushing the ceiling.

'Don't you recognise me now?' she said. 'I'm not quite a Phrygian princess ... I'm Aphrodite. Please don't be afraid. I'm going to leave you now. But listen: I'm going to have a son, our son. I will call him Aeneas, and I'll bring him to you when he is five years old for you to bring up. He will be a fighter, a defender of Troy, a man with a great destiny. Just one thing. Don't boast about having slept with a goddess. When I bring our son to you, you can make up some story about his mother. You can pretend she was one of the mountain nymphs.'

Anchises looked confused. Propping himself up on his elbow, he shaded his eyes with his hand. 'You're leaving?' he said. 'Yes,' she replied. 'You need to understand how it is, Anchises. Your life is so short to a goddess like me. We can't be together. You would grow old in the blink of an eye. Mortals and deathless ones can come together briefly, but we don't exist in time in the same way. Imagine a kestrel, Anchises, think how he races through life as fast as he sweeps through the skies. That's how you are to me. It's best if I go.'

'Right when I first saw you, I thought you were more than a mortal,' said Anchises. 'Why did you lie to me?' Aphrodite smiled, but already she was growing impatient for her own home, her smoking altars on Cyprus. 'Goodbye, Anchises,' she said. Then she disappeared in a rush of golden haze.

Much later, when he was feasting with his friends, Anchises could not resist boasting about what he gradually came to think of as his seduction of a goddess. In his version of the story, afterwards set down by a poet, he was much more bold than he had been in reality. Zeus was so infuriated by the mortal's swagger that he sent a thunderbolt to eliminate him. Aphrodite deflected its full force, saving him from instant annihilation, but ever afterwards he walked with a limp. He was an old man of Troy, and his son Aeneas was Hector's comrade, when Andromache was weaving at her loom. Even then he was still dreaming of his night with the goddess Aphrodite.

Aphrodite, by contrast, gave only the occasional thought to Anchises. She was remarkably devoted, however, to Adonis, during those months of the year when he left Persephone to live with her. The beautiful young man was fanatical about hunting; loved nothing better than to roam the woods and mountains in search of wild animals to stalk and kill. Often the goddess would accompany him, but his mortality made her anxious. She was afraid he'd stray into woodland places that were forbidden, sacred to other gods – she didn't want him killed by his own hunting dogs, like Actaeon. Or by the wild beasts of the forests. 'I worry about you. You're so tender, so fragile, so ... human,' she would say.

Adonis was irritated by her solicitousness. He was a young man: he felt strong and vital and invincible. 'You're not my mother,' he said. 'You really don't need to coddle me like this.' Aphrodite said nothing. A gentle sadness welled up in her heart: she pitied the human, who thought he was the centre of the world, who could not see that he was one tiny, unimportant thread among billions in the great fabric of the universe.

One morning, waking just as dawn broke, Adonis decided to go out without his lover, leaving her asleep in a wooded grove. He dressed himself in his tunic and hunting boots; he slung his hunting horn over his shoulder, picked up his spear, and called softly to his three favourite dogs. That woke the goddess, and she wound her beautiful, deathless arms around him, pleading with him not to go. That's how Andromache showed them – the goddess trying in vain to keep her lover from harm.

He ignored her. Later than morning, he came upon a family of wild boar as they grunted and snickered, grubbing up their food from the soil. Stealthily he approached them, moving nearer and nearer, his spear poised. He threw it at the great bristle-backed sow, the mother of the litter – but missed. At the same time she scented him and, with tremendous speed, squealing with fury, charged – but feinted – then charged again. In his confusion, he didn't know whether to stand his ground or to run. His hesitation cost him everything: she found her mark, her tusks tore at the flesh of his thigh, she pierced the life-giving artery, and she left him there, bleeding out.

Aphrodite was in her swan-drawn chariot, on her way to Cyprus, when she heard his cries of pain. But by the time she found him it was too late. She held him in her arms as his life ebbed away, kissing his eyes, his lips. And as she wept the blood turned into flowers: a lake, it seemed, of short-lived, delicate, scarlet anemones. To this day they spread over meadows in the early spring; they shake restlessly in the breeze as if they want to uproot themselves from their lovely grassy beds and roam the hills.

Andromache next showed Orpheus, as he played the lyre, a fox curled up by his feet. The musician was the son of Apollo and of the Muse Calliope. He could enchant anyone and anything with his artistry. In her tapestry, he was surrounded by the animals and birds who'd gathered to hear his glorious playing. Even the trees – ilex and arbutus, pine and beech – had picked up their roots and lumbered towards him. Among them was a cypress, formerly a youth called Cyparissus, who had been loved by the god Apollo. Cyparissus had adored a mild and gentle stag – everyone doted on the creature, who would boldly come to the dwellings of the mortals to be fed. But, when he was out hunting one morning, Cyparissus had hurled his javelin at that unoffending, trusting animal, not realising it was *his* stag. When he understood his error, he was so distraught he wanted to die; he could not be comforted, even by Apollo. The god at length transformed him into a cypress tree so that he could mourn for ever more. He stands a solemn sentry at cemeteries to this day.

A frog crept close, too: he had once been a human, before being punished by the goddess Leto. At the time, she had been on the run from Hera, who was angry that Zeus had got her pregnant (her children would be the twin deities, Apollo and Artemis). In human disguise, thirsty and tired, Leto had tried to drink cool water from a refreshing pool, but the local people, inhabitants of Lycia, maliciously told her she couldn't, stirring up the water to make it muddy. For that outrage against hospitality, the pregnant goddess turned them into frogs.

Birds flocked through the skies to hear the musician who outdid them in singing: among them, a vivid green woodpecker, who had once been Picus, king of Latium. The immortal sorceress Circe had seen him as she was collecting herbs from a lonely mountainside. He was handsome, a splendid sight as he rode out in his bright green tunic and scarlet cloak, holding his spear aloft. So bewitched was she by his beauty, she dropped her herbs where she stood, staring at him as if transfixed. She conjured up a magical boar for him to hunt, using the illusory animal to bring him to her. But when they came face-to-face, when Circe spoke, Picus repulsed her cruelly, taunting her, mocking her, shaming her, until in anger she transformed him into a woodpecker – his tunic became his plumage, his cloak the red flash of feathers on his head. His piercing call is still shrill and scornful.

Chattering, ebullient magpies came too, in a rambunctious flock: once they had been sisters, nine of them, the daughters of Pierus who ruled Pella in Macedonia. They had dared to compete in singing with the nine Muses, offending the goddesses with their bold and irreligious stories: they claimed, for example, that the Olympian gods had fled ignominiously from Gaia's terrifying son, the snaky Typhon. The Muses angrily turned them into magpies for expressing such heterodox opinions.

Among the crowd of listeners was also Eurydice, a dryad, a nymph of the forest. She loved Orpheus. He was a shy, slightly ungainly young man. But when he played, he was different. He became like a god. His songs irradiated his listeners with despair, joy, passion, elation. He made the lyre vibrate with new sounds. Orpheus loved Eurydice in return, and soon they were married.

One spring day, soon after the wedding, Eurydice was walking by a river. Dragonflies zigzagged through the air. Picus, the woodpecker, screeched with derisive laughter. Wandering in a happy dream, she failed to notice the man leaning against a willow tree, chewing on a stalk of grass.

'Beautiful day,' he said.

Eurydice nodded, and turned away.

'Come on, give us a smile,' he said.

She walked faster. He matched her pace for pace. Dread spread in the pit of her stomach. 'Please, can't you just leave me alone?' she said. 'I'm married. Orpheus is my husband.'

'*Orpheus.* You'll be needing a proper man, then.'

'You know nothing about him.'

'I know everything about him. I'm Aristaeus. We're brothers. Half-brothers. My father's Apollo, his father's Apollo.' He smirked, and reached out, as if to grab her arm.

She ran.

She was fast, Eurydice, like all dryads. She covered the ground lightly, feet kicking up high behind her. Aristaeus went after her, but he was no match for her speed. She felt his steps recede.

But in her relief, in her elation, she failed to spot the adder, basking on the path ahead, its back a sparkling pattern of diamonds, its tongue an elegant flicker. Nor did the snake sense Eurydice until her foot landed right among his coils. Panicked, he flung out his neck, his jaws wide. He bit.

A sting, a shock, a sharp stab in her ankle, pain radiating through her body. She pulled up, crying out. She sank, she fell. Aristaeus saw it all; ashamed, he ran for help. Eurydice felt sick. Her throat seemed to close up, no air ... she couldn't breathe. Her heart was racing. After a while, she was dimly aware of Orpheus's voice telling her he loved her, not to leave him. Darkness spread, shading out the world and dulling its sounds to nothing.

Or perhaps there was ... *something.* After a time, after a confusing, inchoate time of strange, dreamlike impressions – a fire, weeping, lyre music more plangent than she had ever heard before – Eurydice felt herself reconstitute, somehow. There was pain in her ankle, a dull ache. And yet, no flesh, no body. She held up her arm, and inspected her hand: it was there and not there, as if she existed in outline only, like a figure painted on an amphora. She shook her head at the contradictions. Around her she saw nothing but shadows, everything indistinct. Trees, perhaps? A river? She decided to follow it. After a while she realised there was someone walking alongside her, matching her pace for pace. 'Please,' she said. 'Can't you just leave me alone?'

The figure inclined his head. He was wearing a cloak, a traveller's hat, carrying a staff. 'It's not what you think, Eurydice. I'm Hermes. I won't harm you. You're beyond harm. I'm here to guide you.'

'I'm dead then,' she said, understanding.

'You're dead.'

They walked together in silence, along the riverbank; it seemed somehow familiar. 'A trick of the senses,' said Hermes, though she hadn't spoken. 'In so far as you still have them. It's not the river you remember. It's Cocytus. One of the rivers circling Hades. One of the many. There's Acheron; there's Phlegethon, which flows by Tartarus, and runs with flames, not water. Then there's the greatest of them all, Styx. This region is enormous. Marshy. You could get lost for ever here. My job is to bring you to King Hades. Special dispensation. Mostly I just take souls to the banks of the Styx and leave them to fend for themselves.'

They were walking on a high path, which seemed to be part of a complex, labyrinthine network of routes. Hermes led her with complete certainty – though every junction looked exactly the same – sometimes turning left, sometimes right, sometimes heading straight on. Below the paths, a cat's cradle of rivers flowed, murky and uninviting. Reeds grew at their marshy, ill-defined edges. She had the impression of a great open space, though the rolling fog made it hard to be sure. The light never changed. It seemed to Eurydice that they were locked into some eternal, shadowed dusk.

Eventually the landscape changed a little. Stunted little trees began appearing. Then thickened; they were in a wood. Not the verdant woods of her lived experience, which had teemed with insects and birds and plants, but a mean, ungenerous, colourless wood of ravaged trees that leaned as if they'd withstood years of gales. After a time, Eurydice thought she saw something bright in the distance, a warm glow through the chill gloom.

'The Golden Bough,' said Hermes. 'Before any living person enters the halls of the dead, they must pluck it. A gift for Persephone. Not something you will need.' As they got closer Eurydice made out a tree – not a pallid, grey tree like the other trees of the wood, but a magnificent, bristling green elm, with a single golden branch. At first she thought it must have been crafted by a human, or some immortal. But no: the Golden Bough was part of the elm's living substance. She examined it, marvelling at the soft golden buds sprouting from pliant golden twigs.

The tree, she noticed, was growing in front of, and partially concealing, a gatehouse. 'Don't be afraid of what you see next,' said Hermes. 'None of the creatures can hurt you. They're just phantoms. Like you.'

He put his palms to the doors of the gatehouse – a rickety, tumbledown place, the doors seemingly in need of repair. But they swung smoothly open at the god's touch. Eurydice could see that the building was crowded with beings; like her, they were not fully present, not quite substantial. Some she recognised: there were Centaurs; there was a huge serpent, with shimmering scales and dozens of heads that lashed and darted and hissed – Eurydice flinched and had to remind herself that neither of them had flesh, that the creature couldn't bite or hurt her. 'Hydra,' said Hermes. 'She used to live by the lake at Lerna. Heracles and his lover Iolaus killed her.'

Next to Hydra was a lioness, larger than any you'd normally see – but not quite a lioness, since from her back sprouted a goat's head, and her tail, swinging like a cat's, was actually a snake's scaly body. She breathed fire, or the ghost of fire, from both her mouths. 'Chimaera,' said Hermes. 'She lived in Lycia, the land of King Iobates. She was terrifying the local people, so he ordered Bellerophon to get rid of her – in fact he was hoping that Bellerophon would die in the attempt.

'Bellerophon knew he couldn't do it alone: he'd have to tame the winged horse Pegasus, the creature who'd been born from the drops of blood spilled when Perseus killed Medusa. But the horse was strong and untameable, not the kind that a mortal man can break in.

'A seer told Bellerophon to sleep one night in Athena's temple. He dreamed that the goddess had given him a bridle, and told him to sacrifice a bull to Poseidon. When he woke up he was amazed: beside him lay exactly such a bridle, a precious thing with golden cheek pieces. At once he sacrificed the bull as the dream had told him, and dedicated an altar to Athena for good measure.

'After that Pegasus let the human put on the bridle and ride him. Which is how Bellerophon was able to dodge Chimaera's fire-breath, and shoot his arrows at her until she died.'

Beyond these creatures stood a group of tall, stern-faced young women, each with muscular shoulders from which grew magnificent, sweeping wings. Eurydice paused, intrigued. 'Harpies. They are demons. Snatchers,' said Hermes. 'Once, they were ordered by the gods to punish Phineus, king of Thrace. He was blind, but he had the gift of prophecy. He was too accurate for Zeus's liking – told humans more than he thought they needed to know. So he had the Harpies snatch his food away, tormenting him, starving him. That went on until the Argonauts turned up, Jason's crew, the famous adventurers who were on their way to Colchis to try to capture the Golden Fleece. Phineus knew in advance they would be his salvation; he'd been waiting for them. Among the Argonauts were the sons of the north wind, Calaïs and Zetes – the only beings fast enough to chase the Harpies away, right back to their home on Mount Ida, on Crete. But they couldn't catch them, only get close enough, occasionally, to brush their skirts with their fingertips.'

From the gatehouse, Eurydice could see a path leading steeply downwards to the bank of yet another river – this one wide, turbid, a strong current flowing. At its edge a rickety-looking boat was moored. A surly-looking figure stood in the bows. He looked old –

but at the same time exuded a young, green vigour. A god, then. On the bank Eurydice could make out a crowd of shades like herself, jostling, in so far as ghosts could be said to jostle, to get onto the boat, while the god barked out instructions, fending off most of them with his oar. To her shock Eurydice now saw that the crowd stretched out as far as her eye could see: there were hundreds, thousands, perhaps millions of ghosts, like blades of grass in a meadow. 'Charon. The River Styx's ferryman. Only those who've had the proper funeral rites are allowed on board,' said Hermes. 'The others have to stay here. For ever. Come.'

He strode down the path, Eurydice following, and the crowd of souls parted. The ferryman grunted crossly as Hermes hoisted himself into the boat: it rocked dangerously at the god's tremendous weight and now sat alarmingly low in the water. Hermes put out his hand for Eurydice and helped her in. Charon pushed off at once. She turned back and stared at the dead massing at the water's edge. 'Hey, you, wait your turn!' cried out one. 'What do you think's so special about you?' Soon the souls resembled an angry mob, trying to grab at the boat through the muddy water, shouting in their thin, reedy, ghost voices.

Charon ignored them. Eurydice could only look back in horror and pity as the boat creaked and rocked its way to the opposite shore. At the bank stood a huge creature – like a dog, but bigger, with three heads. Three sets of jaws foamed with saliva, three muzzles tested the air, sniffing. As if satisfied, it drew back, whining quietly. 'Cerberus,' said Hermes. 'Not always so submissive.' As soon as they reached the opposite bank, Hermes and Eurydice's fellow passengers meekly joined a long line of other ghosts who seemed to be waiting their turn to enter a fortress-like building. 'Courthouse,' said Hermes. 'King Minos, who once ruled Crete, judges the dead there, assigns them punishments or rewards – or, in most cases, nothing at all. You're bypassing that. Special instructions. Welcome to Erebus.'

On they walked, past what Hermes called the Mourning Fields – a wide hillside, thickly covered by myrtle bushes, where Eurydice could see figures walking among the scrub. 'Most of the souls of the dead end up here. The ones that lived and loved, had what we think of as ordinary, human lives. That's Caenus,' said Hermes, pointing out one. 'He started life as Caenis – a woman. Was raped by Poseidon. Afterwards, persuaded the god to make him a man. Became a great warrior, but died fighting Centaurs. Up there,' he said, pointing at another hillside, 'are more souls of warriors. That's where the best fighters end up.' But Eurydice's eye was fixed on a three-walled bastion, a high tower behind it rearing up iron-dark and foreboding. In front, a roiling, fiery river ran in spate. Atop the massive gates stood a tremendous woman – her hair and arms wreathed with snakes, her blood-spattered tunic hitched up, great wings sprouting from her shoulders, a scourge in her hand. 'Tisiphone,' said Hermes. 'One of the Furies. Guarding the gates of Tartarus. She and her sisters also punish people who have committed murder within their own family. They pursue the guilty like hounds, to the ends of the Earth. The upper levels of Tartarus are where humans are punished. But its chambers descend beneath the mountain for untold miles. At the bottom, the Titans are chained, guarded by Cyclopes and Hundred-handers.' He shuddered. 'Come on, we have to pass through it to get to Hades' palace.'

They crossed a narrow stone bridge over the flaming current. Tisiphone, glowering, flew down in a great rush of wind and beating feathers, and silently opened the creaking gates for them. Stretching into the distance was a grim, haggard landscape. Even to Eurydice's depleted senses, the air seemed fetid. In the distance, she saw a figure struggling to roll a boulder up a steep, barren mountainside. She watched, transfixed – but just as he managed to get it almost to the top, it rolled back down again. A Fury, hovering above, lashed at the unfortunate soul with her whip until he stumbled after it and began the agonising and pointless process of pushing it up once more.

'Sisyphus,' said Hermes. 'When the nymph Aegina was abducted by Zeus, her father, the river god Asopus, tried to find her. In exchange for telling him where she was, Asopus gave Sisyphus a spring, called Peirene. But Zeus punished him for his loose tongue with this endless labour.'

Hermes seemed to be in a hurry; perhaps it was the thought of the Titans incarcerated miles below his feet, disquieting to an

Olympian god. It is true that from time to time, the ground seemed to tremble and vibrate, as if with the restless movement of some immense creature. At any rate, he set a fair pace through the blasted landscape until he arrived at what looked like a sheer mountainside. As they grew closer, Eurydice was amazed to see a tiny wooden door in what seemed to be the solid rock. Another grim-faced Fury appeared, as if from nowhere, a bunch of keys rattling at her waist. Silently, she picked one from the bunch, unlocked the door, held it open and the god stooped to pass through it. As Eurydice followed, she caught the Fury's eye, and something seemed to flash over the winged woman's face – exhaustion? envy? – and then there was nothing but the sound of the door locking behind them.

Now a completely different scene met Eurydice's eyes: a wide plain, covered in pale asphodel flowers. The air was a grey-gold haze, but there was no sense of a broad sky above. 'The fields of the blessed,' said Hermes. 'Your home for all of eternity. A reward for virtue. But first, I need to take you to the house of Hades.'

Eurydice could just discern through the mistiness the outline of a building. As they neared it, she could see that it was indeed a broad, low palace, with porticoes set all around. Following Hermes inside, she found herself in a dim, gloomy hall, at the end of which was a pair of thrones. On one sat a god who seemed to suck the light from the room, his eyes shrouded in the folds of a dark purple cloak: Hades. On the other was a pale-faced goddess, thin and delicate, her face drawn: Persephone. 'Welcome, Eurydice,' she said. 'You have been chosen, as few are, to live here, among the blessed.' As the goddess spoke, Eurydice felt a great wave of melancholy envelop her, and a surge of longing for the upper air, for the sound of birdsong and the breeze on her face. She realised that that longing belonged to Persephone herself.

It was a strange existence, in the palace of the king and queen of the dead. Most days she sat with Persephone as she spun and wove at her great loom. The goddess was hungry for stories of the great world above. Eurydice told her all about her own life, about Orpheus, about his music. If she was not needed by the queen, she would pace around the endless asphodel meadows. The other ghosts she encountered were benign but vague. They had no stories.

Some of them barely knew their own names. Hades she hardly saw, thankfully; if she passed him in a palace corridor, she'd find herself cowering from the darkness that almost shone from him. If only she could live again! A single day on Earth – as a slave, anything! – would be worth an eternity of this. Time drifted on, empty, monotonous.

One day, as she sat with Persephone in her chamber, she heard something that silenced her, mid-sentence, something that sent all the failing senses racing. Persephone too froze, her golden shuttle halfway through the weft; then she rushed to the door. 'It's Orpheus,' she said. 'And he's alive. Come and see.' Eurydice came. It was, indeed, him, Orpheus, his lyre crooked under his arm, a ripple of ghosts walking behind him as he played: he sang of his own passage through the Underworld, how he had found and plucked the Golden Bough; how he had charmed Charon, and sent Cerberus to sleep, and persuaded the Furies to let him pass, while Sisyphus rested for a moment on his rock, and Tantalus ceased to reach for the impossible fruit. As he walked up the palace steps, he changed his song: he sang of how Hades had fought alongside his brothers Zeus and Poseidon against Titans and Giants, how they had divided up the sky, the sea and the Underworld by lot; he sang of Hades as the greatest of gods, because death cannot be withstood, because the souls he rules over are numberless and ever-increasing.

At this, the black-hooded god himself entered his hall and sat down on his great seat; Persephone took her place beside him. It was as if the deathless ones themselves could not resist the trembling, liquid phrases. Eurydice stood at Persephone's side, and wept as her husband sang, though a ghost cannot truly weep, cannot shed the hot damp tears of the living. She wept for her own body, for the sweet sensations she had lost. She wept for the memory of Orpheus's touch. He sang now of her death, of his own wretched grief, the desolation of her friends. He sang of Aristaeus: how, after Eurydice's death, his beloved bees had deserted him, his hives had collapsed. How the youth had appealed to his mother, the lion-wrestling nymph Cyrene, for help, and she had instructed him to find Proteus, the shape-shifting sea god, and hold him tight as he metamorphosed in quick succession from fire to river to beast.

How Aristaeus had done as she had instructed, and never let the god go until he agreed to speak, and how Proteus told him that his bees had fled as punishment, because it was he who had caused Eurydice to die.

Orpheus's song now changed in tone from mournful to urgent, persuasive. He sang of love, which even death cannot destroy. He sang of Hades' own former solitude in Erebus, how he had felt a loneliness so deep that he had forced Persephone to come with him and reign alongside him as queen – even Hades, he sang, is ruled by sweet desire. He sang of how his own love for Eurydice had been cut off as it budded, was never allowed to flower. He begged the rulers of the dead: 'Please, unravel Eurydice's fate, reweave her story. Let her come back to the surface of the Earth with me, and let us live together a little while – such a little while as far as you gods are concerned, but a lifetime for us. And then, in the blink of an eye, she will return to you, as everybody must.'

Persephone leaned towards her husband. They whispered together. Eurydice saw him nod. Persephone raised her hand. Orpheus stilled his lyre and his gaze locked on to Eurydice's; she gazed back, drinking in the sight of his enviable, solid flesh. The queen spoke. 'We are agreed. You may return to the upper air, Orpheus, and you may take Eurydice with you. She will be recloaked in her body, she will live life once more. But you must walk ahead of her, and not turn back, nor may you speak to each other, until you are both on the Earth. If you do turn round, she will be required to return to Erebus, and you will never see her again as long as you live. Now, go: take the path that leads before you.'

Orpheus bowed his head in thanks, then, without speaking, without a glance at Eurydice, turned and walked out of the palace. Through the asphodel a path had opened up, leading away into the haze. Orpheus took it. Eurydice followed close behind, aware that her presence behind him was utterly silent – she had no breath to breathe, and not a grass or flower bent beneath her tread.

They walked for hours through the mist. Orpheus's gaze did not waver from the path. At length the meadow became a hill, which became a mountain, and the path led upwards, more steeply now. Orpheus strapped his lyre to his back so that he could steady himself with his hands, but never did he turn. At long last, Eurydice felt sure she could see a light that was different in quality from the sallow illumination of the Underworld; and what was that rippling through her ghostly limbs – a breeze? She had to clamp her hand over her mouth to stop herself from crying out with joy as she saw that they were entering a broad cave like a tunnel, still leading steeply, perilously up, and at its mouth, yes, was a patch of sunlight. She could actually hear the sound of birdsong, the scream of cicadas, feel warmth on her skin – was it skin? Was she becoming human once more? Orpheus, his human breath laboured, clambered up through the cave mouth. Now he was standing on the surface of the broad and generous Earth.

Which is when he turned. He meant, foolish man, to steady Eurydice as she scrambled up the treacherous scree. He should have let her climb to the surface herself. Eurydice saw his face one last time; she saw joy and triumph and love turn to despair. She felt herself sucked out of his grasp by an inexorable force, she felt herself plunging down, down, down, away from the light, away from the air, away from the flesh of her body, back to the asphodel fields and the dim realms of Hades.

That was the tapestry that Andromache wove, working away ceaselessly until Achilles slaughtered Hector, her husband. Achilles was avenging the death of his beloved companion Patroclus, whom Hector, in turn, had killed.

That day, Achilles chased Hector three times around the city walls – three times past the old fig tree, three times past the springs where the Trojan women used to gather to do the laundry and gossip, before the war changed everything. Perhaps Hector would have survived had the goddess Athena not tricked him. She disguised herself as his brother, Deiphobus; she made Hector think they should turn and fight the Greek together, two against one. But as soon as he took his stand the goddess vanished, leaving him to face Achilles alone. They fought hand-to-hand, until Achilles speared Hector through the neck – the soft, tender, vulnerable neck, unprotected by helmet or breastplate.

Choking on his own blood, Hector begged his killer to return his corpse to his family. Achilles only laughed. 'No funeral for you. I'm going to feed you to the dogs,' he said. 'If I had the appetite, I'd cut you up and eat you raw myself.' Other Greek fighters ran up and surrounded the dying man. Each rammed his sword into Hector's flesh, jeering and mocking, until long after his shade had fled, shrieking, to Hades.

All of this his mother saw from the towers of Troy, and his father too. In that moment they understood that they had lost not only their son, but their entire people: without Hector, they could never win the war. Priam rushed towards the Dardanian Gate – he wanted to demand Achilles give up his dear son's body. But the people held him back; they knew that Achilles, in his anguish and fury, would kill the old king if he could. As news of Hector's death spread through the streets, a great lament went up. Panic and terror engulfed the city, as if it were already being sacked and burned.

Andromache knew nothing of this yet. That morning, strong Hector had embraced her, then stooped to kiss the baby, Astyanax, who had burst into tears, frightened by his father's plumed helmet. Now she was waiting for her husband to return from the battlefield, working to pass the time. Back and forth she went, feeding her shuttle through the shed, pausing only to order the slaves to prepare Hector's bath so that he could wash and rest. She never dreamed he lay dead, face in the dust, killed by Athena and Achilles – until she heard the commotion from outside, and her mother-in-law's voice raised in despair, and she understood. She dropped her shuttle. She left her loom.

HELEN

Helen and Priam + Achilles' rage + Menelaus and Paris fight a duel + Patroclus's death + mourning for Hector + Proteus + Helen and Menelaus return to Sparta + Peleus and Thetis's wedding + the Judgement of Paris + Helen and Paris + the reluctance of Odysseus and of Achilles + Iphigenia at Aulis + Protesilaus and Polydora + Penthesilea + Memnon + the death of Achilles + the delusions of Ajax + the death of Paris + Helen and Odysseus + the wooden horse + Sinon and Laocoön + the fall of Troy + the Trojan women

HELEN

In the time before, Helen would sometimes leave her lover
Paris asleep, slip out of the house, and walk in the dark to
the city ramparts. From atop Troy's walls she'd look down on
the soldiers' watchfires gleaming on the plain, as bright as stars –
a thousand fires or more dotted between the walls and the River
Scamander. More often, though, she'd go there during the day,
standing with the men too old to fight, watching the warriors in
their bloody struggles. Then, she'd set her gaze straight ahead and
walk back to her own palace quarters, ignoring the hiss of insults,
the whispered contempt that rose from doorways and street corners.
Once home, she'd work her loom, making tapestries that showed
the Greeks and Trojans as they fought for the sake, so they said, of
her face.

Often she would watch the fighting with old King Priam at
her side. At the start of it all, she'd pointed out the Greek fighters
she'd known back in Sparta – the great Ajax, bloodthirsty Achilles,
wily Odysseus, old Nestor, and the leader of them all, Agamemnon,
who was married to her sister, Clytemnestra. Then she and Priam
would strain to glimpse Priam's son, her lover, Paris – the man for
whom she'd left her husband, Menelaus of Sparta, the trigger, so
people said, for the war. She would watch Menelaus, too, her veil

hiding her expression. And she'd silently scan the ranks for her half-brothers, the twins Castor and Pollux. She never saw them. She imagined they'd not come because they were ashamed of her. But they were already dead; Sparta's soil held them close.

Priam, despite all he'd lost in the war, was always gentle with her, always tried to protect her from the haters, those who reasoned that if she'd never come to Troy, then the Greeks wouldn't have sent an army to fetch her back, and the men they mourned would still be alive. But Priam – and his eldest son, Hector, Paris's brother – knew that Helen was a pretext. There was always an excuse for war, some symbol or stand-in. It was often a woman; this time it was Helen. What the Greeks really wanted, all along, was Troy's wealth. They wanted the treasuries of her temples emptied out, her women lined up and shared out – soft bodies on which to vent their rage and greed. To Helen, there was an air of unreality about this war, despite the daily stench of death from the funeral pyres, despite the men carried back from the field screaming for relief from their wounds. She sometimes felt as if she were nothing more than a phantom the gods had dreamed up for the men to fight over, while the real her was somewhere else, living a different life.

There in Troy she wove the great warrior Achilles as he sat alone in his tent, eaten up by fury, refusing to fight. That was all because of another dispute over a woman – or, more accurately, two women, Chryseis and Briseis. The Greeks' commander-in-chief, Agamemnon, had seized Chryseis when he'd sacked her city, Cilician Thebes. Her father, Chryses, a priest of Apollo, came to the Greek camp to plead for her return, in front of the whole army. 'May the gods grant that you succeed in plundering Troy and get home safely,' he said to Agamemnon. 'Only please, free my daughter. Accept this ransom. Honour and respect Apollo.'

The whole army roared in approval, urging the king to give way to the priest, to accept the gold he'd brought – but Agamemnon in his arrogance refused. 'I'll not give you back your daughter. She'll die an old woman in my house, working my wife's looms. Get away from here before you make me angry! If you want to stay alive, don't let me find you loitering by our ships again.'

Afraid, Chryses walked away in silence along the beach. But when he reached a safe distance, he turned, raised his arms, and spoke to the god. 'Lord Apollo, hear me now, if you have ever received my sacrifices to you. Punish the Greeks! Send them your arrows to pay for my tears!'

Apollo heard him, and down from Olympus he sprang like the night, his fatal arrows rattling in his quiver. Unseen, he ranged around the Greeks' camp, aiming first at the mules and the dogs, then at the humans, infecting them all with a deadly plague. There seemed to be nothing that anyone could do to stop the disease, which spread like an uncontrollable fire from tent to tent, consuming soldiers, animals, captives, captains. Those who lived in crowded quarters, the rank-and-file troops, the slaves – they were the most likely to sicken and die. Funeral pyres burned constantly.

After ten days Achilles called an assembly of the leaders, and asked Calchas, the Greek seer, to give an opinion on the cause of the epidemic. 'Only if you promise to protect me, Achilles,' he replied. 'Not everyone is going to like what I've got to say.' Achilles promised, and Calchas told the Greek leaders that the only way to stop the plague was to return Chryseis to her father. 'No ransom now!' he said. 'The time for that's over. The only thing you can do is take her home, and sacrifice a hundred bulls to Apollo.'

Agamemnon was enraged at the suggestion. He and Achilles argued, almost came to blows, would have fought with each other had it not been for Athena, who darted to Earth and grabbed Achilles by his hair to restrain him. Agamemnon, in the end, agreed to give Chryseis back to her family, but as compensation he demanded from Achilles a captive of his, Briseis. Achilles had torn her away from the corpses of her husband and three brothers when he'd sacked her home city, Lyrnessus – she'd seen them lying there, their bodies mangled and bloody.

After Briseis, trembling and anxious, was led away from his tent by Agamemnon's men, Achilles refused to fight, and asked his mother, the sea goddess Thetis, to persuade Zeus to favour the

Trojans – their enemy – in the battlefield. But Briseis, like Helen, was just another pretext. In reality it was an old story, one of the oldest: men locking horns over power and status.

Helen wove, too, Menelaus and Paris, as they fought in single combat: her husband and her lover struggling to the death, or so it seemed at the time. Menelaus nearly killed the younger man, was dragging him by the chin-strap of his helmet towards the Greek lines, when all of a sudden Aphrodite plucked the Trojan up in a swirl of mist and sent him back to Helen's perfumed bed. Then she came back for Helen, who was standing with the Trojans on the ramparts, peering through the mist, wondering what had happened to her lover. The goddess disguised herself as an old slave, one who'd worked the looms with Helen years before in Sparta. Plucking at her sleeve, she said, 'He's in his room, waiting for you – you wouldn't think he'd been in battle – he looks ready for a feast, like he's about to go dancing.'

Helen was furious with the goddess, once she sensed the lovely breasts and the flashing eyes behind the disguise. 'What do you want with me now?' she hissed. 'Do you want to drag me off to become the lover of some other favourite of yours – some lord of Maeonia or Phrygia? Why don't you become Paris's lover yourself – or his slave – if you love him so much?'

Aphrodite replied, 'Be very careful, Helen, not to lose my goodwill, if you don't want to be hated by every Greek and every Trojan.' Helen wrapped herself tightly in her shimmering cloak then, and followed the goddess in silence, escaping the notice of the Trojan women. When she reached her chamber, she berated her lover, taunting him for being a less impressive fighter than Menelaus. But he just laughed. 'Helen, stop. Athena helped Menelaus today. Another time he won't be so lucky. You're so beautiful. I want you – even more than the day you left your husband for me. Come to bed.' And she did.

She wove Hector seizing the advantage while Achilles was away from the fighting, breaking through the ramparts built by the Greeks, taking the battle as far as the ships, almost driving the invaders away. She wove Patroclus, when he begged his beloved Achilles to let him lead their band of Myrmidons to battle and save the Greeks from defeat. Patroclus wept in frustration until Achilles softened, comforting him as tenderly as a mother might her child, allowing him to wear his armour, lead his troops – the two had loved each other since boyhood, when Patroclus had come to live with Achilles' father, an exile from his own land because he'd killed another youth in a fight over a game of knucklebones. Then Helen wove the Greeks and Trojans fighting over Patroclus's corpse, after Hector killed him. Patroclus: even Briseis mourned him. Though a warrior, he could be the mildest of men.

Achilles was sent wild with grief at Patroclus's death: it was then that he at last returned to the battle, killing hundreds in the savagery of his impossible, blinding anger. He choked the River Scamander with corpses before fighting hand-to-hand with Hector. That day, Achilles wore fresh armour forged for him by Hephaestus. The shield's decoration was the whole world: the god had fashioned the Pleiades and Hyades shining in the night sky; musicians playing at a wedding feast; city elders judging a murder case; a marauding army encamped outside a city; oxen churning up the black earth as they pulled a plough; reapers harvesting a field of grain; a vineyard full of ripe grapes; lions springing to kill a bull; and a crowd of people dancing, whirling as fast as a potter's wheel, as fast as a spinner's whorl. Helen wove the shield – an artwork within an artwork – as it gleamed on Achilles' arm when he delivered the death-blow to Hector.

Finally she showed Priam bringing Hector's corpse back to the city from the Greek camp. In his passion, in his fury, Achilles kept the Trojan's body, refusing to release it for proper burial. Every day he lashed it to his chariot and dragged it around the city walls, humiliating Hector even beyond his death. Eventually the old king dared to venture into the camp himself under cover of darkness, driving his mule cart right up to Achilles' tent. Achilles might have killed him there and then, but no – the younger man was reminded, for a brief and fragile moment, of his own beloved father, back in lovely Phthia, and both wept, one for his son, one for his father. It was Cassandra, Hector's sister, who, looking down from the city walls as dawn broke, saw Priam's cart trundling back towards the Scaean Gate, Hector's body laid on it – still fresh, still lovely, despite Achilles' attempts to spoil it. She and Andromache rushed down to mourn him. Hecuba and Helen sang for him, too, Hecuba grieving for her strongest son, Helen for her only friend.

All that was in the time before. Things were different, now. Achilles, Paris, Priam, Hecuba, Agamemnon, Cassandra, Clytemnestra – all of them were dead.

But not Menelaus. He was alive. It had taken ten years and thousands of corpses, but he had got his wife back, and a generous share of Troy's bounty, too. After the sack of Troy he and Helen travelled to Cyprus, to Phoenicia, to Egypt, to Ethiopia, to Libya, Menelaus amassing more wealth all the while. But the gods held him back, stopped him from getting home. He didn't know why, until a goddess took pity on him – Eidothea, one of the daughters of the sea god Proteus. She told him that her father could instruct him how to get back to Sparta. 'He won't want to say, though. You'll have to take him by surprise,' she said. 'In the heat of the day he'll have a sleep among his seal flock. Grab him then. Don't let him go, whatever he turns into.' Menelaus did as the goddess said, seizing Proteus and clinging grimly on as he changed into lion, snake, leopard, boar, water, tree – until at last the god grew tired of his protean shifting, and told Menelaus what he needed to know. A hundred cattle would have to be sacrificed to the immortals, said the god, before Menelaus and his ships could be guaranteed a safe passage.

Now they were back in Sparta. Helen spent her days working in her own incense-scented room. There, with her slaves Phylo,

Adraste and Alcippo toiling alongside her, she would twirl her golden spindle, drawing out the thread in long even lengths; she'd store the spun yarn in a beautiful silver basket on wheels embellished with gold. The precious spindle and box were gifts from Alcandre, the wife of Polybus of Egyptian Thebes, a city of unimaginable wealth.

Still Helen wove the war, obsessively, as if it might give up its brutal mysteries once she'd transformed it into thread-made images. She wove the way it had all started – with the lust and greed of two gods, and their quarrel over a goddess's body.

Poseidon and Zeus had each wanted the proud sea goddess Thetis in their bed. They argued bitterly over her, until a prophecy foretold she was fated to have a son who was greater than his father. Both gods were afraid, then. They decided that she must marry a mortal. The man they chose for the honour was Peleus, king of Phthia in Thessaly.

Thetis and her Nereid companions were playing together in the sea, leaping naked through the waves like dolphins, when they saw a strange contraption cutting through the swell towards them – it seemed to them to be plaited from wood, and from it wooden arms emerged, with wooden hands that lashed the waves. Above it rose a great bird's wing, but it wasn't feathered, no, it was a great piece of woven cloth. The immortals swam nearer, curious for a closer look – it was the first ship ever made, the *Argo*. Thetis could see a man staring down at them, at her, seemingly transfixed. It was Peleus. Thetis soon learned that she was to suffer the indignity of marrying him, mere human though he was.

Helen wove the magnificent wedding in Peleus's palace in Thessaly: all the mortals for miles around flocked there, abandoning their ploughs, leaving their vines unpruned. Inside, ivory thrones gleamed, and golden cups glittered. Right in the heart, right in the very centre of the house stood the goddess's bedroom with its ivory-inlaid bed, spread all over with a purple bedspread, woven with scenes from old stories: how on the island of Crete Daedalus had built an intricate, confusing building, the Labyrinth, to house Pasiphaë's son, the half-human, half-bull Minotaur; how Athenian girls and boys, chosen by lot, had been locked inside it as the creature's fodder; how one year the Athenian Theseus had volunteered to come with the sacrificial crew; how the princess Ariadne had given him a sword and a red thread, the means to kill the Minotaur and find his way out of the Labyrinth; how Theseus had promised to take her to Athens, then abandoned her on the shore of the island of Naxos, sailing away while she slept.

The gods of Olympus came to the wedding too, after the mortals had streamed away, their hunger for looking at treasures, for admiring stories told on tapestries, sated at last. Chiron the Centaur brought garlands of flowers grown on Mount Pelion; Peneus, the river god, Daphne's father, was laden with boughs of trees – beech and laurel and plane and poplar and cypress, which, bound together, made a green-tinted bower for the palace entrance. Prometheus came, freed at last from the daily torture he'd suffered when he was chained to the Scythian rock. Zeus and Hera came. The three Fates came – those ancient, white-haired goddesses whom even Zeus must obey: they draw out the thread of our lives from their distaffs, winding it up on their spindles and then – just like that – cutting it. The Fates sang the wedding hymn, foretelling the birth of the couple's son, Achilles, a man who would cause the grief and mourning of so many parents; a man who would make Scamander's waters run red with Trojan blood.

There was one uninvited guest: Eris. The goddess of quarrels and dissension, of bitter argument and strife, had no place at such a feast and yet she came. It may be, in fact, that she always comes to weddings, eavesdropping behind garlanded pillars, squatting resentfully under tables loaded down with jugs of wine. On this occasion, she did something surpassingly malicious. She rolled a golden apple – fruit from the garden of the Hesperides – into the echoing hall, and it stopped exactly between the three goddesses Hera, Athena and Aphrodite, who happened to be talking together. On it were inscribed the words: 'for the most beautiful'. Three shimmering arms bent to pick it up, each assuming, in her immortal vanity, that it was meant for her. An almighty row broke out as the goddesses snatched at the apple, tussling for the pretty prize like badly behaved children. The joy of the wedding was soured. Eris, grimly satisfied, crept away; but she was only doing the will of Zeus, and he himself was bound by the Fates' iron resolve.

Zeus stepped in. 'Hermes,' he said to his son, the messenger god, 'you know Paris, King Priam's son – a shepherd, for the time being, on Mount Ida? Take the goddesses to him, and the apple. Tell him to decide which of them is "the most beautiful".'

Hermes bowed and took the apple. The resentful goddesses, still bickering, hitched their winged horses to their chariots and flew to the mountain slopes. There, dozing on a soft grassy hillock, lay Paris.

The beautiful mortal had no idea that he was really a prince of Troy. After Hecuba had given birth to him, her second-born, she'd dreamed she'd had not a good-natured, squirming baby, but rather one of the Hundred-handers, those terrifying primal deities who stand guard over the Titans, deep in Tartarus. In her dream, the creature had swept up from the depths to Troy, and torn down its towers, laying the whole city waste. The meaning seemed clear: this delightful child would turn out to be the downfall of the city. And so Priam ordered him left for dead on the slopes of Mount Ida.

The slave he'd ordered to expose the baby, though, went back after five days to check on the little body, and found him miraculously still alive. Taking pity on him, he'd brought him into his own house and brought him up as his own. And now, as Paris lay languid in the grass, he awoke to three blazing figures looming over him; four, including Hermes, who hung back with the apple in his hands. The young man listened to the goddesses' question, heard their inducements. Athena, her skin gleaming with olive oil, offered him wisdom. Imposing Hera offered him enormous power and wide dominion. Finally, the myrrh-scented, impossibly seductive Aphrodite offered him the most beautiful woman alive to be his bride: Helen. Of course, Paris gave the apple to Aphrodite. He shivered as he dropped the golden apple into her outstretched fingers, his sunburned hand reaching towards her cool palm. That's what Helen wove: the moment her body became a bribe.

❖

Now she wove how Paris, his true parentage discovered, set sail with his nine ships to find her in Sparta, where she lived with her husband, Menelaus. By then she had long known that men lusted after her, hungering for the perfume of the divine that lingered about her. When she was only a child, Theseus had tried to rape her, and would have succeeded, too, had it not been for her half-brothers Castor and Pollux. Later, when it was time for her to be married, a whole jostling crowd of suitors had come to the palace of her stepfather, Tyndareus. They'd nearly come to blows, this band of rivalrous men – Diomedes, and Ajax, and Philoctetes, and Patroclus, and Odysseus and the rest – all the Greek champions she'd later watch in battle as she stood on Troy's ramparts.

In the end, Odysseus had taken Tyndareus aside, and said, 'I can help you find a way to choose a husband for Helen so that all the other suitors respect your choice – this will end peacefully if you follow my advice. But my price is this – I don't want to marry Helen. I want her cousin. Penelope. Persuade Icarius to give me his daughter. I know he's reluctant to let her marry at all.' Tyndareus had been amazed. 'My niece? But you're here to win Helen. Why on earth would you want Penelope, of all women? She's so ... hard to read. You couldn't call her beautiful, not compared with Helen.' Odysseus, a half-smile at his lips, had just shrugged and said, 'I have my reasons.' Then, after the older man had agreed to his terms, Odysseus had said: 'Make the men swear that they'll help Helen's husband if he ever gets into trouble over the marriage – they'll all promise without thinking, but then they won't be able to raise their fists against each other when you tell them who you've chosen.' The plan had worked. Tyndareus chose Menelaus, the dull, stolid, powerful Menelaus.

Menelaus, suspecting nothing of Aphrodite's bargain with Paris, welcomed the Trojan prince into his house as an honoured guest when he crossed the sea from the Troad to the Peloponnese. Helen had liked him right away: he was so different from the men she'd encountered before, with their sweat and their meaty breath and their talk of weapons and horses. Instead of going out hunting, or exercising with the other men, he would come and lounge around in the room where she and her slaves worked at their weaving. He'd sit there polishing his breastplate and bow, but really he was there for the company: he'd gossip with the women, flattering Helen above all, matching her joke for joke. He was a flirt; charm dripped from him. When Menelaus had been suddenly called away to his grandfather's funeral on Crete, he had pressed Paris to stay on while he was away, and instructed Helen to look after their guest. Of course they'd become lovers, and of course, when he'd asked, she'd left with him. Helen, the inhumanly beautiful, had gone without a thought for her husband, for her child, for her loving parents, because Paris, intoxicating Paris, had become the only thing she wanted. Any thought of armies, chariots and ships – everything that she might have known would follow, sooner or later – meant nothing to her, nothing at all.

In the uproar that followed the discovery of her disappearance, Agamemnon, Menelaus's brother, king of Mycenae, sent his men round the Greek kings, demanding that they make good on their promise to help Helen's husband if he should ever be in need. Odysseus regretted his advice to Tyndareus, his oath to Menelaus. He didn't want to leave Penelope and their newborn, Telemachus; he didn't want to leave his beloved island of Ithaca.

When Agamemnon's representative, the canny Palamedes, came to the island, Penelope told him, with a pretence of anxiety, that her husband was sick – in the head. Meanwhile, Odysseus yoked an ox and a horse together, and tried to plough a field with the incompatible creatures, as if he'd lost his mind. Palamedes' response was to grab Telemachus from his mother's arms and throw the weeping infant down in front of the plough. Of course Odysseus's act was over. He hurled himself in front of the beasts and snatched up the child, soothing the wailing baby – that's what Helen wove, the father cradling his son beside the plough. Odysseus had no choice but to join the army, but he turned over in his mind how he'd get his revenge. Later, at Troy, he framed Palamedes as a spy, forging a letter from Priam to him and hiding gold in his camp. Agamemnon had him stoned to death.

Achilles hadn't wanted to go to Troy, either. Peleus, his father, had heard a prophecy that his son would die there, and so he'd taken him away from Mount Pelion, where Chiron the Centaur was educating him, to the island of Scyros, far from the attention of the Greek leaders – or so he hoped. This time it was Odysseus's turn to expose a reluctant soldier. He sailed to the island and questioned the king, Lycomedes. Everything was denied with a laugh and a shake of the head. But the Ithacan was suspicious. There was something odd, something he couldn't quite put his finger on, about Lycomedes' great band of daughters, who always seemed to be rushing about in a flock, indistinguishable from each other in their long trailing dresses. He decided to test them. He scattered some objects in front of the doors to the great hall and then, concealing himself behind a pillar, waited to see what would happen. As the chattering girls came by he saw them stoop to pick up the spindles and weaving swords he'd left there, inspecting them and discussing the tools expertly. Only one of them reached for the sword – not a weaving sword in this instance, but a gleaming weapon. Odysseus saw the exquisitely dressed figure draw the blade from its sheath with a practised movement, the fine-pleated fabric of her, or rather his, dress falling back to reveal a muscular, scarred arm. That's what Helen wove: Achilles giving himself away because he couldn't resist the glint of deadly, sharpened metal.

Helen now wove the story of Iphigenia, Clytemnestra's daughter, her own niece, at the time the Greek fleet was assembled at the harbour of Aulis, ready to sail over to Troy – but becalmed, no wind to send them there. Days passed and still there wasn't the merest breath of a breeze. The army grew restless and impatient under the blazing, monotonous sun. Only Palamedes and his friend Protesilaus passed the time well, sitting in the shade playing draughts, the game Palamedes had invented. Even that couldn't distract them for ever.

Frustrated, Agamemnon, Menelaus and Odysseus consulted the seer, Calchas. The old man told the captains it was Artemis who had made the sea so flat and glassy, the air so thick and suffocating. She would bring a wind for Troy on one condition: Agamemnon's eldest child, Iphigenia, must be sacrificed on her altar.

Agamemnon's first instinct was to summon the herald Talthybius and issue a proclamation to disband the army – of course he couldn't have his daughter killed. It was unspeakable, unthinkable. But his brother Menelaus reasoned with him, grinding him down until at last he found himself writing to his wife, telling her to send their daughter to Aulis. The pretext he used was that she was to be married, there at the Greeks' encampment.

Agamemnon was in torment. The whole thing was wrong, of course it was wrong. Almost at once he wrote a second letter to Clytemnestra telling her the wedding was off, Iphigenia must stay at home. Menelaus was furious. 'You were happy enough to be everyone's friend when you were going round Greece, recruiting troops,' he said. 'But now look at you – where's your loyalty to me? What kind of leader are you? You've got to be stronger than this. More consistent. Do you think personal concerns can be allowed to get in the way of warfare? This isn't about your daughter any more. The Greeks will be the world's laughing stock if you back down now. There are more lives at stake than Iphigenia's.'

As Agamemnon agonised, word came that she had already arrived – and not just Iphigenia either, but her mother and baby brother, Orestes, too. They were just now washing themselves in a spring, after the long journey, a messenger told them. And what a day of rejoicing it would be! A wedding! As the messenger congratulated them and left, Menelaus watched his brother crumple into despair. And at that moment, the reality of killing Iphigenia, of killing his own niece, swam into focus.

'We can't do it,' said Menelaus. 'You're right. To kill your child for the sake of getting my wife back – it's impossible. Let's do as you say. Let's get Talthybius here. No more expeditions. No more war. This is unbearable.' But Agamemnon turned to him and said: 'It's not that simple. Things are beyond our control. Have you thought about the fact that Odysseus knows of Calchas's prophecy? I know exactly what he'll do. He'll call the soldiers together, tell them about Artemis's demand himself. He'll whip them into a frenzy – they are hungry for battle now, pumped for war and death. They'll want my daughter's blood, I know they will. And if they don't get it, they'll rise up and kill us, all their leaders.'

Meanwhile Clytemnestra and Iphigenia were in an excited, happy flurry. Iphigenia rushed to find her father, hugged him. Then she held him at arm's length and gave him an appraising look. 'Are you anxious, Father?' she said. 'You seem ... upset.'

'It's because,' he managed to reply, 'we're going to be apart for a long, long time.'

'So why not come home? We miss you so much.'

'That's what I want more than anything else in the world. If I had a choice. If things were that simple. Darling, it's hard to explain: there are things I don't want to do. But I have to do them anyway.'

The rest is dreadful to tell. Agamemnon informed his wife that Iphigenia was to be married to Achilles, a worthy match. He tried to send her back to Mycenae – 'Electra and Chrysothemis will need you at home, and this camp is no place for a baby,' he said – but Clytemnestra insisted on staying. 'The girls are quite safe at home,' she said. 'Of course I need to be here. It's my daughter's wedding day. I leave the politics and war to you, Agamemnon. But family – that's my domain.'

Iphigenia's slaves dressed her in a saffron wedding dress. Clytemnestra carried the flaming torch. They walked in procession to the sanctuary of Artemis, where Agamemnon had told them there would be a sacrifice. They were surrounded by heavily armed men – normal, it was a military camp after all, but after a while Clytemnestra felt the tremor of something not quite right, something wild and savage in the air that was being deliberately tamped down. Suddenly she couldn't see her daughter any more over the jostling men's shoulders, their nodding, feathered plumes.

'Let me through,' she ordered. 'I need to be with my daughter.' But strong hands restrained her, men stepped forward in front of her, to the sides of her. She heard a cry of 'Daddy!' saw a flash of saffron and her daughter's body lifted high by soldiers' rough hands – just like when you'd lift a goat high over an altar before sacrificing it to some immortal. Clytemnestra was screaming now, kicking and writhing like a wild thing, trying to fight her way through the wall of bodies to reach her darling child; now she was being pinned down, her hands scrabbling in the dust, and she saw, through a frame of bronze-greaved legs, like a picture, her child. Iphigenia was kneeling, shrieking at her father, the light voice that had once sung to him now twisted by panic. 'Daddy, what are you doing? Please, no, no, I don't want to die!' Rough hands gagged her, forcing her silence, now. Still she tried to reach up, straining to touch her father's beard in supplication, but her hair was being yanked back, her throat arched to the sky – that's what Helen wove – and then came a flash of metal and the saffron dress was dyed scarlet. A gale ripped the screams from Clytemnestra's throat.

Helen wove Polydora, who was married to the first Greek to die as the ships' prows nudged the beach at Troy. That warrior, cut down by Hector as he leaped to shore, was Protesilaus: he'd led forty ships filled with troops from Phylace, from Pyrasus where Demeter has her sanctuary, from flock-rich Iton, from Antron, a town that hugs the shoreline, and from Pteleos, with its meadows where the grass grows knee-deep. When she heard the news of her husband's death Polydora was in their house. It was still only half built – they'd not been married long. There in the hall, its beams still pale and forest-scented, she had sunk to the ground, ripping her cheeks with her nails. Later in her grief she forged a bronze statue in the image of her dead husband, and used to embrace it as if it were him, as if she could bring him back to life; sometimes she dreamed she saw him. But no: the black earth held him tight.

Helen thought of weaving them all, each war widow in turn, thousands of them, until her fingers bled, but she couldn't bring herself to. Instead, she wove the warriors who arrived after Hector's death, determined to fight on the side of Priam, who vainly believed they could save the city from destruction, earning glory for themselves.

There came an Amazon, Penthesilea, daughter of Ares. She'd killed her sister Hippolyta – it had been a terrible mistake, a hunting accident, she'd been aiming at a deer. She came to Priam both to be purified and to forget her shame and grief in battle. In her pride she promised Priam she would kill Achilles, though she'd no idea how brutal he was, how godlike. She came with her band of women – they were happiest when they were galloping across the Scythian plains, they almost lived on horseback, they were rough women and fierce, and the luxurious palace of Priam was strange to them. Andromache, Hector's widow, had been contemptuous when they arrived, welcomed by Priam with a great feast. As she'd watched the Amazons drinking cups of wine, tearing into the platters of meat and bread the slaves had brought for them, she'd muttered to Helen under her breath: 'If Hector couldn't kill Achilles, then what do these women think they can achieve?' But the Trojans rallied to Penthesilea's ferocious cry the next morning when she led them in battle, mounted on the horse that Orithyia, Boreas's wife, had given her in Thrace. The Greeks were taken by surprise, hadn't expected the Trojans to bestir themselves so soon after Hector's death: that day Penthesilea looked like warlike Athena herself, or Eris when she rushes, screaming, through an army, lashing warriors into a frenzy with her war cry. She killed many Greeks – among them Podarces, who'd assumed command of the troops from Phylace after the death ten years before of his brother, the more competent Protesilaus. Penthesilea speared Podarces through the arm and he stumbled from the field, bleeding out among his friends.

The women of Troy flocked to the ramparts and looked down at the bellicose Amazons in wonderment. 'Why are we sitting at home, spinning and weaving?' said one of them, Hippodamia, the half-sister of Aeneas. 'Why aren't we fighting? We're as strong as men, and as brave. We eat the same food, breathe the same air –

look how those women are pushing back the enemy. I'd rather be killed in battle, down there on the plain, than raped and made a slave. So many of our men are dead already. My husband's dead. I've nothing to lose. Let's go down there and join them – let's strap on armour, and fight.'

'Maybe we could if we'd trained all our lives, like those Amazons,' said Theano, Athena's priestess. 'But we wouldn't have the first idea what to do on the battlefield. If wars were won by weaving, we'd have triumphed years ago. Still, the way they're going, we won't need to fight. Look at them – they're going to drive those Greeks all the way back to their ships.'

She was wrong. The Greeks' best warriors, Achilles and Ajax, had not been fighting that morning, they'd been at Patroclus's tomb, mourning Achilles' beloved. Achilles was weeping as he remembered how Patroclus's ghost had appeared to him, just before they'd burned his body on the great pyre, and asked that their bones be buried together. Achilles had tried to hold him in his arms. Three times he'd reached out in longing, and each time the ghost had slipped away like smoke. But Achilles knew that it wouldn't be long now before he was dead too, before their bones lay mingled as Patroclus's ghost had asked.

Now Achilles and Ajax joined the battle, and it was the end for Penthesilea. They stalked her like hunters tracking a leopard; she's ready for them, or thinks she is, yellow eyes unblinking, her elegant tread steady: she's about to explode into a great springing leap, unleashing her claws, her jaws. That's how it was when Penthesilea let loose her spear – but it bounced off Achilles' shield uselessly, no match for the workmanship of Hephaestus.

As Ajax sprang away to defend himself against a marauding pack of Trojans, Achilles and Penthesilea faced each other in single combat. She screamed her war cry again: 'I'm Ares' daughter! Run from me, Achilles, I'm a better fighter than you!' But her father turned his face away.

Achilles raised his ashwood spear: Chiron had made it for him, long ago before the war, in the days when the Centaur had raised the boy, educating him in the arts of healing, teaching him to play the lyre, in the lovely glens of Thessaly. The spear was the one weapon that Patroclus hadn't taken the day he'd borrowed his lover's armour and weapons: no one but Achilles could lift it. He had used that same spear to slaughter Hector, piercing the Trojan's sweat-drenched neck; and now Achilles thrust it with lethal precision into Penthesilea's chest. Blood drenched her cuirass, and she slid from her horse, her war-axe dropping from her hand. As she slumped in the dust, Achilles pulled off her helmet. She gasped for air, choking as she tried to call for help from her neglectful father one last time – and then her life ebbed away. That's how Helen showed them, the two warriors gazing at each other, as one sent the other's shade wailing to Hades.

After that, the Ethiopian champion, Memnon, came to the aid of Troy: his mother was Eos, the goddess of the dawn, and his father, a human called Tithonus. When Eos became pregnant, she pleaded with Zeus to give her lover eternal life. The king of the gods assented – but she had forgotten to ask for his eternal youth. While he was still handsome, Tithonus had lived with the goddess in her palace on the banks of Ocean. But as soon as he started to go grey, she banished him from her bed, though she still took care of him, feeding him ambrosia and nectar and dressing him in rich clothes. In the end, though, when he could no longer lift his withered limbs, when he became a wisp of a thing, nothing but a weak, babbling voice, she had laid him down in a room and left him there, closing the shining doors behind her.

Imagine a river in spate: rain has been falling for days, swelling the waters, and it's rising, running faster and faster, foaming furiously – until all of a sudden it bursts its banks, the flow is uncontainable, and it inundates everything that stands in its way. That's what Memnon was like as he forced his way through the Greeks' lines. He came to blows, there on the Trojan plain, with the veteran Greek fighter Nestor – the king of sandy Pylos, who'd hunted the Calydonian boar when he was young, who'd seen days when warriors were stronger and better than they were now. His son Antilochus dashed in front of him, trying to protect the older man, hurling his spear at Memnon – who dodged it, ducking to the left, though it struck his friend Aethops, killing him. Antilochus heaved up a vast boulder now, and threw it, dealing Memnon a blow that made his bronze helmet ring. But the Ethiopian recovered and sprang forward, stabbing Nestor's son right through the collarbone. No god protected him, no immortal deflected the death-delivering blade. The son bought the safety of his father with his own life.

Antilochus: he had been a young man when he came to Troy, fastest of the fast sprinters. The day Patroclus had died he'd fought grimly, struggling in the field for hours after his friend had breathed his last, not realising. As soon as word came he'd stopped right there as the battle raged around him, and wept, wept with fury and grief. Then he'd dropped his weapons and run to the camp, to Achilles. He'd found him brooding among his ships, wondering why Patroclus wasn't back – he'd told him to return as soon as he'd driven the Trojans from the ships, so why wasn't he here yet? 'He's dead, Achilles,' Antilochus had said. 'Dead, and stripped naked, and Hector has your armour. They're fighting for his corpse.'

Achilles had sunk to his knees, then, and clawed at the earth, smearing his face with dirt and dust. Antilochus had wept beside him, grabbing his friend's wrists and holding on to them tight, afraid that he would kill the man who had brought such bleak news.

Nestor now hurled himself at his son's killer. But Memnon refused to take him on. 'Save yourself to be a father for your other sons,' he said. 'I'm not going to fight an old man.' But now Achilles bore down on Memnon, enraged by the death of Antilochus, and the two men grappled, evenly matched ...

From Olympus Zeus and the other gods watched the champions. Thetis and Eos, each of them in agony for a son, begged him to save her child; the other gods were taking sides too, arguments breaking out all over Zeus's gleaming palace. 'Please, Zeus, if I ever did anything for you, let him live, just one more day,' said Thetis. 'I know his death is near, I know he'll never return to his father's house. My fragile mortal son! He grew so quickly, like a sapling in an orchard, so much stronger, so much more beautiful than any other human, and yet his life is so short.'

Eos cut in: 'A few days ago you were feasting at Memnon's table, enjoying his company, trusting him as you trust so few mortals. He should have stayed at home instead of coming here looking for glory. This war has nothing to do with him. Father Zeus, let him live, let him return to live out his days peacefully on Ocean's banks to feast with you again.'

Down on the plain, Memnon was taunting Achilles. 'No point boasting about your mother now,' he said. 'I'm the son of a goddess too, and my mother is more powerful than yours – she brings day to the world.' Achilles laughed. 'Even Hector died, and he was a better man than you. I killed Hector because he killed Patroclus. I'll kill you because you killed Antilochus. That's how it is, Memnon. You might be strong, the son of a goddess, but today you'll die. I will die soon, too – my fate is coming for me. Some spear or arrow will kill me, right here on the field at Troy.'

On Olympus, Zeus said nothing to the goddesses. Instead, he took his golden scales and in them placed the fates of Memnon and Achilles – then lifted them high for all the gods to see. Memnon's side sank towards Erebus, and Achilles' lifted towards the bright sky. At that moment, Achilles ran Memnon through with the sword that Hephaestus had forged for him.

Eos in her grief sent cold winds roaring down to the Trojan plain: rain lashed the sands, agitated the seas, bent the trees, as if the very forests themselves were doubled up in pain. She flew to the battlefield on her great strong wings and plucked Memnon's body up, bringing him to the banks of the Aesopus in Ethiopia, where she sat weeping, cradling his cold limp corpse in her arms: that's what Helen wove.

As for godlike, savage, gentle Achilles, he would see Eos turn the sky scarlet only once more. The very next day he died. With Apollo guiding the arrow, Paris shot him in the foot. Swift Achilles ran no more; pinned to the earth, he breathed his last. Zeus sent a raging gale to stop the fighting. Through the whirling dust, his men brought his corpse back to the ships, and laid him on a bier. As the grieving

Myrmidons tenderly washed his corpse, they heard an unearthly, piercing cry coming from the sea – they would have run away if Nestor had not told them to hold their ground. It was the goddess Thetis, weeping for her beloved son – the son she'd once tried, and failed, to make immortal to insulate herself against the pain of loss. Thetis and her sisters, the Nereids, brushed aside the mortal men; they smoothed Achilles' hair, oiled his skin, dressed his body in clothes fit for a god. The Muses sang his lament; no one who heard that music could stem their tears. When his pyre at last had burned, when his bones were retrieved from the embers, his friends laid his remains alongside Patroclus's in a beautiful box that Thetis had brought – it was made by Hephaestus, she said, Dionysus had given it to her. These they put alongside Antilochus's remains, and raised a great barrow over all three on a headland above the Hellespont, so that for many years, passing sailors wondered what ancient warriors, what forgotten kings had died there.

Helen now wove Ajax, the great defensive Greek fighter, who desperately wanted to inherit Achilles' miraculous, Hephaestus-forged armour. But crafty Odysseus hankered after it too, and they each made their case before the army leaders. Ajax, though he was by far the better fighter, didn't stand a chance against Odysseus's polished tongue. Ajax told the crowd about his friendship with Achilles, how they'd often feasted together, played draughts together. It was he who'd carried Achilles' body from the field, the day he'd died. He reminded the men of his exploits, how he was second only to Achilles in military prowess. When Hector had sent out a challenge for any Greek to face him in single combat, it had been he who'd strapped on his armour and gone to face the famous Trojan: he'd wounded Hector in the neck, he'd sent a boulder crashing into his shield and had the warrior on his knees, and might have killed him, too, if Apollo hadn't set the Trojan back on his feet ... He'd battled him a second time too: he'd had him down again with another, better, throw of a boulder, one that had sent the man whirling like a child's spinning top. And when the Trojans had fought their way to the Greek ships, it had been he who'd stood high upon the hulls, swinging his spear, encouraging the men: he'd impaled twelve Trojan men that day, one after another.

Odysseus, though, yawned elaborately. 'So many near misses, Ajax. So many opportunities to kill Hector, and so many squandered. The fact is that this war won't be won by brute force. It will be won through sound tactics, planning – and cold cunning. That's where I come in. Without me, Achilles wouldn't have even got to Troy: it was I who tricked him into revealing himself when he was disguised as a girl on Scyros. Or think of the time when Diomedes chose me as his partner to go out on night manoeuvres: out there on the plain I spotted the Trojan scout, Dolon. Thanks to Athena, we trapped the man, questioned him. Harvested intelligence. Then we killed him. We used what we'd learned to kill a whole band of Thracians, freshly arrived as Trojan allies. I still have their horses to prove it. But in any case, I'm not sure if Ajax here is capable of appreciating the artistry of Achilles' shield. He's not intelligent enough. I'm the one who deserves the arms. I'm the one who can really do them justice.'

After the other Greek captains, led by Agamemnon, awarded the arms to Odysseus, Ajax became deranged with anger. He knew he was the stronger man, better in battle. It was he who ought to be taking the arms home to the island of Salamis, a trophy to impress his demanding father, Telamon. He decided to kill them all, his so-called comrades. In the night, while the army slept, he went out with his sword drawn and murder in his heart. But instead of slaughtering his fellow Greeks, he killed only sheep and goats – Athena made it so. After that, in his shame and humiliation, Ajax committed suicide, impaling himself on his sword: that's how Helen showed him, the killer killed by his own hand. He left behind him to fend for themselves Tecmessa, the Phrygian captive woman he loved, and their little boy who'd been born in the camp on the Trojan plain – Eurysaces.

Odysseus was right. It was his cunning that would destroy Troy in the end. A prophecy told the Greeks that the city could be taken on two conditions: Heracles' bow would have to be brought there, and the Palladium – the ancient wooden statue of Athena – would have to be stolen by the Greeks.

The bow of Heracles now belonged to Philoctetes, an archer the Greeks had abandoned on the island of Lemnos at the beginning of the war because of an unhealed leg wound that emitted a terrible stench of decay, appalling and disgusting his comrades. He'd lived there alone for ten long years. But now Odysseus sailed to the island, where he cajoled, flattered and threatened the man until he was persuaded to come to Troy. There Machaon, the son of the healer god Asclepius, tended to his leg and freed him from the awful agony he'd suffered. Philoctetes faced Paris in battle and shot him, killed him. But Helen couldn't weave that: no, the death of her languid, beautiful man was something she couldn't bear to tell.

Helen wove, though, the night she'd been walking incognito through the streets of Troy, when she'd seen two beggars slinking from doorway to doorway. She'd sunk herself into shadow and tracked them, quiet and discreet. She'd recognised them, despite their disguise: Odysseus and Diomedes, undercover in enemy territory. Skilfully she had passed ahead of them, then stepped out in their path, surprising them, pulling back her veil. In secret, in the pitch darkness of an alley, the three of them had talked – she knew Odysseus of old, a man not to be trusted, a man whose words fell like a winter snowstorm, soft but deadly. But she was shrewd too, she knew how to make a deal, how not to sell her knowledge cheap. They had talked for a long while, testing each other, coming at last to an agreement. Then she had led the men silently to Athena's temple, and showed them the door, unlocked and unguarded, to the innermost recesses of the sanctuary.

Inside was the Palladium, an image as old as the city, and its precious symbol: when Ilus, generations ago, had founded Troy, he'd prayed to Zeus for a sign, and the statue had appeared outside his tent as he slept, one hand holding a spear, the other, a distaff and spindle.

The next morning, you would have thought Helen's shock and distress at the statue's disappearance, her mourning for the trail of corpses found in the streets, entirely genuine.

Helen wove, too, the wooden horse that Odysseus's crafty mind dreamed up. One morning the Trojans woke to find the Greeks' camp deserted but for a sea of abandoned tents flapping in the wind, dead campfires, and the still-smouldering pyres where they'd burned their dead. All gone: except for a great wooden horse, standing just outside the Scaean Gate. The Trojans had streamed out to stare at it, and arguments had quickly broken out: some said it should be pulled into the city, others were convinced it must be some trick. Laocoön, the priest of Poseidon, argued it must be burned, at once. Cassandra, Priam and Hecuba's daughter, agreed: the hollow body must surely be concealing soldiers, she said. 'Have we learned nothing in the past ten years? Never trust the Greeks – or their gifts.' But she knew her words were pointless. Apollo, whom she served as a priestess, had wanted to sleep with her, years before. She'd refused and he'd punished her: no one from then on would believe her prophecies, even though they always came true. Her daily anguish, her impossible burden, was to know the disaster that was coming and to be utterly powerless against its force ... She knew that it wouldn't be long, now, before Troy was in flames; she knew she'd be raped in Athena's temple by the lesser Ajax. The son of Oileus would force her at knifepoint, as she clung to the goddess's altar.

Laocoön even threw a spear into the wooden horse's flank, and, as it quivered in the timber, some of the onlookers were sure they could hear the creature sigh or groan. Then Helen herself had circled the horse, calling out the Greek captains' names, precisely imitating the voices of their wives as a test, and the trick would have worked, too, had not Odysseus, hidden inside the structure's belly, clamped his comrades' mouths shut ... it was almost as if he was expecting it to happen.

✤

Just then there was a kerfuffle, a commotion – a group of Trojan shepherds had found a man lurking in the reeds, a Greek, and they were dragging him towards Priam. The king questioned him. 'I'm Sinon,' he said, 'I'm Greek, yes, I admit it, I came here with their army, but believe me when I say I've nowhere to go, no friends left ... Perhaps you've heard of Palamedes. I was his comrade, his kin. Odysseus accused him of treachery, but the evidence was faked. There was a trial, if you could call it that, then he was stoned to death. Priam, you know better than anyone that Palamedes never conspired with you against his fellow Greeks. But ever since then Odysseus has had it in for me. When the Greeks decided to give up the siege and sail home, Calchas the seer told them they'd need to make a sacrifice, just like they had at Aulis – and the chosen victim was me. Odysseus's idea of course. They captured me, tied me up. Prepared the rites, sprinkled the barley ... But I managed to get free. I ran, hid myself in the reeds of that lake all night until your men here found me. I know it's over for me. I'll never see home again. The Greeks hate me, the Trojans hate me.'

Priam took pity on him. 'Greek you may be – but you're not friendless. Consider yourself one of us now,' he said.

He signalled to his guards to let the man go free. 'Now tell us, Sinon. What is this wooden horse for? What had the Greeks in mind when they left it here?' At that, the Greek cast his eyes up to heaven and, tears rolling down his face, said, 'Gods – forgive me for breaking my oath of silence! I have no choice!' Then he turned to the king and said, 'They made it as an offering to Athena. They want to atone for stealing the Palladium. They are hoping you won't drag it into your city. If you do, a prophecy says you'll invade Greece, you'll win great victories. You'll batter down Agamemnon's own city gates.'

Just then, though, a ripple of panic ran through the crowd. People were pointing out to sea – two huge snakes, their eyes suffused with fire and blood, were surging towards them, swimming landwards, leaving a spumy wake behind them. Now they were slinking across the beach, making towards Laocoön, who was preparing to sacrifice a bull to Poseidon. Everyone scattered – but not fast enough, they had one of Laocoön's young sons in their slinky coils, then the other, and they were twisting, constricting, fangs ready to bite ... Laocoön, sword in hand, rushed to help his boys, but the snakes seized him in their deadly spirals, and his face was contorted in agony, his bellow was like a bull's, his arms were straining to wrench away the living bonds. Within seconds there were three corpses by the altar, and the snakes were gliding up through the city streets, as people screamed and scattered. When they reached Athena's temple they slithered inside, then glided out of sight into a crevice in the floor.

There was no stopping the people now: the gods' message seemed clear. Laocoön had surely been punished for arguing that the horse must be burned. Sinon's sinuous story must be true. The horse was dragged into the city. Despite the terrible end of Poseidon's priest and his sons, a wild desire to celebrate took hold of the city; the atmosphere was febrile.

Helen wove how, in the dead of night, Sinon unlatched the concealed door in the horse's hollow body, and the fighting force of Greek captains poured out – Odysseus, Menelaus and young Neoptolemus among them, the last the son of Achilles, the boy he'd fathered when he was hiding on Scyros all those years ago. They found a city dulled by feasting and wine. It was easy work to slaughter the stragglers who were still stumbling home, drunk; easy to kill warriors in their beds; easy to slit the throats of the few guards who slumbered by the gates – which they now forced open, letting in the massed army of the Greeks, who'd sailed back on Sinon's signal.

Soon the city was ablaze. Trojans were strapping on their armour, hurriedly forming fighting bands, but it was chaos. More and more Greeks were swarming through the gates, streaming through the streets, bursting through doors, killing men and boys in their beds, dragging away the girls and women. Drunk on violence, they were indiscriminate in their murder, greedy for bodies, greedy for riches.

❧

Aeneas and his men had climbed to the roof of Priam and Hecuba's palace – the building was surmounted by a tower, and their plan was to work the whole structure loose with crowbars, to send it crashing down on the mass of Greeks who were attacking the palace's huge oak gates. It worked – rubble tumbled in a deadly rain onto the enemy soldiers – but not for long. Others soon came in their place.

Inside the palace, Helen could hear the rhythmic battering of an axe against those oaken gates, now, and then there was a sound of splintering, and yell of triumph, and a band of Greeks clambered through into the courtyard. Women and children scattered, screaming, through the colonnades, but Helen melted into the shadows and watched. There was Neoptolemus – she recognised Achilles' features in him – and Agamemnon, and Menelaus. The Greeks hurled the palace guards aside like flotsam on a stormy sea, and the fires were taking hold, smoke choking the corridors – and still the Greeks came, like packs of hungry wolves.

Right at the centre of the courtyard was an altar dedicated to Zeus, protector of kings, shaded over by a laurel. That's where Hecuba and her daughters flocked, like doves sheltering from a storm, clinging on to the statues – as if the gods would help them now. The king, old man that he was, was strapping on his armour with trembling arms, ready to fight, but Hecuba cried, 'Priam! What are you doing? Are you mad? Not even Hector could save us now, even if he were still alive. Come here, darling – come here with me and hope that the altar will protect us, or else we'll die here together.'

Just then Polites came racing towards them – he was a son of Priam and Hecuba, young and fast, keen-eyed, who'd kept watch on the Greeks for his father, who'd saved his elder brother Deiphobus, once, when he'd taken a spear in the shoulder on the battlefield. Polites was already badly wounded, bleeding profusely – and Neoptolemus was right behind him, aiming his spear for the final blow. The wounded boy collapsed in front of his parents and sisters, vomiting blood. Priam, outraged, furious, screamed at Neoptolemus: 'Monster! Animal! Call yourself Achilles' son? I don't believe it. Even he gave back Hector's body, even he showed some respect for the gods.'

Weeping now, the old man hurled his spear, but weakly, and it was easily deflected by the ringing bronze of Neoptolemus's shield. The young man laughed. 'All right, Priam, you can tell my father, when you see him in Erebus, how I disgraced him. Now, die!' At that he grabbed the old man by his hair and dragged him, slipping through his own son's blood, to the altar. Neoptolemus lifted his sword: that's what Helen wove, that moment before the king was killed and Troy was ended, while his wife and daughters clung to each other, burying their faces in each other's laps so they wouldn't see it.

But Helen, concealed behind her pillar, watched it all. Through the mayhem, her eye caught Aeneas's for an instant, as he ran from that last, futile battle – another guilty survivor. Later that night he would take his old father, Anchises, on his shoulders, and run with his wife Creusa and son Ascanius through the burning streets of Troy, trying to get out, to Mount Ida, there to muster a band of refugees to escape across the sea. But in the confusing melee, in Troy's labyrinth of narrow streets, he would let go of his wife's hand. She would find herself alone, separated from her family. And there in the city she would die, taken by the ravening fires.

Helen at last wove the royal Trojan women as they huddled together, guarded by Greek soldiers beneath the towers of Troy – stripped of all dignity, robbed of their freedom, their humanity, waiting to be handed out to the victors. She wove Hecuba raving in grief for her daughter Polyxena, shamefully killed at the altar to appease the vindictive ghost of Achilles – the girl, though terribly afraid, had gone willingly in the end, knowing that a quick death would be better than a life of slavery. She wove Cassandra, as she stood there pale and muttering, ignored. Andromache was there too, existing in all of her nightmares at once: her son Astyanax, just as she'd always feared, was dead. He'd been snatched from her arms as she breathed in one last gulp of his sweet, babyish smell, and flung from Troy's ramparts.

Rough hands divided the women now, cuffing and kicking them, herding them like animals. Andromache was assigned to her father-in-law's killer, Neoptolemus; Cassandra to Agamemnon, just as she'd foreseen. Hecuba, who was to go with Odysseus, was raging now, nothing like a queen any more, nothing like a human; she was grovelling in the dust, howling like an animal, like a dog ... and now Menelaus came in, looking for Helen, determined to see her dead, and Hecuba screamed at him, 'Yes, kill her, Menelaus, but don't look at her. She'll trap you with those eyes of hers! Her eyes destroy cities!'

That's what Helen wove – the Trojan women as they were torn apart from each other for the last time, and herself standing apart, willing herself to smile at Menelaus, willing herself to stand tall, hoping there was some flush in her cheeks and that, despite her bruises and her torn, filthy clothes, she still had some vestige of her beauty to help her as she argued, now, for her life, turning anything she could to her advantage. 'Think this through, Menelaus,' she said, as calmly as she could. 'If Paris had given the golden apple to Hera, he would now be the master of an empire; if he'd given it to Athena, he would be a shrewd and powerful king, impossible to outwit. Either way, it wouldn't have been good for the Greeks – you wouldn't be master of Troy, as you are now. I admit there have been losses, terrible losses. But you've defeated Paris, he's dead. You won. As for when I left Sparta – instead of blaming me, blame Aphrodite. All of this was out of my hands. It was the gods, it was the Fates, that made me leave you. Paris persuaded me, yes – but I was powerless against the force of his words, powerless against the force of the gods.'

'She came here willingly! She left you for my son! Don't listen to her, Menelaus,' shouted Hecuba. 'She was no victim. No one abducted her. She didn't shed a single tear for you. I used to tell her to get out, to leave, I didn't want her here, my sons were dying because of her, but no, she stayed, I couldn't get rid of her, she loved her Trojan life of luxury, and she loved my son. She betrayed you, Menelaus. Kill her!' But Helen kept looking steadily at Menelaus, even though her hands were shaking, her knees almost giving out. At length he swung his gaze away and said, 'I'll take her with me. I'll kill her when I get her home,' and Helen breathed out, then, in relief, knowing that he'd not do it, that she'd bought time, that she'd persuade him.

✤

That was the tapestry that Helen of Sparta was finishing in her great, high-ceilinged chamber. The palace had just been celebrating her daughter Hermione's wedding to Neoptolemus – though he was still obsessed with his slave, Andromache, who survived and endured, despite all her suffering. Now, from the next room, she heard voices – her husband's, loud and hearty, and others, too, that she didn't recognise.

She listened at the door for a lull in conversation, choosing her moment. Then she pushed open the doors and came in, followed by her slaves, who brought her chair, workbasket and footstool. With a quick glance she took in the guests: a boy who looked exactly like a younger version of a man she knew well, and another youth. 'Menelaus,' she said, 'have you asked the names of our visitors yet? This one is surely Telemachus, son of Odysseus – just a baby when his father left him to fight the war that I was blamed for.'

'I'd noticed the resemblance,' said Menelaus. 'He surely takes after his father – hands, hair, eyes, all of them remind me of my old friend. He couldn't hide his tears when we were talking about Odysseus just now.'

The other young man spoke now. 'You're right. This is Telemachus, Odysseus's son. Forgive my friend if he is being reticent. He is shy; you seem like a god to him. I'm Pisistratus, son of Nestor. We're here because Telemachus wants to know if you have news of his father.'

'So the son of my dear friend is really here,' said Menelaus. 'I loved that man so much I would have given him a city, had he survived, so we could have been neighbours. We would have been inseparable.'

All of them, now, had tears in their eyes. Pisistratus wept for his brother Antilochus, killed at Troy. Menelaus cried for Odysseus – wherever he was. He wept too for his brother Agamemnon – the king who'd won Troy, but died all the same, murdered as soon as he'd arrived home in Mycenae. Helen wept her own silent, secret tears. Then, as the slaves set food on the tables, she got up and mixed the wine. She sprinkled drugs into it – powerful, magical herbs Queen Polydamna had given her in Egypt. Whoever tasted those drugs wouldn't weep any more that day – not even if her mother or father died, not even if she saw her brother, or her darling child, killed. After she'd finished preparing the wine, Helen told the slave to pour it out. Each of the guests spilled the first drops from his cup as a libation, before drinking deeply of the delicious, dark red liquid; so too did the king and queen of Sparta. Helen sat back down on her golden chair. And then she began to tell stories about Odysseus.

CIRCE

Men become pigs ✦ Jason assembles the Argonauts ✦ the Lemnian women ✦ Heracles and Hylas ✦ Argonauts in Colchis ✦ Medea and Jason ✦ Daedalus, Pasiphaë and the bull ✦ Ariadne, the Minotaur and Theseus ✦ Procrustes ✦ bronze bulls and the Golden Fleece ✦ Apsyrtus gives chase ✦ Scylla, Charybdis, Sirens ✦ Arete, Alcinous and the Phaeacians ✦ Talos of Crete ✦ Aeson and the daughters of Pelias ✦ Creon and Glauce ✦ the chariot of Helios

CIRCE

Aeaea is a wooded island with a mountainous interior in the Tyrrhenian Sea. Were you to happen upon it – though sailors hardly ever do – you would find a snug harbour and plenty of fresh water, but you would be wise to leave swiftly. The island is the home of Circe the witch, the daughter of the sun god Helios and the Oceanid Perse. She likes to be alone. The only company she can bear for long is that of her tame lions and wolves, and her slaves, the nymphs of rivers, groves and springs. Her house is a solid, well-built place of stone and timber, surrounded by Turkey oaks, arbutus and pines. If you came close to it, attracted by the homely curl of smoke wafting up through the trees, you'd hear her – her voice is so strong and clear that when she sings, the house itself seems to vibrate. But if you really were this close, you'd already be in danger.

She was singing at her loom one afternoon when a group of shabby, sunburned, underfed sailors approached the house – men who not long ago had been drunk on victory, loaded down with spoils and slaves from the sack of Troy. But the gods had punished them and their king, Odysseus, and sent them much suffering as they tried to sail home to their own rocky island, Ithaca. She heard the mortals as they blundered through the undergrowth towards the door, but she did not stop singing. Instead, with a deft flick of her mind, she sent her lions and wolves streaming out from their lairs to surround them in a coiling sea of sleek, furry bodies.

While the men hesitated, frightened by the wild creatures, she went to her great oak door, unbolted and opened it, and stood there on the threshold. 'You look tired and hungry,' she said. 'Come in and have something to eat and drink. The laws of Zeus demand no less.' In they all trooped, except for one, the canny Eurylochus, who hung back, unseen. He wasn't sure he could trust the beautiful woman – or, surely, goddess – with her entourage of tame beasts. Inside, Circe busied herself, smoothing down soft sheepskin on stools, preparing a meal of barley mixed with honey, cheese and wine.

Circe added certain herbs to this delicious concoction – drugs to make the men drowsy and stupid. As soon as they had taken effect, she struck them with her staff, turning them into pigs. Then she chased them into the pigsty and threw them a few handfuls of acorns and bitter berries. The interruption dealt with, she returned to her loom, where she was weaving a marvellous tapestry, the kind that only a goddess can make.

The textile was decorated with scenes of the adventures of her niece, Medea, daughter of Circe's brother Aeëtes, who ruled over the Colchians, far away at the eastern edge of the Black Sea. The girl was a powerful enchantress, like her aunt Circe: she knew how to find and mix the herbs that bring sleep, madness and death; how to force rivers to run backwards, how to quench blazing fires, to make forests move.

First, though, Circe wove the men who travelled to Colchis, changing the course of Medea's life: Jason and the Argonauts.

Jason's father Aeson was the rightful king of Iolcus in Thessaly, but his brother Pelias had usurped the throne, and Jason had been sent away to the safety of Mount Pelion, where he was brought up by Chiron the Centaur. As soon as he came of age, he returned home, demanding that his uncle give up the throne. Pelias agreed, on condition that he brought him the Golden Fleece – the shining wool of a miraculous ram, the most precious possession of King Aeëtes of Colchis.

Jason accepted his uncle's challenge, and put out the call to the toughest fighters in Greece to join him in his expedition. Heracles, the strongest and fiercest of them all, consented. The Dioscuri – the twins Castor and Pollux – enthusiastically offered themselves. So did Zetes and Calaïs, the winged sons of Boreas and Orithyia. The musician and poet Orpheus came too, bringing his lovely lyre. The craftsman Argos built the ship, the first ever made by humans, and the *Argo* was named for him; Athena taught him how to plait pinewood planks into the texture of a ship, how to weave linen sails and shape wood into oars. The final touch was a beam worked into the keel that had come from Zeus's oracular oak grove at Dodona. The beam – at times of crisis – would talk, offering its prophecies. Hera gave her blessing to the expedition. She was eager to punish Pelias, who had failed to offer her the sacrifices she felt were her due. And she liked Jason: once, when she had been testing the limits of human kindness, she had disguised herself as an old, frail woman, and the young mortal had lifted her up and carried her gently across a river.

On their way to Colchis the Argonauts, as they were called, had many adventures, and saw many extraordinary things.

Circe wove a scene on the shore of Lemnos, where the men were met by an army of women and girls, led by their queen, Hypsipyle. The female population of that island had, after years of mistreatment, plotted revolution, armed themselves and, one bloody night, slaughtered all of the men and the boys on the island. Then they took control. It was easier work, they said, to plough the fields, make speeches in the assembly, and defend their city, than to spin and weave.

The Argonauts sent out a herald to negotiate with the armed women. An agreement was made: the Argonauts could rest on the shore for one night. Early the next morning, though, Hypsipyle summoned an assembly in the marketplace, and, sitting on the great marble throne, began a debate on what to do next. 'I propose we set a good example of hospitality,' she said. 'Let's show these Argonauts how generous a city ruled by women can be. After everything we have suffered from men, I know that some of us would have preferred to have killed these Argonauts as they slept. But I propose we supply the travellers with water and food, in accordance with the laws of Zeus – then wish them on their way.'

But an older woman, Polyxo, who had once been the queen's nurse, stood up, and said, 'My friends, we need to think of the long term. What do you think will happen when we grow frail? The fields won't plough themselves, and our battles won't fight themselves either. It's all right for me – it won't be long before I'm knocking on Hades' door. But what will happen to this city as the years pass? Men, I fear, do have one essential function, however much we might pray to produce children without them. And these travellers who have turned up on our shore – look at them. They are the pick of Greek manhood. Many of them are children or grandchildren of immortals. There are fighters and poets and seers among them. What if we were to welcome them into our city, and offer them a share in it?'

A murmur of approval went up from the crowd. But Hypsipyle spoke up again. 'Polyxo, have you such a short memory?' she said. 'Don't you remember what we suffered? What we fought against? While men ruled here we had no say in anything. We were silenced. We had to ask permission to take even a step outside our homes. We were not allowed to take part in debates. Even if our husbands loved us, their affection was the kind they had for a well-trained horse or a precious diadem. Our bodies were not our own. To justify this treatment, we were told that Pandora, the first woman, was the cause of all the evil in the world – an evident lie! A false myth propagated by a woman-hating poet! Do you really think that if we exchanged one set of men for another that things would change? I believe it is possible to imagine a city in which women and men are equal, but it will not come in our lifetimes.'

'Yes, but to create such a city in the future, we need men, Hypsipyle. Sons,' said Polyxo.

Hypsipyle paused – then spoke again. 'You have a point, Polyxo. In fact I don't think that these travellers would take our city even if we offered it to them: they have their own quest to pursue, far away from here. But I propose a middle path. Let us spin some story to deceive them about the absence of our men. Let us invite them into our city, offer them our hospitality, stage games in their honour. We shall send them away in due course, after a time of celebration and pleasure. And then, in a few months, I think we will be able to look forward to welcoming a new, better generation of Lemnians.'

A cheer went up from the crowd, the assembled women voted in favour of Hypsipyle's suggestion, and the Argonauts accepted the women's proposal, persuaded that the Lemnian men were in temporary exile in Thrace. Games were held: the Argonauts raced and wrestled under the women's watchful, appraising eyes for prizes of precious textiles. Jason and Hypsipyle were struck by one another immediately, and at the end of a night's feasting, after they had heard Orpheus sing songs of love, she took him by the hand and led him to her own quarters. Who knows how long the Argonauts would have spent enjoying the islanders' hospitality, sharing their beds, had it not been for Heracles, who alone of the crew kept away from the women. It was he who stirred the companions, reminding them of their quest.

The reason Heracles avoided the women of Lemnos was his great love for Hylas – a love that also accounted for his decision, later on the journey, to leave the expedition before the adventurers reached Colchis. Heracles had, in fact, killed Hylas's father and taken him in as a boy; later, they became lovers. It is sometimes forgotten that Heracles loved men as well as women; the truth is, Heracles had so many male lovers that it would be quite impossible to list them all. At any rate, this is what happened. Not long after they left Lemnos, the Argonauts anchored at Cius, on the sea of Marmara. Hylas went off inland, a bronze bucket in his hand, in search of fresh water. He found a clear, cool pool, all circled around with reeds, and celandine, and soft grass. He lowered his bucket into the water, but, as he did so, the nymphs of the place – Eunica, Malis, Nicheia – outraged at the intrusion, grabbed his wrists and pulled him under, holding him fast beneath the surface as his companions vainly searched for him. 'What treads on our territory is ours,' they hissed, as the poor man struggled, screaming for his lover.

Nobody heard him. Hylas struggled in vain. At last, when the wind got up, and the *Argo* was ready to sail, the companions reluctantly prepared to leave without him – all except Heracles, who stayed behind to look for his Hylas. But he never found him.

After many more adventures, the Argonauts reached the shores of Colchis, where the River Phasis runs down from the mighty Caucasus mountains and flows into the sea. Jason had decided to approach the city of Aea and the palace of Aeëtes openly, reasoning that there was a good chance that the king would understand his predicament, and offer them the Golden Fleece willingly. To help the Argonauts, Hera did three things – first, she asked Aphrodite to persuade her son, Eros, to shoot Medea with one of his arrows. Second, she made sure Medea stayed indoors, putting it into her mind not to go that day to the temple of Hecate, whose priestess she was. Third, she shrouded the Argonauts in a deep mist, so that as they walked towards the city of Aea and the royal palace, they were hidden from prying eyes.

And what a palace it was – the mist dispersed just in time for the adventurers to admire the splendid, tall-columned courtyard, the sturdy stone buildings, the mighty gates. The most remarkable things in the palace precincts were the four miraculous fountains that Hephaestus himself had built: one flowed with milk, one with wine, one with oil, and the last with mountain-cold water in the summer and steaming hot water in the winter.

As the Argonauts stepped into the palace, Eros landed silent and unseen at their feet, keeping close to Jason. Just as the young men entered Aeëtes' lofty hall, he raised his bow, pulled an arrow from his quiver, and, with unerring aim, shot the invisible bolt into Medea's heart. She stood there, wounded, struck into speechlessness. The sweet pain of love began to flicker inside her, then burst into a fiery blaze – it was like when an old woman rises before dawn and heaps up kindling on a dying fire, making the flames leap up voraciously. Medea gorged herself on the sight of the handsome Jason; and she blushed deeply.

Aeëtes ordered his slaves to prepare food and drink for the travellers, and only then, when all had rested and eaten their fill, did he question them about who they were, and what had brought them to Colchis. Jason took a deep breath and explained their mission. In return for the Golden Fleece, he offered a deal: the Argonauts' help in the Colchians' war with the Sarmatians, who lived to the east of their country in the Caucasus.

Aeëtes smiled, but secretly, he was furious at the young men's presumption. He was tempted to have the Argonauts killed, there and then – but he thought of a more entertaining way to deny them what they'd come for. 'Let it not be said that I am as ungenerous as your uncle Pelias,' said the king. 'I will certainly let you have the Golden Fleece – on one condition. On the plain of Ares I keep two bronze, fire-breathing bulls. For my own entertainment, my habit is to yoke these creatures to a plough, and then sow a field – not with corn, but with a snake's teeth. From these teeth warriors spring up, and I strike them down as they attack. I do this in a day: I hitch my bulls to the plough at dawn, and by dusk I have finished my reaping. If one of you can do as well as me, then I'll happily give you the fleece.'

The task seemed impossible. Nevertheless, Jason agreed: what else could he do? At that moment, though, Medea decided to help him, not just because of the desire with which Eros had infected her, but out of her resentment at being ignored and overlooked by her father – a resentment only increased when she saw him whispering urgently to her brother Apsyrtus and other close counsellors, planning (she correctly guessed) to burn the *Argo* and murder the Argonauts the minute Jason failed to yoke the bronze bulls. Apsyrtus – magicless, feeble, stupid Apsyrtus, who was favoured by their father for the sole reason that he was male. Medea despised him.

She went to her own room, sat down and wrote a letter to Jason, to be delivered by the most discreet of her slaves. Next, she reached beneath her bed and drew out a locked cedarwood box. Inside she kept her most precious and hard-won concoction: a salve of invulnerability. Those who rubbed it on their skin would find themselves far stronger and braver than an ordinary mortal, and immune from harm by fire or the sword. She had adventured far into the Caucasus mountains to find the main ingredient: the sap of a plant that had sprung up from the ichor that Prometheus had shed when Zeus's eagle tore at his innards each day. The flowers of this magical plant were the colour of saffron, the root looked unpleasantly like human flesh. She had harvested its dark juice in a shell from the Caspian Sea, in the dead of night, after bathing in seven streams and singing seven incantations to Hecate.

The girl sat there in her room, turning over her plans in her head, until at last she ordered her chariot and set out for Hecate's temple, where – she hoped, if her letter had reached its destination – she would have a rendezvous to keep.

The temple was set apart from other buildings, right on the edge of the city. Medea concealed her horses and chariot in a stand of trees, and went inside to wait in the dark shadow of the goddess's statue. After a while, she heard the great door of the inner sanctum creaking open, letting in a slice of evening light, and then she made out Jason's sturdy frame, silhouetted. For all her power, she was nervous, now. What had she done by inviting the stranger – her father's enemy – to this secret place? If Aeëtes knew, he would blast her with his magic to the end of the world. What if the stranger ignored her, or laughed at her? The gods knew she'd had a lifetime of that, but she couldn't bear it if Jason were to humiliate her. She watched him step into the temple, as bright and lovely but also as destructive as Sirius, the star that brings intolerable heat on blazing summer days. Hera had made him so handsome that his own companions were spellbound by his beauty.

For a moment they faced each other, silent, the youth and the girl, the adventurer and the witch, like two tall, slender trees on a mountainside: that's how Circe depicted them, alone together that first time.

'You came,' said Medea at last.

'I came,' said Jason gently. 'How could I not?' He smiled, and Medea felt Eros's flame lick and surge inside her.

'The reason I asked you here,' she said, steadying her voice, 'is that I have something that could help you with the task my father's set you. But I'm not sure whether I should give it to you. I do know my father would try to kill me if he found out, if he knew we were even meeting. Can I trust you, Jason?'

The young man sat down on one of the stone benches that lined the wall of the sanctuary, and patted the place beside him. 'Well,' he said, 'whatever path you choose, Medea, please know that I'm your friend. But let's just talk a little for now. Tell me about yourself – what's it like to live here? What's your father like?'

Emboldened by Eros, Medea told how, when she was a young girl, she used to impress her brother with her sorcery – but, lacking magical skills himself, his delight had faded and hardened into envy, fear and suspicion. How her father, who once had indulged and encouraged her, gradually joined Apsyrtus in his cold disregard, telling her that now she was grown, she ought to forget her powers, and prepare herself for a suitable marriage. How her compliant mother and sister lived in fear of Aeëtes and his volcanic rage. She told him how different her dull palace days were from the freedom of her nights, when she roamed the mountains and forests. She described how it felt when Hecate's power coursed through her like lightning. And Jason was enthralled.

'I'm wondering: how much do you know about the rest of your family?' asked Jason, after a while. 'The ones who live far away from here. What about Ariadne? Have they told you about her?'

'My cousin Ariadne? The daughter of my aunt Pasiphaë, who married King Minos of Crete? What on earth is there to say about her? Ariadne doesn't have any magical powers, as far as I know. Nor her mother, for that matter, despite being a daughter of Helios. I expect that's why they married her off to Minos, instead of sending her away to an island on the edge of the world, like they did with my other aunt, Circe.'

'Actually, there's quite a lot to say about Ariadne,' said Jason. 'It's true that she was born without magical powers – but they say she is very clever. She spent a lot of time with Daedalus, and that's who really gave her an education. Haven't you heard of him? He was the great designer and inventor Minos employed in his palace. I say employed – he was kept there, long after he wanted to leave.

'Anyway, he made all kinds of extraordinary things for the king – weapons, mostly, like never-missing arrows and impregnable armour. But then Pasiphaë, came to him in secret. She had become obsessed with a bull – it was Poseidon, they say, who made her mad for the animal, a punishment after Minos failed to sacrifice the creature to him. She wanted to find a way to have sex with this animal. So Daedalus designed a perfect, realistic model of a cow for her. It was hollow, so that your aunt could climb inside it.

'She used it, she had sex with the bull. Nine months later she gave birth to a baby. Except, it wasn't really a baby. It had the head of a bull and the body of a boy – the Minotaur, they called it. Minos asked the oracle what on earth to do with it, and the answer was to order Daedalus to build it somewhere to live. So Daedalus designed and built the Labyrinth: a huge maze of a place, full of confusing, winding corridors. No one really understood the layout, except him. Once you'd got in, you could never find your way out.

'It turned out that what the Minotaur liked to eat was human flesh. Typically, Minos used this to his advantage. After his son, your cousin Androgeus, was killed in Athens, Minos demanded tribute. The Athenians had to send seven girls and seven boys each year to be locked into the Labyrinth. None of them ever came out.

'This went on for quite a long time, until, finally, Theseus, the son of King Aegeus of Athens, volunteered to be one of the sacrificial offerings. Theseus is exceptional. He spent his childhood in Troezen away from Athens, for his own safety, far from Aegeus's enemies. The story goes that Aegeus plunged a sword into a rock when he left him there as a baby: it was to be a test for Theseus when he grew up. Every year from when he was a small boy Theseus tried to pull that sword out of the stone until, when he was sixteen, he finally did it. Then he set off for Athens. On his way there he used that sword to rid the entire territory of Attica of bandits and evil-doers – people like Procrustes, who would entice travellers into his house, and force them to lie on one of his beds. If they were shorter than the bed he'd stretch them until they fitted. If they were taller, he'd cut them to size. Anyway, Theseus got rid of him, reached Athens, and was reunited with his father.

'It wasn't long afterwards that he insisted on going to Crete with the annual offerings. He was determined the sacrifices to the Minotaur shouldn't go on any longer. And he succeeded – he killed the monster, he rescued his friends, and he got home to Athens, where he's king now. But the point is he wouldn't have succeeded, wouldn't have got anywhere, without Ariadne. It was she who helped him. It was she who worked out how to kill the Minotaur, how to kill her own half-brother. She managed to bring Theseus a sword. And she gave him a spool of red thread – he tied one end to the door of the Labyrinth and unwound it as he worked his way deeper and deeper inside the building. That meant that after he'd battled the Minotaur, he knew how to find his way out, bringing the other young Athenians with him.

'After that, Theseus and Ariadne managed to get away together – they reached his ship and set a course for Athens. I'm sure it was difficult for Ariadne. Unimaginably so: her half-brother deserved to die, but he was still her half-brother. And she had to leave her mother and father behind for ever. But you see, Ariadne and Theseus had fallen in love.'

Jason smiled at Medea, and took her hands in his. He left the implications of his story – how a girl had helped an adventurer, betraying her family – hanging in the air. 'It would mean a great deal to me if I knew you were thinking about me tomorrow,' he said. 'I should leave now. The trial starts at dawn, and I need to prepare.' He made to get up, but she said, 'Wait – if I help you, will you take me back home with you?'

'Of course,' he said. 'After everything you've told me, I couldn't leave you here.'

'Do you promise? Do you promise never to let me down?'

'I will never, ever let you down.'

'Then take this,' she said, reaching for the leather pouch that contained the salve of invulnerability, 'and listen to me. Tonight, my father will give you the serpent's teeth that he wants you to sow. When you have them safe, wait until midnight, then carefully wash in the river to purify yourself. Then get dressed, in a dark-coloured tunic, and dig a pit. Sacrifice a sheep over it, then pray to Hecate and set out an offering of honey. Leave the sheep's carcass in the pit, build a pyre over it, and set it alight. At that point, walk away. Don't look back, whatever strange noises you hear. The next morning, rub this ointment into your skin, just as if you were oiling your body after exercise. Grease your sword, spear and shield with it too.

'Just one more piece of advice,' she said. 'When the warriors start to spring up around you, they won't immediately see you. Throw a boulder in among them – they'll fight each other, and that will buy you some time.'

Jason was so grateful and relieved that he truly felt he was falling in love. He reached towards her and kissed her. Then he told her about his beloved but weak father Aeson; he told her about the handsome town of Iolcus, its well-built temples and bustling marketplace; he told her about his land's olive groves, its vineyards, its pastures, and the lovely, sheer cliffs that career down into the foaming sea. 'You will be worshipped like a goddess when we get back home,' he said. 'Everyone will know that it's because of you that their sons, their daughters, reached home alive. And we'll marry, and share our bed together all our days, until death separates us.'

But Jason didn't tell Medea all that he knew about Theseus and Ariadne. He didn't tell her that after the pair escaped from Crete they put in for the night on the island of Naxos. He didn't tell her that early in the morning, before it was light, when Ariadne was still asleep, Theseus ordered his crew to put to sea without her, leaving her all alone on the shore – betraying her, breaking all his promises to her.

Nevertheless, even Jason did not know the whole story. He didn't know what happened when Ariadne woke up, there on the rocky shoreline, feeling the warm sun on her cheeks, discovering herself abandoned. At first she was afraid, confused, panicked. She ran out to the shore, saw Theseus's sail on the horizon, shouted until she was hoarse to try to get them to turn back.

Then she became angry. She denounced Theseus as a liar, an oath-breaker. After everything she'd done for him – giving up her family, conspiring to kill her half-brother. Then she prayed to Zeus that Theseus would become forgetful – just as he had forgotten her. That in the blankness of his mind he would fail to hoist fresh white sails as he approached Athens, the agreed signal to his father, Aegeus, that he was returning alive. The Earth heaved and sighed as she screamed her curses to the winds and the seabirds.

After a time, emptied out by despair and fury, she simply lay there, prone on the Naxian beach, praying for death. Which was when she heard a strange, cacophonous sound – cymbals, flutes, song, laughter. She sat up, looked around, and saw to her surprise a chariot pulled by two leopards, driven by a beautiful, smiling, androgynous young god. All around him his companions, wreathed in ivy, were swaying, ecstatic, lost to the dance. All except for one tremendously fat, drunken figure who was riding a donkey – he was slumped over its neck, in danger of slipping off.

The god was Dionysus. The young mortals were his followers, the maenads. On the donkey was Silenus, not a man but a creature with a horse's tail: a satyr, a lawless, lustful spirit of the wilds. Ariadne stood up, amazed. Dionysus leaped out of his chariot. Mesmerised by each other's gaze, overwhelmed by desire, they walked towards each other, the god and the girl; and in his joy Dionysus flung a new constellation into the heavens, a crown of stars.

And Zeus, it turned out, listened to Ariadne. When Theseus sailed close to the shore of his homeland, Attica, he did indeed forget to change the ship's sails. His father Aegeus saw not white but deathly black linen – the signal that the young people were dead and the mission had failed. In his grief the old king flung himself off the Acropolis, so that when the prince returned home he found a house full of mourning and tears.

So much for Medea's cousin Ariadne and her love for Theseus of Athens. That night, after they had reluctantly parted, Jason did exactly as Medea had told him: he washed, dressed in dark clothing, dug the pit, sacrificed the sheep, made an offering of honey and prayed. Then he set the pyre alight and walked away – so that he heard, but did not see Hecate rise, dark-browed, snake-wreathed, a flaming torch in each hand, while the hounds of Hades coursed up from beneath the Earth and barked their strident chorus.

Early the next morning Aeëtes armed himself in a breastplate that Ares himself had given him, and took up his spear. Then, with his son Apsyrtus steadying the horses' heads, he mounted his chariot, and trotted out to the plain of Ares, his people following him to watch the spectacle.

At the same time, surrounded by his companions, Jason rubbed his skin with the salve of invulnerability, not forgetting to anoint his sword, shield and spear. At first, nothing. But then he sensed a fresh energy suffusing his body. He was like an excitable racehorse: all the animal wants to do is feel the joy of the race, the invincible power of its own limbs. He refused the armour his friends had brought him: he felt like a god, as if nothing could touch him.

Out onto the plain the Argonauts now walked, a magnificent sight: a band of young, intrepid men with their naked leader at their head, a bag of snake's teeth slung round his shoulders. Aeëtes looked momentarily bemused to see Jason so gleamingly confident, but he shook off his anxiety and turned towards the Colchians. 'Today I put this young man to the test,' he cried. 'Let us see whether Jason is worthy of the Golden Fleece!'

He pointed at the wooden plough that was ready at his feet. 'One piece of advice – try not to let the oxen burn their own plough,' he said, with an unpleasant grin. 'May the gods go with you, Jason – let the contest begin!' The crowd roared. Medea, veiled and demure, squeezed her fists and made a silent, passionate prayer to Hecate.

Jason strode across the plain, while Castor and Pollux followed, with the plough in their hands. He scanned the horizon until he saw the bulls in the distance; the rising sun was catching the metallic sheen of their flanks, and their nostrils were sending out flares of scorching light. Jason ran right up to them, threw down his sword and spear against a boulder, and stood ready, his feet firmly planted, his knees flexed. Holding his shield before him, he simply stood there as they charged, as impervious to their strength and scorching breath as a great rock is to the pounding of ocean waves.

The bulls lowered their massive heads and made as if to toss and gore him. But before the first of them could reach him, Jason shot out an arm and grabbed one of his bronze horns. He then gave the animal a violent kick. It was his bare, human toes against a burning, brazen flank, but Medea's salve was so powerful that the bull collapsed to his knees. The other bull received the same treatment. Castor and Pollux hurled the plough towards Jason with their combined strength and then retreated swiftly – the heat was overwhelming, and in their fury and distress, the bulls became like flamethrowers, completely enveloping Jason in their blazing breath.

All the crowd could see, at this point, was a vast fireball in the distance – it seemed that the young adventurer had been annihilated. But suddenly, a shout of excitement went up as they saw the young man emerge from the inferno, his shining skin miraculously unblemished. Even more extraordinary, he seemed to be driving the oxen ahead of him. 'Walk! Go on!' he cried; and the bronze animals, still snorting flames, but calmer now, ambled forward in unison, their necks bent to the yoke. The ploughshare bit into the soil. He had done it. He had tamed the bronze bulls.

Now Jason, holding the plough with his left hand, plunged his right into the leather pouch of serpent's teeth, and started sprinkling them behind him. He worked all morning, and still the back-breaking toil of ploughing and sowing went on; it was only when the sun was beginning to dip that he finished. At last, the deadly crop planted, he let the bulls wander off, and washed himself in the river, then, surrounded by his friends, he worked himself into a battle fury – he made himself as ferocious as a wild boar cornered by hunters, baring her teeth, her mouth foam-flecked.

He did not have long to wait. In the place where he had begun his sowing, the soil seemed to tremble and quiver. Then something large and round seemed to push up from the earth, like a giant fungus as it shoulders its way from the soil to the light. Quickly, though, it revealed itself as the top of a warrior's helmet. Then a face emerged, then an entire body shot up, armed with cuirass, greaves, helmet and sword. The creature shook the soil from his limbs and blinked, momentarily dazed by the light. All around, more soldiers were emerging from the furrows that Jason had ploughed.

Jason ran back to the boulder where he had dropped his own weapons. Already, there was a crop of fifty or so warriors, looking less dazed, now, and more aggressive, stepping towards him with snarls, their swords glinting in the low sun. He picked up that immense rock and flung it into their midst, just as Medea had advised. The men, roaring, turned on each other. It was a dreadful, bloody melee, a mad confusion. Jason's work was to finish off the stragglers, and to hack away at half-grown men, killing them before they could even emerge from the soil. By the time it was over, the plain looked like a forest flattened by a storm. Aeëtes looked on with mounting fury. Before Jason had even finished his deathly task he called for his chariot and galloped back towards his palace.

That night the Argonauts built a great fire next to the river, and drank and feasted to celebrate Jason's success. Early the next day, they said, they would go to Aeëtes' palace and claim the fleece, and then set sail for home.

Medea, however, was desperately afraid. Yes, Jason had completed Aeëtes' task: he'd lived through the day. But she knew the greatest danger lay ahead, while the young men were off their guard, naively assuming that her father was a man of his word. She knew she needed to pre-empt him, tonight. He would plan to kill the young men before dawn.

And so she sent her slaves away, pretending to feel unwell. She packed up her most precious herbs and potions. She said a swift farewell to the room where she had spent her girlhood, then she slipped out of the palace, unseen, silently opening locked doors and gates with her magical incantations. Soon she was out of the city, invisible to all but Selene, the moon goddess, who watched her, recognising a fellow sufferer in love – for Selene still burned with desire for her once-mortal lover Endymion, who slept an eternal sleep, locked in an eternal youth.

The Argonauts were drunk and raucous and singing when she found them. Only Orpheus, she noticed, wasn't joining in; he was sitting apart from the others. As she approached, the men gradually fell silent. One or two attempted to get up to greet her. She ignored them, and threw back her veil. 'Listen to me, Argonauts,' she said. 'This is no time for celebration. My father has no intention of honouring his bargain. The minute you walk into his palace tomorrow morning, you'll be trapped, as good as dead. The only chance you have – we have – is to get the Golden Fleece, now, and leave right away.'

'But that's madness,' said one of the men from the darkness around the fire. 'With respect, lady, we can't. We know that the fleece is held in a sacred wood, guarded night and day by a snake that never sleeps. There's no way we can get it without your father giving it to us. He's treated us fairly so far – there's no reason to think he'll let us down.'

'Fairly? He set Jason a task that would have killed him had it not been for my magic, for my salve of invulnerability. Believe me, my father's word is worth nothing,' she said. 'But you can trust me. I risked my life to help you. Look at this –' she took a pot from her bundle – 'it's a potion. I can use it on the snake. For the first time in its life, it will actually sleep. Then you can take the fleece. And we can leave. But we've got to do it *now*. And then I will come with you, back to Iolcus, and Jason and I will get married as soon as we get there.'

There was an uneasy silence as the men took in the implications of this. It was the first they'd heard of this marriage, this elopement with the foreign girl. 'She's right,' said Jason at last. 'Come on. Let's go. Let's get the Golden Fleece.'

The men quickly put out the fire, boarded the *Argo* and rowed along the Phasis – sobering up fast – until they reached the place Medea pointed out. She and Jason alone went ashore, picking their way through the dark shadows of the sacred wood.

After what seemed like a long time, Jason saw a kind of rosy aura up ahead; at first he thought, with a sinking heart, that it was the goddess Eos bringing the dawn – that they were too late, that they'd be seen. Then he decided that no, it couldn't be the dawn, but maybe it was some far-off barn or mansion, burning. He was incredulous when Medea hissed, 'The fleece.' He started to speak, but she hushed him, and gestured for him to follow her. Soon they were close enough to see it properly, though it emitted such a bright glow that Jason had to shade his eyes. It was huge, too, much larger than the kind of ram's fleece you or I have seen – it was as large as an ox's skin. It was laid out over the branches of a low but spreading oak tree. Coiled around the trunk was a snake. Its body was as thick as Jason's chest. Its scales were like breastplates, hard and gleaming and black. Its eyes were fixed on the mortals. Its tongue flickered.

A rattling hiss came from its belly. It began to unwind its endless length and slink towards them, sinuous as wreathing smoke.

It was then that Jason saw Medea's power for the first time; Circe wove the scene. The young witch stepped out in front of him. And, as the snake slunk closer and closer to them, she lifted her arms straight out in front of her, her palms raised, and began to sing.

It was an unworldly melody, high and strange, almost whining; it seemed to halt the air in the trees, make time stand still. She called on Hypnos, the god of sleep; she flattered him and cajoled him, singing of his great Titan parentage, Nyx, the night, and Erebus, darkness; honouring too his brothers Thanatos, death, and Momos, blame; and his great sisters, the Fates. She described with longing Hypnos's home, the dusky cave on the banks of the River Lethe, where chamomile and poppy grow. She called on him to bring his sweet relief, now, to the serpent that had never slept, to soothe him into slumber, to offer him rest from his constant, exhausting watchfulness.

The charm worked. The serpent seemed to struggle to lift its colossal head, then it stopped moving altogether, though its eyes, having no lids, still seemed to watch the humans. Hurriedly, Medea took her terracotta pot and dipped her fingers into the sticky ointment it contained, smearing it over the snake's head. Then she turned to Jason. 'Go, now – grab the fleece. Don't waste any time. The ointment will help keep him asleep – but not for long.'

Mutely, Jason stepped over the snake's body, clambered up into the oak's lower branches, and tugged at the great fleece until he had it down. Then the two of them ran back to the *Argo*, carrying the fleece between them, their faces golden in its reflected glow. 'Row!' Jason roared. The men bent to the oars.

Soon after dawn Aeëtes received the first reports that the fleece – and his daughter, and Jason – had disappeared. Furious, he ordered his fleet to set out in pursuit, dividing it into separate contingents so that all the Greeks' likely routes were covered. After several days, the ships commanded by Medea's brother Apsyrtus caught up with the *Argo*.

The Argonauts were in despair: the Colchian ships had them trapped on a tiny island at the mouth of the River Istros, a place empty but for a small shrine devoted to Artemis. A delegation of the men approached Jason quietly; Calaïs spoke for them, arguing that the only way to get out of the impasse was to make terms with Apsyrtus, offering to leave Medea on the island in exchange for the Golden Fleece. 'After all,' he argued, 'Aeëtes promised it to you if you managed to plough the field and defeat the warriors – there's surely a good chance that Apsyrtus will agree to those terms.'

It wasn't long before Medea got wind of the idea; she overheard two of the crew discussing it. She confronted Jason. 'How could you!' she said. 'All your soft words, your promises – they might as well have been written on air! You vowed to marry me. We *are* married, in the sight of the gods. I've abandoned my homeland for you, my family. I've sacrificed everything – I have nothing, nothing apart from you. You know that, and you would – what? – leave me here on my own, absconding while I slept? If it weren't for me, you'd be dead, burned to death by my father's bulls. I'm so angry, I could burn your ship now, burn all of you. I hope you die, I hope your children die. I hope you are thrown out of your homeland.' Jason could smell the sour, electric odour of her rage. Her fingers were crackling with power, her eyes flashing with sharp glints of light. He was afraid.

'My love, Medea – calm down, please,' he said. 'I don't like this any more than you. But what can we do? We're surrounded. Your brother has alliances with all the kings near here. We have to think of something, or else we're all going to be killed. Better, surely, that we get out of this alive.'

'*We* have to think of something? It seems like I'm the one who does the thinking around here. And you actually believe that if my father got hold of me, he'd let me live? You haven't the first idea, have you? And you tell me to be calm.'

Bitterly she laughed – then began to stride up and down, gesturing impatiently for Jason to be quiet. At last she said, 'I think there might be a way. A plan that might work. But it's not … honourable.'

'Well, whatever it is, just tell me,' said Jason.

'What you told me about my cousin, Ariadne, gave me the idea. She helped Theseus kill her half-brother, didn't she? Using an unfair advantage, arguably: she gave him a sword and a ball of thread. And still everyone thinks she did the right thing. She's honoured, you tell me, in Greece. What she did was justified, because the Minotaur wanted to kill the Athenians. Well, our situation is the same. My father Aeëtes, my brother Apsyrtus – they clearly want to kill you and the other Argonauts, and probably me too. Which means, it's all right for us to kill him. My brother. Apsyrtus …'

She trailed off, turning away. Then began speaking again, with resolution. 'What you need to do is ask him to come here, bringing only his heralds, as if you're going to make terms with him. It needs to be credible. You're going to have to get ready all the gifts you can offer, just as if you were really making a pact with him over the fleece. And I'll get a message to him, too. It'll say I'm ready to betray you and the Argonauts. It'll say that if he comes here pretending to negotiate with you, I'll steal the Golden Fleece back, and go home to Colchis with him. Then, when he arrives, I'll get him on his own while the heralds are loading up his ship with the gifts. And then you can …'

'Yes, I see,' said Jason.

'And here's what we do next. My father will insist on my brother getting a proper burial. So, we cut up his body. We take the parts, and we drop them into the water one by one. His men will have to collect every single bit of him. That will buy us time.'

They looked at each other. He nodded. They went back to the men; Jason explained what was going to happen. The Argonauts listened, silent, grim-faced. They didn't like it. But they'd promised their loyalty to Jason. He and Medea sent their separate messages to Apsyrtus, and Jason began to heap up the richest gifts he could find – among them a remarkable purple robe that the Lemnian queen Hypsipyle had given him, woven by the Graces. It was the very cloth that Dionysus had spread on the ground when he'd made love to Medea's cousin Ariadne, on the shore of Naxos.

Soon enough, Apsyrtus put in on the island. He accepted Jason's terms, but while his heralds were loading up the boat with treasures, Medea approached him, as if in secret. She told him she'd been abducted by the Argonauts, and would use her powers against the adventurers to help get the fleece back to Colchis.

Which is when Jason appeared and struck the boy down with his sword before he even knew what was happening. Medea couldn't look, turned away. Together, the lovers dragged the corpse of their victim aboard. Then Jason shouted an order and the *Argo* was on the move.

Medea and Jason butchered the boy's body together. Gore drenched the stern, their arms, their faces. Bit by bit they threw Apsyrtus's body into the waters behind them. The Colchian ships delayed to collect each piece, while Hera's fresh wind sent the *Argo* soaring ahead.

It was a silent crew that sailed for home. The days were long, repetitive, exhausting. One night the sacred beam from Dodona began to speak; in its strange, creaking voice it told them to seek out Aeaea, Circe's island, and from her to seek purification for the crime of fratricide. The exhausted men, longing for home though they were, set a course towards the western seas.

Circe wove a scene of herself greeting her niece and her companions on the shore; she had been warned of their imminent arrival by disturbing, blood-filled dreams. Reluctantly she took them in and, slaughtering a pig and sprinkling them with its blood, performed rites of propitiation to soothe the anger of the Furies, who punish murderers. Jason and Medea were withdrawn and evasive when Circe questioned them; nevertheless, with her witch's insight, she saw everything that had happened, and understood how it would end, too.

After they left Circe's island, the companions had many more adventures. Under orders from Hera, the sea goddess Thetis helped them avoid the great whirlpool, Charybdis, and Scylla's hungry, snatching arms.

Scylla normally fed on fish and dolphins that she grabbed from the water with her long arms. But she ate sailors too, when she could get them. Many years before, she had been a beautiful sea goddess. But she had been desired by Glaucus, a mortal fisherman whom Circe herself had lusted for. In her fury Circe had used magic against her rival – in place of legs, Scylla grew a fish's tail, and snapping dogs' heads sprouted from her waist.

Afterwards, Glaucus happened to eat a herb that transformed him into a sea god. Over time he was battered by storms and waves, and shells and seaweed attached themselves to him, so that he came to resemble an ancient, barnacle-encrusted shipwreck.

Circe wove, now, how the companions survived the Sirens, the daughters of the Muse Terpsichore. Their music was marvellous, but rotting corpses were piled up on their shores – bodies of men who forgot to eat and drink because they were so distracted by their irresistible artistry. As the Argonauts passed the coastline, the magnificent beings – half-woman, half-bird – began to sing, some swooping elegantly over the heads of the men, others perching on the cliffs, unfurling their wings. It was only because Orpheus sang loudly over them, blotting out their gorgeous music with his own piercing melody, that Jason withstood the temptation to order the crew to row to the island and their doom.

At length the Argonauts reached the elusive island of the Phaeacians, usually impossible for mortals to find. Here Arete, the wise and strong queen, ruled with her husband, Alcinous. They lived in a remarkable palace, covered in rich bronze, guarded by immortal silver and gold dogs made by Hephaestus. Inside the halls, banquets were lit by flaming torches held aloft by realistic golden statues. The Phaeacian women made exceptional cloth there, their fingers as deft and quick as poplar leaves in a breeze; it was Athena who had given them the skill and intelligence to make beautiful things.

The adventurers enjoyed the islanders' lavish hospitality. But Medea's prickling witch's senses told her there were Colchian ships nearby, scanning the seas in search of her, in search of the fleece. Cleverly, she appealed directly to Arete for help. Later that night, after they had gone to bed, the queen spoke to her husband, telling him how she feared for the girl if she were to be returned to her family. 'We have to protect her. Fathers can be so cruel. Don't you remember how Danaë's father put her to sea in a chest? Think of our own baby, Nausicaa, how lucky she is to have you. You'd always want to help a woman in danger, wouldn't you?'

'Of course,' said Alcinous. 'It's also true that we could easily defeat Aeëtes in a sea battle. But it would be more effective to solve the problem in a way that will be deemed acceptable by the majority of men and gods. We should tell Aeëtes that he can have Medea back if she is still a virgin; but if she's married, she must stay with Jason.'

Shrewd Arete took him at his word. Rising earlier than her husband, she summoned Jason and Medea, and ordered her slaves to prepare sacrifices and a feast. All the customary rites were performed, and, to Medea's joy, the couple were married. The Golden Fleece was the coverlet – shining, miraculous – for their bed on their wedding night.

Not long afterwards, when the Colchian embassy arrived, Alcinous was unshakeable: as a married woman, Medea would not go back with them. The delegation, dreading what would happen to them when they returned home, sought asylum and ended up living happily among the Phaeacians until the end of their days.

Eventually the Argonauts left the comforts of the land of the Phaeacians and resumed their journey. As they approached Crete, they encountered the deadliest danger yet: the island's terrifying guardian, Talos. Years before, Zeus had given the creature to Europa after he'd raped her and left her on the island, pregnant with the baby who would become King Minos.

Talos was a robotic giant, a violent bronze automaton. His job was to pound up and down the coastline three times a day, pulling chunks of rock from the cliffs and flinging them at unwelcome ships. As the *Argo* sailed close to the shore, the giant sent boulders hurtling into the sea around them. Jason cried out the order for the ship to turn, to sail away, even though they desperately needed water and rest. As the ship bucked and listed, Medea shouted to her husband:

'I think I can defeat this creature. It seems to be bronze, impossible to wound – except for one place above its ankle. Can you see it? There's a kind of vein there, and it's unprotected.'

The Argonauts rowed the ship just out of the giant's range. Then Medea stood in the prow, facing the shore, magnificent, like a figurehead, swathed in a dark red cloak. That's how Circe showed her, dwarfed by the vast bulk of the bronze giant, but with bolts of power flaring out of her body, flashing like lightning over the plains on a dark night. She invoked the spirit of Thanatos, and the devouring dogs of Hades, and she harnessed their dark, creeping potency. She pinioned Talos's eyes with her gaze and hurled thoughts of agony into his mind. And the giant, stooping to grab more boulders to throw at the *Argo*, tripped and slashed his ankle on a sharp rock that jutted out of the mountainside. Ichor drained out of his unprotected vein, and with it, his strength. He managed to straighten himself up, and made as if to hurl one last rock at the ship. But then the light seemed to go out of his eyes and he collapsed with a tremendous, deafening crash – like a pine tree smashing down on the forest floor. Later, the Argonauts sometimes thought, or at least said, that Talos tripped by chance, and his demise was nothing to do with the young woman who stood alone to face him on the prow of the *Argo*.

From Crete it was no great journey to Jason's home town of Iolcus. The Argonauts were greeted like heroes, and their exploits immediately became the stuff of poetry, made famous by wandering singers. Pelias was the one person who was by no means pleased to see them, though he put on a show of welcome, throwing great feasts in their honour. He was careful to give the impression that he was preparing to step down from the throne in favour of his brother Aeson, and his triumphant nephew, Jason.

Jason was too busy enjoying his status as Iolcus's most popular adventurer to notice what Medea quickly divined: that Pelias was stalling, and had no intention of handing over power. He was determined, she saw, to use Aeson's frailty as an excuse to cling on to the throne for as long as possible, and that, in turn, Jason had no real taste for the graft and subtlety required of a ruler. So she decided to take action – by using her power to strengthen Aeson.

This required potent magics, and careful decoctions of herbs. Medea searched the countryside, walking for days on the mountaintops of Pelion, of Ossa, where the air is scouringly clear and the shadows fall as sharp as daggers. Here she searched for wild marathon, snake grass, bitter daphne; for crocus root, hellebore, belladonna, mandrake, and the juice of the Pelion ash – the same ash that Chiron the Centaur would later use to make the spear of the great fighter, Achilles.

With these, and certain other plants that only a person with witch-sense can find, she returned to Iolcus. On the night of the next full moon, she sacrificed a sheep to Hecate and began her invocations, summoning her most fearsome powers – to call forth or send away the clouds in the sky; to anger or calm the seas; to make the Earth render up its shadowy remnants, the ghosts of the dead. As she prepared her herbs, pounding and combining them in exact proportion, she called on the monarchs of the Underworld, Hades and Persephone, and pleaded with them not to take Aeson yet, but to delay his descent to their bleak country.

Judging the medicine ready, she tested it by dipping into it a stick of old olive wood: the branch came out sprouting fresh leaves and young fruit. When she gently smeared the potion onto the forehead of her old, sick father-in-law, he seemed to sleep more peacefully, his pain, his bewilderment, his confusion ebbing away. In the morning he woke – still white-bearded, but vigorous now, with purpose and intelligence in his eyes.

All would have been well, perhaps, had it not been for Pelias's daughters. Seeing the change in Aeson, they approached Medea and asked her whether she couldn't do the same for their father. Medea pretended to be flattered, to agree, but secretly, in her boiling rage against the usurper, in her utter disdain for the idiocy of his daughters, she plotted his doom, and theirs. She put on a show for them, pretending to summon magics – instead she was performing a parody of her own witchcraft. She stood over an immense cauldron, stirring it with fake incantations. She slit a ram's throat and heaved the creature in. And then she pulled out a live lamb that she had beforehand hidden in the huge bronze vessel. She turned to Pelias's daughters. 'Come on then, now it's your turn – first you need to slit your father's throat and then, after we've put him into the cauldron, he'll come out a young man.' The credulous girls did as they were told, cutting their father's throat as he slept. Pelias's daughters thus became his murderers, tricked by the witch Medea.

The result of this violence was not, as Medea had hoped, to shore up Jason's power in Iolcus. Instead, in the ensuing scandal, he and she were both forced to leave the city; they sought asylum far away to the south in Corinth, at the time ruled by King Creon. They lived there for several years and together had two sons. But the truth is that there, in Corinth, their relationship began to curdle and sour. It was, perhaps, partly the strain of living away from home. That was true for both of them, of course, but it was much worse for Medea, who was so obviously a foreigner. She tried to fit in, to suppress her magics, to behave like a Greek. But whatever she did she was treated with suspicion, never quite accepted. The Corinthian women avoided her and laughed behind her back at her strange way of dressing and her thick Colchian accent. Sometimes the men more or less openly mocked her – and then, with difficulty, she would swallow back the raging power she felt mounting in her stomach, the crackling of fire in her fingers. After what had happened in Iolcus, she had promised: no more trouble, no more magic.

Jason, meanwhile, lived off his reputation, feasting with Corinth's finest. He began to resent Medea: for her power; for her disastrous manipulation of Pelias's daughters; for the fact that with a foreign wife he would never be quite the man he wanted to be. Increasingly, he spent time away from home, in Creon's palace. It was Creon himself who took Jason aside, and sat with him in the cool of one of the palace courtyards. 'My friend,' he said, 'we can all see you're not happy. Please forgive my interference, but I don't think Medea is right for you. There are so many differences between the Colchians and us Greeks. I can't help wondering if you'd be happier with a wife who shared your own traditions, your own way of life. I know you won't want to hear this, but we're all a little afraid of what she might do. She sits there, apparently so mild and quiet, but we all know her reputation for violence. She's clever, we also know that – though I've never considered that a particularly desirable quality in a woman. The point is: she might be thinking anything, plotting anything behind that veil of hers.

'Now, I'm sure I've offended you by speaking so openly. But as a man, and a Greek, please understand that I'm doing so out of affection and concern for you. I have one more thing to say, and you don't have to answer me now. My daughter Glauce is of marriageable age, and I know she admires you. You know how highly I think of you too. Why don't you consider making a fresh start? With a good, Greek girl. Your boys, too – of course they would be part of our family, we'd treat them the same as our own flesh and blood. And we'd make sure that Medea was dealt with fairly, of course. Think about it. There's no hurry.'

Creon got up and left. Jason was shocked. Could the king really be suggesting something so obviously disloyal, so wicked as leaving his wife? As marrying Glauce, a pretty thing, but no more than a girl?

But as the weeks and months wore on, as he and Medea continued to snag irritably against each other, Creon's suggestion gnawed away at Jason. He began to think about what it would be like to be the king's son-in-law – consulted, included. And he began to tell himself, above all, what it would mean for his sons to have a future without the faint taint of their mother hanging over them. Then there was Glauce. She was pretty, shy and young. So different from Medea, always grim and frowning.

And so the day came when Jason told Creon that he would like to marry Glauce. He officially moved into Creon's house; there was a wedding.

Medea emptied herself into shock and fury. She paced incessantly through the rooms of the house she'd once shared with Jason, beside herself, raging against the day she ever saw him, blaming Aphrodite (as well she might) for all the mad, terrible things she had done ... She prayed not to Hecate, now, but to the ancient, strong goddess Themis, the guardian of oaths. Because Jason had vowed never, ever to let her down. And now he had.

She was finished, she'd say. She wanted to die. She had absolutely nowhere to go. Why, *why* had she been born a woman? Men had it easy. They had freedom. They invented the rules. They wrote the stories and sang each other's praises, they controlled how things were remembered. But they were cowards and liars. They had no idea what real heroism was. Women knew, though: she'd rather fight in the front line of battle three times than give birth. One day things would change – women would be the ones who had the glory, women would be the ones whose exploits were sung to the skies. The idea that Jason got the credit for stealing the Golden Fleece – it was all her doing, her story! The Muses, in the end, would silence the false songs that told of women's treachery, women's duplicity.

If Creon and Jason thought that Medea would accept her new situation in time, they were wrong. Medea's fury was never-ending, a dark shadow that crept from the house and contaminated the city. The women of Corinth, some of them, began to mutter among themselves that she had a point: who among them would be happy to be left for a younger, prettier, richer wife? After she'd risked her life for him, given up so much for him, done so many terrible things, just for him?

In the end, Creon decided that enough was enough. He went to Medea and told her that she had to leave the city – and with her sons. The next day, Jason went to see her. 'Can't you try to understand,' he said, 'that I did this for us, and most importantly, for our children? This was nothing to do with abandoning you, finding someone else, or sex, or love. This was about trying to make our lives work here in Corinth.'

'*Our* lives work? Are you actually trying to say that leaving me has been for my own good? For our sons? Gods, you must think I'm a fool. You don't love our sons, not really. I'm the one who suffered to give birth to them. I'm the one who spends all day with them, who treasures their soft skin, their lovely sweet breath. I'm the one who cares about seeing them grow up to be young men. Face up to what you're doing, Jason: you're abandoning the person who gave up everything for you. All your so-called heroic feats, they were mine. I did them. I'm the author of them. And I didn't care, because I loved you. I wanted to do those things for you. But now you are trampling every vow, every promise you made.'

'Being abandoned is your choice,' said Jason. 'It didn't have to be this way. If you had accepted the situation, you could have stayed here in Corinth, with our sons. This is your fault, no one else's. But look, I will give you money, introductions, we'll find a place you can be safe, settle down.'

Medea looked at him contemptuously. 'I want nothing from you – not your so-called friends, certainly not your money.'

Jason flushed. 'You're impossible, Medea. Do you know what I wish? I wish there was another way for men to reproduce – without women involved. Then we might actually get to be happy.'

'Is that all I've ever been to you – a *vessel*?' said Medea.

Jason had his hand on the door, he was leaving. But as he stepped through it, he could hear Medea's voice calling after him. 'Enjoy your new wife, Jason. But I can promise you, my sufferings will be nothing to yours soon. The gods will see to that.'

He shrugged and walked on, the fool. Those years of living in Corinth had dulled his memory of Medea's abilities, of how far she would go. It felt like another world, another existence, when he'd watched her standing on the prow of the *Argo*, splintering the sky with her power, as she screamed for Hecate and the death gods, and brought Talos plunging to the ground.

That night, Medea stayed awake, plotting Jason's downfall. The next morning, she pretended to everyone that she had finally seen sense; she would go quietly, she'd bear the inevitable with dignity, there would be no grudges. As a token of her goodwill she sent her boys to Creon's house with gifts for Glauce – a golden circlet and a precious dress that her grandfather Helios had given to her. But she had smeared the dress with poison, a sticky, gluey, death-bringing venom, infused with bleak enchantments; the circlet was bewitched, too. When Glauce tried on the dress, turning this way and that to admire the clinging fabric that the light glanced off so prettily, she found that her skin was burning, her limbs shaking. She began to foam at the mouth. She collapsed. The golden circlet seemed to be tightening around her head, crushing it. She tried to claw off the circlet, the dress. When her father grabbed at them, he too became infected by the poison. They died together, in pain and humiliation.

At the death of their king and his daughter the Corinthians started rioting; they were a mob, terrifying in their cries for vengeance. Medea's boys did as they had been instructed by their mother. To keep safe, to keep from harm, they should run to the temple of Hera, where no one would hurt them. But the Corinthians ignored the sanctity of the temple. They turned on those children, they stoned them, kicked them, battered them until they were dead. When Medea heard the dreadful news, the mob was already on their way. They planned to storm her house, rip the foreign witch limb from limb.

But that's not what happened. As the rabble approached, her doors swung open and she came outside. At the sight of her, the mob fell back – they were blinded, burned, by the deadly, shimmering heat that came from her. She had undergone a change. She was a woman no more, but something else – a creature of the cosmos, a comet, a star, a shattering ball of flame. Jason tried to call out to her, blaming her for everything, for the deaths of the children. Medea ignored him. She spoke in a voice of thunder, in her own language – words of summoning-power that she had never used before. And from the furthest reaches of the sky came a dark speck that grew, and grew, and soon became, to the sharper-eyed of the Corinthians, a chariot. An empty chariot, bouncing through the heavens at breakneck speed, pulled by a pair of dragons with green-grey scales from which light glinted and flashed: it belonged to her grandfather, Helios, who sent it to her now, in her time of need.

The dragons soared over the city. The wind from their beating wings lashed the trees into a frenzy. Their baleful cries drowned out the panicked screams of the Corinthians, who scattered. The creatures clawed their way through the air towards Medea as she stood there, lambent, outside her house. Lightly they brought the chariot to a halt in front of her, and she climbed up into it, catching hold of the reins. She called out to the dragons now, exulting in their strength, praising their beauty. Flames licked from their mouths as they rose into the air again. The creatures came to rest on the roof of her house, and Medea looked down at them all: that's how Circe wove her, magnificent, terrible, furious. She looked as if she might speak – but she appeared to think better of it. She shrieked out a command to the dragons instead, and they leapt into the sky. In a moment they were gone, for ever.

Those were the scenes that Circe was weaving as Odysseus's men – or rather, pigs – honked and snuffled and grubbed about for the acorns she had thrown them. Eurylochus, though, hidden in the trees, saw everything, and returned with his story to the Ithacan ship. It wasn't long before Circe heard more mortal footfalls outside her house – this time it was Odysseus, alone. The witch tried to cast her spell of transformation once more, but to her surprise she found that her visitor was immune to her magics – Hermes had given him a sprig of moly, a herb known only to the gods, which acts as an antidote to enchantment.

So she invited the mortal into her house, and they talked, and shared stories, and, after a while, she took him to bed. Later they feasted together, and enjoyed each other's lively, subtle minds. After a longer time than Odysseus would later admit, she turned the pigs back into his men. The other Ithacans, camping out on the shore, were brought to the house, and there were more feasts, more wine.

When the year turned, she sent the men on their way with supplies and advice, telling Odysseus first to visit the Underworld to consult the prophet Tiresias, then explaining how he might plot a route, as the *Argo* had done, past the Sirens, past Scylla and Charybdis. At last she stood on the shore of Aeaea and watched as their sails shrank towards the horizon. Then she returned, relieved, to her solitude and her loom.

PENELOPE

Telemachus ✦ Phemius ✦ Odysseus and Penelope in Sparta ✦ Eurycleia ✦ Argos ✦ an archery contest ✦ the death of the suitors and the slave women ✦ Odysseus and Penelope reunited ✦ Clytemnestra ✦ Aegisthus ✦ Atreus and Thyestes ✦ Agamemnon's return to Mycenae ✦ Cassandra ✦ Electra, Chrysothemis, Orestes and Pylades ✦ the Kindly Ones

PENELOPE

Penelope waited twenty years for Odysseus – and as soon as he returned to rocky Ithaca, he was away again. When he'd met the ghost of Tiresias in the Underworld, on his circuitous journey from Troy, the prophet had told him that after his homecoming there would be yet another journey. With an oar strapped to his back, he must travel, Tiresias had said, until he came to a people who had never heard of the sea. When a wayfarer mistook his oar for a winnowing fan, he should fix it into the earth and make a sacrifice to Poseidon. Only then would he be able to live out the rest of his life at home, in peace.

During that first, long absence, Penelope raised their child, Telemachus, on her own. She ran the household and managed the estates. Stories reached them about Odysseus's exploits at Troy, his ruthlessness, his cleverness, his talent for deceit. After news of the Greeks' victory trickled back to Ithaca, she expected him every day, her heart beating faster at the sound of any fresh footfall.

As time passed, though, other songs began to be sung by Phemius, the travelling poet: how Ajax, the son of Oileus, had raped Cassandra in Athena's temple, souring the goddess's former love for the Greeks into hatred. In these new stories, their homecomings were cursed. Athena had convinced Poseidon to help her, and the god of the oceans had brought many men – including the rapist – to saltwater graves.

And Odysseus? The stories told how he'd set off for home from Troy with his fleet – but then, nothing. He didn't appear in Phemius's more recent songs. He was just a blank space, a no-man, wiped out of the story. Drowned, most likely. Once in a while, a stranger would turn up on Ithaca pretending to be him; she learned how to test such men when hope opened a chink of doubt in her mind. Others would arrive with tales of supposed sightings. He'd been seen in Egypt. He'd been spotted on Crete, or in Thesprotia. He'd been taken by Taphian pirates, sold as a slave. He'd been seen with Phoenician traders. He was rich beyond measure. He'd married a goddess. Or: he was on his way. In a month, in one turn of the moon, he'd be home. He was already here, on the island. She learned to steel herself against the malicious peddlers of rumour, the fraudsters who came looking for a handsome reward for so-called information.

A flock of suitors began to assemble in the house: the great men of Ithaca and the surrounding islands all but moved in, urging her to take one of them as her new husband. She didn't want to remarry. But before he'd left for Troy, just as he was about to climb aboard his ship, Odysseus had taken her wrist and said, 'Look, if the baby grows up before I come back, take another husband.' She'd laughed at the time, jiggling Telemachus on her hip. But now the boy was nudging his way towards manhood, one minute still a shy, uncertain child, the next asserting himself awkwardly against the suitors. Even telling her, to her amazement and irritation, to keep quiet and stick to the distaff and loom.

She had hesitated before she'd married even Odysseus: she often thought of the day when a man she hardly knew, back in Sparta, had put out a sun-darkened hand and taken hers, steadying her as she climbed into his chariot.

He'd come, ostensibly, to try to marry her cousin, Helen, the woman who blinded men with her beauty. But he'd ended up preferring her, the one no one looked at – not when Helen was around, anyway. He'd cut a deal with her uncle, Tyndareus – Helen's father – to win her. That's how he was: always plotting out scenarios, trading favours. She was his prize. She didn't mind: she could understand a brain like that. Her own wasn't so different.

Her father, Icarius – Tyndareus's brother – had pleaded with Odysseus to set up house there in Sparta. He had followed them, even, when they'd set off for the coast, planning to set sail for Ithaca. Odysseus had made no bones about the island: it was unprepossessing, had no wide rich valleys like Sparta's. And yet. There were fine orchards. And it was his. She could see the longing in his eyes.

Eventually, tiring of the ridiculous situation of being pursued by his heartbroken father-in-law, Odysseus had pulled up the horses, turned to Penelope and said, 'I'll not take you from your father if you don't want to come. If you prefer to stay, stay. It's your choice.' She'd said nothing, concealing her churning thoughts. She'd just lifted her veil over her head and set her gaze ahead, into the future.

It was over twenty years ago that she had made that impulsive choice, and for most of them she had been lonely. At least, in recent years, the suitors had given her company of a sort. The skill was to hold them all in balance, to favour one for a while, and then to seem drawn to another, but delicately, not so much as to antagonise the others. She thought of the game in the same way that she considered the designs on her loom: you didn't want to let one element dominate, because that would ruin the effect. Some of her slaves were sleeping with the suitors, she knew that. She didn't like it, but it wasn't as if they had a great deal of choice. Delay: that was the tactic. She'd have to choose a husband at some point, but not yet. Not quite yet.

She came up with a ruse: she told the suitors she'd make a decision, but only when she'd finished weaving her father-in-law Laertes' winding sheet. Ever since his wife Anticleia had died, anxious and miserable about her absent son, the old man had seemed to be waiting for death. He'd moved away from town and gone up to his farm in the hills, where he barely took care of himself. He still tended his orchard, though, growing his apples, pears, figs and grapes. He buried himself in his memories of his son – how, when he was a tiny, curious child, Odysseus used to trail after him, pestering him with questions about the trees, their names, their natures.

Every day she wove that winding sheet, working on a design as intricate as her own involuted, withheld mind. And every night she crept back to the loom by torchlight and unravelled her work – her border of winged horses and flying wind gods coming apart, deliquescing, like a reflection in a pond disturbed by a breeze. At first she found it hard, all that labour wasted. Then she began to savour the repeated motions of doing, undoing and redoing. She enjoyed the way the work never came to completion, never resolved, never had anything definite to say. It was in a constant state of deferral, just like her.

Or not, as it turned out. She kept the suitors in stasis for three years, telling them that work of this complexity took time – which was, of course, true. Then, in the fourth year, some of her slaves, the ones who'd been sleeping with the suitors, let slip what she'd been doing. She had to finish the winding sheet, but it no longer pleased her; it seemed a dead and static thing after all. After she'd reluctantly showed it to the suitors – who weren't interested in its artistry, barely looked at it, were concerned only that it had been done – she folded it up and put it away. And the design – well, that would remain a secret, now, between her and Laertes' corpse.

On the other hand, these days it didn't seem like it would be needed for a while. Athena seemed to breathe vigorous new life into Laertes when Odysseus finally returned.

The return: it had all happened so fast, so unexpectedly, so violently. She'd mainly been anxious about Telemachus at the time. He'd disappeared, without a word, she hadn't seen him for days, until at last the slave Eurycleia, Odysseus's old nurse, had let it slip: the boy had sworn her to secrecy, but she'd helped him provision a ship so he could go off to find news of his father. He came back looking older and more assured; he'd been to see Nestor in Pylos, Menelaus and Helen in Sparta. They'd told him stories about his father at Troy, told him they recognised the father in the son. Helen had given the boy a dress to save for his bride, woven by her own hands. A typically flirtatious move. Penelope had scrutinised it: not bad.

And Telemachus did have news, which he delivered bluntly. He'd gleaned it from Menelaus, who'd heard it from Proteus, the sea god. The last anyone had heard, Odysseus was trapped on the island of the nymph Calypso, without a ship, without a crew, unable to get home. At this, hope, anxiety, jealousy, and murderous, blind fury fought within Penelope's mind. But she didn't let any of it show.

Then two things happened, neither of which seemed important at the time. First, old Argos died – the dog Odysseus had trained as a puppy. He'd been a good hunter, and loyal. Now he was a mangy old thing who could be seen, more often than not, lying outside on the dungheap. She wasn't surprised to see him dead – it was remarkable how long he'd hung on. But she was taken back to find herself moved by the sight of his stiff little corpse, flies buzzing around his vacant, glassy eyes.

Second, the swineherd, Eumaeus, came down to the house from his pigsties with an old homeless man in tow. The suitors proceeded to bully the vagrant – she heard it all from behind the door of the hall. There was an argument: Antinous, the meanest of the suitors, threw a stool at him, lashed out at Telemachus when he dared to suggest he ought to share some food with the old man – which, after all, wasn't even his. The homeless man spun a tale: he'd once been rich, he said, until he'd been taken as a slave when he'd tried to raid a town in Egypt ... Penelope was anxious to meet him, but when she summoned him, he sent a message through Eumaeus that they'd speak alone, later in the day. Which was presumptuous – but intriguing.

She came down into the hall, then. She wanted to get Telemachus away from the suitors, sensing their rumbling hostility to the boy. So she washed and put on fresh clothes, made herself look as alluring as she could, and showed herself to them, deliberately deflecting their attention. Then she persuaded them to go and fetch her gifts. While all that was going on she took a good long look at that homeless man.

That evening, after the suitors had, thankfully, left, she went downstairs again, while the slaves were clearing up after their mess. They set her usual seat by the fire, covered with a sheepskin. Then she and the stranger talked. He seemed full of sadness. He flattered her. He had a way with him. She found herself telling him more than she'd meant to say. She told him about the weaving ruse. She told him about how she would have to choose a new husband, soon. Then she asked him about his family. He said he was from Crete, a grandson of King Minos, no less; he had seen Odysseus twenty years ago and exchanged gifts with him. And that was it. Nothing else.

At that moment, all the emotion that she had so carefully buried inside her, burst out. Her face, sometimes so icy, melted into tears. Later, she would remember how he watched her as she cried, not moving a muscle, no emotion, just an intent gaze. Then, after what seemed like a long time, she wiped her face, rearranged her mind, and tested him. 'If you really saw him, perhaps you'd be able to remember what he was wearing?' she said. The stranger answered: 'Yes. A purple cloak. A tunic, soft and shining as onion skin. The cloak was secured, if I remember rightly, by a remarkable brooch – decorated with a dog holding a fawn in its teeth. Everyone noticed it: the fawn was really struggling, or so you'd think, and the dog so lifelike.' She sobbed again, then. 'I made that tunic, I made that cloak, and I pinned that brooch on his chest. But he'll never be coming back. It was all so long ago.' The stranger looked at her . 'He is coming back,' he said. 'He's in Thesprotia now. He's rich, he's brought treasure. He's alone. All his men – lost. Poseidon punished them, because they ate Helios's sacred cattle. He would have been home sooner, but he's gone to Dodona, to listen to the rustle of the sacred oak leaves, to hear what Zeus has in mind. But I swear by Zeus, and this hearth, that he'll be back. This month.'

She answered sadly, 'No, he's not coming back.' But something was flickering inside her wary brain. She got up and ordered a bed to be made for the man. He asked for a slave to come and wash him – one of the older women, he said, not one of the spiteful youngsters who, spurred on by the suitors, had been taunting him. Penelope called Odysseus's old nurse, Eurycleia. 'Could you wash your master's ... friend's feet?' she said. The old woman did it, and took her time about it. There was a lot of spilled water followed by whispering, but Penelope kept her gaze away.

Afterwards, though, she turned again to him, and said, 'What do you think I should do? My days aren't so bad: I get on with my work, there's plenty to occupy me. At nights, though, I lie awake worrying. Do you think I should carry on waiting for my husband? Or should I marry one of these men? That's what my son thinks I should do. I'll tell you something. I had this dream. Twenty geese came to my yard. They were eating up my grain. I was glad, in some indefinable way, that they were there. Then an eagle came and killed them, and I was in tears. But the eagle said, "I'm Odysseus, I'm here, I'm coming home, and I will kill those suitors." That was it. I woke up. What do you think it means?'

He gave her a long look and said, 'There's only one thing it can mean: he's coming, he'll kill them all.' She replied, 'Maybe. But there are two gates of dreams, they say, one made of ivory and one of horn. The ivory gates bring false dreams, the horn gates, truthful ones. I think this was a false dream. The fact is, I can't put off any longer what I've got to do. I'm going to have to choose. I've decided to set these suitors a challenge. Odysseus used to set up twelve axes in a long row. Then he'd shoot an arrow right through them all. If one of the men in my house can manage to do that, using Odysseus's bow, I'll call him my husband.' He shrugged. 'Do it,' he said. 'I don't think any man here will string that bow before Odysseus comes home.'

It was late. She lay awake that night, though, her mind turning everything she'd seen and heard back and forth. In the morning, the suitors, with depressing predictability, turned up again, and spent another day gorging themselves. The atmosphere hovered dangerously close to violence as the men drank more and more of the household's rich wine. Penelope sat spinning in the corner, silent, watching it all. One of them, a rich man, a real lout called Ctesippus, said he'd give the homeless man a gift. Then – his idea of a joke – he threw an ox's foot at his head. The vagrant ducked with surprising agility and the hoof smacked against the wall. Telemachus spoke up with unusual confidence then. 'Keep yourselves under control! Don't take me for a child. I know the difference between right and wrong. If you'd hit that man I would have killed you.' One of the others, Agelaus, answered, 'Fair enough. We get it. We shouldn't mess around. But a friendly piece of advice. This can't go on. Odysseus isn't coming back. Your mother needs to choose. Then all this will be over. We'll leave you in peace.' Telemachus said, 'If she wants to marry again, I'll be sure to give her a dowry. But I won't force her to do it. She will make up her own mind.' The men began to laugh, roaring drunkenly, hysterically.

Penelope stood up, then. It was time. She realised this with absolute certainty. Had Athena put the thought into her head? She slipped away to her own room, and reached up with her muscular, work-worn hand for the hiding place of an ivory-handled key. She used it to unlock a storeroom, and right at the back she found the bow, still in its case, with its quiver already filled with arrows. She turned the weapon in her hands. Then she gathered herself, wiped away her tears, and went downstairs. Pulling her veil around her face, she said. 'I'm bringing this saga to an end. Listen: there's going to be a contest. Whoever can string Odysseus's bow, then shoot an arrow through the twelve axeheads we'll fix in the floor – I'll call that man my husband.'

While the slaves were setting up the axes Telemachus tried to string his father's weapon out of curiosity. He couldn't do it, wasn't even close; he shrugged, and he handed it over ruefully to the first contestant, Leodes, the only suitor who'd never joined in with the others' bullying. It seemed for a moment as if the bow would bend to his will – but he found he couldn't manage it either, and passed it to Antinous, who called for grease in an attempt to make the bow more supple. Out of the corner of her eye, Penelope saw the homeless man quietly leaving the hall, then, a moment later, returning. Yet another suitor, Eurymachus, had a go. A smooth talker, that one, and a liar; he was sleeping with Melantho, the slave she'd brought up like her own daughter. She'd always supposed that if she was going to have to choose between these men, he would be the one. But he struggled with the bow in vain. Then Antinous said, 'Let's leave it for today. We'll make a sacrifice to Apollo the archer. Then we'll try again tomorrow.'

Just then a voice rang out from the corner of the room. 'I take it you've no objection if I have a go?' The homeless man. There was silence for a moment. Then Antinous jeered, 'You, try the bow? What are you even doing here? Of course you can't try it.' Penelope said, 'Show some respect. If he wants to, let him.' But Telemachus interrupted her. 'It's for me to decide who gets to try the bow. Mother: go up to your room. Bows are for men. Looms and spindles are for women.' She was so taken aback she actually complied. Eurycleia came straight up after her, and shut the door behind them. 'Madam,' she said, 'whatever you do, don't go downstairs.'

That was when Odysseus brought the war back home with him. She heard later how he'd strung the bow as easily as Phemius might change a string on his lyre. How, still sitting casually on his stool, he'd taken an arrow, aimed and shot it through the twelve axeheads – all in one seamless, swift movement. Without taking breath, he'd plucked another arrow from the quiver and aimed again, this time at Antinous. Right through the man's neck the arrow had gone. The cup he'd been lifting to his lips had fallen to the ground, wine and blood drenching the food on his plate. But all Penelope knew at the time was Eurycleia's panicked face as she bundled the female slaves into her chamber, and, with a shaking hand, shot the bolts on the doors. 'Let's spin,' the old woman said. 'Let's weave. And let's sing. As loudly as we can, now.'

Which is what they did. For a long time. But the singing did not blot out the terrible sounds from below – shouting, tables going over, the clash of armour, bellows of pain, the terrified shrieking of men begging for their lives. Eventually came a voice at the door – Telemachus – calling for Eurycleia, just Eurycleia. The old woman hobbled out. Then, after a few minutes, she came in again, grim-faced, and picked out twelve girls to take back downstairs with her. The girls who'd been sleeping with the suitors. Penelope would never see them again. Not alive, anyway. She'd see a pile of corpses;

her boy, her son Telemachus, hanged them. But only after they'd cleaned the blood and gore from the hall. The suitors were all dead. The stupid ones, the kind ones, the bullies, the ones who should have known better, the young ones – all of them. Phemius, the poet who'd entertained them, was spared to sing another day.

Eventually Eurycleia came back upstairs. The old slave was almost hysterical, gabbling about dead bodies, blood flowing. 'My master is back again! The baby I suckled at my breast! I recognised him when I was washing him – that hunting scar he got as a boy – but he swore me to secrecy, said he'd kill me if I said anything. Your husband, mistress! Odysseus! He's back – he was the homeless man all along.'

'I need to see Telemachus,' Penelope managed to say. 'And I need to see this man who says he's my husband.'

The stench of sulphur and blood hit her nostrils when she walked into the hall – someone had tried to fumigate, but they hadn't blotted out the odour of death. How had her spinning place become a battlefield? How had her home become a slaughterhouse? Performing a serenity she didn't feel, she took her usual seat by the fire. The man was there, sitting by the pillar, just like before, when they'd first spoken. His hair was matted in blood. Her boy was there too, wild-eyed, exultant, shaking. Laertes too, astonishingly. The man they said was Odysseus didn't look up, he just gazed into the dying embers of the fire. Penelope said nothing. Then Telemachus broke the silence. 'Mother, this is your husband! Talk to him! How can you be so hard-hearted?'

'If this man really is Odysseus, I will have my own way of proving it,' she said. 'There are things – secrets – only he and I know.' And the man said, 'Leave her alone, Telemachus. She won't recognise me like this, when I'm fresh from the fight. But first we need a plan. The families of the dead men will come looking for blood, and soon. What do you suggest, my boy?' Telemachus floundered, then, but the older man said, 'Here's what we do: we pretend we're holding a wedding. That should deflect them for a while. Wash. Put your best clothes on. Call for music. Get everyone dancing. I'm going to take a bath.'

When he returned to his seat in the fire-lit hall, he looked ... different. Gilded, somehow. Had Athena worked her magic craft on him? It was Odysseus as he had been twenty years ago – not the battle-worn monster she'd just witnessed. Which of these men, she wondered, was her real husband? Both of them? 'You're a strange woman,' he said, with the glimmer of a smile. 'What other wife would behave like this to a husband who'd been away for twenty years? Who'd suffered everything I've suffered?' The fraudulent sounds of celebration – piping and wedding songs – drifted in from the courtyard. She said, 'Strange: you look just as he did, when he sailed away to Troy. You must be tired, though. Eurycleia – make up our bed. Outside, please.'

His face darkened into fury then. 'What are you talking about? Our bed can't be moved – not by any mortal,' he said. 'I made it myself. When I was building this house I took a living olive tree, stripped off the branches, and used it as a bedpost. I built the rest of the bed around it. It's rooted in Ithaca's soil. No one can move it. That's the secret only you and I know. Please tell me some other man hasn't sawn off that trunk and moved it.'

At that Penelope walked over to him and bent to kiss his killer's lips. 'Don't be angry with me. So many men have come here with their lies, pretending to be you. The gods have been so hard on us. It was Aphrodite that made Helen go to Troy in the first place – Aphrodite who's caused our pain, my pain.' They clung to each other, then, and she let relief flood her, the relief that her suspicious, wary mind had held off for so long. She felt like a shipwrecked sailor finally crawling onto the shore – as if all these years she'd been at a stormy sea, tossed about on the waves. Like a traveller who has endured much, but who has, nevertheless, survived.

After that they went to bed together, and told each other stories. Penelope told him about all her years bringing up their son alone, her efforts to confound the circling suitors. Odysseus told her about his decade-long journey home: about the Lotus-eaters, whose fruit made his men forget about home; about how he'd tricked the Cyclops Polyphemus, gouging out his single eye with a sharpened olive trunk as he lay in a drunken stupor. About fickle Aeolus, lord of the winds, who'd helped him, giving him the winds tied up in a leather pouch, while gentle Zephyr alone blew them towards Ithaca – but his men had opened the pouch while he slept, releasing all the other winds, and a storm had tossed them way off course. He told her about the flesh-eating giant Laestrygonians, who had destroyed the entire Ithacan fleet, except for his own ship. He told her about how he'd withstood Circe's enchantments and descended to the Underworld, meeting the ghosts of his mother, and of his comrades at Troy. About the beautiful song of the Sirens, and how he'd escaped the flesh-eating Scylla, and the whirlpool Charybdis. How his companions had been killed in a storm after eating the flesh of the cattle of Helios – but he had washed up on Ogygia, Calypso's island. How the nymph had kept him there for seven years, offering to make him a god, while all he had wanted was to come home to her, to Ithaca. At last Calypso had let him go, though another storm had nearly killed him before he'd found himself on the shore of the land of the Phaeacians, where a girl doing her laundry had found him. She – Nausicaa – had taken him to her royal parents, the wealthy and generous Arete and Alcinous. They had sent him home at last in a ship loaded down with treasure, setting him down on the shore of Ithaca as he slept. How when he'd woken, all alone, he had wept, not recognising the misty beach at all. But then a shepherd had wandered up to him – a shepherd who had turned out to be Athena in disguise.

It wasn't clear to Penelope how much of this she should believe.

Now he was gone again, on his mysterious journey decreed by Tiresias, an oar strapped to his back. And she was alone, working once more at the loom. Her tapestry was woven with a design of Agamemnon's homecoming to Mycenae.

After Agamemnon sacrificed his own daughter, Iphigenia, in return for a wind for Troy, his wife Clytemnestra's grief had almost struck her down. For years, she had been a shadow of a woman, withdrawn from the world, barely able to be a mother to her living children – the girls, Electra and Chrysothemis, and the youngest, the boy Orestes.

But as the years slid by, things changed. Her brokenness repaired itself into something hard and ironlike. Disbelief and confusion were replaced with contempt and loathing. She took a lover: Aegisthus, Agamemnon's cousin and enemy. Years ago, their fathers – the brothers Atreus and Thyestes – had argued over the throne of Mycenae. Atreus, Agamemnon's father, had driven his brother out of the city, but later he'd returned and begged for mercy. Atreus's idea of mercy had been to capture Thyestes' children, slaughter them, and serve them up as roasted meat to their unknowing father. Thyestes, choking on the appalling flesh, had rained down curses on Atreus and his family as he fled the palace with the baby Aegisthus, now his only surviving child.

However, it was Clytemnestra, not her lover, who ran the city with firmness and decision, wrapping herself in a king's authority as if it were a cloak. In her fury, in her desire for revenge, her mind became a net of intricate plots. Scenarios flashed through the landscape of her imagination, one thing leading to another, like beacons lighting up in quick succession across the hilltops.

It was a beacon that first told her Agamemnon was coming home. She'd planned that years before: a series of flaming signals, all the way from Troy, that would warn her when her husband was on his way. The first was on Mount Ida, near the city itself, the second on the island of Lemnos, the third on Mount Athos, and on and on they came in a great chain all the way to Mycenae. She'd set a watchman on the ramparts of her palace, his task to keep lookout, through the long, star-blazing nights, for the final beacon in the relay. Penelope showed him there on her tapestry, beneath the procession of the heavenly bodies whose risings and settings he knew so well, at the moment when he saw the fiery sign leap into the sky. The king was coming.

Clytemnestra was ready for her husband's return: the stage was set. She stood, proprietorial, at the doors of the palace while the crowds gathered in the square below to greet their king. Agamemnon came at the head of a procession of soldiers loaded down with Troy's glinting treasures. The women they'd enslaved followed behind, pale, underfed, clinging on to each other, staring around them uncertainly. As the king arrived at the palace steps he turned to the people. 'The gods brought us victory!' he roared, as the citizens cheered. 'The gods cast their votes for Troy's destruction and the city is still smoking, the air still full of the stench of their wealth. They thought they could take one of our women, but they were wrong. Because of Helen, the might of Mycenae was unleashed against them! The ferocious beast that lay in the womb of the wooden horse – that was us. We were like a lion – and when we sprang, we gorged on the blood of their royal house, strutted proudly over their towers.

'I've learned a lot about human nature over the years. Some people were loyal. Some – less so. I'll pay tribute to my comrade Odysseus, true to the end, even though we had to force him to come with us ... Sadly, his current whereabouts are unknown. However: I'm back! And now it's time to look at the domestic situation here in Mycenae, to reckon up, to see what's been going well, and what needs my attention. But first, as I reach my own hearth and home, I'll pay tribute again to the gods.'

As the people cheered, he made to stride straight into the house, but Clytemnestra, to his evident surprise, stopped him with a smile and a commanding gesture. She turned to face the crowd. 'Everyone: I'm not ashamed to show the way I feel about my husband. Let me tell you what it's been like: it's terrifying when you're alone and your man's away at war, and all you hear is the churn of rumour. If Agamemnon had been killed as many times as I'd been told, he'd be like a fishing net, more wound than flesh.

'I'll admit it: at times I've wanted to take my own life. I have no more tears left: I've cried myself out. I've hardly slept. Whenever I *have* drifted off, it's been only to dream of you, Agamemnon, wounded and killed. But look at you – here you are at last! Come now! Careful, though: feet like yours must not tread on the ground. We can do better for the ravager of Troy. Slaves – quickly, do as I instructed you – make a path for him with tapestries, spread purple cloth beneath his feet. And above all: let justice lead him home! Let me assure everyone here, whatever comes next will be the result of careful planning and consideration. It will be right, and it will happen with the gods' help.'

The slaves hurried forward and unfurled the tapestries: lengths of purple-dyed, intricately woven fabric, which spread like an ocean of blood down the palace steps.

Blindsided by Clytemnestra's transformation from submissive wife to practised politician, Agamemnon stumbled in his reply. 'Well, thank you. Your speech was – ah, how should I put it? – like my absence. Long. But don't treat me like some kind of luxurious foreigner. I don't want to step on precious fabric. That kind of thing is reserved for the gods. I don't want people to think I'm arrogant. It would be wrong to provoke people's envy.'

'What would Priam have done, if he'd been in your position?' said Clytemnestra.

'Walked on the tapestries for sure,' he replied.

'Then do it,' she said.

Agamemnon laughed nervously now. 'I'm not sure this desire for conflict is particularly womanly,' he said.

'Well then, give way with grace!'

'You really need to win this, don't you?'

'If you give way freely, it's you who'll be the winner.'

The king shrugged, and called for the slaves to take off his boots. Then he planted a bare foot on the rippling textiles, fruits of the endless labour of women.

That's what Penelope wove: her cousin standing in triumph before the palace gates while Agamemnon climbed the steps towards her, crushing tapestries as precious as silver, glimmering with sea-harvested purple.

As he climbed the crimson path he turned back briefly, as if he'd suddenly remembered something, and gestured towards a figure in his chariot. 'Bring in that girl, please, and be kind to her –

a slave, but we all know no one is a slave from choice. She's the pick of Troy. The men insisted I take her. She was their gift to me.'

As he reached the palace doors he paused and smiled at his wife. 'Clytemnestra, here I am,' he said. 'Submissive to your will, just as you asked.'

'Ah, now you are truly home,' she said. 'Zeus – fulfil my prayers. Let's get done what needs to be done.'

She stood back to let Agamemnon go inside, then turned to the exhausted-looking figure in the chariot. It was Cassandra, Priam and Hecuba's prophetic daughter. 'Do you speak Greek?' There was no reply. 'Come inside. You're a slave – you must bear it, you know. Even Heracles was a slave, once. In you come now ...' The girl was unresponsive, her face a blank. 'Oh, I give up. I've things to do, sacrifices to make.' Clytemnestra addressed the crowd of citizens: 'Maybe someone can speak her language? Get her to come in, please.'

She disappeared inside the palace. One of the older men came forward and tried, with gestures, to show Cassandra what to do. But suddenly she exploded into words, Greek words, piercing, terrifying. 'Apollo, Apollo!' she shrieked. 'Where have you brought me? – to this house of death, the house of Atreus, house that the gods hate, soaked in blood ... where a father once ate the flesh of his children, oh, oh, *horrible* ... Now what's happening? Something else ... keep the bull away from the heifer – she's going to turn the water red, the net will tighten, she's going to tangle him in her trap. He'll die there in the water, snared in his winding sheet. Oh gods, I wish I were Philomela! I wish I could become a nightingale – be changed – be spared the death that's coming for me. I'll never see Scamander's waters run again – only the rivers of the Underworld for me now, Cocytus and Acheron ...'

She paused, gasped for breath, then stood up straighter, seemed to grow in stature, in authority. 'No more ambiguity! My words won't be veiled like some blushing young girl any longer! Let them be as fierce as the wind and bright as the sun! The woman strikes down the man! She is as strong as Scylla! She is like a lioness! She'll kill me too, for all that her husband has made me his slave, raped me ... But someone will come and murder her in turn, oh yes, I can see that too, it won't be long ...

'My prayer now is to Erebus: make the blow that kills me clean. That's all. I'm going in. It's over. Who cares – I'm only a slave. A tiny life. Just a scratch of chalk on a blackboard, ready to be wiped out.'

She walked inside. The people gathered in the square were shocked, spoke restlessly among themselves – what was happening, what had the barbarian girl said, what did it all mean?

Inside the palace, Clytemnestra led her husband through to the bath, and, with smooth assurance, helped him strip off his clothes. She watched him as he lowered himself into the water, shutting his eyes as the water closed over his battle-worn body. Then she took a net from its hiding place – and threw it, trapping him in its inextricable, snakelike coils. She drew a sword out from the same place and, as he struggled, she slashed him once, twice, three times, and she shivered with pleasure as his blood spurted over her, as welcome and lovely to her as the morning dew that drenches the meadows. That's what Penelope wove: her cousin stained with scarlet, as she turned, flexing her sword-arm, towards the young, pale Trojan girl who had calmly walked into the room.

Clytemnestra's girls Electra and Chrysothemis grew up hating their mother and her crime, loathing Aegisthus. Orestes was far away, growing up with Strophius's son, Pylades, in Phocis – the boys were each other's most beloved companions. Over and over again Electra and her mother had raged at each other, Clytemnestra justifying what she'd done, talking about the terrible death inflicted on Iphigenia, Electra stormily insisting that that had been Artemis's fault, not her father's – he'd had no choice at all. Chrysothemis, though, was different. She preferred to bend to necessity rather than try to resist it. 'I feel the same as you,' she'd tell her sister, 'but we are completely powerless. The only thing we can do is try to survive. That means keeping quiet and staying patient.' A view that Electra regarded with contempt.

Agamemnon's tomb was in a dusty, neglected patch of land outside the city gates. No one was supposed to go there, least of all Electra. And yet she did – she'd steal out of the palace to pour libations and make offerings of grain and honey. Then she'd sit all alone, brooding, letting the terrible vision of her mother felling her father, as a woodsman might an oak, play out in her imagination. She was waiting for the day Orestes would return and plot with her to right the wrongs of the house.

It was Chrysothemis's unwelcome tread Electra heard one day as she kept her vigil at the tomb-side. 'What do you want?' she said, not looking up. 'I've come to tell you to be careful,' said Chrysothemis. 'There's a rumour going round the palace that you're to be locked up. Please, Electra, you need to change your behaviour. At least pretend to be more submissive. I'm frightened about what they'll do to you.'

'As if I care! The sooner the better as far as I'm concerned. Wait though, what have you got there?'

'Offerings, from our mother for our father's tomb. She's worried. Last night she dreamed that she'd given birth to a snake. It suckled at her breast – and bit her. She bled blood and milk.'

'Oh gods – I wonder, does that mean he's coming back? Orestes? Could he be the snake? If only … Chrysothemis, don't pour that libation. Anything that she's touched – I won't have it defiling his tomb. Leave me alone, for the gods' sake.'

Chrysothemis sighed and walked away, but hope was surging in Electra's heart – and then she caught sight of something on the tomb. What was it? A lock of hair? She examined it: the curious thing was that it could have been her own, so exactly did it resemble it in colour and texture. Who'd put it there? She looked around in the dust. Those footprints … They weren't hers, not Chrysothemis's – too big. She crouched over them, comparing them to her own, then started as a shadow fell over her – and stood up to find that a young man, exactly her own height, was gazing at her. 'Electra,' he said. 'It's me. Your brother. Orestes.'

She froze. This youth on the verge of manhood, was it really her baby brother? The child she'd managed to get sent away to safety when he was only tiny? 'Are you playing some kind of trick on me?' she said. 'Who are you? Tell me the truth.'

'You know, really, don't you?' he said. 'I saw you comparing my hair with your own. And here – look at this piece of cloth. You made it. Look at the animals woven into it – your own design.'

Electra gazed at the fabric in wonderment, then, without a word, took her darling brother into her arms – the tiny boy who'd turned into a man. 'Always hold me like this, never let me go,' he said, and they both wept. Penelope wove them like that, brother and sister reunited, clasping each other tight, by their father's tomb.

Electra and Orestes made plans together, now, in earnest. Apollo had told him to come, Orestes said. The time was right. He'd be punished if he didn't take action. Orestes had travelled with his beloved friend Pylades. They decided that the two men should approach the palace, disguised as strangers from Phocis, and tell Clytemnestra that Orestes was dead.

The young men were greeted at the gate, welcomed as guests. They told Clytemnestra the false news; she was taken in, did not perceive that one of the strangers was her own, long-absent child. As she heard them speak she felt impossible emotions roiling in her heart. Grief, terrible grief that her child, another of her children, was dead. And yet – yes, relief. For years she had been frightened Orestes would return and kill her. Night after sleepless night she'd felt the strain of waiting, always on the alert. And then there had been that dream, the one she couldn't shake, the one that had come again and again, about the viper sucking bloody milk from her breast.

It was when Aegisthus summoned the two young men to his quarters, hoping to talk to the travellers from Phocis, that the violence began. Taking him by surprise, Orestes and Pylades struck him down, and the young men emerged, bloodied, from his room, just as Clytemnestra, her heart full of fear, ran into the hall, summoned by her lover's shrieks, shouting for the slaves, for anyone, to bring her an axe.

But the slaves had scattered. Only Electra and Chrysothemis were there. It was a family reunion, of sorts: that's what Penelope wove: Clytemnestra as she began to understand that the young man with the dripping sword was her child. 'You've killed the man I love?' she said.

'It's your turn now, Mother,' said Orestes. 'You want to lie beside him? Your wish is about to come true.'

Clytemnestra never moved her gaze from his eyes, but reaching to her shoulders, she undid the pins that secured her dress and let it fall. 'Yes – my breasts, where you sucked when you were a baby, Orestes, your gums at my nipples. I'm your *mother*, Orestes. Stop this. I gave birth to you. I looked after you. Can't I grow old with you?'

'You killed my father, and you think we can live together? Really? Like – a family?'

'What happened had to happen! It was the Fates – can't you see that? Please: don't kill your mother. You'll be cursed. Oh gods, don't be that viper I dreamed about. Orestes, wait, if you murder me, the Furies will come for you …'

Orestes raised his sword, and hesitated. But Electra screamed: 'Do it! Again! Again!'

Pylades and Chrysothemis turned away. After a while, it was over.

As Orestes staggered back from his mother's corpse, he could already see them beginning to flock, out of the corner of his eye. They'd fade from view if he tried to look directly at them, but they were definitely there, lurking in the periphery of his vision – black-winged, grim-faced women, snakes wreathing their hair and arms. The Furies. As the days and nights passed, they seemed to crowd nearer and nearer, grinning at him – at first he couldn't hear them, but then, soon enough, he was tormented by their voices, their taunts like the constant, maddening barking of dogs. His mother's voice, he was sure he could hear that too; he was sometimes certain he could glimpse her face among the Furies'. She would come to him in his dreams, her body slashed and gaping where he'd struck it.

Electra and Pylades tried to soothe him, but he was disappearing into the dark interior of his mind, moaning and sweating and shaking. Occasionally clarity would return; he'd say the Furies were asleep. At those moments he and Electra would cling together, and it would be his turn to comfort her, and they'd promise to take care of each other.

After a time, even other people began to be able to sense the Furies – like a cold draught or a dark shadow, at first. Soon everyone could see and hear them as they crouched over him, leering, threatening him.

It was Apollo who had told Orestes to kill his mother, and the god must be honoured – and consulted – again. And so the young man journeyed to Apollo's shrine at Delphi, the Furies snapping at his heels like hounds chasing down a hare. 'Lap up his blood, make him pay,' they'd mutter. 'Drag him down, down to the Underworld, mother-killer. No pity for him, no mercy: a mother's blood, spilled, can't ever be gathered up again.'

Once he arrived at the sanctuary he clutched the statue of Athena for safety, where he was protected – enraging the Furies, who cursed the Olympians, those younger gods who threatened their own primal power, a potency that came from Mother Gaia and the blood-bonds knotting together families. While Orestes clung there, Apollo himself argued for Orestes against the black-winged goddesses. 'We punish mother-killers! That's our right, and our task,' they screamed.

'But what about husband-killers? That's a worse crime,' countered Apollo.

'No – the crime is worse when shared blood is spilled. There's no shared blood between husband and wife.'

The deadlock was broken only by Athena, who came in person in answer to Orestes' prayers. She listened to the accusations and counter-accusations. 'This can't go on for ever,' she said. 'This cycle could be never-ending – the children of the house of Atreus slaughtering each other in turn, vendetta breeding vendetta.'

She proposed that Orestes should be tried, in Athens, in a court. Mortal men of the city, chosen by lot, would form the jury. They would hear the evidence, they would vote, they would abide by the verdict. Athena would preside, as was her right, over a court convened in her own city. All of them agreed.

The trial took place on the Areopagus, a high rocky outcrop north and west of the Acropolis. The Furies acted as the prosecution, and began by cross-examining Orestes. 'Do you admit you killed your mother?' one of the winged women asked.

'Yes,' he said.

'Ha – he admits it! And how did you do it?'

'With my sword. I cut her throat.'

'Why did you do it?'

'The god Apollo told me to. He will confirm it. My mother deserved it – twice over.'

'What do you mean?'

'She killed her husband – and my father.'

'Irrelevant! You are alive, aren't you? She didn't kill you. She killed someone who wasn't her blood kin. He's guilty, jurymen!'

Orestes now turned to Apollo. 'I don't deny I killed her. The question is, was it lawful? Apollo – what do you say?'

'It was lawful,' said the god. 'The oracle I gave to Orestes came straight from Zeus. And Zeus's word is law. It was right to punish Clytemnestra for murdering Agamemnon.'

One of the Furies cut in. 'You mean Zeus said it was right for him to murder his mother, because she'd killed his father? But what about the father's crimes – the murder of his own child? You talk of the claims of the father – but what right does Zeus have to pronounce on that? He chained up *his* father, Cronus, and imprisoned him in Tartarus. Do you really think it's right for Orestes to go and rule in Mycenae, in the palace he soiled with matricide?'

'It is true that murdering a parent is a terrible thing,' replied Apollo. 'But understand this: the crime under consideration is *not* the murder of a parent. The mother is not the parent of a child. It is the father who is the only true parent. Look at it this way: it is the father's seed that enters the womb. The womb is only the soil that the plant grows in. The woman is just ... the vessel for the child. We know this because the womb is not even needed! Here is the proof, standing before you: Athena. Zeus gave birth to her himself – no need for a mother. She was born from his head.'

That was it. The evidence had been given, the witnesses cross-examined. The jurymen cast their votes, each man dropping his token into one of two urns. Finally it was Athena's turn. Penelope wove it so, the Furies on the one side, dark wings shining, faces hungry for blood, on the other, the Athenian jurymen; and in the centre, Orestes with the god Apollo at his side, and the helmeted Athena as she held out her shining, immortal hand and let her token clatter into the vessel for Orestes' innocence. 'I am my father's daughter,' she said. 'I will stand beside no woman who killed her husband.'

The votes were equal, for and against. According to the court's rule, Orestes was acquitted. The Furies howled with anger, and raged at the younger gods, who'd dishonoured them, who'd torn up the ancient laws of blood-guilt. They shrieked out their curses: Athens would be blighted, its children would sicken, its people would be massacred. Eventually Athena held up her hand. 'Please! Furies: I respect you. You are older, and of course so much wiser, than I am. But I've my fair share of intelligence, and I have something to say. You claim you've been dishonoured. That we new gods have taken away your old rights. Maybe. Things have changed. But you could change, too. You could become ... kindly. We could give you a home in this city. Right here – under this great rock of the Areopagus. You could be worshipped. You could help make Athens great, help win its wars, help make its people rich. Stay: be persuaded by me. Forget this idea of dishonour. Become milder, calmer. Lose your bitterness. Be loved. Don't be Furies any more. Be Kindly Ones.'

The Furies were persuaded by Athena's subtle oratory, seduced by her offer. Their dance of rage became a dance of joy. They consented to their new role. They allowed their primordial powers, their ancient rights, to drift away. Their harsh, doglike voices became soft, almost inaudible. All their old strength, their old potency, their old loyalty to the rights of the mother, were now harnessed by the city, and put to work making it hungrier for territory, and wealth, and power.

Penelope finished her tapestry. She stood back from it and gave it an appraising look. She thought about her cousin Clytemnestra, the girl she'd grown up with in Sparta. Was she really such a vicious example of womanhood? What would she, Penelope, have done if Odysseus had killed their child? She could easily have behaved in exactly the same way as her cousin, had the circumstances been different – they both possessed a capacity for calculation, for playing the long game, for assuming the mantle of power, for trickery. Perhaps it was only a throw of the dice, an accident of marriage, that had made their lives turn out so differently. And yet here she was, the Ithacan queen sung to the skies by the poets for her loyalty and her patience. Clytemnestra, on the other hand, was a byword for murder and monstrosity.

Yet the poets knew nothing: they had no idea how murderous she had felt when she'd learned of Odysseus's affairs. How very close she'd been to abandoning him altogether, taking one of the suitors, marrying again. How frightened she'd been of him when he'd returned, how shocked by his violence – yes, terror and revulsion, she had learned, could exist alongside love. And what was all her legendary virtue for? In the end, it was about keeping Odysseus's home intact and his property secure. It was about upholding the laws of kingship, the power of men, the customs of inheritance. She thought about the dog Argos – he had stayed alive just long enough to thump his old tail for a minute against the dungheap when he saw his master return home. Was she expected to be a human version of Odysseus's loyal dog?

As for Athena – how she loved her mortal men! How she had fawned over Odysseus, over Telemachus, over Orestes, too. It was no surprise that she had repudiated the rights of the mother, of the woman, of Clytemnestra. The goddess had taken so many shapes, wrapped herself in so many disguises, to help her husband and her son. She'd become Mentor, one of Odysseus's oldest friends – that's how she'd apparently helped Telemachus to summon a ship, to set off for Pylos and Sparta. She'd become a vulture. A pretty young girl. A beautiful woman. A shepherd. A swallow. So much effort! If you didn't know that Athena had no interest in sex, you would think she was in love with Odysseus. The way she flattered him sounded almost like flirtation. If Odysseus could be believed, of course.

Penelope dropped her weaving sword and sat down on her stool. Her son and husband had, so they claimed, seen the goddess repeatedly. But she'd never seen her. She had only her husband's word for it – for any of it – and the only certainty about Odysseus was that he was a compulsive liar. Did Athena even exist? The goddess had put thoughts into her head. At least, that's what she'd always assumed when she'd had a burst of inspiration out of nowhere. Were her best ideas really brought to her by Athena? Or were they, in fact, the product of her own intelligence? The goddess had been born from her father's head, supposedly, but that sounded implausible, to Penelope – like a male fantasy of how a child should be born, without any need for a female body.

Could the universe really be governed by the gods and goddesses of Olympus – with their endless greed for sacrifices, their readiness to be offended, their arbitrary punishments? She'd heard that the Thracians believed the gods were tall and blond, like them; that the Ethiopians understood the gods to be black. Maybe if lions and horses and cows had gods, she mused, they'd resemble lions and cows and horses.

Was Zeus really responsible for lightning? Maybe there was another explanation. Perhaps, she thought, it came from the clashing of the wind and the clouds. Maybe the rainbow was not the work of goddess Iris, as she'd always been taught, but an effect of the light in the clouds. Could rain not be the result of vapour drying from the earth? Was the Earth itself really flat, its edges bounded by Ocean – and if it was, how did the heavenly bodies appear to be revolving around the world? Could the sky not be below us in some way, as well as above us?

She looked again at her loom, at the elaborate scenes she had woven. Then she took the shuttle and tugged on the weft thread, undoing the work. Everything began to unravel. Her stories began to dissolve. When there was nothing left but thread, she left the loom, walked away, and shut the door behind her.

Much later – years later – when the house was abandoned, when the courtyard lay empty, when its roof had collapsed, it was only spiders who still wove there. They caught up the flies in their glistening threads, and their strong webs did not break.

NOTES

ONE: ATHENA

The goddess **Athena** presides over technology and craft; she is the inventor of the loom. Ovid's *Fasti*, a poetic calendar of Roman festivals, for example, describes Minerva (the Roman version of Athena) as '*mille dea ... operum*', the goddess of a thousand crafts (3.833). It also describes her role in teaching humans the arts of woolworking and weaving.

The sources for my account of the creation are Hesiod's *Theogony*, and the openings of Ovid's *Metamorphoses* and Pseudo-Apollodorus's *Library*.

Hesiod's creation story, which scholars place in the era of the Homeric epics, perhaps the late eighth or seventh century BCE, is concerned above all with divine genealogies. Ovid, writing in the era of the Emperor Augustus, the late first century BCE/early first century CE, gives a beautiful, materialist vision of the start of the universe in his epic poem on mythological transformations. It owes a lot to Lucretius's earlier poetic/scientific/philosophical text *On the Nature of the Universe*.

Pseudo-Apollodorus's *Library*, a handbook of mythological stories in Greek prose, was probably written in the first or second century CE. For the convenience of readers, in these notes I have followed the division of the work into books and sections offered by Robin Hard in his translation for Oxford World's Classics, which differ from the divisions made by (e.g.) James Frazer in his Loeb bilingual edition.

I've combined elements of the three sources, slimming down the massive profusion of detail (and long lists of names) in Hesiod, and I've drawn on details from elsewhere: for example, the story of **Hephaestus** being hurled down from Olympus by Zeus is in

Iliad 1.590–5; the image of **Aphrodite** rising from the sea owes something to the glorious Ludovici throne, which can been seen in the Palazzo Altemps, Rome; and Mount Etna as a prison for Typhon is wonderfully described in the first *Pythian Ode* by Pindar. The fifth-century BCE poet celebrated winners of various ancient Games, including the Olympics; they are an important source for mythical stories.

In real ancient Athens, the annual Panathenaic festival included the dedication of a sacred peplos, or robe, to the small olive-wood statue dedicated to Athena Polias (the goddess as the protector of the city, or *polis*). This moment is depicted in the culminating scenes of the Parthenon frieze. The weaving was said to have taken nine months, and was undertaken by women and girls. Some historians of Greek religion also think that there was also a larger weaving made every four years, which may have been draped over the colossal (around ten metres) statue of Athena in the Parthenon, or hung behind it. These textiles were woven with scenes from the gods' battle with the Giants, the 'gigantomachy', which is why the episode forms the central scene of the weaving that my Athena makes. The poet of *Ciris*, a work in the *Appendix Vergiliana* (a collection of Latin poems once attributed to Virgil), describes the peplos in this way: 'Thus in order are woven the battles of Pallas [Athena], the great robes are adorned with the trophies of the Giants, and grim combats are depicted in blood-red scarlet. There is added he who was hurled down by the golden spear – Typhon …' The poet then announces an intention of creating an analogous artwork – a 'woven' poetic tale about nature.

I've simplified the story of the origins of fire given by Hesiod in his *Theogony* – there, Prometheus steals it back for humans after Zeus takes it away, having become angry at the apportionment of meat during sacrifices.

Hesiod is the originator of the story of **Pandora**. He tells it twice – once in *Theogony* and once in his poetic farming manual, *Works and Days*. In both cases his Pandora is accursed, opening her clay jar (a not very occluded metaphor for her vagina) to bring misfortune to men. Hesiod, in general, is baldly misogynist in a way that Homer, say, is not (nor does Pandora feature in Homer). I have taken the liberty of switching the story around, using her name – meaning 'she who gives all' – to suggest that she in fact allows men to discover their true humanity in all its moral complexity. For Hesiod, before women came along to wear menfolk down, male humans inhabited a golden age where none of them aged and the Earth gave up its fruits spontaneously.

My **Prometheus** owes a lot to the play *Prometheus Bound*, traditionally attributed to Aeschylus, in which the eponymous protagonist describes his rebellious desire to teach skills to humans. At the very start of the play, he is bound to the rock by the reluctant **Hephaestus**. There is a chorus of **Oceanids**.

The story of **Demeter and Persephone** is closely based on the *Homeric Hymn to Demeter*. The thirty-three *Homeric Hymns*, once attributed to Homer himself, are songs mostly composed in the seventh and sixth centuries BCE to honour individual gods. The *Hymn to Demeter* is one of the few ancient Greek texts to give a female character a 'quest' narrative that seems to echo both the *Iliad* (Demeter's Achilles-esque rage and withdrawal) and the *Odyssey* (the goddess's journeys and habit of dissembling). The *Hymn to Demeter* partly operates as an aetiological poem, explaining the foundation of the Eleusinian Mysteries, an important mystery cult based in the town of Eleusis near Athens.

The stories of **Phaethon** and **Pyrrha and Deucalion** are drawn largely from Ovid's *Metamorphoses* books 2 and 1 respectively.

The idea of humankind as simultaneously magnificent and destructive is most eloquently expressed by the fifth-century BCE dramatist Sophocles in the famous choral ode in *Antigone* at lines 322ff.

TWO: ALCITHOË

Alcithoë is not, admittedly, a household name. She and her sisters, the **daughters of Minyas** of Orchomenus, appear at the start of the fourth book of Ovid's *Metamorphoses* as deniers of **Dionysus**'s divinity. They are weavers, and they keep on weaving while other women rush out of their homes to worship the god.

The fact that Dionysus's female followers upset normal domestic arrangements and gender roles – abandoning their looms and shuttles, stung by the god into heading into the mountains – is an important aspect of Euripides' great play *Bacchae* (see for example lines 118–19). The play tells the story of how the god's mortal cousin, **Pentheus** of Thebes, denies Dionysus's divinity and is duly punished. *Bacchae* was probably written in Macedonia around 406 BCE, where the writer spent the last year or so of his life; it was produced posthumously in Athens at the Great Dionysia, the most important annual festival devoted to the god. Over three days, three playwrights would compete against each other with four plays each – a trilogy of tragedies followed by a riotous 'satyr play', featuring a chorus of the lascivious, ithyphallic creatures.

In *Metamorphoses*, the daughters of Minyas sing songs as they weave, and thus become a device for the embedded telling of a number of stories, including that of **Pyramus and Thisbe**. My Alcithoë's subject is a 'history' of Thebes up until the arrival of Dionysus (although I have embedded a long flash-forward to the stories of Oedipus and his children). Sources for this material include, along with *Bacchae*, the epic *Dionysiaca* – the longest extant poem of Graeco-Roman antiquity at 20,426 lines, organised in forty-eight books. The poem, which tells the story of Dionysus beginning with the foundation of Thebes by his maternal grandfather, Cadmus, was written in Greek in the late fourth or early fifth century AD by Nonnus, an inhabitant of Panopolis in Egypt, the modern city of Akhmim. A new English translation is forthcoming, by Robert Shorrock, Camille Geisz, Mary

Whitby, Tim Whitmarsh and Berenice Verhelst, and I am grateful to have been allowed to consult an early version.

Europa's rape is the subject of one of Titian's greatest works, painted for Philip II of Spain in the 1550s. Her billowing pink shawl is a feature of the scene from antiquity onwards. The story is told at the end of book 2 of *Metamorphoses*.

The episode of **Cadmus and Typhon** is in book 2 of Nonnus's *Dionysiaca*. Cadmus's visit to Samothrace and to **Electra** and **Harmonia** are in books 3 and 4.

The story of **Io**, which Cadmus narrates to Electra in *Dionysiaca*, is also told in book 1 of Ovid's *Metamorphoses*, book 2 of Pseudo-Apollodorus's *Library*, and in Aeschylus's play *Prometheus Bound*, from where come the details of Io's travels, including to the land of the 'swanlike' **Graeae**, as Aeschylus calls them.

Cadmus is said by many Greek sources (including Herodotus, in *Histories* 5.58) to have brought the alphabet with him from Phoenicia. It's true that the Greeks adapted their alphabetic writing system from that developed in Phoenicia.

Dirce – sometimes considered not a spring but a person (or a person who becomes a spring) – was the aunt of Antiope, whom she treated badly. Antiope's children by Zeus (he raped her in the guise of a satyr) were **Amphion and Zethus**, the builders of the walls and seven gates of Thebes. They later killed Dirce because of her cruelty by strapping her to the horns of a bull. This is the subject of the famous *Farnese Bull*, a Hellenistic sculpture group in the Naples Archaeological Museum.

The notion that **Tiresias** is descended from one of the **sown men** is in Pseudo-Apollodorus's *Library* (3.6.7), as is the story of his transformation into a woman. Why is Hera so angry at his response to the question about sexual pleasure? There are various theories.

I have borrowed Nicole Loraux's from *The Experience of Tiresias: The Feminine and the Greek* (1995, translated by Paula Wissing).

According to Diodorus of Sicily (*Library of History* 4.66.5), Manto, sometimes known as Daphne 'wrote oracular responses of every sort, excelling in their composition; and indeed it was from her poetry, they say, that the poet Homer took many verses which he appropriated as his own and with them adorned his own poesy'. *Mantis* is Greek for prophet, from which comes our adjective mantic and the name of the praying mantis – so called because of its posture, with folded forearms, as if in prayer. Diodorus' *Library* was a compendium of universal knowledge from mythological times to 60 BCE. Only fifteen of the original forty books survive.

The source for **Oedipus and Jocasta** is Sophocles' masterpiece *Oedipus the King*. The precise date of the play is unknown, though it was likely premiered in 430 or 429 BCE; his career in the theatre was long, lasting at least from 468 to 406 BCE. Aristotle thought it the most exemplary of Greek dramas. It was not, however, part of a winning trilogy at the Dionysia.

Oedipus's eventual death near Athens is the subject of Sophocles' *Oedipus at Colonus*. The story of **Polynices and Eteocles** is told in Aeschylus's *Seven Against Thebes*. The attempted burial of Polynices by his sister **Antigone** is the subject of Sophocles' *Antigone*. The detail about Harmonia's necklace being used to bribe Eriphyle is in Pseudo-Apollodorus.

Actaeon's story here draws on Ovid's *Metamorphoses* book 3. The story is also told in the Callimachus *Hymn* known as *The Bath of Pallas* and in Nonnus's *Dionysiaca*.

Some of the **Semele** story is from *Dionysiaca* book 7. In ancient accounts it's usually the jealous Hera who persuades Semele to ask Zeus to show her his thunderbolts; I've invented the notion that Semele does it deliberately, perhaps knowing the likely outcome.

Ino's role in the early care of Dionysus and transformation into a sea goddess is recounted in Pseudo-Apollodorus, 3.4.3.

The **early days of Dionysus** are largely taken from the *Homeric Hymns* to Dionysus, 1 and 26. The **Ampelus** story is in books 10, 11 and 12 of Nonnus's *Dionysiaca*. *Ampelos* is the Greek word for vine. Dionysus's Asian travels are listed in the god's opening speech in Euripides' *Bacchae*.

The story of **Dionysus's kidnap** comes from the wonderful seventh *Homeric Hymn*, to Dionysus. I've invented the idea that it's on this particular ship that he makes his way to Greece. There is a magnificent kylix, or cup, made by the Athenian potter Ezekias in the 540s BCE, which shows a similar scene to the one I've had Alcithoë weave. It's in the collection of the Antikensammlungen in Munich.

The story of **Dionysus in Thebes** and his encounter with **Pentheus** is from Euripides' *Bacchae*. The image of **Agave** striding down Cithaeron with her son's head impaled on her staff is one of the most unforgettable in Greek theatre. Imagine the 'head' as the actor's mask.

The transformation of the tapestry of the **daughters of Minyas** is in Ovid's *Metamorphoses* book 4. The women explicitly deny Dionysus's divinity, just like Pentheus; for my purposes I have suggested they are too busy concentrating on making their artwork to heed his call. The idea of the god disguised as a maenad comes from Antoninus Liberalis's *Metamorphoses*, a work dating from the second to third centuries CE.

THREE: PHILOMELA

The story of **Philomela and Procne** is told in its fullest surviving form in Ovid, *Metamorphoses* book 6. It was also the subject of a largely lost play by Sophocles called *Tereus*. Sophocles' play, it is thought, established the sisters as the lens for the story. Relationships between sisters are also important to Sophocles' plays *Electra* and *Antigone*. In those plays each pair of sisters is somewhat contrasted – Antigone and Electra characterised as the 'strong', decisive ones, Chrysothemis and Ismene as their 'weaker' foils. In Ovid's version of the Philomela and Procne story, at least, the sisters show unusual solidarity.

I've borrowed the sisters' desire to become birds from one of the beautiful choruses in Euripides' *Hippolytus*, 732ff. Anne Carson has it thus: 'I long for the secret sunwalked places, / and a god to take me up high / amid high birds flying, / to rise and soar / over sea coasts / and rivers / where sad girls / pitying Phaethon / drop into the deepblue wave / their amber tears, their brilliant tears.'

The story of **Iphis**, told in *Metamorphoses* book 9, is one of a handful of myths in which characters are changed from male to female or vice versa. (Other characters who undergo such a transformation are Caenis and Tiresias.) On the face of it, Iphis might be read as a mythical precursor of a modern transgender experience. However, a thoughtful essay published in the journal *Eidolon* by a transgender classicist, Sasha Barish, suggests that the story – positioned in *Metamorphoses* as it is among a number of stories about impossible or unnatural loves – may be more troubling than it first looks. One might also note that the change from female to male is required, in Ovid's telling, because to him the idea of two women loving each other is so novel as to be unthinkable: '*femina femineo correpta cupidine nulla est*' – no woman has been seized by desire for a woman, the poet asserts.

This is why I have left open what happens at the end of the story. Some blessing from Isis is given, but it is up to the reader to decide what nature of blessing that is. I take my cue from another line in Ovid's story (*Metamorphoses*, 9.711–13). '*Facies, qam siue puellae / siue dares puero, fieret formosus uterque*' – 'Iphis's appearance, whether you think it that of a girl or a boy, would be beautiful either way.'

The stories of **Echo** and **Narcissus** are told in Ovid's *Metamorphoses* book 3.

The story of **Pygmalion** is in *Metamorphoses* book 10. In Ovid's version, Pygmalion and the statue have a happy ending, and a child. Ovid's statue was made from ivory; mine is based on the famous Hellenistic statue of Ariadne that you can see in the Vatican Museums (it also features in my book *Red Thread*). According to a dialogue called *Erotes*, attributed to Lucian, one man who came to see the real nude marble statue of Aphrodite at Cnidus, by the famous Athenian sculptor Praxiteles, was so aroused that he ejaculated over it, leaving a stain on her thighs. That's what inspired a gory detail here.

Heracles dressed in women's clothes and spinning for **Omphale** is mentioned in Propertius's *Elegies*, 4.9; and the wardrobe swap in Lucian, *How to Write History*, 10. In the British Museum there is a Roman wellhead showing Heracles in a dress, lifted to show his erect penis, 'in erotic pursuit' (as the museum puts it) of a woman.

Euripides' play *Alcestis* tells how she offers to die instead of her husband Admetus, and is brought back to the world of the living by Heracles, who wrestles Death and brings her home, veiled, to be recognised by her husband.

The story of **Deianira**'s accidental killing of her husband **Heracles** is told in sources including the Hesiodic *Catalogue of Women* (which also includes the story about Periclymenus, Nestor's brother, who could disguise himself as an ant, a bee, an eagle or a snake – and who, when he lost the favour of Athena, was killed by Heracles in a battle outside his father Neleus's city walls).

The main source here, though, is *The Women of Trachis* by Sophocles. In that play, the actual Labours (the most famous thing about Heracles) are compressed into a single speech in flashback, while the story focuses on how this great hero is inadvertently killed by his wife. There is a wonderful Renaissance painting by Jan Gossaert (in the Barber Institute, Birmingham) that does something similar: it shows Heracles and Deianira sitting together, she about to present him with the poison-infused tunic that will kill him. Heracles' famous Labours are hinted at through a partially concealed carved frieze on the bottom of the stone bench on which they are sitting, which inspired my approach here. In some versions of Heracles' story the Labours were undertaken to expunge the crime of killing his first wife, Megara. But Homer, in *Iliad* book 19, says it is because of Hera: she extracted a promise from Zeus that whichever of his mortal descendants was born that day would have dominion over his neighbours. She delayed the birth of Heracles and it was that day that Eurystheus, Zeus's grandson, was born. So Heracles was obliged to be subservient to his kinsman.

It is Pseudo-Apollodorus's *Library* that reports that Deianira drove a chariot and knew the arts of war. Heracles' immortality in everlasting peace with Hebe as his wife is described in Pindar's first *Nemean Ode* and the Hesiodic *Catalogue of Women*.

Atalanta's story is told in Ovid's *Metamorphoses* books 8 and 10. Other sources include Pseudo-Apollodorus's *Library* and Callimachus's *Hymn to Artemis*, which mentions her dispatch of her attempted rapists. Melanion is sometimes known as Hippomenes. The detail of Atalanta's snatching the apple 'like a Harpy' is taken from the Hesiodic *Catalogue of Women*.

The story of **Pyramus and Thisbe** appears for the first time in surviving literature in Ovid's *Metamorphoses* book 4.

The much, much lighter-toned story of **Eros and Psyche** comes from the second-century CE Latin prose-fiction work *The Golden Ass*, by Apuleius, a writer from Madaurus (modern M'Daourouch, in Algeria). The scenes I've had Philomela weave – the council of the gods and the wedding feast – are among those that you can see on the ceiling of the loggia in the Palazzo Farnesina in Trastevere, Rome, a magnificent work by a group of artists including Giulio Romano.

The story of **Procne and Philomela** is undeniably grim. Ovid's version is grimmer than mine: he offers a truly horrific tongue-severing scene. Shakespeare borrowed details from this story for *Titus Andronicus* – both the idea of serving up someone's sons for dinner, and the notion of rape followed by a mutilation. His Lavinia's tongue is cut out – and her hands are also severed so that she cannot write down (or weave) her story. However, she manages to indicate the story of Philomela in a copy of Ovid's *Metamorphoses* to communicate what has happened to her.

The child-killing here is perhaps, as in Euripides' *Medea*, a woman's weapon of last resort against patriarchy – a way of disrupting the father-to-son transfer of prestige, power and property on which society, in these stories, depends. (Though you could also see the episode as a masculine projection of terror about women's undeniable control over one human function – that of childbirth and the care of young children.)

Ornithologists will note that female nightingales do not in fact sing – but don't let that kind of detail ruin a good story.

FOUR: ARACHNE

The story of **Arachne**'s weaving competition with **Athena** is told at the start of Ovid's *Metamorphoses* book 6, and I've followed Ovid's account quite tightly right up until the descriptions of the two contestants' tapestries, including the rainbow simile. I've borrowed from Ovid on the makers' themes, but altered the precise contents of their works – though Ovid does present **Athena and Poseidon's contest** as the centrepiece of the goddess's tapestry.

Colophon and **Phocaea** are both in Ionia, Greek cities on what is now Turkey's western Mediterranean coast. **Purple** was a byword for luxury in the classical world, often associated with Phoenicia (modern Lebanon). I was lucky enough to learn about the process of producing 'Tyrian purple' through visits to the National Museum of

Beirut and the Archaeological Museum of the American University, Beirut, some eighty kilometres north of Tyre itself.

Ixion's story is told in sources including Pindar's second *Pythian Ode*. It was the subject of a number of lost tragedies – Aeschylus and Euripides both dramatised the story. A fragment of Aeschylus's lost *Women of Perrhaebia* includes the detail of 'drinking cups, wrought in gold and silver'. Diodorus of Sicily recounts the tale too (4.69.3–5).

According to Hyginus's *Fabulae*, none of the gods consumed Pelops's flesh at **Tantalus**'s dinner party except for Ceres (the Roman name for Demeter). Hyginus (*c*.64 BCE–17 CE) was a freedman of the Emperor Augustus. His *Fabulae* are regarded as somewhat simplistic student notes on his original, more learned mythographical treatises. (A different version is offered by Pindar in his first *Olympian Ode*: the gods cannot possibly have been cannibals, he writes; instead Pelops must have been abducted by Poseidon, who wanted the mortal as his lover. Later, he recounts, Poseidon helped Pelops win Hippodamia as his wife, which involved beating her father Oenomaus in a chariot race. Pelops and Hippodamia became the founders of the royal house of Mycenae.)

Tantalus's punishment is described in the *Odyssey* (11.582–92).

Niobe's story first appears at the very end of the *Iliad* (24.602–9), where she is brought forward as an example of extreme grief in the remarkable scene when Priam, king of Troy, steals into the Greek camp and persuades Achilles to let him have his son's body. Other versions are in *Metamorphoses* and Pseudo-Apollodorus's *Library*. The number of her children varies wildly; I've stuck to Homer's tally. The detail of the rock's enclosing her like 'clinging ivy' is from Sophocles' *Antigone*. There is a remarkable Roman fresco of the killing – Apollo picking off the humans as they try to flee on horseback – in the Naples Archaeological Museum, originally from a house in Pompeii.

For the **Marsyas** story, I've broadly followed the version in Diodorus of Sicily (3.59). Ovid has a famous, and famously grisly, description of the flaying in *Metamorphoses* book 6. I've also drawn on Jusepe de Ribera's painting of the scene in the Capodimonte Museum in Naples.

The story of **Daphne** is told in Ovid's *Metamorphoses* book 1. The transformation is the subject of numerous artworks, including Gianlorenzo Bernini's extraordinary sculpture in the Villa Borghese, Rome.

There are various versions of the location for **Orithyia**'s abduction, and I've chosen that of the sixth-century BCE mythographer, Acusilaus. The scene of the rape itself, on the banks of the River **Erigonus**, is offered by Apollonius of Rhodes in the *Argonautica* (late third century BCE), 1.215ff. There is a beautiful amphora in the collection of the Antikensammlungen in Munich showing the abduction.

Creusa describes her rape, denouncing Apollo, in Euripides' play *Ion*, 881ff. The story told here is closely based on that play, including the particulars of the rape and the description of the blanket with its Gorgon-and-snake pattern, rather poorly made by the inexperienced young girl: weaving provides this plot with its means of resolution. (In a play rather deeply concerned with textiles, we also find descriptions of elaborate hangings that decorate the banqueting place where Ion narrowly misses being poisoned. These depict the heavens, complete with Helios, Nyx, the Pleiades, Orion, the Great Bear, the Hyades and Eos; a sea battle between Greeks and foreigners; various half-animal, half-human creatures; deer and lion hunts; and Cecrops and his daughters. In addition, at the start of the play the chorus of Athenian women admire the sculptures in the sanctuary at Delphi, saying that they recognise the scenes depicted from stories told at the loom – we might imagine them singing as they work, or even weaving the stories.)

The Arcadian **Callisto**'s story is told in Ovid's *Metamorphoses* book 2 and *Fasti* (2.155ff), and by Pseudo-Apollodorus (*Library*,

3.8) who gathers up the threads of various disparate traditions relating to her. My version is most closely aligned to that given by Pseudo-Eratosthenes, in turn citing a lost work of Hesiod, in the compilation of star myths called *Catasterisms* – a first-century BCE precis of a lost original, probably not by the actual third-century BCE Eratosthenes. Fiona Benson's poem '[transformation: Callisto]' is a remarkable, raw reworking of the Callisto story.

One of the rapes woven by Arachne in Ovid's *Metamorphoses* is **Leda**'s. Eroticising the scene has proved irresistible for male painters, sculptors and poets over the centuries; for a different point of view, see Lucille Clifton's Leda poems. Supposedly Leda also slept with her husband the day she was raped by the swan, so while Zeus is Helen's father, Tyndareus is Clytemnestra's, and often Castor and Pollux's too.

The story of **Ganymede** is told in the *Homeric Hymn to Aphrodite*, 201ff.

Pseudo-Apollodorus (*Library*, 2.4) tells the story of **Danaë**, and **Perseus**'s conception in the shower of gold. It's another popular subject for artists, including Titian: see his version at Apsley House in London. In his *Ode* 3.16, Horace, the first-century CE Roman poet, shares **Acrisius**'s cynical interpretation of the gold. The particulars of the chest come from the painting on a mid-fifth-century BCE Attic hydria (by the 'Danaë painter') in the Boston Museum of Fine Arts. The little song sung by Danaë to Perseus while the chest is on the sea is taken almost word for word from a fragment of a lovely poem by the sixth-century BCE poet Simonides of Ceos.

The scene on the beach with **Dictys** and the fisherman draws on surviving fragments of Aeschylus's satyr play *Net-Haulers*.

Pseudo-Apollodorus picks up the story now (*Library* 2.4.2). The **Graeae** – sometimes a pair, sometimes a trio – are often depicted as grotesque old women. But the saffron-coloured dress and the 'beautiful cheeks' are courtesy of Hesiod in *Theogony* (270), who also tells us they were grey-haired from birth. He offers two named sisters, Enyo and Pemphredo; Deino is added by Pseudo-Apollodorus (who also has Pephredo, instead of Pemphredo). The fact that there are encounters with three different trios of supernatural females, plus such an array, even overkill, of magical objects, suggests to modern commentators that mythographers may have gathered together variants on the tale to make a single, somewhat congested story. I've reflected this slightly overdone quality in my version of Perseus's encounters with the Graeae and the **nymphs**, who aren't usually this knowing or sarcastic.

The notion that the nymphs live 'north' is my invention – the locations for these events are vague but distant. The Graeae seemingly live near Scythia in *Prometheus Bound* but they can also be found near Lake Tritonis in North Africa.

In archaic and classical Greek art, and texts such as Pseudo-Apollodorus's, **Medusa** and her sisters, the **Gorgons**, who, like the Graeae, are daughters of the sea gods Ceto and Phorcys, have tusks, hands of bronze, wings and scaly heads. Sometimes, though, Medusa is depicted as a beautiful winged woman, such as on a *pelike*, a kind of wine jar, by the fifth-century BCE painter Polygnotus, now in the Metropolitan Museum of Art. In Pindar's tenth *Pythian Ode* she is described as 'beautiful-cheeked'. In Pseudo-Apollodorus, Athena guides Perseus's hand to kill Medusa. In Ovid's *Metamorphoses* (4.791–803) we are told that the beautiful Medusa acquired her snaky hair after Neptune (the Roman equivalent of Poseidon) raped her in Minerva's (Athena's) sanctuary. The hair was Athena's punishment. Following Polygnotus's example, I've not given her the snaky hair, but I have borrowed the rape and Athena's enmity.

Hesiod's *Theogony* (270ff) also tells us Medusa was raped by Poseidon and that when she was killed by Perseus, two creatures were born – the winged horse **Pegasus** and the warrior Chrysaor. The western pediment of the sixth-century BCE temple to Artemis on Corfu – now in the island's Archaeological Museum – shows her with her two offspring.

According to Ovid, Perseus's next stop is the Titan Atlas, whom he turns to stone (the Atlas mountains). Then he comes to **Ethiopia**. For the Greeks, this was a distant southern land, only vaguely located, which gradually came to be associated with the Nilotic territory south of Egypt – more like modern Sudan than modern (and landlocked) Ethiopia.

Cetos, the great sea creature, gives his name to cetology, the study of whales. 'The gallant Perseus, a son of Jupiter, was the first whaleman,' wrote Melville in *Moby-Dick*. Cassiopeia and Cepheus eventually became constellations – Cassiopeia, with its 'W' shape, is particularly easy to spot in the northern sky.

Some of **Arachne**'s statements of religious scepticism are borrowed from Ion's speech in Euripides' *Ion* (429–51). The spidery punishment is in *Metamorphoses* (6.139–45).

FIVE: ANDROMACHE

The details of **Andromache**'s story here come from *Iliad* books 6 and 22. In the latter she is at her loom, working at a textile woven with an intricate flower pattern, when the news comes that Hector has been killed. When she realises what has happened, she rips off her headdress and drops her shuttle: one of the great devastating moments in literature. The Greek word for the flowers that she is weaving is a little-used one – *throna*. It comes up in Theocritus's second *Idyll*, with the idea of their having magical powers, being used in a love spell. In my version she is weaving a kind of wish-fulfilment, if not quite a love spell – tales about nature that take her beyond the confinement of Troy's city walls, and love stories.

The specific memory of her wedding day is gleaned from a work (fr 44) by the Lesbian poet Sappho (c. 630–570 BCE). The idea of the women at their looms, speculating on which Greek will drag them away by their hair, comes from Euripides' *Iphigenia in Aulis*, 786–91.

The story of **Alcyone and Ceyx** first appears, in fragmentary form, in the Hesiodic *Catalogue of Women*, where Alcyone and Ceyx impiously address each other as 'Hera' and 'Zeus' and are duly punished by being turned into birds. My version is more indebted to Ovid in *Metamorphoses* book 11, where the tale becomes a tender love story.

Ceyx is the Greek for gull or tern, so that is the bird that he must have originally been turned into. The speech I've given Alcyone against sea travel is drawn from some of the details in Horace's *Odes* 1.14, in which the narrator hopes that his friend, the poet Virgil, will reach his destination unharmed. Ceyx borrows some arguments in reply to this speech from Shakespeare's *Sonnet* 39. The land of the Cimmerians is described in the *Odyssey* book 11. My moaning doves and murmuring bees are borrowed from Tennyson.

Baucis and Philemon and **Icarus** are stories told in Ovid's *Metamorphoses* book 8.

The story of **Hyacinthus** is told in *Metamorphoses* (10.162–219) but details also come from two books written in Greek, each, confusingly, called *Pictures*, each by a different person called Philostratus, each describing mythological-themed works of art. They were perhaps members of the same Athenian family, perhaps grandfather and grandson. The elder Philostratus was working in the third century CE. A fragment of a poem by Bion of Smyrna (thought to have been working in about 100 BCE) has the god trying to use ambrosia and nectar to revive his lover.

Adonis's fate is narrated by Ovid in book 10 of *Metamorphoses*. The story is also the subject of a poem by the Hellenistic poet Theocritus, who was writing in the third century BCE. In his fifteenth *Idyll* he describes two women who attend the festival of Adonis. They admire tapestries so marvellous that the figures depicted on them seem to move. Bion of Phlossa, another Hellenistic poet, wrote a *Lament for Adonis*, full of baroque details of **Aphrodite**'s extravagant grief. Titian painted Aphrodite wrapping her arms around her lover, trying to stop him from hunting alone – one of his Ovid-inspired series commissioned by Philip II of Spain.

The wonderful *Homeric Hymn to Aphrodite* is the source for the story of **Aphrodite** and **Anchises**. I've given Aphrodite a few of Anchises' lines. The story of their son, **Aeneas**, is told in the great Roman epic, Virgil's *Aeneid*.

The story of **Orpheus and Eurydice** has two main sources: Virgil's *Georgics* (4.453–527) and Ovid's *Metamorphoses*, book 10. The version in *Georgics* is centred around the Arcadian beekeeper Aristaeus, who causes her death. In Pindar's ninth *Pythian Ode* **Cyrene**'s story is told. There is often a fox at Orpheus's feet in Roman mosaic depictions of the scene.

The story of **Picus** is in *Metamorphoses* book 5, that of **Leto and the frogs** in book 6; the **magpies** are in book 5.

The geography and nature of the Underworld are substantially drawn from the *Aeneid* book 6 and the *Odyssey* book 11. I have taken the liberty of giving Eurydice the traditional male character's role of descending to the Underworld and being shown the sights by a guide, a role I've given to **Hermes**, who does traditionally accompany the souls of the dead. (The Cumaean Sibyl performs the tour-guide role for Aeneas in Virgil's epic, and Virgil does it, in turn, for Dante in *The Divine Comedy*.)

The story of **Bellerophon**, **Pegasus and Chimaera** is recounted in more detail in the *Iliad* (6.119–211). The detail about how Bellerophon tames Pegasus using the bridle with its golden cheek pieces come from Pindar's *Olympian Ode* 13.

The story of the **Harpies** is from Apollonius Rhodius's *Argonautica*, written in Alexandria in the third century BCE. His Harpies also spoil Phineus's food and leave a disgusting smell wherever they go. On Greek vases Harpies are sometimes depicted as women with magnificent wings; or else as birds with women's heads. **Furies** are often shown as winged women wearing tunics and boots, with snakes wreathed in their hair and around their arms.

Sisyphus is encountered by Odysseus in the *Odyssey* (11.593ff), and his story is also told in Pseudo-Apollodorus's *Library* (1.9.3).

It is Ovid who, in *Metamorphoses* book 10, asks **Hades and Persephone** (in their Roman versions, Pluto and Proserpina) to reweave the fate of Eurydice – '*retexite fata*'.

SIX: HELEN

At the *Iliad* 3.125–9 we see **Helen** at her loom weaving the contests between the Greeks and the Trojans onto a great double-folded purple textile. **Iris** comes to her in disguise, hurrying her to the ramparts to join **Priam**, where she points out for him various Achaean (Greek) warriors (somehow implausibly, since this is supposedly the tenth year of the war). This is an episode known as the teichoscopia (the 'looking down from the walls'). There follows the single combat between **Menelaus** and **Paris**, ending with Aphrodite's rescue of Paris. It's at the end of book 8 that comes a magical description of the Trojans' fires burning at night like stars. I've invented the notion that Helen leaves her house at night to look at this scene.

Helen's feeling that 'the real her' is somewhere else entirely is a reference to Euripides' play *Helen*, in which a phantom made by the gods elopes with Paris, causing the war, while the real Helen, blameless and faithful, is spirited away to Egypt. Euripides' own source was probably the earlier lyric poet Stesichorus's poems about Helen.

In this first tapestry, made at Troy, I've imagined Helen weaving some of the principal events of the *Iliad*. The shield of Achilles is described (at far, far greater length than I have done here) at *Iliad* 18.478ff. The *Iliad* does not tell us whether Achilles and **Patroclus**'s loving, passionate, intensely close relationship is also a sexual one, though the surviving fragments of Aeschylus's play *Myrmidons* are explicit, with Achilles, heartbroken, recalling sex with his lost companion. Pseudo-Apollodorus recounts the knucklebones episode (3.13.8). The *Iliad* ends with **Cassandra**, **Andromache**, **Hecuba** and finally Helen mourning **Hector**.

The **Eidothea and Proteus** episode is described in the *Odyssey*, 4.361ff. Helen's golden spindle and silver box on wheels are described at 4.120ff.

Hermione's conflict with Andromache, who bears Neoptolemus a child while she remains childless, is the subject of Euripides' play, *Andromache*.

The decision to have **Thetis** marry Peleus is told in Pindar's eighth *Isthmian Ode*. The encounter between Peleus and Thetis and the wedding scene is drawn from poem 64 by the first-century BCE Roman poet Catullus. I've retained Catullus's continuity error (if the *Argo* was the first ship, how come Peleus and Thetis's bedspread depicts Theseus and Ariadne on board a boat?). The *Chrestomathy*, by a writer called Proclus (date unknown), includes a summary of the various lost parts of the epic cycle. One of these lost poems, the *Cypria*, about the early part of the Trojan War, contained the scene of Eris at the wedding of Peleus and Thetis, as well as that of the **Judgement of Paris**. These events are also narrated in Pseudo-Apollodorus. That Athena has her skin rubbed with olive oil and Aphrodite is doused in perfume comes from Callimachus's fifth *Hymn*, to Athena. The particularities of Hecuba's dream are taken from Pindar's fragmentary eighth *Paean*.

The story of **Helen's suitors** is told in Proclus. A slightly different version comes in Euripides' *Iphigenia in Aulis*, in which **Tyndareus** himself devises the plan to avoid bloodshed and Helen herself chooses Menelaus.

At *Iliad* 6.321ff, Paris is looking after his weapons indoors with Helen when Hector bursts in and berates him for his unmilitary indolence. I've borrowed some of that spirit here. Helen's feelings on leaving Sparta owe something to Sappho's wonderful poem known to us as fragment 16, which begins, in Stanley Lombardo's translation: 'Some say an army on horseback, / some say on foot, and some say ships / are the most beautiful things / on this black earth, / but I say / it is whatever you love.'

The **ploughing** story is in Hyginus, *Fabulae* 95. Sometimes **Palamedes** is said (including perhaps in a lost play about him by Sophocles) to have been the inventor of board games – and indeed he is seen at the start of Euripides' *Iphigenia in Aulis* playing draughts with Protesilaus.

Iphigenia's story is told in *Iphigenia in Aulis*, a powerful play about political calculation and moral compromise, first performed soon after Euripides' death in 406 BCE, in a trilogy with *Bacchae* and the lost *Alcmaeon of Corinth*. For the sacrifice itself, I've turned to the bleak tone of Aeschylus's *Agamemnon* (227–57). I note that girls who, like Persephone, call on their fathers in time of need in Greek myths often do so in vain.

Protesilaus's story is from the *Iliad*, 2.695–710. Polydora is named as his wife in the *Iliad*, and as Laodameia elsewhere. Pseudo-Apollodorus (Epit.3.28) has her creating an image of her husband in her grief, receiving a visit from his ghost – then committing suicide. 'The more competent Protesilaus' – there's a nod here in my phrasing to Alice Oswald's wonderful poem *Memorial*, a version of the *Iliad*.

There is a manuscript of the *Iliad* on which a scholiast notes the first line of a continuation of the poem's story: 'So they busied themselves with Hector's funeral. And an Amazon came, / a daughter of Ares the great hearted, the slayer of men.' (M.L. West's translation.) The scholiast was referring to the next poem in the epic cycle after the *Iliad*, the lost *Aethiopis*, which concerned itself with the exploits of the Amazon **Penthesilea** and the Ethiopian **Memnon**, both killed by Hector. Proclus in the *Chrestomathy* gives us a plot summary, and Quintus of Smyrna's rather laborious epic poem *Posthomerica*, written perhaps in the late fourth century CE, tells their stories in his books 1 and 2. He includes a debate between Trojan women on whether they should emulate the Amazons and take up arms. There is a beautiful sixth-century BCE amphora in the British Museum by Exekias, showing Penthesilea's death. Some versions of the story have Achilles falling in love with Penthesilea as she dies. Readers might note that earlier in this volume (in 'Philomela') Hippolyta was killed by Heracles, not by Penthesilea. Consistency is not a strong suit of the Greek myths.

Tithonus's story is told in the *Homeric Hymn to Aphrodite* (218ff). William Congreve translates the end of the story thus: 'Lock'd in a Room her useless Spouse she left, / Of Youth, of Vigour, and of Voice bereft.' **Antilochus**'s act of sacrifice is described in Pindar's *Pythian Ode* 6.28–42 (and indeed in Quintus of Smyrna). How he brought the news of Patroclus's death to Achilles is told at the junction of books 17 and 18 of the *Iliad*.

Aeschylus, Sophocles and Euripides each wrote lost (alas!) plays about Memnon. Aeschylus's *Psychostasia* seems to have had Zeus **weighing the fates** of him and Achilles (as he does the Greeks' and Trojans' in the *Iliad* book 8) to decide which one should live, while **Eos** and **Thetis**, their goddess mothers, pleaded their respective sons' cases. I've based Thetis's appeal to Zeus on her words in books 1 and 18 of the *Iliad*. At 1.424 it is mentioned (by Thetis, as it happens) that Zeus is feasting with the Ethiopians. I've made Achilles speak to Memnon with something of the spirit with which he addresses the young Trojan Lycaon in the *Iliad* 21.107ff. There's an early fifth-century cup in the Louvre by Douris and Calliades showing winged Eos lifting her son's body, pietà-like. The account of Achilles' funeral is at the start of the *Odyssey* book 24.

Sophocles' play **Ajax** is about the madness, anger and suicide of the fighter after the arms of Achilles are awarded to **Odysseus**. This story opened Lesches of Mytilene's lost epic, the *Little Iliad*, according to Proclus's *Chrestomathy*. Ovid in *Metamorphoses* book 13 imagines their arguments (including the idea that only Odysseus is a sufficiently able critic to understand the artistry of the shield). There is a beautiful amphora potted and painted by Exekias in the Vatican Museums, showing Ajax and Achilles playing a board game. Ajax's single combats with Hector are described in the *Iliad* books 7 and 14, the battle at the ships in book 15. A scholiast on Aristophanes' *Knights* mentions that it was Ajax who carried Achilles' body from the field in the *Little Iliad*. Book 10 of the *Iliad* has the story of Diomedes' and Odysseus's killing of Dolon.

Sophocles' play **Philoctetes** (409 BCE) is about Odysseus's trip to Lemnos with Achilles' son, Neoptolemus, to convince the pain-ridden archer to bring Heracles' bow to Troy, an episode that was also part of the *Little Iliad*.

Helen recalls meeting Odysseus, disguised as a beggar, in Troy in the *Odyssey* book 4; the **Palladium** is described in Pseudo-Apollodorus 3.12.3. In the *Iliad* book 3 the Trojan Antenor describes Odysseus's way of speaking as like snowflakes falling in a winter storm. I've made Helen an active accessory to the theft of the Palladium.

The whole narrative of the **wooden horse** is sung by the poet Demodocus at the court of Alcinous and Arete in the *Odyssey* book 8; the fall of Troy is the brilliantly vivid story of Virgil's *Aeneid* book 2. The episode of Helen imitating the Greeks' wives' voices is told by Menelaus in the *Odyssey* book 4. '*Timeo Danaos et dona ferentes*' is a famous line from Virgil – 'I fear the Greeks even when they bring gifts'. Virgil has it uttered by a character called Capys. However, I have given it to **Cassandra** here since, in Pseudo-Apollodorus's account, it is she and **Laocoön** who argue against bringing it into the city. It is in that work that the story of her rape by Ajax 'the lesser', son of Oileus, is described (not to be confused with Ajax 'the greater', son of Telamon).

The moment in the *Aeneid* when Aeneas locks eyes with Helen is considered by some scholars to be interpolated. He will indeed leave Troy, losing his wife **Creusa** in the confusion en route, but taking his father Anchises and his son Ascanius. After many adventures he will reach Italy, fight a war, and found the dynasty that will later establish Rome.

The fates of **Andromache, Cassandra, Hecuba and Helen** – notably those who mourn Hector at the end of the *Iliad* – is the subject of Euripides' *Trojan Women*. Here we see Helen and Hecuba arguing about the former's fate with Menelaus. I've also drawn on the *Encomium of Helen* by the fifth-century BCE Sicilian-born philosopher Gorgias, a rhetorical set piece that argues for Helen's innocence. Euripides' grim play *Hecuba* sees **Polyxena** sacrificed; Hecuba herself, it is foretold, will turn into a dog. As Anne Carson puts it in the introduction to her translation, 'There is nowhere else for her to go but out of the human species.'

Back in Sparta, I've had Helen emerging into the hall where Menelaus is entertaining **Telemachus** and **Pisistratus** precisely at the moment she does so in *Odyssey* book 4, which I now follow quite closely until the end of the section. When I describe the effects of Helen's drugs I follow Emily Wilson's translation in using the feminine pronoun, though translators usually offer 'his'. It is not specified in the original that we are talking about male experience; indeed, the context is somewhat more suggestive of female experience.

SEVEN: CIRCE

In the tenth book of the *Odyssey*, when Odysseus's men find their way to the house in the woods on Aeaea, they hear singing. 'It was Circe, / the goddess. She was weaving as she sang, / an intricate, enchanting piece of work, / the kind a goddess fashions.' (Emily Wilson's translation.) It's my invention that **Circe** should be weaving the stories of her various female relatives, especially that of Medea, her niece.

The story of **Medea** and **Jason** draws on two main sources – the *Argonautica* by Apollonius of Rhodes (late third century BCE) and

Euripides' *Medea* (431 BCE). I also love Pindar's account of the story, in his fourth *Pythian Ode*, which predates both Apollonius and Euripides.

The *Argonautica* forms a kind of prequel to the Euripides play, and presents a very different character – not the furious, vengeful, wronged woman of the earlier tragedy but an innocent, virginal creature who, at the same time, wields dark and fantastic magical power. On the whole, I've made her more calculating and less of an ingénue than Apollonius; and I've given her some cause for her resentment of her father and brother.

The story of **Hypsipyle** and the **Lemnian women** is taken from the *Argonautica*. Apollonius's picture of female power is not a flattering one, and I've made the women much more competent than he does, but it is he who says they find the work of ploughing and soldiering easier than Athena's tasks (i.e. spinning and weaving). I've updated the debate between Hypsipyle and **Polyxo**, the conclusion of which, in Apollonius, is that the Argonauts ought to be offered the city.

The story of **Hylas** and **Heracles** is told in *Argonautica*, but it is also the subject of the thirteenth *Idyll* by Theocritus.

It was Plutarch, writing around the turn of the first and second centuries CE, who said that Heracles had so many male lovers that it would be impossible to list them. This was in his philosophical dialogue on desire, *Amatorius*, where he also argued that the most warlike nations are the most amorous, and wrote of the erotic love between comrades-in-arms.

I follow Apollonius in having Jason tell Medea about her cousin **Ariadne** – in fact I have made Jason's economy with the truth much more obvious than it is in the original. But that's only one version of the story. Sometimes, when **Theseus** returns to his Athenian father as a young man, Medea is already installed there as **Aegeus**'s wife, and tries to kill him (it is to Aegeus and Athens that Euripides has Medea flee at the end of his play, which can't be done in my version, as Aegeus is already dead). The timelines in the various versions do not match up – for Euripides, the Ariadne/ Theseus story must have happened after, not before, the Medea/ Jason one.

For the gruesome episode of **Apsyrtus**'s death, I follow Apollonius in having Medea making a plan to trap and have Jason kill her half-brother. (I've invented the notion that she uses Ariadne's example to justify her actions, but the echoes between the two stories are clear.) The flinging of body parts into the water is described in, among others, Pseudo-Apollodorus and Ovid's *Tristia* book 3. The detail about the cloth that Ariadne and Dionysus once lay on is from Apollonius. Roberto Calasso, in *The Marriage of Cadmus and Harmonia*, writes of the cousins Medea and Ariadne: 'They never met. But they touched each other through a fabric.'

The story of **Scylla** and **Glaucus** is told in Ovid's *Metamorphoses* book 13. The description of Glaucus is borrowed from Plato's *Republic*, 10.611d. Socrates uses the story to make a philosophical point – he is comparing the accretions that attach to a person's soul to the shells and seaweed that stuck to Glaucus.

The description of **Arete** and **Alcinous**'s palace is from *Odyssey* book 8 – including the description of the Phaeacian slave women as especially skilled textile makers. Arete's catalogue of girls mistreated by their fathers is from Apollonius, though she doesn't mention their own daughter, Nausicaa.

Medea's exercise in rejuvenation is described in Ovid's *Metamorphoses*; so too her dispatch of **Pelias**. I drew the catalogue of Medea's herbs from 'Medicinal Plants of Mt Pelion, Greece' by David Eric Brussell, *Economic Botany*, vol. 58, Supplement (Winter, 2004), pp. S174–S202.

If one knows anything about Medea, it tends to be that she kills her children. This is what happens in Euripides' *Medea*, and it's that great play that has come to be regarded as the 'definitive' text about her. But in the surviving fragments of the many other lost plays about Medea, as Matthew Wright points out in his *The Lost Plays of Greek Tragedy* (vol. 2, Bloomsbury), we see 'an extraordinary multiplicity of Medeas. It is impossible to say which of these versions, if any, was regarded within antiquity as offering an authoritative portrayal, but it seems to me that in the ancient world no one ever created, or intended to create, a truly definitive version of the character or her story.'

Medea did not always kill her children. It can plausibly be argued that Euripides was creating a bold new plotline in his version of the story. (Another playwright, Neophron, also has her killing her children – we have fragments of his play, but it's not known for sure which of the two came first.) In some versions, it is the Corinthians who kill the children. The second-century BCE scholar Parmeniscus, for example, suggested that they did so because they were unwilling to have Medea as their queen; he even said that contemporary Corinthians bribed Euripides to have Medea kill them in his play (better for the city's reputation). A lost play by a writer called Carcinus, described by Aristotle, seems to have had Medea falsely accused of killing her children when she had in fact sent them away for safety.

The **chariot pulled by dragons** is the climactic endpoint of Euripides' *Medea* and a favourite scene for Greek pottery painters: see for instance the remarkable Lucanian (southern Italian) calyx-crater (*c.*400 BCE) attributed to the Policoro Painter, now in the Cleveland Museum of Art, Ohio.

Back on Aeaea. In the *Odyssey* book 10, it is the notoriously dishonest **Odysseus** himself who narrates his encounter with **Circe**. In his story (told to the Phaeacians) **Hermes** has given him a special herb, moly, that makes him invulnerable to her spells. When he arrives at her house, he moves to attack her with his sword but Circe suggests they go to bed together. Odysseus refuses to sleep with her until she frees the men, which she immediately promises to do. Afterwards he refuses to eat until the men are freed. My version of Circe is a notch less desperate, and my Odysseus slightly less eager to see his pigs resume human form.

EIGHT: PENELOPE

The key text for **Penelope** is the *Odyssey*, in which she cuts an intriguing, sagacious and often opaque figure, with a mind full of thoughts to which we are not always privy. In particular, it is unclear from the text precisely when she recognises the disguised Odysseus as her long-lost husband. It is at least possible to infer that she does so – on some level – before the official (as it were) recognition scene in book 23. The first part of the chapter uses Odysseus's arrival at his own palace in book 17 and onwards as its basis; but it sees the events unfold from Penelope's point of view.

When **Odysseus** visits the Underworld in book 11 of the epic, Tiresias gives him the prophecy (122ff) about the **winnowing fan**. By contrast, a further iteration of the epic cycle, the lost *Telegony*, by Eugammon of Cyrene, tells a story of Circe's son by Odysseus, Telegonus, who kills his father in ignorance with a spear that has the barb of a stingray as its point. Telegonus ends up with Penelope, and Telemachus with Circe.

Phemius in the *Odyssey* 1.325 is indeed telling a story of the Greeks' return from Troy and their punishment by Athena. It is a case of Homeric self-referentiality, since the *Odyssey* itself is a story of a Greek's return home from Troy. The song brings Penelope no pleasure – she asks him to stop, but Telemachus intervenes, by saying 'Go in and do your work. / Stick to the loom and distaff. Tell your slaves / to do their chores as well. It is for men / to talk, especially me. I am the master.' (Emily Wilson's translation.)

Poseidon fights alongside the Greeks at the start of the *Iliad* book 15, until he's called off by Iris, sent by Zeus.

In the *Odyssey* 18.270, Penelope recalls being told by Odysseus that she should choose another husband when Telemachus becomes a man.

The story about **Icarius** following Penelope and Odysseus is recounted by Pausanias in his *Description of Greece* (3.20.10–11). The merits and demerits of **Ithaca** are teasingly laid out by Athena in the *Odyssey* 13.236–49.

Ellen Harlizius-Klück told me that when she weaves in the public spaces of the Museum for Plaster Casts, Munich, visitors – surprisingly – do not on the whole come and scrutinise what she's doing. *I do, I undo, I redo* is the name of a series of tower-like sculptures that the artist Louise Bourgeois (the daughter of tapestry restorers) made for Tate Modern, London, in 2000.

Anticleia's ghost appears in the *Odyssey* 11.188ff. **Laertes** and the tiny Odysseus in the orchard comes from: *Odyssey* 24.339–446. **Winged horses and flying wind gods** – these are borrowed from the design shown on the skyphos, or cup, in the Museo Civico, Chiusi, Tuscany, by the Penelope Painter (see also Introduction, page 13). On the other side, Eurycleia washes Odysseus's feet.

In the *Odyssey* 17.290ff, **Argos** recognises his old master and dies. It is one of the most touching episodes in the poem and one of the crucial 'recognition scenes', in which loyal slaves, family members and this old pet recognise long-lost Odysseus. **Eurycleia** recognises Odysseus at 19.468.

The idea that Penelope makes this **second tapestry** after Odysseus has left again is my invention. The story of Clytemnestra and her husband's homecoming, and the revenge taken on his mother by Orestes, meanwhile, is the subject of Aeschylus's trilogy the *Oresteia*, first produced in 458 BCE. (He moves the action from Mycenae to Argos.) The dramas drew on a lost poem of the epic cycle called *Nostoi* (*Returns*) by Agias of Troezen, which dealt with the homecomings of Greeks after the Trojan War, especially that of Agamemnon. The *Odyssey* is of course also a homecoming or *nostos* (the Greek word that gives us nostalgia, 'return pain', an intense ache for home). The poem is infused with references to the catastrophic return of Agamemnon, which is strongly contrasted with Odysseus's more successful return to Ithaca.

A speech by a **watchman** opens Aeschylus's *Agamemnon*, the first play of the *Oresteia*. The trilogy is full of knotty imagery relating to nets and cloth. The unfurling of the purple tapestries, the battle of words between **Agamemnon and Clytemnestra**, and his foot hitting the precious cloth: these events form one of the most thrilling scenes in Greek drama.

The next part of the *Oresteia* is *Libation Bearers*, the story of Orestes' return to Argos, the reunion between him and **Electra**, and his killing of Clytemnestra to avenge their father. This territory is also covered in Sophocles' play *Electra* and indeed Euripides' play of the same name.

There is a glorious first-century CE Roman sculpture of **Pylades** and Orestes, arms around each other, known as the San Ildefonso Group, in the Prado, Madrid.

The **Furies** gather at the end of *Libation Bearers* and will form the Chorus in the third play of Aeschylus's *Oresteia*, *The Kindly Ones*, which begins in Delphi, and then changes location to Athens for Orestes' trial for Clytemnestra's murder.

For the **Areopagus** and the **trial of Orestes**, I've followed *The Kindly Ones* fairly closely. A fascinating reading was made of the courtroom scene by Johann Jakob Bachofen in his *Das Mutterrecht* (*The Mother-Right*, 1861). The trial is convincingly read as a symbolic defeat of an old matriarchal order (embodied by the female chthonic deities, the Furies) in favour of a newer, patriarchal order represented by the 'young' gods, Apollo and Athena.

Mentor – our word mentor is derived from this character. Athena disguises herself as him, taking Telemachus under her/his wing, at

Odyssey 2.398. She becomes a vulture at 3.372, a young girl at 7.19, a beautiful woman at 13.288 and 15.157, a swallow at 22.239.

Penelope's scepticism is my invention, though it is true that she, unlike her husband and son, never actually sees Athena in the *Odyssey*. Her theories and speculations, however, are not invention: they are drawn from the ideas of pre-Socratic philosophers, a disparate group of thinkers, many of whom lived in Ionia (the western seaboard of modern Turkey) in the sixth and fifth centuries BCE. They were almost certainly influenced by the western flow of mathematical learning from Babylon and the Near East, and in their writing – which survives in only fragmentary form – we see a certain scepticism about the role of the gods, and attempts to explain phenomena by purely natural, rather than supernatural, means. The observation about Thracian and Ethiopian gods comes from the Xenophanes of Colophon (c. 570–c. 480 BCE); so too does the thought about animals' gods and the explanation of the rainbow. The theories about lightning and rain come from Anaximander, who lived in Miletus in Ionia in the sixth century BCE, so too the idea that the sky is not just above us but around us.

The final image of the spiders inhabiting the empty house is from Philostratus the Elder's *Pictures*, 2.28.

FURTHER READING

For Greek and Roman texts in translation, the first port of call is the Penguin Classics and Oxford World's Classics series. In addition, I recommend Emily Wilson's pacey, intelligent translation of the *Odyssey* (W.W. Norton, 2018); Stanley Lombardo and Diane Rayor's translation of Callimachus's *Hymns, Epigrams, Select Fragments* (Johns Hopkins University Press, 1988); Helene P. Foley's translation of *The Homeric Hymn to Demeter*, which also includes commentary and essays (Princeton University Press, 1994); Anne Carson's translation of Euripides, titled *Grief Lessons: Four Plays* (NYBR Classics, 2008); and a one-volume translation of sixteen Greek plays by scholars including Emily Wilson, titled *The Greek Plays*, edited by Mary Lefkowitz and James Romm (Modern Library, 2016).

The Loeb Classical Library of parallel Greek or Latin and English texts is particularly useful when it comes to fragments, for example the remaining scraps of the lost poems of the epic cycle: *Greek Epic Fragments*, edited by M.L. West (Harvard University Press, 2003).

Online, the Perseus Digital Library (perseus.tufts.edu) is a resource for Greek and Latin texts together with out-of-copyright commentaries and translations, and hyperlinks to dictionary tools.

The Dictionary of Classical Mythology (Penguin, 1991), an edited version (by Stephen Kershaw) of a classic 1950s work by Pierre Grimal, is a useful one-stop reference book.

For a sense of the sheer multiplicity of stories that are substantially lost to us, or exist only in fragments, I recommend Matthew Wright's accessible *The Lost Plays of Greek Tragedy* (two volumes, Bloomsbury, 2016/19). And if you want to get serious, try Robert Fowler's *Early Greek Mythographers* (two volumes, Oxford University Press, 2001/13), and Timothy Gantz's *Early Greek Myth* (two volumes, Johns Hopkins University Press, 1996).

On the history of spinning and weaving, the best all-round introduction is *Women's Work: The First 20,000 Years: Women, Cloth, and Society in Early Times* by Elizabeth Wayland Barber (W.W. Norton, 1996).

On the significance of Greek myths in general, a good place to start is *Classical Mythology: A Very Short Introduction* by Helen Morales (Oxford University Press, 2007); *The Gods of Olympus: A History* by Barbara Graziosi (Metropolitan, 2014); *Battling the Gods: Atheism in the Ancient World* by Tim Whitmarsh (Faber, 2016); *Antigone Rising: The Subversive Power of the Ancient Myths* by Helen Morales (Wildfire, 2020); and *Pandora's Jar: Women in the Greek Myths* by Natalie Haynes (Picador, 2020).

'Reading Ovid's Rapes' is a seminal essay by feminist scholar Amy Richlin, collected in *Pornography and Representation in Greece and Rome* (Richlin, ed., Oxford University Press, 1992). The 1985 essay 'What Was Penelope Unweaving?' by Carolyn Heilbrun, collected in her volume *Hamlet's Mother and Other Women* (The Women's Press, 1991), helped me find a way to tell these stories.

ACKNOWLEDGEMENTS

Thank you to my inimitable agent Peter Straus and his colleagues at Rogers, Coleridge and White.

Thank you to the best of editors, Bea Hemming, who, sitting outside the King Charles I pub in King's Cross, London, in early August 2017, said, 'Why don't you do a book of Greek myths?' To the entire team at Jonathan Cape, including Suzanne Dean, Neil Bradford, David Eldridge, Katherine Fry, Anna Redman Aylward, Ilona Jasiewicz. Thank you to Dan Franklin.

Thank you to Chris Ofili for making drawings of such rare beauty. It is an honour to share these pages with you. Thank you to Tamsin Wright and Kathy Stephenson.

Thank you to colleagues at the *Guardian* who made possible and tolerated my absences: Katharine Viner, Jan Thompson, Pippa Prior, Randeep Ramesh, Jonathan Shainin, Clare Longrigg, David Wolf, Alex Needham, Charlotte Northedge, Liese Spencer and Carey Evans.

Thank you to Mary Harlow for fielding my questions on ancient textiles, and helping me play around with a drop spindle and a warp-weighted loom. Thank you to Ellen Harlizius-Klück: she generously spent a morning showing me her work with the Penelope Project on ancient textiles, part of the Research Institute for the History of Technology and Science at the Deutsches Museum, Munich. Thank you Frank J. Nisetich (and Pindar) for the epigraph.

Thank you to two remarkable institutions: the American Academy in Rome, where I was made so welcome as a visiting fellow in 2018; and Gladstone's Library in Flintshire, where I was a writer-in-residence for the month of February 2020, looked after so well and warmly by everyone there. I am extraordinarily fortunate to have been able to complete my residency before the Covid-19 pandemic meant the library's temporary closure. Thank you, Peter Francis, Louisa Yates, and the whole team.

Thank you to two dear friends for being my first readers: Fiona Bradley and Sara Holloway.

Thank you to James Davidson, Tim Whitmarsh and Paul Cartledge for so generously reading the manuscript with expert eyes. You have saved me from many errors, and those that remain are my own.

Much help has been given, wittingly or unwittingly, by friends, classicists and writers (some being all three), including Richard Baker, Nick Barley, Andy Beckett, Francis Bickmore, Kate Bland, Emma Bridges, Xan Brooks, Aditya Chakrabortty, Agnes Crawford, Sarah Crown, Susanna Eastburn, David Fearn, Barbara Graziosi, Mark Haddon, Sophie Hay, Jon Hesk, Keith Miller, Camilla Norman, Charlotte Schepke, Ali Smith and Gary Younge.

Thank you to Cynthia Smart for being my first teacher of Greek and Latin. Thank you to the late classicists Jasper Griffin, Oliver Lyne and Michael Comber, who taught me about classical literature when I was a student. I was lucky enough to learn alongside three goddess-like women – Emma Christian, Antonia Potter and Emily Wilson – as well as Joshua St Johnston, who has been an inspiration these past thirty years.

Thank you to my beloved father Peter Higgins, who instilled in me (aged eight, over a badly composed thank-you letter, with reference to Evelyn Waugh) that the work of a writer is to redraft.

Thank you to my beloved mother Pamela Higgins, who died in November 2018. To her I owe more than can be expressed.

Thank you to Rob Higgins, for the first book of myths, and thank you, Pam Magee. Thank you to Rupert Higgins and Dawn Lawrence for keeping me alert to the natural world. Thank you to the ever-stimulating Miriam, Isaac and Simeon Bird, and to Zora Bird who arrived in August 2019 bringing delicious distraction.

Thank you to my wonderful nephew and nieces – James and Emma Higgins, Tilda and Eleanor Lawrence – to whom this book is affectionately and proudly dedicated.

Thank you most of all to Matthew Fox, for listening with love.

GLOSSARY OF NAMES AND PLACES

Each entry concludes with a reference to the page in the main text on which the character or location first appears.

Acheron – one of the rivers of the Underworld p.163

Achilles – the best Greek fighter in the Trojan War. Son of Peleus, a mortal, and the goddess Thetis p.150

Acrisius – king of Argos, father of Danaë p.132

Actaeon – grandson of Cadmus and Harmonia, son of Autonoë and Aristaeus p.72

Admetus – king of Pherae in Thessaly, husband of Alcestis p.93

Adraste – one of Helen's slaves in Sparta p.183

Aea – capital of Colchis, ruled by King Aeëtes p.216

Aeaea – far western mythical island inhabited by Circe p.231

Aeëtes – son of Helios, king of the Colchians p.63

Aegeus – king of Athens, father of Theseus p.220

Aegina – daughter of Asopus, abducted by Zeus; gave her name to the island in the Saronic Gulf p.167

Aegisthus – cousin of Agamemnon, lover of Clytemnestra p.257

Aeneas – a Trojan ally, son of Anchises and Aphrodite. He will found the dynasty that will one day establish Rome p.158

Aeolus – master of the winds p.256

Aeson – father of Jason p.212

Aether – the light upper air p.22

Aethops – a comrade of Memnon in the Trojan War p.195

Aetolia – a region in central Greece, at the north-west end of the Gulf of Corinth p.97

Agamemnon – king of Argos (or Mycenae), leader of Greek forces in Trojan War, brother of Menelaus p.177

Agave – daughter of Cadmus and Harmonia, mother of Pentheus p.72

Agelaus – a suitor of Penelope's p.252

Agenor – king of Tyre, father of Europa and Cadmus p.57

Ajax – (1) 'the Greater Ajax', son of Telamon, from

Ascanius – son of Aeneas, sometimes called Iulus p.204

Asclepius – god of healing and medicine p.199

Asopus – a river in Boeotia, and a river-god, father of Aegina p.74; 167

Atalanta – a hunter from Arcadia, devotee of Artemis p.96

Athena – Olympian goddess of technology, strategic thinking, winning p.21

Atreus – king of Mycenae, father of Agamemnon and Menelaus p.257

Atropos – one of the Fates p.15

Attica – the territory round Athens p.121

Augeas – a king of Elis, whose filthy stables were cleaned by Heracles p.95

Aulis – mustering point on the coast of Boeotia for Greek forces bound for Troy p.188

Autonoë – eldest daughter of Cadmus and Harmonia, mother of Actaeon p.72

Bactria – region of central Asia (part of modern Afghanistan and Pakistan) p.76

Baucis – hospitable old woman, married to Philemon p.150

Bellerophon – rider of Pegasus, killer of Chimaera p.164

Boeotia – a region of central Greece, location of Thebes and Orchomenos p.55

Boreas – the north wind p.49

Bosporus – the strait connecting the Black Sea and the Sea of Marmara p.61

Cadmus – Phoenician founder of Thebes, brother of Europa p.56

Caenis – a nymph, later transformed into Caenus, a man p.167

Calaïs – son of Boreas the north wind; an Argonaut p.165

Calchas – a seer with the Greek troops in the Trojan War p.179

Callidice – daughter of Metanira of Eleusis p.36

Calliope – Muse of epic poetry p.160

Calydon – a town in Aetolia ravaged by the Calydonian boar p.97

Cassandra – prophetic daughter of Priam and Hecuba p.182

Cassiopeia – queen of Ethiopia, mother of Andromeda p.143

Castor – brother of Pollux, half-brother of Helen p.97

Cecrops – first king of Athens; half-man, half-snake p.121

Celeus – husband of Metanira, ruler of Eleusis p.37

Centaurs – half-human, half-horse beings p.93

Cepheus – king of Ethiopia, father of Andromeda p.143

Danaë – daughter of Acrisius, mother of Perseus p.132

Daphne – daugher of Peneus, the river god, later a laurel tree p.132

Dardanians – a people of the Troad, closely related to (or sometimes the same as) the Trojans p.157

Deianira – second wife of Heracles, daughter of King Oeneus of Calydon p.93

Deiphobus – brother of Hector, son of Priam and Hecuba p.171

Demeter – Olympian goddess of the harvest p.23

Demophon – son of Metanira, foster-son of Demeter p.37

Deucalion – son of Clymene and Prometheus p.48

Dia – wife of Ixion, mother of Perithous p.122

Dictys – brother of Polydectes, husband of Danaë p.135

Diomedes – son of Tydeus, one of the Greek warriors at Troy p.180

Dionysus – god of wine, theatre p.55

Dioscuri – Castor and Pollux, sons of Leda and Tyndareus, Argonauts p.131

Dirce – a spring of Thebes p.63

Dodona – Zeus's oracle in Epirus, north-western Greece p.213

Dolon – a Trojan scout captured and killed by Diomedes and Odysseus p.198

Dryads – nymphs associated with trees p.49

Echo – a nymph condemned to repeat others' words p.90

Eioneus – father of Dia, victim of Ixion p.122

Electra – (1) one of the Pleiades, daughter of Atlas p.59; (2) daughter of Agamemnon and Clytemnestra p.257

Emathion – king of Samothrace, son of Electra (1) p.59

Enaesimus – a young hunter killed by the Calydonian boar p.97

Enceladus – a Giant p.32

Endymion – mortal lover of Selene p.46

Eos – goddess of the dawn p.22

Epimetheus – Titan brother of Prometheus, husband of Pandora p.27

Erato – Muse of love songs p.15

Erebus – the kingdom of the dead, also known as Hades (which is also the name of its immortal ruler) p.35

Erechtheus – king of Athens, son of Pandion p.126

Eridanus – a mythical river in the far west, sometimes associated with the Po p.48

Hamadryads – like dryads, the nymphs of the forests p.49

Harmonia – daughter of Aphrodite, wife of Cadmus of Thebes p.57

Harpies – 'snatchers', winged women p.165

Hebe – Olympian goddess of youth p.25

Hecate – goddess of fertility, witchcraft p.33

Hector – eldest son of Priam and Hecuba, husband of Andromache p.149

Hecuba – wife of Priam of Troy, mother of Hector, Paris, Cassandra and others p.149

Helen – daughter of Zeus and Leda, sister of Clytemnestra p.131

Helios – Titan god of the sun, father of Phaethon, Circe, Aeëtes, Pasiphaë p.22

Hellespont – the Dardanelles p.197

Hephaestus – Olympian god of craft and the forge p.25

Hera – queen of the Olympians, protector of the family p.23

Heracles – strongest of human fighters, son of Zeus p.32

Hermes – Olympian trickster and messenger god p.27

Hesperides – keepers of a garden of golden apples in the mythical far west p.25

Hestia – Olympian goddess of the hearth p.23

Hippodamia – (1) daughter of Oenomaus of Elis, wife of Pelops p.59; (2) daughter of the Trojan ally Anchises, wife of Alcathous p.192

Hippolyta – an Amazon, wife of Theseus p.95

Hundred-handers – Titan giants p.22

Hyacinthus – a Spartan boy loved by Apollo p.155

Hyades – rain-bringing star cluster in Taurus p.181

Hydra – a multi-headed venomous serpent from Lerna p.94

Hylaeus – a Centaur p.97

Hylas – Argonaut, lover of Heracles p.215

Hymen – god of the marriage ceremony p.88

Hyperboreans – inhabitants of a mythical land beyond the north wind p.25

Hypnos – personification of/god of sleep p.153

Iambe – slave of Metanira p.37

Ianthe – a Cretan woman, married to Iphis p.89

Iapetus – Titan father of Prometheus and Epimetheus p.22

Iasius – Arcadian father of Atalanta p.96

Lethe – a river of the Underworld p.153

Leto – Titan mother of Apollo and Artemis p.26

Leucothea – sea goddess, formerly Ino p.75

Liriope – a nymph, mother of Narcissus p.90

Lycia – a region in Asia Minor, in what is now southern Turkey p.160

Lycomedes – king of Scyros, father of Deidamea p.188

Lydia – a region of Asia Minor, in what is now central-western Turkey p.93

Macedonia – a region north of Thessaly p.161

Machaon – healer son of Asclepius p.199

Maenads – ecstatic followers of Dionysus p.55

Maeonia – Lydia p.180

Maia – daughter of Atlas, mother of Hermes p.27

Malis – a nymph of Cius p.215

Manto – prophetic daughter of Tiresias p.64

Marsyas – a Satyr and aulos player p.123

Medea – daughter of Aeëtes, king of Colchis p.212

Medusa – one of the Gorgons p.140

Melanion – husband of Atalanta p.98

Meleager – son of Althaea and Oeneus of Calydon p.97

Melicertes – son of Ino and Athamas, later a sea god called Palaemon p.75

Melpomene – Muse of tragedy p.15

Menelaus – king of Sparta married to Helen, brother of Agamemnon p.149

Merope – (1) one of the Pleiades, daughter of Atlas p.59; (2) adoptive mother of Oedipus p.65

Metanira – wife of Celeus of Eleusis, mother of Demophon p.37

Metis – Titan goddess of shrewdness p.22

Momos – god of/personification of blame p.228

Morpheus – son of Hypnos, who appears in dreams p.154

Mycenae – city in the north-eastern Peloponnese, home of Agamemnon and his family p.187

Myrmidons – Achilles' fighting force at Troy p.181

Narcissus – son of the nymph Liriope p.90

Nausicaa – daughter of Arete and Alcinous of Phaeacia p.233

Naxos – south Aegean island, largest of the Cyclades p.184

Peleus – one of the Argonauts, king of Phthia, husband of Thetis, father of Achilles p.96

Pelias – uncle of Jason p.212

Pella – city of ancient Macedonia p.161

Pelops – son of Tantalus, brother of Niobe p.123

Penelope – daughter of Icarius, wife of Odysseus, mother of Telemachus p.187

Peneus – a river god of Thessaly, father of Daphne p.125

Penthesilea – an Amazon, daughter of Ares p.192

Periclymenus – brother of Nestor p.93

Perse – one of the Oceanids, mother of Circe, Aeëtes, Pasiphaë p.211

Persephone – daughter of Demeter and Zeus, wife of Hades p.33

Perseus – son of Danaë and Zeus p.134

Phaethon – son of Helios and Clymene p.43

Phaistos – a city in central-southern Crete p.88

Phasis – river in Colchis p.216

Phemius – a poet/singer on Ithaca p.245

Philemon – hospitable old man, married to Baucis p.150

Philoctetes – Greek archer in the Trojan War p.186

Philomela – daughter of Pandion, king of Athens, sister of Procne p.87

Phineus – a king of Thrace p.165

Phlegethon – a river that runs with fire in the Underworld p.163

Phocaea – a city in Ionia p.119

Phocis – a region of central Greece, containing Delphi p.261

Phrygia – a region in Asia Minor (in modern Anatolia, Turkey) p.123

Phylace – a place in Thessaly ruled by Protesilaus p.191

Phylo – one of Helen's slaves in Sparta p.182

Picus – a king of Latium p.161

Pierus – a king of Pella in Macedonia p.161

Pirithous – a Lapith, friend of Theseus p.97

Pisa – a town in Elis (not to be confused with the modern town in Italy) p.136

Pleiades – a cluster of stars, like their sisters, the Hyades p.59

Pollux – Argonaut, brother of Castor, one of the Dioscuri, son of Tyndareus and Leda p.97

Polybus – king of Corinth, adoptive father of Oedipus p.65

Sipylus – a mountain in Lydia; the rock into which Niobe was transformed p.122

Sirens – half-woman, half-bird creatures with beautiful voices p.232

Sirius – the dog star, the brightest in the night sky, heralding hot summer days p.218

Sisyphus – a mortal condemned to heave a rock up a mountain in the Underworld p.167

Stheno – one of the Gorgons p.142

Stymphalos – a lake west of Corinth p.95

Styx – greatest of the rivers of the Underworld p.39

Taenarum – promontory on the tip of the central peninsula of the south Peloponnese (modern Mani) p.110

Talos – a bronze giant, guard of the island of Crete p.233

Talthybius – a herald on the Greek side in the Trojan War p.189

Tantalus – a Lydian, a thief of the gods' ambrosia and nectar p.122

Tartarus – underground region of Hades/Erebus where Titans were imprisoned p.22

Taurus mountains – a range in southern Turkey p.57

Tecmessa – a Phrygian woman, captive of Ajax p.198

Telemachus – son of Odysseus and Penelope p.187

Tereus – king of Thrace, husband of Procne, father of Itys p.87

Terpsichore – Muse of dance p.15

Tethys – Titan ocean goddess p.22

Thalia – Muse of comedy p.15

Thanatos – god of/personification of death p.93

Theano – Trojan priestess of Athena p.193

Thebes – (1) city in Boeotia founded by Cadmus p.59; (2) a city in the Troad, original home to Andromache and Chryseis p.149; (3) a city in Egypt famed for its wealth p.183

Theseus – son of Aegeus p.184

Thesprotia – a region of Epirus on the west coast of Greece p.246

Thetis – sea goddess, mother of Achilles, wife of Peleus p.179

Thisbe – a young woman of Babylon p.100

Thrace – an area bounded by the Aegean on the west, the Black Sea on the east, the sea of Marmara on the south, and the Rhodope and Balkan